YELLOW DAY

By

William J. Douglas

ISBN: 0-75964-310-5

This book is printed on acid free paper.

1stBooks - rev. 06/27/01

ACKNOWLEDGEMENTS

For their assistance, support, and ideas in writing this novel I would like to thank:

My wife, Joan, for her concepts, thought, and critiques of the evolving manuscript

My daughter, Stephanie, for her dedicated review of my final manuscript

Joan Jones; her kind and insightful reading of just a few chapters are deeply appreciated

Donna Micelli, for her editing and thoughtful critique of the first half of my manuscript

My daughter, Elizabeth; her reaction of approval made me believe in writing this story

My son, Bill; his sense of humor inspired a number of thoughts in this book

While the author has referred to the names of public figures and personalities, titles and words from cinema and theater productions, private and public and institutions, commercial brand names, and locations in this book, none of the characters are real and all of the incidents are fictional.

William J. Douglas
March 28, 2001

—1—

On a morning in mid February, Jim awoke to the music of the clock radio alarm tuned to a classical station. With closed eyes he listened to the melody. He often recognized the composer and sometimes the name of the piece. He smiled at the soft strains of *Fur Elise*. A few feet away the narrow gap of a window served as a portal for icy winter air. Under a thick quilt, a shield against the cold room, Jim lay enjoying the warmth. After stretching his back and calf muscles, a habit from rehabilitating a lower back injury, he rolled over and peered through squinting lashes. The clock said 6:02. He struggled with the thought of leaving his cozy cocoon, but it was time to start the ritual.

He dressed and completed a stretching and exercising routine to warm-up tired muscles. He stood and slid his arms into the windbreaker, then knelt to retie the loosened knot in his sneakers. After slipping on the stocking cap and gloves he started for the door, and then stopped, remembering the time in Texas when he locked himself out of a fully automated motel. With nobody around to help, a major commotion ensued for almost an hour before he got back into his room.

He walked back to the small desk, picked up the key, placed it inside his glove, and stepped into the hallway. Through the clear plastic bags hanging on each doorknob he read the words, *USA Today*. The stairs deposited him in an empty lobby with a vacant reception desk. Crossing the lobby he stepped into the cold February air. A misty fog, common at this time of year, rose from the damp snow lining the driveway, producing halos around lights that hung from invisible poles. The limited sight distance, about fifty feet, and the morning darkness created a mysterious atmosphere. *What would the morning bring?*

At home, Jim jogged two and a half miles around a neighborhood loop every other day, and tried to fit in a morning run when away on travel. The aerobics and full sweat of strenuous exercise made him feel good, and missing a run caused a guilt trip. His travels had produced a variety of different and interesting running experiences, including the mall in Washington, Grant Park in Chicago, the beaches of New Jersey and Cape Cod, and overseas in Paris, London, Warsaw, and the Scottish Highlands.

While Jim had stayed at the Larchwood Inn several times, this would be his first opportunity to run in its surroundings. Estimating distance on strange and hilly terrain was difficult, and time provided more certainty to the length of the run. He checked his watch, 6:20, and stepped from under the canopy of the inn onto the driveway, beginning the outbound leg of his 25-minute loop in a slow trot. He trudged along at about one mile every ten minutes. Looking over his shoulder, the lights of the inn faded from view. *Remember the landmarks and look at the street signs.*

Behind him, the inn faded into the fog. A historic nineteenth century mansion near the ocean in a small Connecticut town, it had four guestrooms. Its personal touches included a welcoming note on the unlocked door and quiet tones of classical music when entered the small lobby. Passing the registration desk, which reminded him of the British Comedy Series, *Fawlty Towers*, he'd settle into his favorite, the Lincoln Room, with four poster bed, memorabilia, and furnishings of the Civil war era. A bottle of wine and a surprise desert set out for guests each evening added to the pleasure of the visit. The Larchwood was comfortable, like home.

No matter where he ran, after the outward leg of twelve or thirteen minutes Jim would turn to retrace the course and complete the run. The fog continued its surrounding grip as he made a few turns, mentally tracking them between glances at his watch. At 6:32 he looked for a landmark ahead, a definitive point where he would turn and begin the return. Choosing a stop sign at the next intersection, he crossed over the road and completed his U-turn, keeping on the left side of the road.

Today it didn't seem to make much difference; there had been no traffic.

After several winding turns, puffing his way up the hilly suburban road, he arrived at an intersection and looked up for the street name. *Davison, is this where I turn? No, not yet.* At the next intersection he looked up again and decided to keep going. Another familiar sign said McCalum. Jim hesitated, and then turned under the sign. The mist and darkness of morning provided few navigation clues. Now everything began to look different; new hills he didn't remember, and new houses replaced those he saw on the way out. *Was it just the fog, or are they different?*

Jim trotted downhill as a dog barked in the distance, causing him to tense. Then his foot moved backward, of its own will and as if a roller skate, and his body lurched ahead. As Jim's face accelerated toward the street he thrust out his arms to break the fall. Crashing into ground, he winced at the pain in his knee and wrist. He felt foolish, and cursed his stupidity in a whisper. "Damn I didn't need this." He felt a sting in the palm of his hand and removed a glove. The key edge, like a saw blade, had sliced the flesh between the forefinger and thumb.

He sat up, moved the wound to his lips, tasting blood while surveying his injuries. The distant barking grew louder so he tried to stand. A shadowy figure moved across the misty lawn to his left. The dog sounded big. A Doberman twice his size attacked Jim, at the age of three, and the fear of that incident never went away. He tried to raise himself from the street as the barking grew louder and more ferocious. The shadow drew closer. Jim's fear won over the pain and he rose to his knees to face the racing animal as it approached, now about ten feet away. As Jim lifted his arms to cover his face, the dog let out a piercing yelp and slid to a halt, made a few whimpers, and then started barking again. In the faint glow of the streetlight, a short distance from where Jim knelt, he spotted the row of small flags separating him from the snarling dog.

On hands and knees, Jim backed away with slow, cautious movements. Then he heard a faint sound of approaching footsteps. The barking resumed with a tone of increasing anger. Jim forced his attention away from the dog, toward the direction of the footsteps. From the darkness he noticed an emerging image, faint, coming up the hill. He watched a slender figure become visible through the gray mist, drawing closer, and stopping the other side of the road, about twenty feet away.

Jim called, "I could use some help!" The dog's barking and snarling competed with his plea as he awaited a response. The blurred image crystallized into a figure moving toward him in black pants and a yellow windbreaker. Dark hair protruded from under a ski cap; still no sound of a voice. The figure approached with caution, maintaining distance.

Jim felt pathetic. On his knees with a dog a few feet away, he knew he looked and sounded pathetic. A soft voice asked, "What happened?"

"I tripped. I may have injured my wrist and knee; this dog is about to chew me up."

"Don't worry, he won't cross the fence line." The voice had a sound of assurance.

"How do you know?"

The woman in the yellow windbreaker moved closer, "I run by here all the time. The invisible fence is only a week old. Kaiser is mean, but the fence works. He won't cross."

Jim rose to one knee and then stood, watching Kaiser with care. House lights went on. The dog moved along the line of flags, barking and snarling. "I hope you're right," Jim said. Then he looked over at her. "Thanks".

"I didn't do anything," she said, "maybe calmed you down a little. May I help you."

"Well, you could tell me where I'm going. I got turned around in the fog and everything looks different."

She moving closer, asking in her quiet voice, "Where do you want to go?"

"I'm staying at the Larchwood Inn."

4

"Not far, but you were going in the wrong direction."

"I thought I knew the street signs. I guess not." Half the street still separated him from the woman.

He watched her look him over, reducing the distance between them. He felt like a real sight, knee showing through the ripped sweat pants, scratched face, rubbing his wrist, licking his palm. "Come on, I'll take you there. Can you run?" she said.

"I never run; how about a slow trot? I'm Jim Dulles."

"Ellen Cramwell. Let's go."

At a slow pace, he followed her lead. When they approached the sign, McCalum, he had used to mark his way he said, "This is where I turned."

"But the wrong way," she replied.

He nodded. The road went both ways, and in the fog he hadn't noticed the second sign on the other side of the street.

They continued for a short time as the sky began to take on a lighter tone. The fog persisted but the rising sun began to brighten the sky. When the canopy lights of the inn became visible, Jim realized he would have been looking for a long while.

"I was really in left field!" he said between puffs. Then, as they slowed to a walk, "Coffee?"

"That would taste good right now, but it has to be quick, I'm a little late."

"Sorry, my fault."

"No, that's not it. Usually I'd have plenty of time, but tomorrow is Yellow Day. It's a special day for the kids. I have some work to do to get ready for the festivities."

"Oh, how many kids do you have?" he said, with a sigh. He knew she was too good to be true. "And what's Yellow Day?"

"I have eighteen of them..."

"B...but?" he stammered, taking a deep breath and turning to her with a questioning look.

"And Yellow Day is a day of hope. We're past the mid-winter point, and it's to remind us that spring is near." She laughed, "Oh, the kids; I teach second grade."

Jim exhaled with relief. "Well, I would have believed eight or ten."

She jabbed his ribs with her gloved hand. "Oh, would you?" They both laughed.

They helped themselves to coffee from the setup in the lobby, for early risers, and moved to a corner sofa.

Jim glanced at Ellen's dark hair bound in a ponytail and her large, brown, doe-like eyes. She wore no makeup, and her sculptured face, and pink lips and cheeks against a white, clear skin along with her slenderness indicated a healthy life style; that of an athlete.

As they sat down, Jim said, "So, tell me about Yellow Day."

Ellen smiled. "Everyone, teachers, staff, and students, wear something yellow. We have an assembly after lunch and serve cake. It's a fun day."

"Sounds like it," he said.

He told her about the business conference he would attend in a few hours. The time slipped by as they chatted, and then she raised her arm, revealing a slender wrist, to look at her watch. He noticed she wore no ring.

"It's time to go," she said.

"School time for you and conference time for me."

They rose and walked toward the door. He extended his hand and found hers softer than he expected. He liked soft hands and held hers a little longer than he should have. "Thanks again."

Ellen nodded and smiled; then stepping down the stairs she tugged on her gloves and cap and started down the path toward the road.

He felt his heart sink. "Ellen?" he called.

After only a few steps she stopped and turned, dark hair swinging over her shoulder. She looked up at him.

"Dinner tonight?"

"Sorry, I can't. Yellow Day tomorrow. I have to meet with some of my teacher friends and get things ready."

It wouldn't be Yellow Day for him. He planned to leave tomorrow at noon. They stood facing each other. In another second she'd run off.

"How about tomorrow?" he blurted.

Ellen looked up at the torn sweatpants and bloodstained knee. *The poor guy!* She started to say, "I can't," for a second time, remembering a business appointment on her schedule. But clipping off the "t" it came out "I can...work it out."

"Great! How do I find you; you know I get lost easily".

"Just find Kaiser and then turn right on Hillside. Large, gray house; 1228."

"I'll be there. 6:30 okay?"

She nodded, turned, and jogged into the gray mist. Realizing the time, she picked up the pace and made a fist with her right hand, thinking of Jim's lingering touch.

Due to her morning diversion, Ellen's run took a different route. She wound her way through the neighborhood until she turned one last corner, onto her normal course, planning to finish in the usual way, with a full sprint for the last quarter mile. When she reached the top of the last hill, her house came into view. As she neared the intersection, a green sedan sat at on the right side, about half a block down the street. It was not there when she started out. She looked straight ahead, at the car, wondering if someone was inside. At the intersection she turned right, with her eyes still on the car. Slowing to a trot she scaled the stairs of the porch and opened the door. Inside, she ran into the foyer, and then through door on the left, into her office. She peered through the curtains, but discerned no movement in the car. Ellen shrugged and went upstairs to shower to prepare for school.

A short time later, Ellen hurried toward her car and climbed behind the wheel. At the intersection, she glanced right, at the empty street. During the five-minute drive she turned her attention to school. The morning adventure wouldn't disrupt her day, but it gave her an interesting lunchtime story for the teachers at Ethan Allen Elementary School.

All of the teachers looked forward to the excitement of Yellow Day. This year Ellen mentored Molly Gavin, a young and enthusiastic first year teacher. Ellen enjoyed Molly's energy and vitality. She thought back to the morning a few days earlier. "How was your weekend with Byron, Molly?"

Molly blushed, "We had a great time. Went to the Main Point Café and enjoyed hearing Donna sing an opening set for the Golden Warriors' performance. Then we went to dinner and hung out with friends."

"Sounds great." Ellen longed for a fuller social life, like Molly's, but she enjoyed talking with Molly, and liked her great enthusiasm.

Molly nodded and then asked, "Ellen, can you help me with some ideas for Yellow Day?"

"Sure, you're welcome to borrow my file. And don't forget to request yellow paper for all of your worksheets. I'm cutting paper for the window flowers now. Do you want to borrow my tulip and daffodil tracers?"

"Why are the flowers so big?"

"Oh, the kids like to trace and cut them out, and then we put them in the windows. They look great! And Karen and Judy have the kids make yellow paper chains to hang from the ceiling."

"Well, I'd better get busy! I thought I'd just have to help at the staff social and not plan things for the whole day! What else should I do?"

"You can put out yellow paint for one of your work centers. I'm having the Room Mothers bring yellow juice, yellow napkins, and cookies or cupcakes with, of course, yellow icing. Last year they were great and sent in yellow Jell-O Jigglers. The kids loved them!"

"I'm getting a late start. It'll be hard for me to catch up with all of the things you're doing."

"I'll let you share some of my things."

Later at lunchtime, Ellen entered the cafeteria and found a spot among her usual group. Opening her brown bag she spread the assortment of vegetables, fruit and pasta salad before her. When she mentioned her encounter with Jim, Karen immediately asked the expected question, "Was he cute?"

"I didn't notice," brought a chorus of guffaws and snickering.

"That means he was," Barb said, one of the members of Ellen's second-grade team.

"I'll take another look when we go to dinner," Ellen replied.

They reacted with an exchange of glances and oohs, continuing their friendly banter.

"Dinner is it? Well, aren't we moving fast?" Karen teased.

Ellen began to blush. She had trouble with these casual discussions about men.

Barb added, "Definitely a fast track."

Soon they were all taking their shots and attacking her with an onslaught of good-natured kidding. After they had spent themselves with their first round of jibes Ellen took the opportunity to respond.

"Okay, okay, you guys are all jealous. Why don't you get up some morning and run with me and share my adventures?"

"Oh no, not me. I need my beauty sleep," Karen laughed.

"I'm not a morning person," Judy said, another of the pack.

"Call me when an adventure starts and I'll be there," Barb said.

Ellen responded to this one, "Sure, stand by for an early call from my cell phone tomorrow."

Jim's meetings were uneventful, but he enjoyed networking with people of common interests. He thought more about his dinner plans than he did about anything else. During the lunch break he located a shopping center, drove over and returned in time for the afternoon sessions.

After a quick dinner Jim returned to the inn for an evening of reading and watching CNN and CNBC. He walked out to the small lobby and filled his glass, then sipped and surfed between Larry King and Geraldo. They were each hammering away at the latest headline story about a scandal in the President's selection of a cabinet member.

The wine made him drowsy.

This would be a fun day for Ellen. The new principal had proclaimed dress down for Yellow Day. Ellen slipped her yellow sweater over a yellow turtleneck, and then slid on the freshly pressed khakis and sneakers, completing the look.

Ellen pulled into the Ethan Allen School parking lot smiling with thoughts of yesterday and at what lay ahead. The American Flag flapped in the strong wind, today sharing the flagpole with a another flag, a yellow Smiley Face. School windows made a statement with their bright yellow flowers, hearts and butterflies.

As she entered the school, a sea of yellow outfits filled the halls and classrooms amid the raised level of chatter brought on by the day's excitement. In the Cafetorium, a combined cafeteria/auditorium, Ellen passed the long tables covered with yellow tablecloths and stared at the centerpiece. *Who brought the daffodils? What a nice touch!*

Placing her miniature Cheese and Lemon Danish rolls on the buffet table she inhaled the aroma of fresh brewing coffee in three pots, thanks to Jack the custodian, who had started them at 6:00 AM. Pitchers of orange juice, the feature beverage, flanked the coffeepots. Across the room Ted, a first grade teacher wearing a yellow apron and chef's hat, flipped a round of his famous buttermilk pancakes at a table laden with scrambled eggs, muffins, bagels, fresh-cut fruit, and more flowers.

Ellen sought out her teammates. Karen wore a bright yellow blouse and a yellow plaid skirt, and Larissa appeared in a sweatshirt, a summer skirt, and nylons, all yellow; and her pride and joy, the old Keds sneakers spray-painted yellow. Coffee in hand, Ellen spotted Molly. "What do you think about Yellow Day?" she asked.

Molly, all smiles, raised her voice above the happy din. "This is crazy! But it's fun!"

Ellen motioned and led the way, "Come on, sign the tablecloth." Molly returned a puzzled look. This was a Yellow Day tradition. Molly followed Ellen to a long table covered with a yellow bed sheet. Names and dates appeared at random locations on the sheet. "Find a place and write your name," coached Ellen. Then, every year you'll add a tally mark. Look, here's Bobbie Stiles' name. She was the kindergarten teacher who started this whole tradition. And when she retired she wrote the date again, for a final time."

"Wow! She taught here for twenty years!" exclaimed Molly in awe. Then she leaned over to find a spot and signed her name and the date.

Ellen smiled, remembering her own inaugural signing six years earlier.

After an hour of socializing and having breakfast, the Principal, Mrs. Stuart took the stage, wishing the teachers a "Happy Yellow Day!" Then Ellen entered the queue to refill her coffee cup and headed for her second grade classroom.

A short time later her group of excited children tumbled into the room she greeted each arriving child. "Happy Yellow Day, Bobby! Happy Yellow Day Sue!"

"Happy Yellow Day, Miss Cramwell!" said Jamie, one of her favorites, handing Ellen a small pot of primroses.

"Thank you, Jamie! I love flowers! I'll put this on my desk."

Throughout the day the school swarmed with squealing children and staff clad in yellow. The children who had forgotten about the event were conspicuous with makeshift yellow ties and ribbons fabricated of crepe paper. The cafeteria staff entered into the fun with yellow macaroni and yellow juice, and served a yellow cake for dessert.

At the end of the day, when the festivities ended, Ellen sat at her desk and cleaned up for the evening. She lifted her briefcase and another small one containing her portable computer, and started down the hall. In the silence of her car, thoughts of dinner with Jim ran through her head.

She climbed the stairs and entered her apartment. As the door swung open, she dropped her cases on the floor, near a small table. A wall clock showed 5:35. *Less than an hour.* She headed for her bedroom to prepare for her date. *I wonder what he's like?*

Jim woke again to the soft music. The dial read 6:00, an oversight; he had forgotten to change the alarm for another hour of sleep. He turned off the music and closed his eyes. *Only for a few more minutes.* When he looked at the clock again, the green numbers displayed 7:40. *Damn, now I'm late.* He jumped out bed, showered, dressed, had a quick breakfast. He would be late for the morning session.

During a break at noon, he drove back to the shopping center again. Along the way he found Kaiser and his flag fence, and then explored the neighborhood, including a drive by Ellen's house. He admired the old colonial style building. A huge structure, it seemed too big for her to live in alone.

He spent the afternoon working at his computer, and then at five o'clock he stopped. After dressing, Jim observed his reflection in the mirror, thinning hair, light brown, with a few traces of gray. Exercising had kept his weight down but not without a struggle. Recalling the first impression, of lying in the street, sucking on a bleeding hand, clothes torn, lost, and at the mercy of a dog, he shook his head, smirking at this image. *Cool guy.* He started down the hall, planning a timely arrival at Ellen's.

Jim drove up the quiet, wooded lane to the intersection at the corner of Ellen's house. He turned right and parked at exactly 6:30. He picked the package off the seat and got out of the car. Slipping on his all-occasion raincoat he smiled at the *London Fog* label. As he started across the street, the door opened and Ellen came down the steps, catching him off guard. She wore a dark coat and slacks, a yellow sweater visible at her neckline. He smiled and held out his package as he crossed the street, greeting her at the curb with, "Happy Yellow Day!"

Ellen accepted the package with a look of pleasure on her glowing face and continued toward the car. Jim turned and followed her lead back toward the car, puzzled at how she took control of his arrival and their departure.

When they drove off she opened the package containing a single, yellow rose. "This was very nice of you, Jim. It's delightful."

"Normally it would have been red," he replied. "Where to?"

"A small local restaurant. You'll like it."

"You lead the way."

After a short drive they reached an intersection at the edge of the residential neighborhood. It looked like the center of a thriving community of the Revolutionary War era, with an old Post Office and a few shops on one side of the street, and on the other, one of the quaint old restaurants that populates New England. A white building with black shutters and a black sign with gold letters, Brookfern House. A porch ran the full length of the front of the building. Along one side a small brook and a waterwheel added to the charm.

"I see the brook. What about the fern?" Jim asked.

"Come back in the summer and you'll find lots."

"It's a date." He noticed her smile.

When they walked up the stairs onto the porch, candles flickering in windows evoked a warm welcome. Jim opened the door and the aroma of food and sounds of soft music greeted them. Turning to her Jim nodded, "This is a good start."

"It gets better."

Jim took her coat and handed it to the attendant behind the opening. Then, as he removed his raincoat she stared at him, a large smile appeared on her lovely face. He gazed at her, aware of his own red-faced grin, as her smile turned into a full laugh, exposing her white teeth through lips painted a soft pink. They stood there in yellow sweaters, two beacons illuminating the room.

"The flower, and now this; it's something to remember. The teachers will be buzzing tomorrow when I tell them."

"I wanted to share the spirit, but I thought maybe you'd change and I'd be solo," he said. "I'm glad you didn't."

"Well, lets make our entrance and give everyone else a laugh," she answered, placing her hand under his arm and leading him toward the dining room.

There a gray-haired man wearing a blue blazer greeted her. "Ellen, good to see you!" He gave quick glance at Jim. "I have a nice place for you."

A candle and a small red rose adorned every table. Ellen seemed to know everyone, nodding and greeting several of the diners as they moved toward a window table with an ocean view. Although they sat in an out of the way corner, eyes from all of the tables were directed their way. "Looks like the yellow twins have created quite a stir," he said.

Ellen laughed, "It's all your fault. You just like being the center of attention."

They each ordered a seafood dish from the Inn's specialties, and Ellen chose a nice white wine. Jim sometimes had difficulty with conversation, but not tonight. Ellen made him comfortable, and he liked her sense of humor. He was surprised and pleased by the ease with which they talked; conversation with her had an unforced, genuine and natural quality of old friends, even after such a short time. Starting with her surprise answer to his question on her kids, followed by the gentle nudge to his ribs at his reply, he felt a warm rapport had developed between them. He wondered what Ellen thought about him.

Ellen took her first opportunity to survey Jim. He had a pleasant face, blue eyes, and brown hair, and seemed trim for his age, kind of handsome. What was he, maybe forty, forty-five? Attached in any way? He had to be. "Lots of travel in your job? What do you do?" Ellen asked.

"Mostly driving in the northeast; a little flying. I work for ECD, an Information Services Company located in Chicago, Electronic Computer Data."

"I've heard of them. The owner is a billionaire."

Jim nodded and continued, "I have an office in my house, outside of Philadelphia. It's set up with a telephone, computer, fax, and copier. I write, create business plans and presentations, and manage consulting work for clients. I spend lots of time on-line exchanging e-mail and documents with people all over the world. ECD has a great network and lots of bright people to work with."

"How do you like working at home?"

"It would be hard to go back to a traditional office work style. I have great flexibility in the use of my time as long as I deliver documents, respond to phone calls promptly, and keep the projects running."

"Sounds interesting, but don't you miss having some people around to talk to?"

"I talk to people a lot, but it's almost always by phone. I get to travel every two or three weeks to meet with real people face-to-face, like I am this week."

"I don't know, it sounds kind of lonely."

"It's not lonely, but it is different. I meet new people every day. You don't have to be in the same place to conduct business. I'm probably in two or three teleconferences every week involving six or eight people, all in different locations. The hardest part is setting up these meetings and getting everyone to attend on time. You get pretty good at it after a while. And I probably send and receive twenty or thirty e-mail messages a day.

"Do you have a secretary, or admin, as they say these days? Who helps you out?"

"There are people in our business group who are assigned to help with those things. I make my own travel arrangements by computer and through the company travel office, and I have phone numbers to order supplies and to help me with computer problems. I really believe this is the future. The business world is competitive and you have to do things better, faster, and cheaper than everyone else who's chasing your clients."

Ellen thought for a second and then remarked, "It's a lot different from my world. I can't imagine trying to teach my second graders without being there with them."

"But don't you have a computer at home, and computers in your classroom?"

"Yes, I have a computer at home. I use it for e-mail, mostly, and some for teaching. The kids at school are really good at using them. Most of them know more than I do."

"Lots of those kids will all be working at home and they'll figure out ways to do things that will make my setup look like the dark ages."

She liked the way he linked her world to his. "You may be right."

Jim looked at her and said, "What about you? Tell me your story. Why teaching?"

"You sound like my father. He wanted to set me up with a job in his business, but I never took the bait. I wasn't sure what I wanted, but I knew what I didn't want."

"What business?"

"Here in Connecticut. He does engineering design and manufactures parts for the automotive and aircraft industries."

Jim nodded, then he asked, "Why second grade? Why not sixth, or eighth, or high school?"

"I like the younger kids. Those are the formative years where you can instill a desire for learning. High school might be interesting because it's more like an adult relationship, but not quite. I'm happy where I am. You, know, I did work in Philadelphia for a while."

"You did? Tell me about it."

Ellen gave a short synopsis of an earlier job and then their conversation wove among a variety of topics from movies to books, travel, and college. The waiter cleared the table and placed dessert menus before each of them.

"I usually don't do this, but pick one out and I'll help you out," he said, scanning the options.

"I usually do. I'll accept your offer. How about coffee?"

"Sure."

Ellen chose a chocolate mousse with raspberries and whipped cream served in a large wineglass. They took turns dipping into the soft creamy mixture with long spoons until they were each scraping the edges of the glass for the remains.

Ellen smiled at Jim, "For someone who doesn't usually do this, you performed quite well."

He put down his spoon, "I said I didn't usually do it, not that I didn't like to do it. I love desserts, and I've had more than my share. I try to have some discipline and limit my intake to special occasions. This one is special." He glanced into her eyes and then looked at her empty coffee cup. "More?"

"No, that was just right."

After the drive back Jim parked the car and they walked toward Ellen's house. Jim noticed the glowing porch light near the front door. Earlier, when Ellen came down the stairs to meet him the light was off. They walked to the top of the stairs and she turned to him, holding her yellow rose.

"Jim, it was an evening I won't forget. Thanks for everything."

"You chose the restaurant, I couldn't have done that well; and when I'm traveling, it's rare to have company at dinner. It was fun, especially the Yellow Day stuff."

"Yes, especially that."

She moved to the doorway, pushed it open, and then turned to him again. He took the cue and leaned toward her, moving his hand behind her head, drawing her to him and pressing his other hand on the doorframe. Jim inhaled her fragrance as her lips, soft and warm, met his. When he moved his hand it touched her earlobe and something slid through his fingers, making a quiet plop as it landed on the carpet inside the door. The distraction almost caused him to pull away, but it could wait for a few seconds.

When their faces separated he reached down. "You dropped something," he said, handing her an earring.

"I know," she took it from him in her gloved hand.

"Goodnight Jim; it's late and I have my second-graders early in the morning."

He caught the message, took a step back and said, "Me too, I have to get out early." Then, taking her hands in his, he gave them a squeeze, smiled and nodded. In three quick steps he was onto the street.

"Jim?" she called.

He looked over his shoulder.

"Call if you ever get back here," she said.

He nodded, turned, waved, and continued on, smiling and with heart beating a little faster.

—2—

On his drive back to the inn, Jim thought about the events of the evening. It had been pleasant, like spending time with someone whom he might have known for years. The absolute comfort with Ellen stirred memories of another, long ago. *Had it been long enough?*

A few disturbing questions clouded the evening. Why did she come down the stairs before he could get to her door? She seemed in a hurry to get into the house. Who turned on the light? Despite their comfort with each other they had not gotten too personal. If it were a female housemate, why wouldn't she want to introduce her? Was she living with a guy? Why did she accept Jim's invitation to dinner? And she asked him to call. As his car entered the parking lot he glanced at his watch, only 9:30.

Jim sat on the bed across from a small screen television. He considered himself a world class channel surfer. Mulling over the evening he clicked from channel to channel. At 11:30 he returned to the lobby for a second glass of wine, hoping it would help him fall asleep.

He awoke to a gentle melody, tired and confused after a restless night. After a shower and shave he listened to his voice mail. Then he dressed and connected his computer to the phone outlet to read and respond to e-mail messages. A short while later he packed and checked out of the inn.

The drive home took five hours from door to door. He could have made it in three or four by air, but flying had its schedule uncertainties and all of the aspects of parking, handling luggage, waiting in line, checking in, and passing through security. They made traveling unpleasant. The car-phone, every hour or so, kept him touch with events until he got back. He had more time to think about yesterday. *It was a great evening. But was she holding something back? But she asked me to call.* He continued his ruminations as the broken white lines slid by.

That evening Jim opened his day planner and located the reminder message. He dialed the number. After several rings he heard a click, and then another ring. Then a harsh, male voice answered. "Hello." Jim felt himself start on a downswing.

"I'm calling for Ellen."

The man's voice was gruff. "She's not here."

"Do you know when she'll be home?"

"No, but it'll be late."

"This is Jim Dulles. Will you please tell her I called."

"Yes." Click. The line was dead.

The conversation, if that's what it was supposed to be, had been terse. *Who was living there with her? Could this guy be mad that she went out with Jim? She has to be involved with someone.*

The following morning in Jim's basement office, a radio played classical music while he worked at the computer. Immersed in the financial plan for a new business offering, he heard the doorbell ring. Swinging his chair from the keyboard he stood and ran up the stairs. As Jim swung the door open, a police officer wearing a gray shirt and black tie confronted him. A second officer stood behind the first. *What's this about?* Jim tensed, thinking of his children, hoping he was wrong.

The large policeman, looming in the doorway, said "I'm Sergeant Olsen," then pointing to his associate, "and this is Officer Dunn. Are you Jim Dulles?"

"Yes, I am. What is it?"

"We want to talk with you."

"What do you mean? What's going on?" Jim pulse began pounding.

"Do you know Ellen Cramwell?"

Astonished by the unexpected question, Jim replied, "Ellen, yes, I just met her a few days ago."

"We want you to come with us to the police station to talk about it."

"What happened? Is there something wrong?"

"You'll find out when we get to the station."

"To the station? Can't we talk about it here?"

"No, we have some questions to ask you."

Jim stood, staring at the officers; then he said, "I have to shut off the lights and my computer and get my keys."

When Jim turned to walk away, Olsen said, "Wait a minute!" Both policemen entered the door. Olsen signaled for the other officer to follow Jim and then said, "Go ahead."

As Officer Dunn watched, Jim returned to his office, shut down the computer, turned off the radio, and then the lights. Jim and the officer returned to the top of the stairs where Jim removed his keys from a small box on a table near the door.

Outside, they approached the police car conspicuous in the driveway. *The neighbors will be wondering about this.* Jim asked, "Now can you tell me what happened?"

"You'll find out soon enough. No more questions," replied Olsen, opening the car door.

They drove in silence as the car wound its way through the suburban streets. Jim stared ahead, his thoughts on the wonderful evening, then on driving back home to his work routine; now this surprising occurrence. *What's going on?* Maybe Ellen had been in a car accident or...but they didn't have to take him to the police station to tell him that. No, this was about a crime. Without warning, he had been thrust into the middle of something unusual. *What happened to her? Was she hurt, or worse? Is this a dream?* Incredulous, he pondered the situation presented by the police, one he would never have imagined.

When they arrived at the Radnor Township building, the police examined Jim's driver's license and asked a few basic questions. Then they led him to another room, and directed him to sit at table opposite the uniformed Sergeant Olsen, another heavyset man wearing a shirt and tie, and a young woman wearing dark slacks and a gray sweater. As Jim's mind raced as he mulled over the possibilities, Sergeant Olsen asked, "Okay, how do you know Ellen Cramwell?"

Overcome by his own thoughts, Jim did not hear the sergeant.

"How do you know Ellen Cramwell?" the officer asked again with emphasis, glancing at his two partners.

Now, conscious of the question Jim replied, "I met her on Monday." Then he related the events of the two days in Connecticut, the morning encounter in the fog, dinner on Tuesday, and then his drive back Wednesday.

"Did you go inside her house?"

"No."

The inquisitors exchanged glances.

"I didn't!" he iterated.

"Your fingerprints were inside her house."

Jim took a deep breath. "Fingerprints! What do you mean? Why are you talking about fingerprints? I wasn't inside her house; only on the porch by the door." He noticed their reaction to his answer, the eye movements.

Olsen continued, "Ellen Cramwell is missing. She hasn't been seen in two days. You saw her the day before she disappeared. There are several witnesses who can describe you."

The color, yellow, came to Jim's mind and the word, conspicuous. *How did they get my fingerprints?* Then he remembered. His fingerprints were on record as part of a top clearance required for consulting work he'd done for the Defense Department. But he hadn't been in her house. *How could they be inside?*

The police questioned him for an hour, taking notes and repeating the questions in different forms. His answers were the same. When they finished, Sergeant Olsen said, "We're finished for now. But we may want to talk with you again. Don't go anywhere."

"What does that mean?" replied Jim. "I may have to travel on business."

"Don't go anywhere unless you tell us."

"I didn't do anything. Are you arresting me?"

"No, we just don't want you disappearing, too."

"I'm getting a lawyer."

"You can call a lawyer. If your lawyer wants to talk to us, ask for Sergeant Olsen. We'll take you home now."

On the drive back to his house, Jim recycled the events of the past few days in his mind. A chance meeting with a woman, now someone he wanted to know better; a new excitement in his life now shattered by uncertainty. *Where is this going?* The police car slowed and entered Jim's driveway.

Jim Dulles came from a small town near Pittsburgh, a place like many others where coal and steel provided the jobs, and high school football, the weekend entertainment. He lived with a large family group where three generations occupied the same house. In high school, a knee injury in the first game of his senior year ended Jim's aspiration to play football at Penn State, but his interests in mathematics and science led him to apply to the engineering college. He concentrated on academics after that and became a spectator and student of Penn State football.

Jim had established a strong group of high school friendships and found it hard to leave them behind. He also dated a number of different girls in high school, but he left for college without a serious attachment.

Among the new friends he made in college, Aaron Moskowitz emerged as the best. Aaron came from Brooklyn and his parents were from an area he called Russia-Poland, because the border would change after each new conflict, much like the Balkans in the 1990s. Jim and Aaron discussed their Polish connection many times. They attended synagogue services and Catholic Mass together on a few occasions. Their connection regarding Penn State football, movies, and their academic directions established a strong friendship cemented by their common sense of humor. They spent countless hours watching *Boris and Natasha*, *Rocky and Bullwinkle*, and Peter Sellers movies. They met during their freshman year and laughed their way to graduation, never having a serious argument or exchanging words that they regretted. Jim cherished this unique relationship.

Aaron didn't have a driver's license when he met Jim. During their junior year, Jim taught Aaron to drive and helped him buy a new car. They decided to take a few courses during summer school and both landed jobs in the engineering laboratory, running tests, grading papers, and assisting with equipment maintenance. As summer school came to a close in mid August, Jim connected with a group of students from the Philadelphia area who planned to spend a week at one of the ocean beaches of southern New Jersey. Jim thought Aaron might like to join the group.

Aaron was measuring the alignment of a pressure test setup when Jim walked into the lab. Jim asked, "How'd you like to go, down the shore?"

"What's, down the shore?" replied Aaron.

"It's where Philadelphians go in the summer."

"You mean to the beach."

"You go to the beach, they go, down the shore."

"What shore?"

"New Jersey, of course; for a week. Al Capers; remember him?"

"Sure."

"He has a house in Ocean City. He's getting a group together to pay for the house he rented. Upstairs, downstairs deal; guys downstairs, girls upstairs. He asked me today and I told him I'd talk to you. It's a cheap way to have some fun and forget school for a while."

"Sounds good. I'm in." Aaron was unattached, like Jim.

"You can drive," Jim said.

"So that's the con," Aaron said.

"No con. You always wanted to drive somewhere, now that you have a car."

"Okay, okay. Anyhow, I'll feel safer. I'm a better driver than you are."

"Yeah, sure. Have you paid the repair bill from your collision yet?" Aaron had a minor fender bender trying to park the first week after he bought the car.

"That was no collision. And it wasn't my fault."

"Yeah, yeah; that parked car slammed into you."

"I had the right of way."

They both laughed.

On a Saturday morning in August, Aaron's blue-green Oldsmobile entered the driveway to Jim's house, a basement apartment he shared with another student. Standing out front, Jim picked up the two canvas bags at his feet and called to Aaron, "Let's go, down the shore."

As they started east from State College, Jim unfolded the roadmap and started his navigation duties. He liked geography and found maps intriguing and an interesting way to pass the time; he always searched for faster ways to get there. And he knew Aaron was happier behind the wheel, thrilled with his new mobility and making up for his late start at driving.

After a pleasant drive across Pennsylvania the traffic increased as they passed through Philadelphia and then worsened as the shore vacationers aggregated into a slow crawl for the last thirty miles. The rental houses changed hands on Saturday and the arriving vacationers crowded the roads inbound for their week of fun in the sun. It was afternoon when Jim, pointing and naming streets, brought them to the front of a gray, two-story house one block from the beach, their destination. The bright sun and clear sky signaled the start of a great week.

On the porch, Al Capers with a beer can in his hand called out, "What took you so long?"

Jim replied, "Hey, we're not local yokels like you are. We're right on time."

"Have a beer," said Al. Then he grabbed two of their bags. "Follow me. Pick out a bunk that doesn't look like it's taken."

Aaron and Jim obliged with the beer suggestion, lifted their remaining luggage, and climbed the steps to the porch into a comfortable house where they would spend the week. Jim asked who else would be there and Al recited a list of names, some familiar, some not. Al added that there were two couples, but all of the others were unattached. Aaron set out to introduce himself to some of the new roommates. Jim tossed his bags on a small cot and explored the house to get his bearings.

A short while later Jim walked toward the beach, trying to find the rest of the group. A waving arm attached to a cute body caught his attention. He walked toward the familiar face with the qualities of a classic shore specimen; short, sun-bleached hair, blue eyes, perfect smile, and a great tan contrasting a white bathing suit. Jim could see why Jeannie was Al's true love.

Jim unfurled his blanket and parked himself next to her. "Hi, Jeannie, your new neighbor is here." As they chatted he gazed out at the crashing waves; each accompanied by its own roar blended with shrieks of bathers who climbed and bobbed like corks on the wet, rolling mounds. A blue sky and gentle breeze added to the shore experience. He lay back, closed his eyes, and began to relax.

He heard Jeannie's voice, "Jim?"

His eyes opened. "I must have dozed off. How long has it been?"

"About ten minutes, I guess. I figured it out when you stopped answering my questions."

"Sorry."

"No need. I'm going for a swim. Want to come?"

"Sure." Jim rose to his knees and scanned the water line. His eyes locked on a green bathing suit with someone who looked great in it. She was sprinting in toward Jeannie's blanket, chased by one of the guys he remembered seeing on the porch.

"Who's that?" Jim asked.

"Gail Nardelli; interested?"

"I don't know her, but I'd like to."

Jim and Jeannie turned their heads to watch the sprinters dash by the blanket.

"Sorry," said the girl in green, kicking up sand while sliding to a halt. Then she said, "Jeannie, who's the new guy?"

"This is Jim. Jim, Gail."

"Hi," Gail said.

"Hi." Jim looked into Gail's eyes and fell in love.

That week for Jim was about having fun. He got his first taste of salt water, and saw little of Aaron, who seemed to be having a good time. He spent most of his time with Gail, but had to fight off the competition, consisting of everyone downstairs that just met her and half the other guys on the beach that wanted to. But after two days everyone accepted them as a pair to be left alone. She would be a senior and they would both graduate next year.

As they walked along the beach one evening Gail asked, "Why haven't I ever met you before? You know Al and Jeannie pretty well, don't you?"

"Good question. I know Al, but just met Jeannie a few weeks ago. And I haven't known Al for very long."

"Jeannie's my best friend," Gail said.

"She seems nice."

"She is; she introduced me to you."

Gail smiled. "What made you come this week?"

"Don't know. Needed a break, and had to find out what, down the shore, meant."

Gail chuckled. "Well, this is it. Ocean, sun, sand, girls, boys, beer, and time."

"I've never heard the formal definition. Is that what it says in the dictionary?"

"Doesn't appear in all dictionaries. Only the ones printed in Philadelphia."

"How about you; do you do this every summer?"

"Since I can remember. My family comes here every year and I started this group thing since I've been at Penn State."

"I wish I had known about it sooner."

"Better late than...What about you? Where do you go if not down the shore?"

"Up to Lake Erie, or to the mountains; fresh water lakes. The salt is strange to me. When I took that first mouthful, wow!"

She smiled at his twisted face. "I've been to the Poconos a few times. That's fun, too."

"We'll go the mountains sometime."

She responded with a smile and a twinkling eye, "I'd like that."

During the drive back, Jim couldn't stop talking about Gail. Aaron listened and nodded.

"I guess it's pretty obvious I'm hooked," Jim said.

"Really? You could have fooled me. I thought this was just a casual thing. It's not like she's on your mind or anything like that."

Jim laughed. "Well, then let me tell you about her."

"Okay, okay. I've had enough. I've never seen you like this. She must be something special."

"Special, she really is."

As the excitement of the week wore off and reality set in, Jim began to worry. Was this just a summer shore romance that would fade in the fall? After a few weeks he found that Gail had not yet returned to school. He spent the next week thinking about her and waiting for her to appear, and to pick up where they had left off.

Registration for the fall semester started the following week. In the large ancient auditorium, Rec. Hall, Jim and Aaron handled the paperwork for freshmen and sophomores. During a lull in the activity Jim said to Aaron, "I'm taking a break; ten or fifteen minutes."

"Ok. I'll take one when you get back."

Jim rose and walked across the crowded floor among the scurrying students. In front of him, Gail stood in one of the many lines. Butterflies swarmed in his stomach. When she saw him he waved. She smiled back and nodded, but didn't stop talking to the guy in the white sweater who stood next to her.

Jim started toward Gail but decided not to interfere just then. At that moment, Jim decided to find a way to make Gail the woman in his life.

Jim's enthusiasm turned to disappointment. When he phoned Gail, she seemed friendly but cautious, more like a casual friend than someone with whom he had shared some of his deepest thoughts. It soon became obvious to him that she didn't want to proceed as fast as he did. He began to wonder about her feelings toward him. Maybe he had it all wrong. It was too good. He wanted to recapture the magic of that week. Perhaps it would never happen.

One afternoon, midway through the semester, Jim and Aaron sat in a booth having coffee at the Corner Room Restaurant. After sharing some of his frustrations concerning Gail, he asked Aaron for his thoughts.

"Back off Jim. You're in a full court press. Go back to a zone. If she's right for you and you for her, you'll get together. Give her some breathing room."

Jim remembered his conversation in the car with Aaron. He had never stopped pressing. Aaron was right, time to back off.

He found it hard not to call, and made conscious decisions to restrain himself, but he took Aaron's advice. Gail's caution had a reason, and he hadn't taken the time to discover that reason. He decided to slow down, let her talk, and listen. Patience might take him where his eagerness had not.

During the second semester, Jim's last, recruiters from all over the United States arrived on campus to find the raw talent that would shape the future of the companies they represented. Jim began a job interviewing process in late February that ran through April. In a sellers market, an engineering graduate with good grades could attract a number of lucrative offers, and Jim had finished well up in his class. He scheduled several first round interviews and accepted four invitations to visits companies where specific positions would be defined and offers made. After trips to Indiana, Ohio, and Connecticut, Jim arranged to visit Aerospace Controls, a company in Valley Forge, Pennsylvania.

He called Gail and told her about his plans. "What do you think of Valley Forge?" he asked.

"It's very nice. I hear the living is expensive, but the park is beautiful. We've gone there for picnics."

Jim wondered who she meant by, we.

"My Dad worked near there and the family sometimes celebrated birthdays and had family picnics there, or else in Fairmount Park."

Relieved by her response, Jim replied, "Well, this will be my last interview. Want to come along?"

"That would be fun. I could visit home while you're down there. Okay."

A few days later Jim stood at Gail's apartment door. "Ready to go?" he asked.

She smiled. "Yes, I've been looking forward to it."

He liked the words, but there seemed to be an element in her tone, one he couldn't put his finger on. Was it forlorn?

A short time later as they headed east on route 322 Jim started the conversation. "I think we've had lots of fun together, Gail. Don't you?"

"Yes, starting with the shore."

"Somehow we haven't talked about the serious things lately."

"Like what?"

"Like after graduation; and why you seem so cautious about me."

She looked at him and he started to dread the direction of the conversation. He was pressing her. He decided to say nothing more. *Slow down, Jim and let her talk.*

After five minutes of silence, Gail turned to him and said, "Find a place to stop."

He had not expected such a serious response, and it scared him. *What am I getting into?*

A short time later he exited the highway and drove to an ice cream stand. He carried the two cones to a small picnic table where she sat. The mountains and a small pond provided a scenic view. When he sat across from her wondering what was to come. *Let her start, and listen.* They licked their ice cream but neither spoke.

Gail looked out over the mountains, avoiding his eyes. "You deserve to know this."

I deserve; this sounds serious.

She took a deep breath and drove right to the point, like ripping a Band-Aid off to shorten the pain. "I have a young child who lives with my parents. That's why I never took you to meet them. Nobody at school knows, not even Jeannie." She spoke without looking at him.

The words made him numb; out of control, like drowning in one of those ocean waves, unable to catch his breath. Silence. Time passing. Ice cream running down his hand.

"I didn't want to lead you on and hurt you," she continued. "But I didn't want you to leave either."

He said nothing, but recalled the first time he saw her, a beauty in a green bathing suit, a picture of innocence flirting on the beach, a flower that he wanted to pluck. *Innocence?* He couldn't find the right words so he remained silent. They sat looking off into the distance, finishing their ice cream. Then he finally spoke, "How? How did it happen?" He wanted her talk about it. He wanted to listen.

"I had a high school romance and got into a bad crowd. They were drinking too much and I wanted to belong, to fit in. He seemed like a nice guy. One night we went too far with the drinking, and with...." Her words trailed off to silence.

Jim started to comment. Stopped. *Listen.*

"We're an Italian Catholic family. I remember how I was shaking when I told my parents. I hurt them so badly. They reacted first with screaming and anger, then crying and anguish."

Jim pictured the scene, and imagined himself in that situation with his own family. He didn't want to think about it.

31

Gail continued looking off into the distance, and then she spoke again, "For a month you could cut the tension; it dominated everything that happened in our house. I was afraid to be there and spent a lot of time anywhere but there. Every time I walked in the door I felt...I think the word is angst. After a while my mother came around and then my Dad. Tension breaking. More crying, this time, me."

He noticed her glance at him, fleeting, and then she looked out to the mountains again. "Finally, realization that they had to deal with the situation. And above all, love, for a daughter and a grandchild. Mom and Dad helped me covered up my condition until June. I faked sickness and left school a few weeks early. That summer we took a, vacation, and the baby was born at the end of August, in Scranton. I stayed at my aunt's house. After that, my parents said they wanted me to have a normal college life, as normal as possible under the circumstances. They said they would take care of the baby. I couldn't believe them, after what I had done. God, I cried when they offered to do that."

"Gail, they have to be very exceptional people. You said it, love for a daughter and grandchild. You're lucky to have that kind of love." Then he asked, "Jeannie doesn't know?"

"I met Jeannie my freshman year. I wanted to tell her, but was afraid. I didn't want her to have to carry my secret. And if I told her someone else might find out and I'd be destroyed."

"Boy or girl?"

"Girl; Tracey; my mother's name is Theresa."

"So she'd be three now?"

"Yes, she'll be four on August 26th."

"Must have been tough for you." His shock gave way to empathy. She looked so vulnerable, sitting there opening her soul to him.

"Yes, and for my family. They wanted a big wedding for me, with grandchildren later. I gave them no wedding, and now they're second parents to Tracey."

"What happened to...your boyfriend?"

"He bailed out. I thought I knew him, but I was a child. He joined the Army; I never heard from him. He went to Vietnam, was ambushed and died, kind of a hero."

"Did he know about Tracey?"

"Yes."

"Do you think he'd have come back to Tracey and you?"

"I'll never know."

"So, this explains your caution with me."

"Yes, but mostly because I was afraid to tell you; of what you would think."

A feeling of comfort, that she had confided in him, competed with disarray, about this young woman whose history had a dark spot that he would never have expected. He wondered if he could be ever deal with it.

"I'm sorry, Jim" she said, her eyes becoming glassy. A small drop of ice cream ran down her chin.

Jim felt Gail's relief at sharing her secret. He reached over with thumb, wiped it off and tasted it. "Black raspberry," he said. Then he took her chin between his thumb and forefinger and drew it gently toward him. She leaned forward, accepting the invitation and they shared a soft kiss.

They drove the rest of the way lost in their own thoughts, making occasional small talk. He dropped her off in Philadelphia and set her suitcase down on the walk in front of her house. "I have to get out to Valley Forge," he said.

She accepted his hint. "Thanks for the ride, Jim. See you Sunday."

"Okay, I'll call you when I'm ready."

Gail hauled her suitcase toward the stairs. He got back into the car and turned the key. As he drove away, a picture appeared in the rearview mirror, a small child climbing into her mother's arms.

The following morning, a full day confronted Jim, including interviews, lunch at a great restaurant near the park, and a drive through the beautiful Main Line suburbs of Philadelphia. He was driven through some of the neighborhoods and provided

33

with a folder of materials to help him with a move into the area. Everything about the job impressed him: the people, the work, the opportunities, and the pay. An evening dinner with a group of prospective colleagues, a few of them recent hires, ended the exciting day. Compared with his other interviews he rated it his first choice, and in the back of his mind, lurked the proximity to Gail. Although he had made the decision to accept, he needed to get a formal offer, which would come within a week. He liked this because it would remove him away from the whirlwind recruiting courtship for a few days, where he could evaluate the offer without all of the pressure. He agreed to reply within a week of receiving it.

That evening, Jim returned to the hotel, changed clothes and packed for the drive back. He picked up the phone. After several rings he recognized Gail's voice. "Hi," he said.

"Oh, Jim. Thanks for calling," Gail replied. "How was it?"

"Really good. Even better than I expected."

"Are you going to take it?"

"I think so, but I need to get a letter offer, first."

"Oh, is that what you expected?

"Actually, I wasn't sure. At a few of my other interviews they gave me a letter offer on the spot. They asked for my reaction, and it was a little uncomfortable. This was better."

"Well, I'm sure it will be a nice offer."

"I hope so." He changed the subject, "What about going back? Will you be ready tomorrow morning?"

"Sure, I can take the train and meet you in Paoli. You won't have to come all the way back here. Would that be better?"

She was making it easy for him. "Sure. But how about Wayne instead? I looked at some nice neighborhoods there this afternoon and know my way to the station. It's a little shorter train ride for you, and I plan to explore the town for a few hours in the morning by myself."

"Okay. Wayne it is. What time?"

"Anytime after 10:00. Let's see." He fumbled through a folder of materials, and then found the train schedule. He ran his

finger across the table of times posted for Saturday. "Wayne;
how about 10:22? You leave 30th Street at 9:40"

"I'll see you there."

"Okay, goodbye, Gail."

"Goodbye, Jim."

The next morning, a warm, spring day, Jim explored the
residential areas where he would look for a place to live. His
feelings about the job were confirmed. He liked the
neighborhoods and the proximity to a large city by train or a
short drive. At 9:30 he found a parking spot and took a leisure
walk to explore the town. At 10:10 he stood on the outbound
platform looking up and down the tracks, four pair, the main line
for the Pennsylvania Railroad. A short time later, a horn
sounded and a locomotive light appeared inbound, toward
Philadelphia. He watched the mass of metal roar by, raising dust
and pieces of paper in its wake, hauling a string of freight cars
from points, west, reminding him of childhood days. A few
minutes later a commuter train appeared in the distance, heading
in the other direction. The string of old, maroon cars slowed
down and screeched to a halt. When Gail emerged from the
second car he waved and walked toward her.

She smiled and said, "Hi."

"Hi, right on time." He lifted her suitcase and carried it to
his car.

A short time later they passed through the tollbooth for the
Pennsylvania turnpike and then veered left onto the entry ramp,
toward Harrisburg. Gail asked about his morning exploration
and then about his interviews. Jim answered and kept the
discussions light, steering clear of serious talk. After Harrisburg,
Gail slept for about an hour, or at least she seemed to be dozing.
He wondered if it was just a way to keep from talking. Thankful
that he didn't have to keep making up topics to stay away from
the real one, Jim appreciated the silence,

—3—

Ellen peered through the curtains as Jim walked across the street toward his car. She still felt the gentle tingle of his kiss, thinking she'd long remember this evening. He energized her in a way that she had not experienced for some time. She watched his car drive away. *Will I ever see him again?*

After turning off the porch light she walked down the hall past the room where a screen flickered. As she started up the steps a harsh voice called, "Oh, you're back. I turned on the light."

"Yes, I noticed," she said, looking back over her shoulder. A man watched the flickering screen, a can of beer in his hand.

Ellen awoke to the chirping sound, blinked her eyes, and squinted at the lighted dial. She inhaled the pleasant aroma of brewing coffee, timed to start ten minutes before the sound of her alarm clock. She turned off the alarm, slid from the warmth of the bed, and swung her legs to the floor while glancing at the chair where the clothes she would wear today were laid out. Entering the kitchen barefoot, in a white nightgown, she poured a fresh mug of coffee. She stood by the counter and sipping the coffee as she scanned her lesson plans for today's classes. After finishing half the mug, she dressed in her usual jogging clothes: panties and jogging bra, a tee shirt, tight black running pants, and a turtleneck shirt. Ellen wore bright running shoes, blue and gray, with reflectors to for running in the dark. She pulled them over her thick, white socks, completing her cold weather running ensemble.

Ellen ran four of the five weekdays and once on the weekend. Jogging kept her fit and gave her time to think. She ran along two different routes: one hilly, through the residential area to the west where she had encountered Jim, the second course, flatter land along the ocean where she would run this morning.

After taking a day off for early arrival on Yellow Day, Ellen wanted today's run to be a strong one. She returned to the coffee counter, raised the mug to her lips, and drained the last drops. She placed it on the counter. Downstairs, in the foyer, she lifted her blue cap, gloves, a yellow windbreaker, and an orange reflective vest from the pegs near the exit where she kept them. The layers would keep out the icy air and wintry breezes and hold in the heat the body generated from the exercise.

When she opened the door and stepped onto the porch to face the cold winter morning. After a deep breath of the salt air, she zipped her windbreaker and swiped her right glove over the small bulge in her right pocket. She slipped on the vest, tugged her cap down on her head, and pulled the gloves over her hands.

Five minutes of warm-ups completed her preparations. She scanned the empty street as she walked down the porch steps. *Ready to go.* She crossed the street, turned right and made a quick left at the intersection. While checking her watch, she broke into a slow trot, counting the first 200 steps, and then she picked up the pace to normal running speed for her five-mile run.

The fog, which seemed lighter than it was two days ago, reminded her of the encounter with Jim. She smiled at the memory of their Yellow Day. They had connected within a very short time. He was kind, interesting, intelligent, and had a great sense of humor. They shared the pleasure of running. But, what was wrong? How could he not be married or somehow involved? She told him that she had once lived in Philadelphia, but they had not gotten into the details of their lives. She pondered over the likelihood of seeing him in Connecticut again, or of a phone call from him.

The road turned down toward the ocean, along a road never more than a quarter mile from the water, and often less than fifty feet. Houses positioned sparsely along the road, rose above the defining the terrain of low dunes covered by scattered shore grasses and shrubs. The white spire of the Congregational

Church rose before her, a striking landmark signaling her approach to the halfway point of her course. She neared the small village of shops and stores, all dark in quiet anticipation of the day's activities, feeling comfortable among the familiar surroundings.

As her feet slapped down on the brick-paved walkway through the Town Square, Ellen's thoughts returned to the evening with Jim. He had warmth she couldn't resist, so different from Kevin; Jim was just as handsome but also kind and considerate, evident even from their short time together. She couldn't think of anyone else who would have bought a yellow sweater on the spur of the moment. She liked his style.

Then she reflected on her first meeting with Kevin. He, too, had swept her off her feet with his worldliness and Irish humor. She had misread him, and now questioned her abilities and inexperience in judging men. Maybe she should be more cautious about Jim.

Ellen passed through the square with its old cannon and historic Revolutionary War monument, the point in her course where she turned back. She circled the monument and began the return route. It included a half-mile through a secluded area among the dunes, a place she called her quiet spot. The soft breezes and sounds of birds created a peaceful haven in the early evening, just before sunset, and in the morning, the best times to enjoy its wooded serenity. It became her habit to include this short stretch as part of the return course.

The sunlight climbing from the ocean started to brighten the morning sky when Ellen turned off the ocean road. As she removed the keys from her left pocket, another habit, preparing for the home stretch, the sound of an approaching vehicle broke the silence of the foggy road. She looked forward and saw nothing, then over her shoulder at a pair of headlights appearing through the mist, moving toward her along the narrow, tree-lined lane. An occasional car sometimes passed during her morning runs. Although reflectors made her visible, Ellen moved as far to the left as she could while glancing over her shoulder at the oncoming headlights. As the car crept along, she slowed down and tried to peer through the passing window. The vehicle moved past her slowly, as if searching for a spot, and then stopped. As she neared, the window on the driver's side rolled down revealing the large, round face of a man. He leaned out and beckoned to her with his hand.

Ellen grew cautious and stopped, maintaining a position on the edge of the road and eyeing the driver, who appeared to be alone. An obese man stared at her through the open window. She felt confident she could outrun him if he made a move, and she'd go back in the opposite direction.

"Where's the Cobb Fish Market?" the man asked.

While jogging Ellen had often been asked to give directions, it came with the territory of being a runner. Still, she kept her distance and leaned over to reply, placing her hands on her knees and staring back at the man. She started to point down the road when a cracking sound behind her, like a breaking limb, awakened her senses. When she turned to look, she felt a heavy grasp on her right shoulder and smelled the leather of a large, gloved hand, confirming the danger; at the same time the car door swung open toward her and the man started to get out. She tried to pull away but the man exiting the car reached out and took hold of her arm, knocking her keys to the ground. As she struggled the gloved assailant slid her cap over her face, engulfing her into darkness. His gloved hand covered her mouth and then she was lifted and placed in the back seat of the car. She heard a tearing sound and felt the hand on her lips replaced by tape before she could scream. Next, the tearing sound of more tape, tightness as they wrapped her wrists behind and then her ankles, and dread, of what might follow.

The whole incident took less than a minute, not a word spoken, after the request for directions. In the persisting silence she sensed only the sound of the car engine and her own breathing. The excitement and fear of the incident clouded her observations. She realized she couldn't remember the color and model of the car, and cursed her lack of attention to these details.

After a few seconds she started to count to get some sense of elapsed time; it helped her calm down. She felt the car taking numerous turns and lost all sense of direction.

When the car stopped, she mentally noted the number 1,287, a little over twenty minutes. They dragged her out of the car and carried her into a building and up a set of stairs. Terror overtook her when they tossed her onto a bed. She imagined the worst when a pair of hands removed her reflective vest and then pulled up the sleeve on her jacket. She started to struggle and felt her watch slide over her fist. A moment later she heard the door close and then footsteps on the stairs; and silence again. Ellen lay in darkness, immersed in terror, and uncertainty.

Jane Van Adams, one of five children in a wealthy family whose money came from the insurance business, had not wanted for physical comforts throughout her life. She chose to go to college at Wellesley, or rather it was chosen for her, following a long tradition of Van Adams women. She and Dave Cramwell (Caramelli) met as opponents in a college regatta. Dave had first become interested in sailing because of its scientific and engineering principles while Jane learned the fine points of sailing from her father, whose yacht, Brittany, was known as the one to beat in races in Narragansett Bay and Long Island Sound. Dave admired Jane's inherent sailing skills, while Dave's technical understanding of how to manage the challenges of wind and water impressed Jane.

Dave, raised in Boston, lived in an environment far different from Jane's. He chose Northeastern University for economic reasons. It had a cooperative education program in engineering, providing full-time employment for six months of the academic year. It extended the time required to graduate but it paid his tuition and living expenses, and left him with extra money for entertainment. He spent much of it on Jane.

The Van Adams family viewed Dave social status as a threat to all that they had tried to instill in Jane. Dave didn't have the cultural background the Van Adams family wanted for their daughter, nor the wealth to take care of her and raise their grandchildren in a manner that they deemed appropriate. But Dave's warmth with people and his genuineness, assets inherited from his large Italian family, were contagious. At first, the Van Adams clan began by treating him with suspicion, resisting his efforts toward Jane. Then, with cautious friendliness, they began to admire his determination and ambition, as he continued his courtship of Jane while completing his education at Northeastern. After the Jim's award of a graduate scholarship to MIT, his qualities couldn't be denied, and their attitude changed to one of kindness and willing acceptance of Jane's choice.

Dave and Jane wanted a large family. When they discovered that Ellen would be an only child, a somber, unhappy period followed. Jane became consumed by reading to Ellen from the age of one. When Ellen was five, Jane began the outings to the museums, art galleries, and gardens around Connecticut and trips to New York. As Ellen grew older, Dave and Jane invested themselves in her well being. They viewed their actions as protective and loving, unaware that they had become managers of her life.

Always athletic, Ellen liked playing tennis and swimming but not with any degree of regularity. She participated in games, but was not an avid competitor in organized sports. During her first year at St. George's, a private girl's high school, Dave bought her an expensive pair of running shoes as a Christmas present. Within a few months, running became her passion. She emerged as a strong, competitive runner on her school team at distances of two to ten miles, and filled in shorter distances when needed.

Dave and Jane started Ellen sailing as a child, presenting her with a small boat on her tenth birthday. After Ellen learned the basics, they allowed her to explore the feel of sailing on a small lake while Dave or Jane served as her crew. Dave taught and quizzed her on the technical aspects of sailing, and created exercises to challenge her, and to help her attain imp... Lessons included leverage, using the sail, centerboar... and their own weights as examples; using tools to re... and keep it fit for sailing; and buoyancy and flotati... hull, water, and flotation gear. She could never be su... lesson would begin, but she knew that each time ou... create a new problem to solve.

One morning as they tacked into a stiff wind Da... back at Ellen and said, "Today's lesson is on navigatio... you to look around and get a feeling for where you are."

"Okay." Ellen scanned the lake, shoreline, and sky, ... noting her position and the positions of the other boats.

"Now close your eyes," he said.

"What? Why would I do that?"

"That's today's lesson. I want to know how long y... sail with your eyes closed."

"Why?"

"Suppose you get lost at night or in a fog. You have to be able to estimate in order to survive."

"Estimate what?"

"What are the key elements I've taught you about navigating?"

"Knowing where you are, your heading, and what time it is?"

"Well?"

"We're in the middle of the lake; we're heading northwest, and it's about 10:30."

"Good. How will you know with your eyes closed?"

Ellen thought for a while. I can guess from our heading and our position when I close them."

"And."

"I could guess how long they were closed."

"Do you have to guess?"

She thought again. "I could count," she said, raising the inflection on the word, count.

"Good! Then close them and count. I'll let you know if you're getting too close to trouble."

After counting to eighty Ellen started to feel a sense of anxiety. At 120 near panic set in and she said, "I'm opening them, Dad; I have to!"

They repeated this exercise a few times and before the day ended she managed a count of 250, including a couple of course changes at Dave's command. Proud of her progress, Ellen continued to include this exercise along with the others when she sailed with him.

Over the years, Ellen learned Jane's propriety, grace, and love of culture. Following her junior year in high school, Jane and Ellen traveled to Europe for two months, visiting the Hermitage in St. Petersburg, the Louvre in Paris, and then spending a full month in Tuscany to experience the wonders of the Renaissance. Dave joined them twice for one-week visits, finding a way to mix pleasure with the demands of his position as CEO of Cramwell Industries, a successful company he founded after fifteen years as an engineer in the automotive industry.

After that summer, Ellen began to rebel from her elite life style and she started looking for a college that would nurture her interests in art and also her desire to experience a different world. She visited a variety of schools in the east from Maine to New York, mostly on drives with Jane and Ellen's best friend, Annie Nowik. Despite her rebellion she fell in love with Mt. Holyoke in the western hills of Massachusetts. Although she accepted early admission, second thoughts followed her throughout the summer before her freshman year. Annie, a free spirit whose love was drama, made her choice, Yale.

The sound of Ellen's heartbeat thundered in the otherwise silent room. Tense, listening for the door to open at any instant, she lay in artificial darkness. The pounding subsided and she began taking deeper breaths. *They're gone for a while.*

She tugged and strained at the tape bindings but they resisted her efforts. She tried to remove her cap by sliding her head against the mattress, but it remained firmly over her face, secured by tape. After a few tries she gave up the struggle to save strength, and lay still on the lumpy bed. *Who were they? What did they want? Not my body, they could have had that by now. It has to be money.*

She realized they would expect her wealthy father to pay. But with all of the uncertainty in these situations they still might harm her, or worse. Tears filled her eyes. Exhausted, helpless, and out of control, she began to sob. *Come on, Ellen; think! Get a grip!* She took a deep breath, and another. The sobbing stopped. Her mind began working again. She relaxed and reached a tranquil, dreamy state.

A cramp in her calf startled Ellen to awareness. The aborted run and change in routine began to take effect; the discomfort of bound hands and legs worsened the aches and pains in her body. *How long have I dozed?* It must be mid morning. *God, I need a shower!* And now the pressure of her bladder began to create a new problem. She tried to put it out of her mind, but it would not go away. The pressure turned to pain.

Oh, I've got to pee. Where are they? I can't hold out much longer. If they don't come back soon I've got to do something. She struggled again to free her ankles and wrists but this made it worse. The pain in her abdomen grew more intense increasing her frustration. She struggled to scream but the tape sealed her lips. *Damn, duct tape, it's everywhere!* Tears filled her eyes again. *Someone help me!*

Ellen began wiggling, rolling, and bouncing her feet. Nothing helped. She lay silent for a minute, making up her mind. Then, moving her feet a few inches she pressed down with her elbows to raise her buttocks and slide them toward the edge of the bed. She repeated this a few times until her feet hung over the edge of the bed. After one more move they touched the floor. She pressed her elbow to her side, felt the hard object in her pocket, and shielded it from what was to follow; then she rolled over and allowed herself to drop the floor next to the bed with a quiet thud. Soon she lay in a pool of her own making, as the warm dampness on her thighs moved down her legs and up her back. After a while the pain went away. Disgusted with her action she remembered her mother's training. "Always be a lady," Jane would often say. She didn't feel like much of a lady right now.

Damn, I'm pissed! Her disgust changed to a forced a smile pressing against the tape on her mouth. *In more ways than one.* She managed a silent laughter before the anger returned. *You bastards are going to pay for this!* She rolled over once, and then again, away from the bed. She lay on the floor and relaxed. Then, she forced into her mind thoughts of her past, as she lost sense of time.

During Ellen's first semester at college the same feelings that stifled her during high school re-emerged. She began having second thoughts about her decision. Maybe she had taken the easy way out. Resentment grew against her parents for their strong influence on her personality, attitudes toward morality, and the manner in which she made decisions. By the second semester she became more comfortable with her life on the lovely wooded campus. Free from parental control and surrounded by young women with various backgrounds and life styles, some similar and others differing from hers, Ellen began to emerge as a person.

Ellen majored in Liberal Arts and expanded her interests in art with a focus on Renaissance History. She loved to paint in watercolors and oils, and discovered a teacher, Mr. Zinman, with whom she formed a special bond. He encouraged her to break away from the basic realism of her structured childhood into experiments with impressionistic and surreal painting. She responded and his continuing support fostered her progression into an accomplished artist. She established casual friendships with a few of her artistic classmates, but couldn't replace Annie, a friend in whom she could confide. She had a mild crush on Zinman, who was twice her age, that she talked about to Annie constantly. "Come on Ellen, get real," was Annie's comment. "It's obvious that you need a man."

One day after class she approached Mr. Zinman. Comfortable with him and still experiencing the frustrations of a college freshman, she now wanted to confide in him. As they walked, she described her childhood and expressed her anger. "I'm a child," she said. "I can't think for myself. My parents think for me, and I'll never do the kind of things the other girls around here do."

"Like what?" said Zinman.

She had never spoken like this to any man other than her father, and she began to shut down. *Here I go, being a wimp again.* But she mustered her courage and spoke, "Like drink without feeling guilty, and..."

"And, what?"

"Well, you know," she couldn't bring herself to say the word sex, or sleep with someone. She paused in embarrassment, suspecting he knew where she was going.

He said, "If there's anything they're doing that you think is admirable, do it. If not, don't. Besides, they do those kind of things out of insecurity."

She appreciated his abstractness and looked at him, waiting for more, but he did not elaborate.

Then she said, "Insecurity, I feel like the insecure one!"

"I don't know anything about your family, but you didn't fall off a tree. Someone helped formulate how you look at life and how you behave. Don't resent them for that. Be yourself and take a closer look at these women whom you seem to admire. Make sure they deserve your admiration. You have lots of time to experiment with your life; it doesn't have to happen before you're a sophomore."

After that she began to view him as someone she could trust. The conversation ended her doubts about Mt. Holyoke and set the stage for her development as a woman. She began to relax and enjoy herself, confident that she was free to make choices, the first step in growing up. When peer pressure got the best of her, she would seek out Zinman. There were several women professors whom she also admired, but she didn't view as friends. Having a man to talk with made her feel like an adult.

Ellen dated on occasion, but developed no serious relationships in college. There were opportunities to meet any number of young men from the countless schools throughout New England. Most of them, as insecure as her freshman classmates, exhibited a shallowness that made her anticipate the end of a date. A few were sincere but without personality, others hit on her in an open and clumsy fashion. She saw only a few of them more than once and began to feel that she had set her standards too high. This, she blamed on her mother.

Ellen continued to run in competition, including two marathons, and during her junior year she tried out for the Olympics, missing the cut at the finals in Los Angeles. Disappointed, but not devastated, she continued her competition at the collegiate level. And just running for the exercise on the campus that she had grown to love gave her great pleasure.

Nearing her senior year, Ellen began to think about her future. She had visited Annie on a number of occasions. She liked Yale and the New Haven area, and the coed life style would be a welcome change. The opportunity beckoned to achieve the experience at life that, through the actions of her parents and her own choices, she had been denied. Annie had a strong influence on her decision.

One day on a visit home, Ellen's father approached her again about entering into his business. Her refusal was polite. "I want to go to graduate school, Dad".

Dave replied, "That's fine, Ellen. We'll help you do that. But, if you ever want to talk about my offer, it's always open."

Ellen decided that teaching would be her career and applied to Yale, majoring in childhood education and art. It was a safe career choice that would allow her to maintain her art interests, and it gave her two more years to defer the life choices that would come soon enough.

Ellen planned to live alone in New Haven, but after a little coaxing she moved in with Annie. She remained apprehensive about Annie's different life style. The fact that moving scared her resurrected Ellen's feelings of insecurity. *Here I go again. I wish I could have a session with Mr. Zinman.*

At 5' 7" Ellen had a long, graceful stride that attracted attention as she raced across the quadrangle or anywhere around the campus. During her first week in New Haven she ran toward her apartment in the middle of a closing sprint, thinking of what might lie in store for her in her new life. As she approached the stairs of her walk-up, the door opened. A young man, tall and red-haired, looked down at her as she finished the run. Ellen started up the stairs.

"Hi," he said.

"Hi," she replied as they passed. She watched for a few seconds as he started down the street and then she went inside.

"Annie, I'm home!"

"How was the run?" Annie called from the next room.

"Great. Who's your friend?"

"Oh, that was Kevin Reardon."

"I've never seen him before."

"I think this is the first time he's come over."

"Anything going on between you two?"

"He's in my drama class. He came over to pick up some notes."

"Anything more?"

"Well, Ms. Holyoke sounds interested."

"Just a question; I only saw him for a second on the stairs," Ellen said, feeling herself turn red, and knowing that her blush was evident to Annie, who had a natural instinct to tease. Ellen sighed with appreciation when Annie backed off.

"Well, come to our rehearsal tonight I'll introduce you."

"What time?"

"We'll leave at 6:30."

Lying on the floor, Ellen tensed at the sound of footsteps. A door opened and closed followed by the click of another door. Someone approached. *Are there one or two of them?* Hands reach under her armpits and lingered there, a little too long. Uncertain what to expect, she cursed the control they had over her. They dragged her across the floor against the resistance of her heels, acting like brakes. She pressed her elbows inward, shielding her right hip. Released, wobbling, she fell to the floor. Then she felt tape removed from her wrists. Footsteps, the door clicked. Alone again.

Ellen stretched her arms. After many hours of being bound, her muscles ached. She pulled at her cap, exposing her eyes to the light. Pain. Her eyelids slammed shut. She opened them with caution, trying to readjust to the sense of sight. After a few seconds she began to scan the appearing images, a floor of white tile hexagons, a white porcelain toilet, tub, basin, and a large cast iron radiator. Metal bars shielded a window covered with gray paint, and on the floor, sat a tray with a sandwich and a glass containing a dark liquid.

She raised her head, sat up, pulling at the tape on her ankles. She pealed it away and stretched her legs. Her knee touched the radiator and reflex jerked it away. Then she rose to her feet. A light bulb on the wall illuminated a sheet of yellow paper taped above the basin, where a mirror should have hung, but didn't. The words issued a command: "YOU HAVE TEN MINUTES. WHEN YOU HEAR THREE KNOCKS STAND WITH YOUR BACK TO THE DOOR. DON'T TURN AROUND!"

What to do next? I have less than that, now! She sprang into action, first emptying her pockets and then pulling off her running clothes, counting as she carried out her tasks. She spotted a small bar of soap on the wash basin. Turning on the basin faucets, and then in the bathtub, she threw her clothes into the tub, created lather with the soap, and sloshed them in the lukewarm water. She wrung the soap from the clothes, transferred them to the basin, and rinsed and squeezed out each piece. At the count of 156 she began to spread her clothes on the radiator. Then at 182, satisfied with the job, she checked the drawers, but found them empty. Then she stepped into the tub, turned on a lukewarm shower, and began to lather her body with soap with. After a quick scrubbing she rinsed away the suds, stepped from the tub, and dried with a dim, gray towel that may once have been white. She pressed the towel to the wet clothes, against the heat of the radiator. *This will have to do.* Then she wrapped herself in the towel and tucked it in under her arms.

Ellen opened the sandwich to find a slice of ham and another of cheese smeared with mustard. Grimacing, she took one hesitant bite, then devoured the rest. She took a sip of the dark, sweet liquid, cheap cola. She counted 420. *Running out of time!*

Ellen turned on all of the faucets to full strength. Then she reached down to pick up the small cell phone, a gift from her father. "Carry this with you," he had told her, "it's the best insurance around." Folded into the closed position, the size of a pager, she carried it in her purse and made a practice of leaving it in her windbreaker at night for her morning run. *Thanks, Dad!*

She sat in her towel gown, back pressed against the door, tapping the speed dial for her father's office. At the count of 525, a faint ring sounded through the background noise of rushing water. She heard three loud knocks, then pressure of the door against her spine accompanied by the sound of the turning doorknob. Ellen returned the pressure, while lowering the phone antenna and folding the phone. "Please, two more minutes! I'm not dressed yet!" She winced. *Ooh! I shouldn't have said that!*

The door pressure increased and she resisted until the pressure eased. "Please!" She cried out. Then, she heard one loud knock on the door, a sound of authority that seemed to say, "You have one!"

She lifted the damp clothes from the radiator, pulling on panties, running pants, and jogging bra in rapid succession. She ducked her head into the turtleneck, popped her head out the other side, and pushed her arms through the openings, completing the quick change. She jammed the phone into the waistband of her pants just below her waistline, sliding it down toward her thigh, then turned off the faucets. Three knocks and the doorknob turned again. Tying the jacket arms around her waist and knotting the sleeves on her right hip, she managed a makeshift skirt. Then, taking a bite from the sandwich and a sip from the glass, she stood, chewing, with her back to the door as it swung open.

Annie's friends and her theater life always intrigued Ellen. Her own subtle art form, conducted to the sound of soft classical music in a painting studio, on a beach, or while watching a sunrise from the porch of her family's summer house, contrasted with Annie's far-out performance art, on a stage full of characters dressed in gaudy costumes. Annie's, on the edge, life style scared Ellen but it also excited her.

A few people sat here and there, on the portable bleachers surrounding the stage of the small, black box theater when Ellen and Annie entered. She spotted Kevin Reardon and tried to look away, but she felt Annie tugging her arm to make the introduction.

Ellen felt herself change color when Reardon looked her over. "You're the runner," he said.

"That's me," she replied with a calm voice, trying to disguise her pounding heart.

They shook hands and he said, "Hang around and watch the show."

"Okay," Ellen replied, climbing up a few rows and taking a seat. A group of students ran through a series of scenes while a woman, the director, called out instructions from a high stool at the corner of the stage. She lectured on bringing feelings into a role, and recalled a poignant moment in her life to illustrate the lesson. Ellen spent the next two hours watching the performance take shape, intrigued by the process. Most of the time her eyes fixed on Reardon. He seemed so confident.

After a few casual encounters, Kevin and Ellen began to date; soon they were seeing each other several times a week. Kevin Reardon, a tough, kid from Queens, graduated from New York City College. He had the gift of blarney and always the right word for any occasion. His quick responses to any situation differed from Ellen's. She analyzed things before reacting to them, afraid of saying something stupid. She liked his fast, on your feet, reaction. Sure of himself, and different from any other guy she knew, Kevin seemed to care little for what others thought about his views and his actions. Ellen didn't know how to put herself first like he did; she always worried about how her behavior might affect others. She wanted to learn from him how to have such confidence.

One evening they sat on a couch in his apartment after another night of rehearsals. He reached for her hand and looked into her eyes. "Why don't you stay here tonight?" he said.

"I don't think so," she replied.

"What are you afraid of?"

"Nothing," Ellen lied. She had never been in bed with a man.

"Afraid your parents won't approve?"

"I do what I want," she snapped. She remembered her conversations with Mr. Zinman.

Kevin pressed his argument "Come on, don't you think it's about time you really did what you want?"

"Not tonight, Kevin," she said rising toward the door.

He released her hand and shook his head with a wry smile that indicated scorn. This scene, and variations, played several times over the next month; Kevin's badgering drove her closer and closer to the decision she knew would come. And then one night she said, "Yes, I'll stay." She noted the smile on his face and wondered what he thought. He said nothing.

The next morning when she entered her apartment Annie waited, a cup of coffee in her hand. "Well, you've finally spent a night with Reardon," Annie said, her words matter of fact.

Ellen didn't reply, but nodded and walked into her room. *It wasn't supposed to be like this.*

It became easier after that and she spent many evenings with Kevin, feeling that she was now in love with the man she would marry. They became inseparable, and they traveled to Boston and New York on several weekends as fall turned to winter. They talked about marriage and came to a tacit understanding that it would happen when they finished graduate school. Ellen called home one day and told her mother about Kevin.

"Why don't you bring him home at Thanksgiving?" Jane asked.

"Okay, I will."

They made the short drive from New Haven in Ellen's white Audi, a graduation gift from Dave and Jane. When they entered the drive to the Cramwell house, Kevin whistled and said, "This is some cottage!"

"I told you my father had money."

"But this is more than that. This is big time bucks! I had no idea."

"Well, now you can marry me for my money," she said, noting the smile on his face.

When Jane met Kevin, Ellen watched her mother's reaction to his routine. Jane wasn't buying it. Jane made up her mind quickly about people, and Ellen knew that her mother had already made her decision about Kevin. After dinner, when Kevin and Dave went outside for a walk around the property, Jane and Ellen sat at the table.

"Tell me more about Kevin," Jane said.

The inquisition started. Ellen took a sip of coffee, then provided a scarcity of facts about his background.

Jane continued probing with a mother's questions. "What about his family?" Jane asked.

"I haven't met them yet."

"Do you know anything about them?"

"A little. His father is in some kind of export business, and his mother works in a bank."

"What's Kevin's future?"

Ellen's defenses went up. "He's an actor and he's also studying to be a director. He has contacts, and I can teach. We'll be fine."

"You won't be fine. Have you thought this through? Living on a teacher's pay with a struggling actor for a husband."

"I've never met anyone like him. He's different, and I love him."

Ellen's parries countered Jane's challenging thrusts in an emotional discussion that lasted until the door opened. Dave entered followed by Kevin.

Thankful for the rescue Ellen asked, "So, what have you two been doing?"

"Surveying the south forty," Kevin said.

Ellen noticed Dave's quizzical reaction.

"How about some coffee?" Jane asked.

Ellen nodded at her mother. *Stalemate.*

The next day as Ellen's car moved down the long driveway, she leaned forward and looked out the side view mirror. Dave and Jane waved from the stairs. She knew her mother disapproved, but that her father wasn't yet ready to make a definitive stand. Jane went with her intuition, but Dave, very analytical, was still in data collection mode. Ellen realized it would be a while before she heard her father's opinion.

In mid-December, Ellen made plans to visit her parents in Hartford again for a family Christmas. Kevin asked her to stay with him during the holidays, but she resisted.

He often chided her about this, family thing. Kevin shouted "You were home for Thanksgiving!"

"I know, and I want to be home for Christmas."

He shook his head and walked away. Ellen compromised by spending Christmas with Kevin; then she drove to Hartford a few days before New Years' Day and spent the holiday with her family.

After the holidays, Kevin and Ellen resumed their usual routine and things went well for a while. But Ellen's concerns grew over the frequent arguments. This was so different from the relationship she had seen between her parents. Then Kevin would do something romantic with flowers or a quiet dinner to rekindle her enchantment. At these times she rationalized that things would work out; she'd prove that her mother was wrong.

At the beginning of Ellen's second year at Yale, an opportunity arose for Kevin to direct a new drama at a New Haven theater. He faced strong competition for the position. Kevin was an operator. Ellen saw that he didn't include competing in his style; he preferred to work around the competition by playing the angles. Kevin felt that he had a lock on the job, but after hearing the bad news he spent a long night of drinking at a local watering hole.

When Ellen heard the knock and opened the door, she discovered a couple of Kevin's friends propping him up for deposit at her apartment. "What happened?" Ellen knew the answer to her question. Rip-roaring drunk, he probably bellowed his laments to an audience of both friends and strangers.

"He didn't get it," Kevin's friend, Carl verified her suspicions.

Ellen took Kevin in her arms. "There'll be other opportunities," she said.

"The hell there will!" he said. "I had this one all lined up; Ted let me down." Ted, a high school friend who had gone to Fordham, now attended Yale. He had control of the production.

Kevin broke away from Ellen and staggered across the room. "Damn!" he shouted.

"Who got it?" she said.

"Tommy Conlan; hot shot from Northwestern. Thinks he's great! Bullshit, he hardly knows Ted. I thought Ted was my best friend."

"Maybe he is," Ellen said.

Kevin turned and glared at her, "What do you know about it?"

"Ted is a good guy. I'm sure it was a tough choice for him."

"What's to choose. You go with your friends."

"What about talent and objectivity?" She surprised herself by the challenge.

He turned with mouth open and shaking his head, "That's nothing to do with it; and whose side are you on?"

"I'm on your side, but..."

"But what? I'm not good enough?"

Ellen understood Kevin's weaknesses. She also knew Tommy had a great reputation and the talent to support it. She didn't want to continue down this track. "Kevin, you'd have done a fine job, but you lost. Now you have to forget it and move on."

"You sure aren't giving me any warm feelings about this," he replied with arms spread, palms upward.

Carl squirmed and looked away.

Ellen tried to defuse the situation. "Kevin, you've had a lot to drink; take a shower and go to bed. You'll feel better in the morning."

"Gotta go," Carl said. "Good night Ellen. So long Kevin; tough break."

"Yeah, tough break," Kevin snarled.

When Carl left, Kevin staggered into the bathroom and slammed the door.

"I'm going now; will you be okay?" Ellen asked, raising her voice. Silence.

"Kevin?" She heard the shower turn on and knew he was brooding and wouldn't answer, best to leave him alone. She wrote a note and placed it on the table, and then walked to the

56

door and opened it. Looking back once more she raised her voice, "Good night, Kevin!" Then she walked out.

Kevin met her at the coffeehouse the next morning, still in a foul mood. He brooded for two more weeks before this particular incident faded from the scene. But whenever his schemes for directing assignments or acting roles failed he'd raise the roof. Each time Kevin blamed someone else for his failure, and argued with Ellen about her inability to devote herself to him and to his success.

In her first serious relationship, Ellen had no basis for comparing it with another that might be better, or worse. Her doubts lost out to her own fear of failure, and worse, of facing her mother. Then, in the spring, Kevin was cast in major role for theater engagement in Boston. Favorable reviews might get the production to New York. It seemed that things were on the upswing.

Ellen and Annie sat in the fifth row as the curtain rose on *Pretension*, with Kevin as Sean Flaherty, a role made for him. Annie leaned over and whispered, "Here goes!"

When the first act ended, Ellen and Annie smiled and said nothing; the enjoyable story had wonderful aspects; but their exchanged glances required no words. After the final curtain, Annie whispered to Ellen, who stared straight ahead. "Oh, oh; this is going to be a problem."

With eyes closed, Ellen nodded.

At Kelly's, a small bar down the street from the theater, the cast of *Pretension* downed a few and the room bubbled with opening night excitement. Ellen and Annie pushed their way through the crowd and spotted Kevin, the consummate mixer, strutting and acting the star, talking with everyone, hugging and kissing all the girls, glad-handing and backslapping the guys. When Kevin spotted Ellen and Annie he broke away from his entourage. He kissed Ellen, then Annie, and stepped back spreading his arms. "Well?"

Ellen gave her rehearsed response, "It was good!"

"Annie?" Kevin asked.

"Yes, good; quite good," she said. Ellen recognized her forced enthusiasm.

Kevin seemed to miss it. He nodded and took a swallow of beer. Someone tapped Kevin on the shoulder. He spun around, laughed and charged off, calling to Ellen and Annie over his shoulder, "See you later; have a drink."

Annie's eyes opened wide, she tilted her head with the palms of her hands raised. Ellen shrugged and wrinkled her brow. They both shook their heads. "Let's have a drink," Annie said.

The following morning, when *The Boston Globe* arrived, Ellen read the review with apprehension. The critic started with an upbeat summary of the story, directing, and staging, but flattened Kevin's wooden performance of an Irish immigrant. Ellen put the paper down. "Hold onto your hat; he'll be mad as hell," she said.

"I'd say pissed, big time," Annie said.

Hearing Kevin's voice on the intercom a few minutes later, Annie took her cue to leave. "I'm outta here! Fill me in." She rose and bolted for the door.

As Kevin stomped in Annie made her exit before he could say a word. Ellen suppressed a smile to the sounds of Annie's fading footsteps. *Annie exits stage left. What timing!*

Kevin slammed the door, facing Ellen across the room. He shouted, "You agree with that bastard, don't you! You never support me! Last night you said, good, but you didn't meant it!" He walked to her as his bellows echoed through the room. His eyes revealed a lack of sleep, and he needed a shave.

Ellen stared at him, prepared for a long tirade. *This is getting old.*

He roared, "Come on Ellen, stand up for me!"

"Kevin, don't take this so hard. We'll get through it." She emphasized the, we.

"This isn't about us; it's about me!"

It's always about you. Ellen reached out to hold him but he turned away. She dropped her arms in silence, waiting for him.

Turning toward her, Kevin took two more steps, placed his hands on her shoulders and pushed her back to the wall. "What is it with you? I thought you loved me!" he screamed.

So did I. Ellen looked into his eyes, searching for words.

"Well, say something!" he continued. He squeezed her harder.

She raised her hands but couldn't reach his arms to break the grip. "Kevin, please stop! You're hurting me!" Then she slid her back down the wall breaking free from him, for a second.

Kevin reached down and pushed, sending Ellen sprawling before him. The realization hit her harder than the floor did. *I can't do this any longer.*

"Oh, Ellen!" he said, extending his hand.

She rose without taking it. "Kevin, I'm leaving now."

As she walked away he took three steps, grabbed her by the waist and spun her around. "Where do you think you're going?"

Another scene from the melodrama of their relationship; a soap opera with a series of angry scenes each starting with his flare-up fading into her appeasement. She hung on because she wanted to change him, to show her mother. But Kevin had the lead and Ellen's part consisted of bit parts, reacting. She remembered Mr. Zinman's counsel and the word, insecurity. Ellen's shoulders ached from his heavy-handed squeeze. Her head throbbed from bouncing off the wall and she rubbed her sore elbow. She imagined herself one day explaining a black eye to Annie. Backing away from him, shaking her head Ellen spoke. "Anywhere but here." She forced calmness to her voice, masking the fear in her tingling body.

Kevin stepped toward her as she retreated. "Damn you! You're abandoning me now, just when I need you!" he screamed.

"There you go again, blaming someone else! I'm not abandoning you; you're creating a situation I can't live with! This can't go on!" She walked to the door.

"Come back here!" he shouted. "You can't walk out!"

"That's just the point, Kevin. Somehow I managed to remember that I can." Damn it, her mother was right. She'd deal with the embarrassment later. This hurt but she felt good. Then she realized the comedy of the situation. *I live here!* She turned to Kevin and said, "Don't be here when I get back. It's over." She noticed the stare of disbelief in his eyes.

A short time later Ellen stood behind a car across the street when Kevin appeared in the doorway. She watched until he shuffled out of sight. Then she crossed the street and climbed the stairs to her apartment. Later, when Annie opened the door, Ellen's good feeling had worn off.

With tears in her eyes Ellen asked, "Oh, Annie, what have I done?".

"You tell me."

"I broke up with Kevin." Ellen's tears swelled over and ran down her cheeks. Pressing her chin to her chest, Ellen made a plea for sympathy and understanding.

When Annie took a step toward her, Ellen expected a big hug. Instead Annie spread her arms and belted out in her best Broadway voice, **"It's a hard knock life!"**

A smile started at the corners of Ellen's mouth as she raised her chin. Before Ellen's transformation could continue Annie continued, **"The sun'll come out, tomorrow!"**

Ellen lost it. She burst out laughing at the performance, Annie at her best, literally. Now came the hug and the giggles. Ellen's sense of resolve returned at the clear message from Annie. She agreed with Ellen's decision.

Over several weeks, Kevin called many times, but Ellen hung up each time after just a few words. Then the calls stopped.

After a while Ellen decided she had a call to make. She punched the familiar sequence of numbers and listened for the ring.

"Hello," Dave answered. Ellen heard music, Gilbert and Sullivan.

Glad that he picked up she said, "Hi, Dad, it's me."

"Ellen, good to hear from you. What's up?"

Not yet. She started with her efforts at getting a teaching position, followed a discussion of her art. Then they talked about the movies that Dave and Jane had seen. They drifted into a variety of subjects. She liked to talk to her father. After a while Ellen realized she had to get to the point. "Dad, I have something important to tell you."

"And what's that?"

She paused, mustering her courage over the silence. *I can't delay any longer; he'll get worried.* She mustered the words; "I've broken up with Kevin."

After a pause at the other end of the line, he said "Well, maybe it's for the best." His calm response showed no obvious reaction.

"Yes, it just wasn't working out," she said.

"I hope you're taking it okay."

"Yes, I am."

"Well, this is important; I'm sure you'll want to talk to your mother."

She didn't. *Time to bite the bullet.* Ellen heard her mother's voice in the background, "What's going on?" and then "Ellen?"

"Did Dad tell you?" Ellen said.

"Tell me what?" her mother replied over the faint sounds of a tune from *The Mikado.*

Ellen spoke in even tones, "I broke up with Kevin." *Damn it Mom, you were right.*

"I think you've done the right thing," Jane said, without obvious emotion. After a pause, she continued, "Your father and I were just having a glass of wine."

The sound of background music stopped, and for a few seconds, holding a silent phone, Ellen formed a vision of her mother covering the mouthpiece and jumping up and down, wagging her head, and doing a little dance of celebration. Then, her mother's voice resumed, "I meant to tell you about..." and in accordance with usual protocol, they began a conversation that lasted an hour.

Ellen awoke after a restless night. *What time is it?* Bound and blindfolded, her back and arms ached from the severe, unnatural position. Damp clothes added to her misery. She thought of the, million bucks, analogy. *God, I feel like...fifty bucks!*

She heard a door open again, like yesterday, followed by footsteps. This time the tray contained a cup of coffee and a hard roll, and the message, FIVE MINUTES.

At the count of 150 Ellen lowered the toilet lid, sat down, and with excited anticipation, dialed her father's number. Then she remembered, jumped up and sat down with her back against the door as the ringing signal started. The programmed voice droned its emotionless message "You have reached..." She clenched her fists in silence. *I want to talk to him, to anyone!*

Then the voice, "Dave Cramwell, please leave a message at the tone."

She spoke in whispers, suppressing her anxiety, "Dad, I'm in an old house. It's about a 20-minute drive from the Shore Road, but I don't know the direction! They grabbed and blindfolded me! We probably drove about 30 or 40 miles an hour. I can't remember the car; I think it was white, foreign! Lots of turns! My phone batteries are low and I have to go. I hope they don't find my phone. If they don't... I'll try to call again later. Help me, Dad!"

Not enough time for another call. She returned the phone to its hiding place against her thigh, then, gulped down the lukewarm coffee and a stale roll. She stood with her back to the door, listening for the knock that came, and then the squeaking hinge. Like Pavlov's dog, she had learned the routine.

Jim walked up the stairs to his house as the police car started around the driveway and toward the street. His mind raced, recreating the past three days in a blur. *What should I do?* He opened the door.

Michael, his sixteen-year-old son greeted him. "Hey, Dad; a police car? Where were you? What's up?"

"Radnor Police. They asked me some questions about someone I know."

"Who's that?"

"Her name is Ellen Cramwell. I met her the other day and now she's disappeared. They thought I might have some information."

"Wow! What do you think happened to her?"

"No idea."

"Where does this Ellen live?"

"In Connecticut."

"Didn't you just come back from there?"

"That's when I met her." Michael's questioning look asked for more. "That's it. We had dinner and I came home the next morning. I'm going up to Connecticut to see if I can help."

Michael nodded.

After Jim packed for the return trip he sat in his office facing the computer screen, trying to focus on his work, but with little success.

—**4**—

As the final days of Jim's senior year at college melted away, he felt a strong melancholy for the friends and life that would soon fade into the past, just as the fear of leaving home a few years ago had become a faint memory. His sadness mingled with the guilt of distancing himself from Gail, but his life plan didn't include assuming the responsibilities of an instant family. He wanted to extend the freedom of his college years, and to live his youth a little longer. He buried the guilt by concentrating on good grades for his final semester, and on preparing for his new job.

Through the spring Jim and Gail had only a few casual encounters over coffee, and exchanged a wave now and then as they passed on campus. When he told her about the job in Valley Forge, she responded with news of her own. She would start with the *Philadelphia Inquirer* on the Sunday edition. Graduation loomed three weeks away.

One day Jim opened the mailbox and found a small square envelope among the usual bills and junk mail. The invitation from Gail's parents started with, THANK GOD SHE MADE IT, PLEASE JOIN US IN A CELEBRATION,...The family gathering would occur on the first week of September. A note from Gail said, 'Welcome to Philadelphia. Hope you can be there. Gail.' Placing the envelope on his dresser he marked the date on his calendar.

On graduation day Jim's parents beamed with pride at his accomplishment, one of the first generation of college graduates on either side of the family. His sister Pam, younger by six years, joined them. After two days of excitement, the family's visit ended in the driveway of Jim's apartment. When they finished their farewells and climbed into the car, Jim's mother called out through the window, "Be careful, and don't forget to write and call!"

"I'll call, don't worry Mom. Dad, I'll come home in August for a week. Find a nice course and we'll play a few times."

"Sure, Jim. Can't wait to see if you've straightened out that hook. Swing a little slower; maybe take a lesson," the standard instruction from Dad. "Yeah, Dad. I'll see you in August. So long Mom, Pam!" They drove off with waves at Jim, standing on the curb.

Jim spent his last summer of freedom on a driving vacation with Aaron through the western states. Aaron wanted to take what he called, a major league trip; they had spent weeks planning it and making reservations at a number of youth hostels.

After two months of driving, sightseeing, and just having fun, they returned to State College in the heat of mid August. Jim spent the next day packing and preparing for his last evening with Aaron, a farewell dinner at The Tavern, their favorite restaurant. Jim's feeling of melancholy settled in again as he looked across the table at his good friend.

"We had a special thing, Aaron."

"I've never met anyone like you, Jim."

"I'll miss the football."

"First game's in two weeks."

Coming from two different worlds they always enjoyed the connection of those three months every fall. They shared a pitcher of beer during dinner, and finished with cigars and then liqueurs to celebrate an end and a beginning.

The following morning after a final breakfast, Aaron headed east and Jim drove west again, this time toward Pittsburgh for another week of dinners, picnics, golf, high school friends, and family gatherings. The continuous activity following two months on the road was more than Jim could handle. He caved in; sleeping for almost sixteen hours after the last event was over.

He woke on a Monday morning for one more round of packing to start another drive, to his new life. When his loaded car stood in the driveway the tension of another departure filled the air. After countless hugs and kisses, Jim's mother with tear in her eyes said, "Philadelphia is so far, Jim. Try to get home once in a while. And call us when you get there."

Sitting in his basement office later that afternoon, Jim called Ellen's house. After two rings he heard a woman's voice.

"Ellen?" Jim asked. His heart jumped.

"No, who wants her."

"I'm Jim Dulles."

"Oh, the one from Pennsylvania."

"Yes." *How do they know about me?* "Whom am I speaking with?"

"This is Ellen's mother, Jane Cramwell."

"You sound just like her. I'm sorry about Ellen. The police here told me about it this afternoon."

"You went out with her, didn't you?"

"Yes, for dinner. We met while jogging the day before. Can you tell me what happened? Is there any news?"

She spoke in a soft voice. "The police don't want us to talk about it. Ellen has disappeared; that's all we know."

Jim asked, "I want come up there and help?"

"What could you do?"

He could understand her apprehension, but continued, "I don't know, but I can't do much down here."

"You hardly know her. Why would you be interested?"

"I haven't known her for long, but we had a very nice evening. I tried to call her yesterday."

"I'm not so sure you should be coming around here and getting in the way. Why don't you talk with my husband."

"Sure, how can I reach him?"

"You can call him at his office." She provided the phone number.

"Thank you. I'll call him. And I hope everything works out well, and soon."

"Goodbye."

Jim hung up and redialed. After two rings a woman's voice answered, "David Cramwell's office."

"Hello; this is Jim Dulles I'd like to talk with Mr. Cramwell. Mrs. Cramwell gave me this number. I know Ellen."

"Just a moment, I'll see if he is available."

After a short pause Jim heard a man's voice, "Hello. You're Jim Dulles? The police told us about you. What do you want?"

"Mr. Cramwell, I met Ellen earlier this week and went out to dinner with her the night before she disappeared. The police questioned me today because they found my fingerprints in the house. I can't figure out how they got there. I didn't go in. I left her at the door and haven't seen her since. I was shocked to hear about this. I'd like to help."

"I'm not sure how."

"Do you mind if I come up there and try?"

"Suit yourself; but the police may not be very happy about it."

As the bathroom door closed, Ellen removed the tape from her eyes and started counting. She sat on the floor with her back resting against the door and slid the tray to her side. A sandwich and a can of orange soda sat on the tray along with a note, FIVE MINUTES. She knew the drill.

Ellen took a swallow of the soda and a bite of sandwich, then turned on the basin faucets. Raising her knees at her chin, she unfolded her phone, raised the antenna, and dialed 911.

A voice responded after three rings, "Emergency Operator."

Ellen whispered, "This is Ellen Cramwell. I've been kidnapped. I don't have much time; they're coming back soon".

"I can't hear you, can you speak up, please?"

After the frustrating response, Ellen gritted her teeth. She increased the intensity of her whisper. "They'll hear me if I talk louder."

"Where are you?"

"I don't know? You have to hurry. I only have a minute."

"What's your name again?"

Ellen clenched her fist and shook her head at the questions, "Ellen Cramwell!"

"Just a minute."

She grew tense; the delay seemed forever. "State Police." She heard the beep of the recorder.

"I've been kidnapped. I don't know where I am; it's about 20 minutes from the Shore Road. I don't know the direction."

"Can you speak up?"

"Damn, do I have to give directions to everyone! I've been kidnapped This is a cell phone." They'll hear me if I talk louder.

"Where are you?"

"I don't know."

"What do the kidnappers look like?"

"I don't know I was blindfolded."

Ellen heard footsteps. "I have to go. Help me!"

She pressed END and slid the phone into its hiding place. After three knocks, she stood again, following the script.

Jim planed an early start for his trip back to Connecticut. After packing, he climbed into bed. Who knew where this adventure would take him? He lay back on the pillow and dozed.

On a September morning Jim's Pontiac exited the turnpike again, five months after his interview in Valley Forge. Stopping at the tollbooth he asked the uniformed attendant, "How do I find Old Eagle School Road?" She pointed and waved her directions.

Jim nodded, said "Thanks," and drove off.

Earlier in the summer Jim had returned to the Philadelphia area to locate an apartment a few miles from work. Today he would move in his sparse belongings and prepare for his first day at work. The following morning he found himself immersed in the day's activities, filling out forms, meeting co-workers, setting up his office, getting photographed for an ID badge, making selections from the variety of fringe benefits, and completing an application for a Secret security clearance. Late in the afternoon he found an opportunity to sit at his desk. *Where did the day go?*

After removing a few textbooks from last box and placing them on the bookshelves, he checked off his list of completed items. Satisfied with the progress, he opened his small planning calendar. When he turned the page he stared at his note, Gail's Party. *Oh my God, I forgot!*

Jim looked at the clock, almost 5:00. With a knot in his stomach, he dialed her number.

"Hello," a man's voice answered.

"This is Jim Dulles. Is Gail there?"

"Just a minute."

After a short wait he heard her familiar voice, "Jim! I thought you fell off the edge! Where are you?"

"Hi. I'm at work. It's been a great summer, on the go since graduation day. How about you; down the shore?" An image passed through his mind; she ran across the sand, at their first meeting.

"Of course, where else?" After a pause, she continued, "I've started my job, and I've been planning the party. Are you coming?"

"Wouldn't miss it," he lied. The feeling in his stomach eased.

"Tomorrow at 6:30. And don't eat. You won't stop once you get here."

"Tomorrow at 6:30. Could you remind me how to get there?" He wrote the directions on a small pad.

At 5:30 the next day Jim started toward the city on the crowded expressway. He looked forward to seeing Gail, but with a sense of uneasiness. The suppressed issues rose into his consciousness: Gail, the ice cream, the confession, her fragile contrition, and then his reaction. Now he had to deal with it.

He had forgotten the neighborhood but not his quick departure, nor the image in the rearview mirror. With heart pounding he walked down the tree-lined street looking for the address. When he found it, he took a deep breath and climbed the stairs. Jim pressed the doorbell and stood back from the door. It swung open and he smiled at the picture of Gail standing in the doorway, beautiful as ever. "Hi," he said.

"Jim, you made it!" She stepped onto the porch and reached for his hand.

He closed the gap, took her hand, and then opened his arms in an invitation. When she accepted, he enclosed her in his arms, taking in the scent of spring flowers and the gentle feeling of her body pressing against his. He waited an extra second an ended the embrace. As they separated he took her hand. *God, she's beautiful!* He felt her gentle squeeze.

Gail said, "Now for the introductions. Pay attention, you'll be quizzed on them."

"Can I take notes?"

She laughed, "Sure. Do you have a pencil?"

They walked into the room to a cast of what seemed to approach a hundred. *Was I that late?* The guests milled around, laughing, holding glasses and encircling a table filled with foods of all kinds; pasta, ham, turkey, vegetables, breads, cake, on and on. Gail dragged Jim around for an hour introducing Jim to her parents, then to uncles, aunts, cousins, and friends. He followed, hanging onto her hand, remembering few of them, except for two lovely cousins, one a tall blond with great looking legs, and the other with rich, auburn hair, and a clear resemblance to Gail. After the introductions, they made a loop around the table filling their plates.

When Jim and Gail finished their buffet dinner, Gail stood and reached for his hand, pulling him to a standing position. She said, "Follow me, there's someone else I want you to meet." Jim took a deep breath as Gail ushered him into the next room. There stood a tall, dark haired guy about his own age or a little older. Before Jim could get too upset, she made the introduction, "Jim, this is my brother, Mike."

Jim sighed with relief as Mike extended his hand and asked, "Enjoying the party?"

"Sure am. Hard to choose from all of the great food."

"Looks great! I just got home from work. Haven't had a chance to eat yet."

"Don't let me stop you."

Mike laughed, "I need a shower, and then I'll be ready. See you later."

After Mike left, Gail said to Jim, "And there's one more; come on." Jim tagged along behind her to the bottom of a stairway, where she raised her gaze upward and called, "Come on down!" in an encouraging voice.

Jim looked up to see a little girl in a green dress with matching ribbons in her dark brown, curly hair. Responding to her mother's request, the child began by placing one of her black Mary Jane shoes on each step and then the other, while holding the rail with both hands. As this vision of a miniature Gail, continued down the stairs, Jim exclaimed, "My God, Gail! That's you minus about 20 years!"

Gail's cheeks turned red as she whispered, "Eighteen." Then in a full voice, Gail said, "Tracey, this is Jim Dulles. Say hello."

The girl looked like a little angel. She extended her hand and said, "Hello. I'm Tracey Nardelli."

Jim stooped down to view her at face level. "I know. Your mother told me about you. But she didn't tell me you were so pretty." He held her tiny hand in his. "I like those shoes."

"Thank you."

"Aren't those Mary Janes?"

The girl looked down, "No! They're mine!"

71

Jim laughed and turned to Gail, who smiled at the response. The feeling, the one he had when he first saw Gail down the shore, returned. Another Nardelli had captured his heart.

After that evening, Jim and Gail began to see each other again, and soon, Jim drove to the Nardelli house several times a week. The leaves fell and the weather turned cold. Gail invited Jim for Thanksgiving dinner, another festive affair with Nardellis from everywhere and reciprocal family members from her mother's side, the Donatos.

After dinner, Jim and Gail took a walk around the neighborhood. The cold evening offered a refreshing change from the warm and crowded indoors.

"Mamma Mia, I can't believe I ate the whole thing!" Jim acted as though he was exhausted.

"You were an eating machine. 'Ooh, Turkey'!" Gail giggled.

With pink faces from the November air, they laughed and continued down the street holding glove-covered hands. Walking in silence, a nervous Jim analyzed the consequences of his next act. He came to a halt. Gail took the cue, stopped and looked toward him, a quizzical look on her face. They stood in the shadows of a tree with the light of a street lamp peeking through the branches.

"What is it?" she asked.

Jim reached into his pocket while she watched. Then he lifted Ellen's left hand and removed her glove. He raised her hand to his lips, and then looked into her eyes. "Let's do it, Gail," he whispered, covering her hand with his. He held a diamond ring between his thumb and index finger.

Gail gasped at the ring. With tears rolling down her cheeks, she said, "Jim, are you sure? I don't know what to say."

"How about, yes?"

She nodded her head. "Yes! Yes! Yes!" as Jim placed the ring on her finger.

In April, the Nardellis and Donatos convened again for another feast, Gail's wedding celebration. Jim's contingent included relatives from Pittsburgh, Aaron, new friends from work, and old friends from high school and college, including several he met at the week, down the shore.

In May, after the honeymoon, Jim initiated the legal process of adopting Tracey, which took almost six months. On the day she became Tracey Dulles, Jim made plans for a family dinner at a nice restaurant. When Jim started down the stairs, Gail stood next to Tracey at the bottom. Gail stooped down and whispered to her daughter. Then Tracey called out, "Let's go...Dad!"

Jim stopped his descent. Her words penetrated his soul. He ran a knuckle across each of his eyes, and looked down at them, the loves of his life. Beaming, he resumed his descent, to start a new chapter in that life.

Jim and Gail had two more children: Elise, born after they had been married two years and then Michael two years later. Gail and Jim had a house built about three miles from Jim's work, a colonial style on an acre of ground. They worked at landscaping and building a large porch in the back of the house. Gail had Jim install bird feeders to create the gathering place for all sorts of birds in the winter and then squirrel feeders to keep them away from the birds. Cardinals were Gail's favorite birds. The same pair seemed to return every year and nest in the back yard. The family went down the shore every summer for two weeks, the first for family only and the second, called, anything can happen week, when the kids invited friends. On that week, all kinds of kids packed the shore house every night. The question of the day was, 'Who's coming and who's going?'

Jim's job brought the challenges of the cold war era into clear view. He worked with a group of engineers and systems analysts that formulated defense strategies against intercontinental ballistic missiles. They faced the problem of intercepting an attacking missile arriving at four miles per second! The interceptor would be armed with a nuclear warhead. The calamity of such an engagement boggled his mind. The accuracy of the radar, the speed of the computers managing the engagement and the costs of attacking and defending became the daily issues of his work. Computer simulated engagements were won or lost by making the costs of attacking or defending too high.

Jim could handle the engineering and scientific issues to do his job, but he had a lot to learn about business. After two years, Jim took advantage of a company benefit and took a partial leave of absence, which he spent attending the Wharton Business School in Philadelphia to obtain an MBA in Information Sciences. When he returned to full-time work, Jim received a promotion, which placed him at a different level. As a requirement for obtaining a Top Secret security clearance, he scheduled a trip to the police station to have his fingerprints taken.

One summer evening at the shore, after a cookout on the second floor patio of a newly built, rented apartment, Jim sat back in the canvas chair with eyes closed. Feeling mellow and satisfied, he nursed a final glass of wine. Gail and the children stood at the rail facing the darkening sky over the ocean and taking in the soft sounds of surf and smell of salt air. He reached up to touch Gail's hand, and she responded with a soft squeeze. Tracey noticed this exchange and smiled at her father. Jim looked into Tracey's eyes and spoke in a quiet tone. "This is as good as it gets."

Jim coached a Little League team and helped with the girls' field hockey. Gail worked with Girl Scouts, and they participated in countless school events and neighborhood gatherings. Jim's business travel kept him away from the family on occasion, but he sometimes found ways to parley business trips into family vacations. Gail's parents dropped by frequently and Jim and Gail visited Jim's parents near Pittsburgh at least once a year. Jim and Gail scheduled trips to New York during the period between Thanksgiving and Christmas to take in a

Broadway show, have dinner, and spend the night. During these getaway sessions they often found time to meet with Aaron for drinks or dinner and an evening of conversation and updates of the year's events. After dinner at one of these meetings Aaron, who had remained a bachelor, raised a glass to toast his friends. "Here's to your life of, happily ever after."

On a cold November evening after work Jim walked into the house to find Gail sitting on the sofa with a glass of wine in her hand, a bottle and another glass on the table, staring out the window. Jim knew Tracey would be at volleyball practice, but the conspicuous absence of Elise and Michael made him wonder. *Something's up.* Gail's formal greeting reminded him of those occasions when one of the kids got into trouble at school or elsewhere. He poured a glass of wine and sat down.

"What is it?"

Gail took a long swallow. "I went to the doctor today."

Jim's stomach flipped, as his fear of the unknown stirred. He listened while she related the results of her recent checkup, followed by blood tests and a biopsy. Gail always had a quality of exuberance, but when she finished, she sat looking down at the floor with stooped shoulders, a posture of defeat. Jim searched for a reaction. He stood and walked to her, then took her in his arms. She began to sob. *How do I deal with this?*

Soon the nightmare of dealing with cancer started, altering forever their family life. Gail's mother moved in to take care of Elise and Michael. Tracey, denying her mother's illness, turned inward and spent too much time away from home. She turned into a rebellious teenager, coming after midnight and often missing the meals prepared with love by Gail's mother. Jim, angered by her lack of consideration, struggled to find the correct way of dealing with her. When he tried to work around the pressing demands on his time due to work, business travel, Gail, and the children, there just wasn't enough of him to go around.

Gail fought for two years, her body invaded by the disease, chemicals, and radiation. The beautiful girl Jim had met on the beach deteriorated to a gaunt, weak, and depressed shell of her earlier self. A pink stocking cap made her self-conscious; not wearing one made her feel worse. Neighbors took care of the kids, and drove them to Little League, field hockey, soccer, and volleyball, and to music and dance lessons. They also pitched in with food, preparing and delivering meals, and often visited with Gail and her mother throughout her struggle. Jim had long conversations with the kids to prepare them for the worst. He wanted them to deal with it, and make it a little easier to move forward, through the difficult period that would follow. The children often responded with tears and refused to accept the unfairness. After several tortuous sessions discussing the subject, Jim saw that they began to accept the reality, Mom was going to die.

One day Jim walked into Gail's bedroom. She strained to form a weak smile. With his heart aching for the woman he loved, Jim forced an air of composure. He faked a smile and sat down next to her. "How was today?"

She looked into his eyes, resignation on her face. "A lot like yesterday. There won't be too many more, Jim."

"Yes there will; lots," but he knew she could see through him.

In a weakened voice, Gail said, "Jim, promise me something."

It got his attention. "You name it." He took her hand in his.

She continued. "Find someone after I'm gone."

His stomach churned, he couldn't be hearing this.

Then, with a twinkle of her old smile, she added, "but not too soon."

His throat tightened and he held back the tears. He would never forget what she said, their last conversation.

The funeral in March challenged the sadness of the event with uplifting tones, celebrating her life while grieving her death. Laughs echoed through the church when family members recalled incidents that made Gail memorable. The building resounded with hymns of joy. But none of this could stop the tears, which somehow flowed in greater measure amid the effort to keep the proceedings upbeat.

When they returned to the house Jim mingled with the visitors, shaking hands, and nodding to their comments of solace. Jim spotted Aaron entering the living room and caught his eye. Jim worked his way to a corner where Aaron joined him.

They clasped hands, and then placed their free arms around each other. "Thanks for coming, Aaron."

"Jim, you know I wouldn't miss this, but I wish I didn't have to be here."

"I know, Aaron."

"How are the kids handling it?"

"I've worked at it, but I'm not sure how well I've prepared them."

"This is something you don't prepare for. I remember when my brother died. I was just a kid. It was hard to handle. I couldn't believe it was happening. I just wandered through it, and after a while, it was over, and life continued."

"Seeing her near the end was painful. She had so much strength, but this was a fight none of us wins."

"At best, we put it off."

Jim paused, and nodded. Then he asked, "So, how are you doing?"

"Still playing the horses and suffering through the Penn State losses. But Joe finds a way to win most of them. Let's take in a game next year. It's been a long time."

"That sounds like a good idea."

"I'll find a schedule and send it to you. And you can come up to New York in the fall. Bring Tracey."

"Life goes on. I'll talk to her about it."

After mingling with the hoard of relatives and friends who filled the house, Jim needed some air. He went out and sat on the porch gazing at the property that he and Gail had chosen and cared for, recalling the good times, and wondering what might now follow. Lost in his thoughts, he looked up to see his sister, Pam, sitting down next to him. She had flown in from her home in Hawaii.

"So, where do you go from here?" she asked.

"That's what I'm trying to figure out."

"Well, I know this may be a little too early, but I'd like you and the kids to visit with Rob and me this summer. You guys need a break."

Jim and Gail always wanted to go to Hawaii but somehow never found the time. He thought about her love of the beach, how she would have enjoyed it. *We should have made time*.

"I'll have to make arrangements at work, and I don't know if the kids would really want to go, and there's our annual trip down the shore." He said the words without emphasis, like an old Philadelphian.

"Give it some thought. There's still time to plan it for this summer."

"Okay; thanks Pam. It's really a good idea, but it will take some sorting out."

"I know. Give us a call when you want to talk about it."

A range of reactions greeted him when he asked the kids about the idea, Michael, uncertain, Elise, negative, and Tracey adamantly opposed. Her mother's girl had been going to the shore since the age of one. It would threaten the link to Gail. "She just died and we're already forgetting her!" Tracey screamed.

Jim started to argue, "No, Tracey; that's not it. She wanted to go to Hawaii sometime. We just never made it. The trip will be for her, to remember her."

It didn't work. After a few more discussions, Jim recalled Aaron's advice. He stopped bringing up the idea. The family began to accept the hollowness of Gail's loss, and to repair the wounds of her departure.

One Friday evening at the end of May, after shutting down his computer, Jim climbed the stairs. He expected the usual commotion; all of them clamoring for a favorite. Which should it be: pizza, hoagies, Chinese, or Mexican? But when he reached the kitchen and started to look for them, the kids were nowhere to be seen.

He poured a glass of wine and sat down to the evening news. After a while, the strange silence made him suspicious. He checked the ground floor and then he went up to the bedrooms. After finding the other rooms empty, he approached Tracey's closed door and called out, "What's going on in there?"

"Nothing," Michael replied. When he said, nothing, it meant, something.

"Everyone in there?" Jim asked.

"Yes," Elise replied.

"We'll be right down," Tracey said.

Now what? He shrugged and returned to the news, wondering. A few minutes later he heard the footsteps. Then Elise's face appeared, peeked around the corner, made eye contact, and disappeared. After that, he heard a scurry of activity and giggles they burst into the room presenting him with a scene he would never forget. Michael wore a Hawaiian shirt and strummed a ukulele; Elise wore a grass skirt, and Tracey a long gown and a flower in her hair.

"Dreams come true, in blue Hawaii!" the trio sang.

He got the message.

In July they flew from Philadelphia to Chicago to change planes for Honolulu. Jim cashed in all his travel miles for Business Class seats. Jim and Michael sat together, and Tracey sat with Elise, across the aisle. After boarding the plane in Chicago an incident occurred. A bird flew onto the plane disrupting the pre-departure safety and security process. The nervous bird fluttered along the ceiling as passengers ducked their heads. The frightened little creature always found a way to elude its pursuers, always landing just out of reach. Laughter filled the plane as the crew chased down the aisles after the feathered stowaway.

Remembering Gail's love of birds, Jim seized the opportunity. "Mom's trying to get on," he said to Michael.

Michael sat up and called to Tracey and Elise. "Hey guys, Mom wants to go with us!" he called.

The girls laughed at Michael's comment, and Tracey replied, "Dad said she always wanted to go to Hawaii."

When they arrived in Honolulu, Pam and Rob greeted each of them with a plumeria lei and an the welcome, "Aloha." They drove to the Kaneohe Marine Air Station on the northern part of Oahu, where Rob served as a Navy Captain. Pam and Rob had two children Terry, 11 and Sandra, 9 near the ages of Elise and Michael.

Jim and the children spent two glorious weeks living more as residents than as tourists in beachfront officer quarters. To Michael's delight they watched the jet fighters take off in pairs every morning from the back yard. Every time he saw a bird he'd call out, "Mom's here! Hi Mom!" Jim would reply, "She is, Michael."

On several mornings they took a short walk through the dunes to a body surfing beach with terrific waves, and they cooked out on the grill almost every night, living in the casual Hawaiian life style Pam and Rob delivered. One day at the beach, Jim looked at Tracey, now approaching the age when he first met Gail. He marveled at the resemblance; eighteen, she was preparing for her first year of college at Brown. This could be their last summer together. Jim remembered his own youth, when adventures to the homes of college friends during the summer replaced the family outings, and that first trip down the shore. Tracey would be starting the same adventure soon; too soon.

While Elise and Michael had cousins their ages to hang out with, Tracey faced the awkward zone between the foursome and the three adults. Jim approached Tracey as she gazed across the blue Pacific. "Having a good time?" he asked.

80

She seemed deep in her thoughts and it took her a moment to reply. "You have no idea, Dad. This has been great. This is paradise. Why would anyone want to leave it?"

"That's a big change from your first reaction to coming here."

"I'm sorry. Losing Mom had a big effect on me. It just seemed too fast, and we always went down the shore. God, I was going there with Mom before you ever went there. It was our place in the summer; and now it's different." After a few seconds she continued, "Dad, I'm, glad you talked us into it."

"You had a lot to do with it. Don't think I couldn't figure out who orchestrated the, *Blue Hawaii*, number."

Tracey laughed, "That was pretty good, wasn't it?"

The evening sky, like an impressionist painting, invited their upward gazes to find rabbits, alligators, angels, and even, *Popeye*, in the clouds. One evening Jim raised a can of beer to his lips and took a long sip, looking at the canvas in the sky, and made a statement, loud enough for the group to hear, "This is nice, but maybe we should have gone down the shore."

Michael responded, "No way, Dad! The shore's nothing like this; this is way cool! The only thing better was when Mom was with us."

Jim looked over at Elise and at the same time saw the smile on Tracey's face. "How about you Lizzie? What do you think about it?"

"It's Elise, Dad! I'm eight you know."

"Okay, Elise. How do you like the trip?"

"I'm glad we came, but I miss Mom."

"So do I sweetie, so do I. But she's here with us, I can tell. She was the one who planned all these things and made us a family. We have to carry on with the good start she gave us."

"Will we come back sometime?" Elise asked.

"Could be," he answered, looking out over the ocean and then up to the darkening sky.

Rob interrupted his thoughts, "Don't forget, we're going snorkeling tomorrow at Hanauma Bay."

Jim said, "I forgot about that."

Rob replied, "Let's take a jog around the neighborhood to get in shape for the diving."

That evening as the group trotted around the neighborhood Jim exclaimed between puffs, "I've gotta get in shape."

The two weeks flew by and then the time to return arrived. They stood in the airport boarding area as Pam passed out another round of leis, along with an, Aloha, for each of them. As they walked down the aisle on the plane Michael took Jim's hand to get his attention and asked, "Hey, Dad, they said, aloha, when we got here; now shouldn't it be, goodbye ha?"

Jim suppressed a laugh, "Yes, Michael, maybe it should. I'll have to write Aunt Pam about that."

On the return trip the two seasoned travelers, Elise and Michael, asked to sit together on one side of the aisle. Jim, settling in next to Tracey, whispered Michael's aloha comment to her. He grinned when she burst out with an uninhibited laugh, so much like Gail's, a sound he had not heard for a long time.

Jim slammed the hatchback of his metallic silver Saab. He called to Michael, who watched from the stairs. "I'll be away for a few days; I don't know how long. I'll be staying at the Larchwood Inn; the number's by the phone. I called Tracey and left a message asking her to come over and stay with you for a few days. I left Elise a message, too. You can call and fill them in." Elise was in her first year at Princeton.

Jim rolled down the window as the car started to move, "Call if you need me; I'll try to phone in the evening to stay in touch, but don't count on it every night. Who knows what will happen up there?"

Michael waved, "Okay. See you, Dad! Good luck!"

As he approached the tollbooth for the turnpike Jim became caught up in his thoughts. *Why am I doing this? I hardly know her. What am I getting into?*

Jim thought about the chance meeting and the dinner, then remembered Gail's words: "Find someone after I'm gone. But not too soon." The thought made him smile. It had been eight years. *Maybe I have, Gail; and I don't want to lose her. Help me find her.* These thoughts recurred to him again and again as he crossed Pennsylvania, New Jersey, and New York. Between thoughts he made a few calls, including a message for Elise. Then he dialed information and connected to the Radnor Police.

A monotone voice answered, "Radnor Police, Corporal Saunders."

"Hello, this is Jim Dulles. I was at the station a few days ago and spoke with Sergeant Olsen. Is he there?

"No, he's off today. Would you like to speak with someone else?"

"There was an Officer Dunn."

"Yes, just a minute."

After a brief wait, Jim heard the officer speak, "This is Officer Dunn."

"Officer, I'm Jim Dulles. Remember me?"

"Sure do. What do you want?"

"I wanted to notify you that I'm on my way up to Connecticut to meet with the Cramwell family."

"What? You're not supposed to leave town!"

"I know, but I talked with the Cramwells about coming up, and decided I should go there."

"Why?"

"I want to make it clear that I'm not involved, and that I want to help."

"I have to report this to Sergeant Olsen."

"Fine. He can reach me in my car. I'll give you my number."

After providing the information Jim hung up.

When the phone rang two minutes later, Jim smiled. *That was quick.* He pressed the send button and answered after the second ring, "Hello."

"Mr. Dulles, this is Sergeant Olsen."

"Yes I expect..." before he could finish Olsen started a tirade while Jim listened, waiting for the Sergeant to stop talking.

When he did, Olsen said, "Mr. Dulles? Are you still there?"

Jim waited a few seconds and then said, "Yes, I am. Are you finished?"

"We told you not to leave town without calling us."

"I did call, and I gave this number so you could contact me. Look, I'm sure the Cramwells will have the local police there when I arrive. I'll tell them you want to talk with them."

"Make sure you do that." After a short discussion, the conversation ended.

When the door closed Ellen removed her blindfold at the start of another five-minute session of privacy. A minute later she opened her phone as the faucet ran. After one ring he answered, "Hello." Her father's voice filled her with hope.

She whispered with excitement, "Dad, it's me! Thank God you're there!"

She listened to his anxious reply. "Ellen, I got your message yesterday! Are you okay? Where are you?"

"I don't know; all they let me see is a bathroom. The window has bars on it and it's painted and so I can't see outside. It's an old house; early eighteen hundreds, I'd say."

"We've notified the police and played the message for them, and they have a copy. We've been hoping you'd call again."

Another voice interrupted. "I'm Sergeant Burns. Are they harming you?"

"Only the aches and pains of being tied up all the time. They free now and then for five minutes in the bathroom, and give me sandwiches and drinks. That's where I am now. It's the only time I can call. I only have another two or three minutes left. I tried 911 yesterday, and..."

"We know, but now we have someone waiting for calls to this phone. There'll always be someone here to pick up."

"Is there anything you can do, or that I should do?"

"Try to keep calm and don't do anything to upset them. From your call, we found the cell you're in and we're starting a search. We only have a general idea where you are, but we have to pinpoint it."

Ellen wanted to shout, but whispered, "Great! How long will that take?"

"It could take a day to make the search and to be sure we've located the house; we have to be careful not to scare them."

"Okay. Anything else?"

The kidnappers will try to call your father. There will be someone with him to help handle the call. We'll let you know what to do after we've heard from them. For now, don't do anything. Wait until you get instructions from us."

"Okay, but I can't leave my phone on. An incoming call might possibly alert them. Besides, my hands are always bound with tape and I couldn't answer it."

"Call when you can. We'll be standing by for your calls. Now, can you tell us what do they look like?"

"They keep me blindfolded when they're around. I haven't seen them, except for a heavyset man. He drove the car and stopped for directions as I was running on Wednesday morning. He had light hair and a round face. I only saw him for a second, about five foot eight. He climbed out of the car after another man grabbed me from behind. They blindfolded me and put on the floor in the back seat of a car."

"Is there anything distinctive about their voices?"

"They never talk. They write notes." Ellen became conscious of the sound of her voice, now rising above a whisper from the excitement of making contact. *Too loud.* She stopped talking for a few seconds, then lowered her voice. "And they keep me in the dark, literally, except in the bathroom. I can't be much help to you. I don't know how many more calls I can make. My battery is pretty low. They'll be back soon. I have to go now. I'll try again tomorrow, but I can't be sure when."

"We'll give you more instructions when you call."

"Bye, Dad. Love you." Ellen disconnected.

"Love you, Ellen."

Jim stood at the front desk of the Larchwood Inn, checking into a room. After he unpacked and had quick lunch, he took a walk around the property to stretch his legs. Invigorated by the chilly air, he returned to his room to make the call. A man answered, "Hello." Jim recognized Dave's voice.

"This is Jim Dulles. I'm at the Larchwood Inn. May I come over?"

"You didn't waste any time. Do you know how to get here?" Dave sounded annoyed.

"I have the address. I'll find it."

"Wait; let me give you the directions." It sounded like an order. Dave described the route.

After a drive of about an hour, Jim started down a tree-lined drive toward the Cramwell house. He scanned the scene confronting him, one that suggested wealth. He imagined his own feelings in dealing with something like this. How might the Cramwells react? They had only one child. What's the possible dollar value of her life? Would they pay? Had they requested a specific amount of money? Kidnappers acted with irrationality. What kind of people are these? He thought of the dangers she might experience, in particular, at the time of the actual cash exchange.

Jim stopped the car, slammed the door, and hurried toward the house set among trees and shrubs in spacious surroundings. He approached the entrance, stepped under a gracious, canopied portal, and pressed the button. The sound of soft chimes announced his arrival. In a few seconds, the door opened and a young woman appeared.

"Mr. Dulles?" she asked.

He answered, "Yes. Jim."

"I'm Maria. Please come in. I help Mrs. Cramwell with the housekeeping."

She led him through an expansive foyer into a large room furnished with sofas, a piano, several chairs, and two large paintings that looked expensive. Polished hardwood floors provided a tasteful break to the oriental carpet, soft to his step. Four large windows offered a view of the grounds. He walked to the first, a panorama of shrubs, trees, and expansive lawn that would be breathtaking with color during spring and summer.

Maria invited him to sit down. "Mr. and Mrs. Cramwell will see you in a few minutes." Jim nodded and took a seat from which he looked around the room, at the elegant furnishings. Soon Maria returned pushing a teacart stocked with tea, coffee, cookies, and scones. "Coffee?" she asked. When he nodded she poured a cup.

A short time later, as he munched on a cookie, a woman entered the room. Older and shorter than Ellen, and with lighter hair, but with a clear resemblance. Her patrician look, tasteful, casual dress, stylish hair, and impeccable makeup drew Jim's gaze. She looked tired, and her face showing the strain of her ordeal. Two men followed her into the room; one, gray haired and wearing a sweater, and a step behind, a younger man wearing a suit. Jim rose from his chair as the group approached.

"Hello Mr. Dulles," the woman said, extending a hand toward him, "I'm Jane Cramwell, this is my husband, Dave and Detective Carl Lawson."

"Jim," he said, feeling a familiar softness in her hand followed by the contrasting strong grips of the two men.

"Sit down Jane, you're tired," Dave said. "This has been hard on both of us," he continued, looking at Jim.

Jim interjected, "Before we start, Detective Lawson, I have something to tell you." Three pairs of eyes locked on Jim. "I spoke with the police, and I'd like you to call a Sergeant Olsen in Radnor, Pennsylvania."

"Why is that?"

"He's a little upset that I came up here, and I think it would help if you talked with him." Jim provided a phone number.

After this minor diversion, Jane continued, "Mr. Dulles,...Jim," she said, "thank you for coming over. I realize you just met Ellen."

"I'm more surprised than you are that I'm here," he said. "I don't know how I can help, but I'd like to, in any way that I can."

A tense silence followed his words. As Jane dabbed her eyes with a tissue, the detective scrutinized Jim while Dave Cramwell, non-expressive, comforted Jane. Dave's demeanor made Jim remember a business school course he had taken in Negotiating. Don't give away anything. Let the other guy talk; make him uncomfortable. Cramwell would have aced that course. Jim also measured the detective's apprehensiveness. I have to sell myself. He broke the silence. "I'd like to tell you why I'm here."

Jim described his meeting with Ellen and responded to a few questions. Jane listened with apparent interest but both men seemed skeptical. Jim felt they wanted to associate him with Ellen's disappearance. If so, why would he have come here? Maybe they considered his arrival as a ploy to divert them away from his involvement. He wrapped himself in a convoluted set of, what ifs. *This is too confusing. This guy's making me sweat and I'm just trying to help.* When he finished his story a silence followed. Jim reached for his coffee, waiting for a reaction.

Jane spoke, "How can you help?" It was an intelligent question, and better than outright rejection.

Jim responded, "I don't know. Do you have any idea where she is? Have you heard from her or from anyone?"

The detective spoke before Jane could reply. "We're the ones to be asking the questions, Dulles. We'll tell you what you need to know and nothing more. It seems kind of strange that you first met Miss Cramwell on the night before she was reported missing. And now you'd come here when you hardly know her."

Jane spoke between sobs, "Dave, where is she? What can we do? I want her back."

Dave replied in a comforting voice, "She's a smart girl; she'll take care of herself. We'll hear more, soon." Then, looking at Jim and in a skeptical tone, "I don't know what you plan to do around here."

Jim decided on a wide-open approach, "Well, she's been gone for what is it, two or three days now? The Radnor Police picked me up on Friday morning. They didn't tell me anything other than Ellen was missing and my fingerprints were found in her house. I think there's a good chance someone may be looking for a ransom. I assume you've searched her house and surroundings and that she doesn't disappear as a matter of routine. If I could see her house maybe I can be of some help; maybe with my fingerprints."

Detective Lawson spoke, "What do you think you can accomplish? We've had professionals through the place three times. We don't want amateurs in there destroying evidence."

"I'm concerned for Ellen and for myself. She didn't seem to want me to come inside when I picked her up and dropped her off. She made a point of not inviting me in, yet I'm told my fingerprints were found inside. I wasn't inside. I want to make that clear, and maybe I can prove it."

Jane said, "Mr. Lawson, I don't see how it matters. We've been there since Ellen left, and you can take the same precautions with...Jim. Dave, don't you agree?"

Until then Dave, expressionless, seemed like a scientist gathering data, intent on being objective. He said, "As long as the police agree it's okay with me. Why don't we all go over."

Lawson said, "No, you and Mrs. Cramwell wait here in case there's a call. I'll have someone come over to stay with you while I escort Dulles through your daughter's apartment."

—**5**—

After returning from Hawaii Jim started jogging to keep his fitness from deteriorating further. He also tried to resume his usual business routine, but the demands of work made it hard to be both a father and mother. Another promotion added to his responsibilities, and the need for more business travel and late evenings at work increased the separation from to his children. When Tracey started college he realized how little time he had left to restore his family relationships. He needed to take action, to change things before they went too far. He began searching for another job, one that would accommodate his needs.

He started by calling the family together and explaining what he wanted to do and why. They sat in the living room in front of the fireplace in an uncommon gathering. He wished he could be with them in this manner more often. Tracey leaned back in the sofa across from Jim, while Michael and Elise sat on the floor.

Jim started in a slow and calm manner, "Guys, I need to talk to you." He sensed their anticipation as they stared at him. "I haven't been doing a very good job with you since we came back from Hawaii. My work is taking too much time and I want us to do more family things."

No response; he had the floor. "I decided to make things better. I want to find a way that will let us spend more time together, the way we used to."

"When Mom was here," whispered Elise.

Jim took a deep breath. He didn't want to start down that path. "Mom will always be with us," he said. "We won't forget her, but now I have to take on the things she did that made it fun to be part of the Dulles family. We've lost some of that, but she wouldn't be happy if we didn't work to restore it. It won't happen by itself. It's like when you hurt a muscle and you have to exercise to get it working again."

Tracey stepped in, "Are you planning on getting married, Dad?"

Jim laughed. "No, not that. I'm not even seeing anyone." He saw the composite relief from his answer on all three faces. "No, what I plan to do is change jobs. I need to find a way that we can spend more time together. I don't think it will happen where I am."

"Are we moving?" asked Michael.

"No, I don't want to do that, unless something comes up that will help us with the first objective. No, I'd rather stay here. I think you would, too, wouldn't you?"

They responded with nods.

"Okay then. I'll tell you everything that's happening, and the first is that it's going to be worse for a while. I'll have to spend some time with interviews while I'm still working, and you can't talk to anyone about this. I promise I'll make it up to you, but I have to find the right job or else I'll stay where I am until I do. The job has to let us be together more, and that may take some time."

He sensed their relief. He remembered Tracey's thought. They missed their Mom and moving or any other change would be traumatic. "Are you with me on this?" he asked.

More nods; they seemed glad it was over.

For almost six months he searched newspaper ads, networked, and made phone calls, which lead to several personal interviews in the Philadelphia area. He squeezed them into an already demanding schedule. None of the interviews resulted in what he wanted, so he started to plan a broader job search.

One day at work the phone rang. "Jim Dulles speaking."

"Jim, this is John Fry; remember me?"

"John, yes, it's been a long time." John was an interesting guy. Jim didn't know him very well but liked him. They worked together on one project and hit it off. John was an Air Force pilot who retired and moved into industry. He called it a nice gig, collecting a salary and retirement pay. He had lots of great flying stories.

91

John replied, "Five or six years. San Diego, wasn't it?"

"Yes, I think you're right. What are you up to these days?"

"I'm at ECD; do you know who they are?"

"Sure, I've met a few of their people over the years. Interesting company. What are you doing for them?"

"I'm setting up a new group. That's why I called."

"What kind of group?"

John described ECD, his position with the company in San Francisco, and the two other guys he recruited in Houston and in Washington, D.C. "Jim, I think you'd fit in nicely, that is, if you're interested."

"Doesn't cost anything to listen. Tell me more."

By the end of the conversation Jim agreed to send a resume.

A week later John called again and Jim asked, "We want to interview you. Can I have someone contact you and set one up?"

"Sure. Where do I go?"

"Nowhere, it will be by phone."

"That's it, just a phone call?"

"Yes, by a professional recruiter. Her name is Debbie Browner. She interviewed me and she's good. Be ready for some tough questions. I can't tell you what they are, but you'll do fine."

After a few more days, Debbie called. She asked Jim to choose a time when he had two hours, and they made arrangements for the following afternoon. He went home for lunch and stayed for the call. John was right; Debbie put him on the defensive with a strong phone presence and a set of questions designed to test his response in dealing with a variety of situations. When he paused to gather his thoughts he heard his heart beating. *I'm glad she can't see me.* Her reactions to his answers, and the fact that they shared a few laughs, made Jim believe that the session went well. He called John afterwards and described the interview.

A few days later Sue White from ECD called. Jim's heart accelerated when she said, "I'm sending you a job application form. You also have to take a drug test. I'll enclose a list of laboratories near you."

The speed and organization of the process impressed Jim. After returning the application he scheduled the test, arriving at the laboratory one morning on route to a business appointment. Jim reacted with surprise when the nurse asked for a urine specimen; he made it clear they were to take a hair sample. After a questioning look she made a series of phone calls to the laboratory headquarters. Then she faxed his request form and received in response, a set of test protocols. It soon became obvious the lab had no idea how to take the test. That afternoon when Jim called a second lab located at a large hospital in Philadelphia, he verified that they understood the sampling requirement.

A week later he sat in a chair while a lab technician using a straight razor shaved a tuft of his hair about 100 pieces, three inches long, right down to the scalp. The sample contained six months of his chemical history, and could not be deceived by any short-term action he might take to avoid the detection of drugs in his body.

After two more weeks, a letter from ECD arrived. He called it a Mafia offer; one he couldn't refuse. He would earn twenty per cent more with an upward possibility of forty-five per cent, have excellent benefits, and could work at home. Sue White called to arrange the delivery of a computer, fax, copier, and printer to his house. She sent him a catalog and a charge code for ordering supplies by phone. He would be responsible for having phone lines installed and setting up his office. The occasional travel caveat caused him some apprehension, but the rest was just what he wanted. He started the second major change in his life one year after Gail's death.

After a week of training in company procedures, getting familiar with is computer, and meeting the team, Jim returned home. The job turned out to be a good choice. Jim spent most of his time at home so he could handle domestic issues, cleaning ladies and plumbers, shopping, and being home when school let out.   He started to cook, borrowing Gail's recipes and experimenting with some of his own ideas. He liked getting comments from Elise and Michael about his new creations, and from Tracey when she came home during semester breaks. He took on the role of Mr. Mom while maintaining his role as their Dad.

Her well-tuned body now felt like a cacophony of aches as Ellen attempted to twist and turn to a more comfortable position. After spending only ten or fifteen minutes a day on her feet, along with a lack of exercise, she had stiff and sore shoulder and back muscles, numb feet, and cramps in her calves. The itching from the tape served as a continuous annoyance. She consumed the food, barely edible, only as an alternative to starvation. A serious departure from a regimen of exercise and sound dietary habits had shocked Ellen's physical and mental system. And lying on the bed, bound and gagged, he felt like one of the beached whales that she had seen on the Connecticut shore.

Rolling to her side, she listened to the sound of an opening door, breaking the silence. She envisioned the usual bathroom and a sandwich routine. Footsteps drew closer and then stopped at her bedside. Hands removed the tape from her wrists and then from her ankles. Instinct made her stretch in an effort to ease the soreness in her body.   As she prepared for a walk to the bathroom in darkness, something different occurred; her cap lifted, uncovering her eyes. She tensed at the departure from the routine.

Ellen sat up and blinked to gain focus, excited by prospect of seeing her captors. Two men stood beside the bed in silence, one tall, the other heavier and shorter, with heads covered by black hoods.   They looked like medieval executioners, even more mysterious than she had imagined. She stared in awe at the eerie sight, trying to gather her thoughts. The tall one then pointed at the wall next to the bed. She turned to a computer on a small desk. She stood and walked to it surprised at the familiar screen setup, her computer! The note on the screen said: READ THE INSTRUCTIONS. SEND THIS MESSAGE TO YOUR FATHER. TELL HIM YOU'RE SAFE. WHEN HE SENDS FIVE MILLION DOLLARS BY ELECTRONIC TRANSFER TO THE BANQUE SUISSE FEDERATED, ACCOUNT 13339864411, YOU WILL BE RELEASED. WE MUST RECEIVE THE TRANSFER BY NEXT TUESDAY. AFTER WE VERIFY THE MONEY IS IN THE ACCOUNT WE WILL SEND INSTRUCTIONS ON HOW TO FIND YOU.

She read the words and then looked up at the two mysterious figures. "I have to go to the bathroom," she said.

The tall one pointed to the bathroom door. Then he raised an index finger for a second, and then swept it in a circle above his watch. *One minute, not enough time to make a call.* Caught using the phone would be a disaster, the loss of her only advantage. She couldn't afford that, and their reaction to finding the phone could bring other consequences, ones she didn't want to think about.

Ellen exited the bathroom, sat down at her computer and read the note again. "I need to connect the phone to send the message," she said.

The taller of the hooded figures keyed in the words below the instruction message: CREATE THE MESSAGE FIRST. CONNECT TO THE PHONE LATER.

She nodded, placed her hands on the keyboard and opened her e-mail program. The hooded men moved in to watch the monitor. *How should I phrase the message?* Could she convey additional information about her status without arousing their suspicions? It would take more time to be clever, and they would read her message carefully before sending it. She decided to be brief and follow their instructions.

DAD,
    I'M OKAY. THEY WILL RELEASE ME AFTER AN ELECTRONIC TRANSFER OF FIVE MILLION

DOLLARS IS SENT TO BANQUE SUISSE FEDERATED, ACCOUNT 13339864411. THEY WANT THE MONEY BY TUESDAY. AFTER THAT THEY'LL CONTACT YOU ABOUT HOW TO FIND ME.

PLEASE RESPOND THAT YOU HAVE THIS MESSAGE, AND THAT YOU WILL COMPLY WITH THIS THE INSTRUCTIONS.

ELLEN

"Do you want me to send now?" she asked.

The taller man leaned over her shoulder to read the message. Then he nodded, reached over her and clicked back to the instruction message screen and placed his hands on the keyboard. Ellen stared at the words, ONLY THE MESSAGE. NOTHING MORE!

Ellen unplugged the jack from the phone on the desk and inserted it into a port on her computer. She started a communications program, and logged on. Then she selected the message and pressed the SEND Command.

She turned to the hooded head. "Can I please have my hands free? And use the bathroom whenever I need to?"

The taller man turned off the computer; then he nodded. Ellen suppressed a smile. She would take advantage of this mistake.

Detective Lawson's car turned onto the familiar street and stopped in front of Ellen's house. On the porch the detective placed a key in the lock and swung the door open. Jim thought back to his departure a few days ago and to Ellen's words to him as he walked away.

"Here, wear these," Lawson said, disrupting Jim's reverie. "And don't touch anything unless you ask. We want to keep things as they are."

Jim nodded and stretched the rubber gloves over his hands. He entered the house, surprised to see a wide foyer, more like a lobby. Through an archway a television screen reflected the light from a window. Jim detected a faint odor of stale cigarettes. Several doorways surrounded the foyer and a wide stairway at the end rose to a landing. Two sets of stairs branched to the right and left to the floor above. Jim followed the Detective up to the landing and to then the second floor.

Lawson pointed at a door, and said, "Someone broke into her apartment, but we didn't find anything out of place. It doesn't seem that they were looking for anything. Kind of puzzling."

To the right, Jim looked into a small kitchen. A pot of coffee and an empty mug sat on a counter top. A briefcase sat on the floor near a small table. Jim's heart skipped a beat at the sight of a yellow rose, fully opened, in a tall vase on the table.

"Where were my fingerprints?" Jim asked.

"Downstairs, by the door, on an earring that sat on that table, and on the paper in the waste basket.

"What kind of paper?"

"Some kind of wrapping paper."

"Oceanside Florists? I think I can explain my fingerprints," Jim said with confidence. He described their Yellow Day date, the flowers, dinner, and the dropped earring at the doorway. He skipped the details. Lawson listened and nodded. Jim finished and then asked, "May I look around?"

"Just look," Lawson commanded.

The Detective followed Jim into the bedroom. A soft chair contained clothes, laid out for dressing. Jim continued his exploration of the other rooms. After a few minutes Jim asked, "Where is her computer?"

"We didn't find a computer in the house or in her car," Lawson said.

"She has one. We talked about it at dinner. Maybe it's at school."

"I'll check."

Jim continued to look around while Lawson made a call. When he hung up the phone, Lawson said, "We didn't find a computer at school either."

"Are the Cramwell's calls being monitored?" Jim asked.

"Yes."

"What about his computer?"

"What do you mean?"

"Unless there's a good explanation for why it's not here, it's possible that whoever has Ellen also took her computer. You're expecting they'll contact the Cramwells by phone, but I think it'll be by computer."

Lawson stared at Jim, nodding. "That's possible. We'll talk to the Cramwells about it."

As they exited Ellen's apartment, Jim noticed the other doors off the hallway. "Where do those go?" he asked.

"They're apartments. She rented them out."

"Are they occupied?"

"No."

After sending the message to her father, Ellen looked forward to the freedom of movement she had requested; instead, they changed the routine again. They bound and blindfolded her, then carried from the room. She counted thirteen stairs pounded out by heavy feet, heard a door open, and then inhaled fresh air for first time in three days. This small pleasure came to an abrupt end on the floor of a car covered by a heavy blanket. The car door slammed and she sensed the motion. *They're moving me! Where? Now what do I do? I have to start all over!*

Lawson's car squealed to a stop in the large, multi-story garage. Jim sat in the front seat, the Cramwells in the back. They parked in a spot designated, Cramwell Industries, and walked a short distance to the garage elevator. It took them up two flights to a lobby where Dave Cramwell waved a magnetic card at a wall-mounted device to activate a green light. A pair of glass doors parted providing access to the lobby. They entered another elevator and Dave pressed 24.

Jim eyed the surroundings, admiring the tasteful décor of Cramwell Industries headquarters. The fading light of the winter evening shone through a high glass ceiling above the spacious lobby. Plants and modern paintings decorated the area furnished by comfortable chairs and coffee tables. At the end of the lobby stood a large reception desk outfitted with a bank of computers, security monitoring screens, and telephones. Large glass doors served as the gateway to the executive offices.

Dave waved his magnetic card again to activate another set of sliding doors and led them to secretary's desk in front of an office with the name, David Cramwell, and next to another glass door. An understated design of geometric wallpaper, lighting, and artwork complemented the dark wood of a massive desk, a small credenza and a large, black leather chair.

Dave sat down at his desk and turned on the computer. He clicked and scanned the e-mail in box and found five new messages. He sat back when the name, Ellen Cramwell, appeared next to one of the messages. "A message from Ellen!" Dave exclaimed.

They gathered around the monitor as the screen filled with her brief note. The words appeared, "Dad, I'm okay. They..."

"Thank God!" Jane cried out.

Lawson spoke, "You called that one, Dulles."

Jim replied with a sense of satisfaction, "Now that they've sent the message, there's a phone record of the connection. You can locate the point of origin of the call."

"What do we do now?" Dave asked.

Lawson replied, "We have three calls from Ellen's cell phone, all from the same cell. We're looking at about five square miles of Connecticut right now. This call will pinpoint the location."

Jim asked, "Has she been in contact by cell phone?"

Lawson answered, "Now you know, Dulles. And if you're part of this, she's lost her advantage. I may have to take you into custody."

"I'm not part of anything. What e-mail service does Ellen use?"

Dave responded, "I don't know."

Jane's answered Jim's question, confident and hopeful, "CONN Data."

Lawson keyed a number into his cell phone. "Jackson? Look, we have some progress here. Locate CONN Data; they're a computer e-mail service. Get a record of Ellen Cramwell's calls and find out where her last message came from. It should be in the cell we're searching. Tell me what you find out." He disconnected.

Dave gazed at the message from Ellen. "Five million dollars! That will take some time, especially over the weekend."

"That's why they gave you until Tuesday. I think you should reply, as she requested," Jim said.

Dave looked at Lawson, "What should I say?"

The detective answered, "Tell them you can't start anything until Monday because your bank is closed. Then ask them how they'll deliver your daughter?"

Dave pressed the REPLY icon and keyed in a message following Lawson's directions. "How does this look?"

Lawson and Jim read the message, nodding. Jane, peeking over their shoulders, commented with a feminine viewpoint. "It's too negative. You'll scare them. You're setting up roadblocks and asking questions. First say something positive, like you intend to comply with their demands."

The three men exchanged glances. Lawson said, "She's right."

Dave made the fixes and after unanimous approval clicked SEND. A stream of electrons headed out to the cyberspace cloud, their connection to Ellen.

Ellen started counting when the car began to move. At 4,000, exhausted, she'd just have to call it a long distance and estimate the time. The car moved at highway speeds but she couldn't even estimate the direction. She heard whispers but no discernable voices. Her mind raced with questions. *How will the police locate me now? Will my phone close enough to a cell antenna to transmit and receive, have enough battery power to reach them again? Will they release me after Dad pays the ransom? Or will worse things happen?* As the engine droned, the discomfort of her confinement produced a new round of aches.

—6—

When that pain of leaving Kevin had diminished, Ellen acknowledged her mistake, staying with him too long. She and Annie created a list of lessons learned, like Commandments.

Don't ignore key character flaws or assume they are easily changed.

Don't accept abuse or humiliation.

Don't rush to commit to someone.

Take steps to leave when the signals are clear.

Ellen resolved to recite them when and if the time came to evaluate another relationship.

Following her breakup with Kevin, she turned her attention to studies and art, and she began to search for a teaching position, concentrating on locations in the Northeast. During the autumn months, she made a number of written inquiries, but discovered no firm opportunities. Most of her letters met with the usual response, a perfunctory request to submit a resume and transcript, and wait until spring when staffing requirements crystallized.

When she called home to talk about her plans, Dave again extended the offer to enter the family business. Ellen appreciated his generous offer of a good income and a comfortable life style, tempting, but not for her. She also recognized that her parents hoped that their only child would live nearby. She needed to prove her own ability and demonstrate that she could succeed without family connections.

Although Ellen realized that this was a bridge she couldn't possibly burn, she refused her father's offer with tact. "Thanks, Dad, but I want to create a career in tune with teaching and art. If it works out, fine; if not, I'll reconsider in the future."

A short time earlier Annie found an opportunity at the Arbor Theater in Philadelphia. This new and dynamic organization under the leadership of Tommy Conlan and an associate, Joel

Cohn, looked like an ideal vehicle to help start her acting career. Annie once said to Ellen, "Conlan and Cohn; it just sounds like a successful theater pair." The company of actors performed for moderate wages in exchange for experience, credentials, and opportunity to participate in the growth of this new venture. Annie traveled to Philadelphia to audition. After landing a part, she returned to look for a place to live.

One afternoon over coffee, Annie told Ellen about her plan for another apartment hunting excursion to Philadelphia, the following weekend. "Up till now I've been sticking to the downtown area," Annie said. "This time I'm going to try a few places near the University of Pennsylvania."

Ellen asked, "What's Philadelphia like? I've never been there."

"I like what I've seen. It's nothing like New York, but it's so close to New York that lots of people from the area commute to work there every day. I expect that I'll be going to New York frequently, to see shows and to audition."

"Sounds like a perfect location for you."

"I think so. Why don't you come down and take a look with me?"

Ellen paused, "Are you serious?"

"Sure. The trip will be good for you. If you drive we can be there in less than four hours."

"This weekend?"

"That's right."

"Where do we stay?"

"Tommy has been letting me stay at his house. I'll tell him you're coming."

"As long as it's not an imposition."

"It's not. I'll call."

Ellen wasn't so sure, and she had some reservations about making the trip. But after Annie assured her they had a place to stay, and also tickets to an Arbor Theater production, Ellen began to look forward to it.

A few days later as Ellen and Annie drove down Interstate 95, Ellen related her career options. "Annie, I'm at a loss for what to do. My Dad wants to set me up with a nice management track job in his company. I don't know if I'll find anything in teaching that will pay the rent. What should I do?"

Annie replied without hesitation, "Take his offer and keep looking. I wish I had a rich Daddy that would set me up like that."

"You always have a simple solution, Annie."

"Look, I'm not the philosopher you are. I've been scratching it out all my life. It would be nice to have a soft job and no worries about money."

"But what about your acting? Would you give that up?"

"No, probably not. I can talk theoretically to you, but if the rubber hit the road and I couldn't make a go of it, I really don't know what I'd do."

"Then, maybe I should reconsider taking his offer?"

"Ellen, you have to figure it out. You need to make decisions. The way you did with Kevin. That was a big step for you."

"Yes, it was. I think it was my first decision of any consequence."

"Well, this is going to be the second. It's a fork in the road that will change your life. Kind of frightening, isn't it? But, as Yogi Berra says, when you see a fork in the road, take it." They laughed.

"Annie, I can't imagine you, scared. You're out there, always knowing what you want and how to get it."

"Ellen, find me someone who isn't scared and I'll show you a corpse. We're all scared and putting on facades to hide the fear. It's called acting."

"And you're an actor."

"Sure, all the time," Annie laughed.

"I have to learn how to act. I'm too tight."

"You're Ellen. Don't change, I like you that way. To me you're a rock, with good taste, wonderful parents, family money, and a nice car. That's not bad. Tight, is not the right word, maybe caring, considerate, or sweet, which seem to have fallen out of fashion; but they're an important part of you."

Ellen reacted with surprise to Annie's comments. As much as they confided in each other, she viewed this as a new plateau. Being with her again had been fun. After more than ten years of friendship, seeing so much of each other during that time, Ellen felt a pang of sadness at leaving Annie. "Annie, let's make sure we stay in touch," Ellen said.

"We'll find a way; e-mail and phones, and travel is pretty cheap, no matter where we are."

"Yes, no matter where."

Arriving in Philadelphia, Annie navigated until they found their way to Tommy Conlan's apartment, located near the University of Pennsylvania. After getting set up in a spare bedroom Ellen and Annie set out to explore the sights. They got lost.

"You told me to turn right!" Ellen spoke in a raised voice.

"No, I didn't!"

"Well, what do we do now?"

"Keep going, we'll come to the river." When they did Annie regained her sense of location, and a short time later they arrived back at the apartment.

That evening, they attended a performance of the Arbor Theater. Annie planned to have the Arbor crowd meet Ellen afterwards. When they entered the reserved room at a nearby restaurant, they found it packed with about twenty-five people having drinks and an assortment of snacks before dinner. Because of Annie's recent arrival to the company, Ellen expected that she had few acquaintances. But Annie waved to a few familiar faces and began mixing with ease. Tommy took special care to escort Ellen around the room and introduce her as, Annie's teacher-friend. He made a considerate effort to assure Ellen's comfort in this group of strangers, a striking contrast to Kevin, who would have let her sink or swim under similar

circumstances.   She recorded Tommy's consideration and
kindness as essential in any future relationship.

When they sat down for dinner, Ellen took a seat next to a
woman she hadn't yet met. The woman said, "Hi, I'm Sheila;
and you're Annie's friend, aren't you?"

"Yes, Ellen." They shook hands.

Sheila asked, "What do you think of this crowd?"

"Different; fun," Ellen replied.

"Oh, we know how to have fun!"

When Ellen remarked, "Annie will fit right in," she and
Sheila both laughed.

What do you teach?" Sheila asked.

"Nothing yet. I'm majoring in Art Education, so that's what
I'd like to do."

"Have you looked around here?"

"No, this is my first trip here with Annie."

"My roommate's from Penn, that's the University of
Pennsylvania, and she teaches at The Mayfair School, in
Westown."

"What's Mayfair?"

"It's fairly new, and run by a Penn graduate. She's always
looking for recent Ivy Leaguers like you and other top-notch
graduates in the Philadelphia area. Doesn't pay a lot but it's
enough, and it could be a start. Do you want me to talk to my
roommate?"

An unexpected surprise, in Annie's words a, fork in the road.
"It can't hurt," Ellen said.

"Like chicken soup."

Ellen laughed. "Thanks! I'll remember that one."

Ellen spent the rest of the evening mingling with this
interesting and somewhat bizarre group; Annie's world, so
different from her own. She entered into snippets of
conversation with lots of people, names Annie had mentioned,
and who could now be attached to real faces.

The dinner proved fruitful for Annie, who latched to the arm
of a guy with long hair and leather jacket. Ellen couldn't quite

count all the earrings. They approached Ellen, each holding bottles of beer. "Meet Jerry," she said to Ellen. "We're heading to the White Dog Café; want to come?"

Ellen found herself relaxing and enjoying the evening, but after the drive and the evening's activities, exhaustion won out over the temptation of joining Annie. "Thanks, but I could use some sleep."

"Okay." Annie seemed relieved at Ellen's refusal. "Can you find your way home, to Tommy's apartment?"

"If you give me some directions that were a little better than this afternoon."

"Touché," replied Annie. "Alright, we'll take you there. Mind if we use your car?"

"Just don't get lost."

After the weekend adventure Ellen and Annie drove back to Connecticut on a pleasant Sunday afternoon. Ellen liked traveling with Annie; she made interesting conversation and always had an amusing comment. Under a clear blue sky, they chatted about Ellen's first taste of Philadelphia and about Jerry, Annie's new love.

A few days later the phone rang. "Is Ellen Cramwell there?" the caller asked.

"This is Ellen."

"I'm Peggy, Sheila's friend. Remember Sheila, from the Arbor Theater?"

"Oh, yes, Sheila. Are you her roommate?"

"Yes, I am. She said you were looking for a job teaching art."

"Well, that's the idea. But there's not much out there."

"Tell me about it. Last year I was in your shoes."

"But, something came up for you, right?"

"Yes, Mayfair. It's a private, coed elementary school. Lots of reading work and dealing with kids who've had a hard time with traditional academics."

"I don't have any real background in that area."

"I know, but you haven't heard the whole story. Dr. Suskind needs an Art Teacher, and she wants one cheap."

"Well, now we're talking."

"Dr. Suskind likes to get recent graduates with good grades from the best schools. It's kind of a boot camp, but the experience would be good, and it could lead to better things."

"What do I have to do?"

"Get me a resume and a transcript fast. Do you have e-mail?"

"Yes, but the transcript will have to be mailed."

"FedEx it."

Ellen, the artist, grew cautious. This felt like business; the pace, much like her father's, moving too fast.

"Do you always operate this way? Everything ASAP."

"This is how it works. Dr. Suskind has had four or five interviews for the job and hasn't made up her mind yet. If you wait too long, she may, and it'll be too late. If you really want a shot you have to play the game. Believe me; you'll like this place and you'll learn a lot. It's enough to live on, and according to Annie, that's not your biggest problem."

"So, Annie has been my agent on this deal?"

"Not just your agent but your sponsor, PR Man, and godmother. She thinks you're the best!"

Ellen decided to play the game. The fast lane opened because of Annie. She hit the accelerator, "Okay, you've got it. Send me an e-mail message, Annie has my address, and include the mailing address for the transcript. I'll reply with my resume and get the transcript out tonight."

After two days the phone rang again. It was 10 AM. Annie picked up and then said. "Just a minute. Ellen, it's for you!"

Ellen took the phone, "Hello."

"Miss Cramwell, this is Dr. Suskind from Mayfair School in Westown, Pennsylvania. I received your transcript and resume yesterday."

"Oh, yes. You move quickly."

"Well, we try. We're at the end of the recruiting cycle for the fall semester and need to fill a few positions that are left. Would you be interested in coming down to talk about one of them?"

Ellen sensed a real opportunity. "Well, you know I want to teach Art. Is that possible?"

"Yes, we have one position left and will need to make a decision within the week."

Sheila's information was correct. "I can be down tomorrow."

"We'll want to see you about nine o'clock."

God, they don't know how to slow down. I'll have to leave this evening! She considered asking for an afternoon interview and a morning drive, but had second thoughts. She remembered her Dad's words, be flexible; be responsive. That's how you win in business. Getting the job was business; the teaching could come later.

"I'll be there; but I need directions."

"I'll e-mail them to you. I have your address. See you tomorrow. Have a safe drive." She hung up.

Ellen hung up the phone, her head spinning. *Wow!*

After lunch, Ellen packed while Annie made a call arranging for Ellen to stay at Tommy's. Then Annie coached Ellen on taking the interview, ending her instructions with, "Remember; acting!"

Ellen arrived in Philadelphia at 7:30 that evening. Tommy left a note for her to pick up the key at the apartment next door. By 10 o'clock Ellen closed her eyes and entered a deep sleep.

Ellen's car moved with high speed along a dirt road. Next to her sat a guy in a baseball cap with the interlocking letters, N and Y. Annie sat in the back seat. The car approached a traffic signal and Ellen slowed down at the red light. Beyond the light, two wide highways departed at forty five-degree angles. Ellen peered at two signs, confused by the posted speed limits of 85 along each road. A group of children beckoned on one road, her father on the other. Annie leaned over the seat and screamed at the guy in the baseball cap, pointing to the right. He shook his head and pointed to the left. Ellen sat frozen at the wheel. The light turned green. A car behind Ellen honked and a voice yelled out, "Make up your mind, lady!"

Ellen sat up, straining her eyes at the clock next to her bed, 5:50. She shook her head. *That was interesting! Time to get up.*

As Ellen's car wound through the suburban streets she searched for the entrance to the school. She spotted the large sign, The Mayfair School, and turned into a long drive lined with azaleas, rhododendrons, tulips, and other spring flowers. The wonderful colors appealed to her artistic senses, contrasting the New England spring she had left just yesterday.

She parked in front of an old brick mansion that looked like a French chateau. When she opened the car door, screams and laughter of children at play made her smile. She stopped to watch the field hockey game in progress, a comfortable feeling, reminiscent of her private school days. As she passed through the large white door she glanced at her watch, 8:55. *Right on time.*

After a short wait, a secretary escorted Ellen into Dr. Suskind's office. Dark paneled walls separated by large colonial windows rose to a twelve-foot ceiling. Reproductions of art masters lined the walls, and a large desk covered with books and work in process exuded the aura of action. On a coffee table in the center of the room, a vase of fresh flowers and a plate of small pastries separated pots of coffee and tea. Ellen stepped toward the two inviting chairs as a striking woman moved in earnest across the floor. Her reddish-brown hair took two paths, one clasped in a bunch atop her head and the other, flowing over her shoulders. A blue dress exposed shapely legs, and golden buttons gave a military aura to her appearance. Blue spectator shoes completed the outfit of a well-dressed woman. Her nails and lipstick showed perfect grooming, and her beaming smile, an air of supreme confidence.

With hand outstretched and piercing eyes, she greeted Ellen, "Denise Suskind."

Ellen had expected she'd introduce herself as Doctor, which everyone used when referring to her. Responding to her firm grip and warm smile Ellen said, "Ellen Cramwell."

"Have you had breakfast?"

"Yes, but that looks great. Some tea and a pastry would be nice."

"Have a seat," Dr. Suskind said. Then she poured the tea for Ellen and coffee for herself.

"Well, tell me, who is Ellen Cramwell?"

Ellen paused at the question, wondering what part of her life should she talk about first? "I'm an artist who wants to teach and likes to run." *Good answer?* She wondered about the length of the pause.

The conversation moved at a comfortable pace to Mt. Holyoke, Yale, and her childhood in Connecticut. Then Dr. Suskind said, "Cramwell Industries; are you related?"

Ellen sensed that she already knew. "Yes, David Cramwell is my father."

"I raced against him; he's a real competitor. Have you inherited that?"

This confused Ellen; her father didn't run. Then she caught it. "I sail for fun, but I think the competitive part came out in my running. He got me started."

"Well, he wouldn't remember me, but I remember him," Dr. Suskind said.

Don't be too sure. Then Ellen realized the play at modesty. If Dr. Suskind always opened this way she'd be hard to forget.

The conversation continued until 10 o'clock and then Dr. Suskind said, "I'd like you to meet some of the staff."

Ellen felt she had made the first cut. They stood and started toward the door.

Dr. Suskind asked a final question, "What's your philosophy of education, Ellen?"

Ellen paused for a few seconds. *She knows how to put people on edge!* She didn't have a pat answer for this one. She remembered that one of her Education Classes dealt with teaching attitudes and educational policies. She dug into her memory, "Each child has individual needs," she said.

Dr. Suskind smiled, "Enjoy your day. We'll talk again when you're ready to leave."

Pleased with her answer, Ellen smiled. *Second cut.*

Most of the teachers Ellen met seemed very nice and kept the discussions light, but a few of them probed into her background. Ellen expected the younger teachers would perceive her as another of Dr. Suskind's prodigies and a threat. To her surprise, she sensed none of that and found them to be quite pleasant. After a tasty lunch at a nearby inn and meetings with two more teachers, Ellen enjoyed a tour of the school. Except for the old mansion, most of the facilities were new, and had a modern architecture style, set in wooded surroundings. When the day ended, she felt comfortable with her performance and enthusiastic about the possibilities that Mayfair offered.

At three o'clock Dr. Suskind looked up as Ellen entered her office, "Well, what did you think?"

"You have a great staff and a beautiful setup here," Ellen answered.

"Would you like to be part of it?" The frontal attack again.

"Well, yes...sure."

"Then you are! Welcome to Mayfair!"

This woman raised the meaning of, fast track, up another notch. There could be no thought of refusing or negotiating. The salary and other conditions of employment seemed inconsequential, as Ellen nodded and smiled through the rest of the session.

In the lobby outside Dave's office, Jim paced the floor in concert with staccato clicks of large clock as the second hand swung through its relentless path. Sitting at his desk, Dave tried to focus on the computer screen between sips of coffee and occasional munches of a ham sandwich. A few hours had passed since Dave's e-mail response, but it felt like a day. Jane lay back in a soft chair with her eyes closed. As Jim turned for another lap, the chirp of Lawson's cell phone broke the nervous silence.

The detective lifted the phone and spoke, "Lawson." He listened, grunting, "uh huh," a few times, and nodding to the remote caller. Jane opened her eyes to watch Lawson speak, and Jim entered the office. "Send a detective over to Cramwell Industries," Lawson ordered. He hung up the phone and spoke to the Cramwells. "They've located the house. I'm going over to plan our move. I want you both to stay here and wait for phone or e-mail messages. You can call me if you hear anything."

"Okay," Dave said, placing his hand on Jane's shoulder as she let out a sigh.

"I'd like to come with you," Jim said to Lawson.

"No, this is police business, Dulles. You stay here. Besides, I want you out of the way and in sight of the Cramwells. Do you have a cell phone?"

Jim removed the phone from his pocket and replied, "Yes."

"Give it to me. I don't want you making any calls." Lawson then turned to Dave. "Mr. Cramwell, don't let Dulles use your phone. A detective is on his way over. You'll have to go down and let him in. Mrs. Cramwell, you answer the phone if it rings in the meantime. Don't agree to any actions unless you talk to me first. I'll call when we have our approach for entering the house ironed out." He walked out of the office.

A short time later a detective arrived. After another hour had passed the phone rang. Jane, filling the wastebasket with paper cups and food wrappings, stopped her chores. The detective signaled to Dave, and Dave pressed the speakerphone button. "Cramwell Industries, Dave Cramwell." Jim listened as the familiar voice announced, "It's Lawson. I have more news. We entered the house at about ten o'clock. Nobody there."

"Are you sure you had the right one?" Dave asked.

"Yes, we are. We were on the phone with CONN Data for over an hour. They sent a specialist in to search the computerized phone logs. He located the call in the log, and it allowed us to find the address. The house was in a part of the cell we hadn't looked at yet, abandoned. A phone was installed recently under the name of John Jones; we suspect it's a bogus name. We're trying to locate the owner of the house."

"What did you find there?" Dave asked.

"When we approached the house was dark; no lights on. We staked it out for about half an hour and listened for sounds of activity. Then we picked a lock and entered. Nobody inside, but it was the right house. It fit the description of the bathroom and the bedroom your daughter gave. It looked like they left a few hours ago, right after they sent the e-mail to you."

"What are you doing now?" Jim asked.

"We're checking for fingerprints and car tire tracks. The location is pretty desolate. There's a gas station and convenience store at the nearest intersection, but that's almost a mile away. We'll continue to look for someone who may have seen them. And we'll wait for their response to your e-mail, or for another call from your daughter."

When Dave hung up he said, "What a setback! So close."

Jim replied, "Whoever they are, they're not dumb. They probably planned the move all along."

Jane sat back in a chair and closed her eyes; "We have to start all over again."

After what seemed like several hours Ellen sensed the car slowing down, then stopping; she heard whispers. A short time later she felt the car beginning to move again, now at a slower speed, then the sensation of a sharp turn, moving at a crawl for about five more minutes, and stopping once more. She repeated the sequence in her mind and committed it to memory.

Car doors opened and slammed and cool air entered the car when the back door opened; heavy hands lifted her out of the car, unbound her feet and raised her to standing position. She teetered behind the pitch black of her blindfold until a hand nudged her to walk, and then controlled her direction through the icy air. Ellen detected a distinctive scent of pine. The mysterious hands guided her to stop, and then up a set of four stairs. She heard a door open.

Inside, still as frigid as the outdoors, she remembered the same musty odor from the buildings at summer camp. They led her up a flight of stairs and opened another door. After that, a metallic jingling and a tightening on her ankle; then footsteps and the sound of a closing door.

Ellen stood in the stillness of the dark silence, straining to listen for sounds. After a short time she removed the tape and slid the cap from her head. Her eyes adjusted to the dim light; moonlight shined through a window revealing walls made of rough logs. She started toward the window and felt resistance to her step. She looked down at a pale glint; then she knelt, and felt the thick metal of ankle clasp attached to a chain. She tugged at the metal links, tracing them to a thick tube frame at the head of an old metal bed. Its chipped white paint and rust indicated age and neglect. A dark blanket lay on a bare mattress. She felt like a circus elephant, chained to a fixed range of movement. *At least I have some mobility, and thank God, no blindfold!*

Ellen turned from the bed, feeling her way through the darkness as the chain slid along the floor behind her. She opened the door to a closet where a few rusty wire hangers dangled from a bent rod. She jiggled the knob on a second door; when it wouldn't turn, she realized it was the entrance from the stairs. Opening a third door she peered into the dark and discovered a bathroom; they had honored both of her requests. *Thanks!*

She returned to the bed, wrapped the blanket around her shoulders and then shuffled to the window. She reached out to feel the, barely warm, iron radiator below the window. Gazing out into the black night at a desolate, wooded area she wondered where they had taken her. She noted the position in the sky of the shiny moon.

Only a few minutes had passed since they had left her alone. She heard unintelligible voices of men talking from the floor below. She guessed it would be several hours before they brought her breakfast, so she removed the cell phone from its hiding place. Standing by the window, she flipped it open, keyed in her father's number, and then sent the call. A faint ring sounded through a crackling sound. Then, through the crackling, she heard her father's voice, "Hello."

In a strong whisper said, "Dad, this is Ellen! I'm very far away, four or five hours! I'm in a cabin! It's a heavily wooded area!"

He replied with assurance, "Keep up your courage. You're doing fine. They found the house where they held you, but (*crackling sound*).

"It's hard to hear you, Dad. My batteries are low, and I'm probably in a remote area that isn't very well covered by cellular."

"We (*crackle*) e-mail".

"What?"

"Just (*crackling*) you again, I promise."

"Dad, I don't know how many more calls I can make. This may be the last one."

"Try again (*crackle*)...ing."

"Dad? Can you hear me? Dad?" She heard no reply. She said once more. "Goodbye, Dad. Please help me!" The light of the phone dial cast a tiny, friendly glow. Ellen pressed the power button and stared at the phone dial as the glow went dark, ending her connection to a safer place. After hiding the phone, she returned to the bed and stared at the uninviting site, a bare mattress and a stained pillow. She sat on the bed, put on her cap and gloves, folded the gray blanket into two layers, and wrapped herself in it. She tucked her knees into a fetal position and closed her eyes. As the frigid air attacked the warmth of her tiny haven, she moved legs, arms, and hips, trying to create heat from the friction. After a while, exhaustion overcame her shivering struggle and she slept.

Ellen listened to the click of an opening door. A man in a yellow sweater entered and smiled. A field of yellow flowers waved in the wind, visible through the doorway. She stood and walked toward a stranger, somehow familiar, extending his hand. She stopped and looked over her shoulder at a mirror reflecting the appearance of a beautiful woman in a blue and white dress. A yellow ribbon held her hair together. Pleased at the vision, she turned and reached for the man's hand, raising her eyes toward his face. A black hood stared at her. Startled, she recoiled and stepped back, but the hooded man moved closer. As she backed away she felt the resistance of a wall and a chill running up her spine.

Ellen's eyes opened. She sat up in the daylight-filled room. Her gaze turned to the door, then down to the breakfast on the floor. She ate the stale bread and mealy apple, and drank lukewarm coffee. *Tomorrow I've got to be awake when they deliver it. Hot coffee!*

After the meager breakfast, Ellen pressed her face to the window and looked left and right, then at the snow beneath large pines and firs, and up at a clear blue sky. She made mental notes of the position of the rising sun. *If I could only get outside and free of the chain!*

She lay down on the floor and stretched calf muscles, hips, and shoulders to the clinking sounds of the clumsy chain, experiencing strange pains, unusual kinks, and tight muscles from her days of confinement. After stretching she rose, longing to run in the open air. She lifted a length of chain from the floor and began to jog around a miniature track counting each short lap around the room. This would have to do, for now.

—7—

After a sheltered youth, a measure of independence, and a failed romance Ellen called this next chapter to her life, the Mayfair Years. She enjoyed the variety of two lives; living with Annie in the city where she experienced the, out on the edge, crowd and also the beautiful and quiet Philadelphia suburbs, where she worked at her art, and her teaching.

Shortly after the fall semester started Ellen invited her parents to visit and see the new life she had begun. In mid-October the Cramwells came down for a weekend. On a charming Saturday morning of autumn leaves, warm sun, and fall flowers Dave drove and Ellen pointed the way to Mayfair. Teachers often came in on weekends to catch up on work. Word of the Cramwell's visit had spread; Ellen wondered how many of them peeked through their windows at Dave's Jaguar cruising up the drive.

"This is lovely," Jane said, remarking at the picturesque beauty of the surroundings.

"I knew you'd like it," replied Ellen. "What do you think, Dad?"

"Seems like a class operation; the grounds look manicured, and that costs money."

"You don't want to know the tuition. Dr. Suskind can afford the manicurists. By the way, she wants to meet you."

"Oh?"

"Yes, she raced against you."

"I don't remember anyone named Suskind. What's her first name?"

"Denise Abrams Suskind."

"Denise Abrams! She was a tiger. She could sail!"

"Really?" Ellen replied.

"We called her, Horatio!"

Ellen knew he'd remember. "Well, she remembers you. Anything between you two in college?"

Dave gave an uncomfortable glance at Jane. "Nothing important."

"What was unimportant?" Ellen asked. She liked this way of relating to her father.

"Oh, nothing."

Jane reacted. "Yes, David, there was something. I didn't know about this." Calling him David, her mother's signal for getting into serious discussions.

"Well, neither did I. And that was before I knew you. I didn't know Denise Suskind was Denise Abrams."

"But now you do."

He replied, "Later, let's look around."

Ellen took him off the hook. "Okay Mom, we'll get him later. We'll give him a little time to get his story straight." She smiled at her father.

"Better be good," Jane said.

Ellen ended the probing with, "Come on, let's look at my classroom."

After showing her parents around the school, Ellen noticed the signs of approval in their smiles. Dave said, "Ellen, you look happy here."

"Very! I'm learning so much. This is a wonderful first job!"

Jane picked up on the comment, "Are you thinking of your second job already?"

"No, but this probably isn't a career position. It's a small school and Dr. Suskind is out in the market every year looking for new graduates. It's a buyers' market. I'll stay as long as I'm enjoying it."

Dave broke in. "Sounds like you've learned something, Ellen. Take care that you don't get too comfortable, and don't be afraid to change; and my offer is always open."

"I know, Dad. Thanks."

Jane took her turn. "Don't get her jumping from job to job. She just got here!"

"And she should stay here for a while, as long as she's happy and learning," he replied.

A door opened at the far end of the classroom and Dr. Suskind appeared in the doorway. Ellen saw her polite smile, waiting to be acknowledged. When Ellen made eye contact, Dr. Suskind said, "May I say hello to your family, Ellen?" Ellen watched her mother's careful observation as this arresting woman approached, suspecting it would be from the top down. Her hair bounced in rhythm to quick steps and her bright red lipstick surrounded a beaming white smile. She wore a red polo shirt with a yacht club emblem and a white and blue striped sweater over her shoulders, white duck slacks pressed to a neat crease, and boating loafers. The red of her fingernails matched the lipstick. Ellen recalled the day she first met Dr. Suskind. She knew how to make an entrance.

"So that's Horatio," Jane whispered.

With a sneering smile, Dave shook his head and returned her whisper, "Too much information can sometimes be a bad thing. This is one of those times."

Ellen smiled. *Getting interesting, Jane meets Denise!* "Dr. Suskind this is my Mom and Dad."

"Denise Suskind," she shook Jane's hand, and then Dave's. "Well, we're happy to have Ellen with us. She has taken control of our art program."

The gracious compliment made Ellen blush, but this time with pride. They chatted about Mayfair, its mission, how it started, and current direction. Denise Suskind had big plans and she shared them with everyone who would listen. After half an hour she excused herself, "You want to spend time with Ellen. It was nice talking with you."

Dave took the initiative, "Dr. Suskind, we seem to have met some time ago."

"Yes, I'm surprised you remembered."

"Nice seeing you again."

"Yes." She smiled and nodded, and turned for the door. She waved and closed it behind her.

"What a woman," Jane said, "personality type, A. But she didn't say much when you said you knew her, Dave."

"I told you, it was no big deal."

She still wondered what was between Denise and her Dad. Later at dinner, Ellen took the initiative from her mother, "Okay, Dad tell us about it; you and Denise."

Dave looked down at the table, and then sat back in his chair. "Nothing much; we were at a party after a regatta and I was doing my imitation of Horatio Nelson, one arm, singing, *He is an Englishman*, from *Pinafore* and all that; drinking beer and having a good time. Denise walked over and joined in. Then she did her, *Three Little Maids*, from *The Mikado*. She did all three of them. She was good. We had a great time and I walked her home that night. That's it."

Jane chimed in "That's it? You didn't date her or anything?"

Dave sat, thinking.

"Out with it, Captain," Jane gave the order.

"Admiral."

"What?"

Ellen laughed at a smiling Dave and said, "Nelson was an Admiral."

"Admiral? Well, he may soon be a Captain," Jane replied with a stern look. Jane also knew how to play.

"No, I saw her a few times after that, and I liked her. She was bright, interesting, and fun to be with. But," then he looked at Jane, "after that you swept me away."

"I thought it was the other way around," she replied. "I don't know. Why didn't she say more when we met her?" Jane probed.

"She's got class, Mom; didn't want to embarrass Dad and appear too friendly. How long ago was that, Dad?"

"Twenty five years, more or less."

Ellen took the plunge, "Did you kiss her, Dad?"

Dave made a slow turned to his daughter, and with a devilish smile, said, "An Englishman never tells."

Ellen grinned at her father, and shook her head. Jane's eyes narrowed, displaying a pretended wonder. Then they all laughed.

In the Cramwell's living room, Jim sat with Jane's sister, Sandra, sipping coffee and awaiting news. Although slightly taller than Jane, her sister had an obvious resemblance and exhibited the same propriety and a warm friendliness. She flew in from San Francisco after hearing of Ellen's disappearance. She seemed to remain in the background, helping Maria handle the household issues and responding to Jane's needs. As they chatted, Jim saw in Sandra, a woman of confidence, someone who would be a comfort at this time of need.

The jingling phone halted their conversation and the room became quiet. Jim felt the rising tension in the room. Dave pressed the speaker button. "Hello."

"Hi. This is Detective Lawson. We've located your daughter again."

Dave covered the phone. "They've located Ellen again!" Then he said, "Let me turn on the speaker phone so we can all hear."

The sound of Lawson's voice followed, "She's in the Adirondack Mountains in New York near the town of Lake George. If she calls you again tell her to dial 911. The emergency operations organization there has been briefed about the situation and they'll be prepared for her calls."

Dave spoke with apprehension. "Our connection was very poor last night."

"I know, I listened to the tape. But if they don't move, we'll locate her again. It's a heavily wooded area; not many houses to look for but hard to find the ones that are there."

"How long would you expect?" Jim asked.

It could take a day or two, if we're lucky. She said her battery is low, so we may not get much more from her. As long as they don't know about her phone, they'll feel pretty safe, that far away. But if they get nervous and run, we're back to where we were, or worse."

Jane asked, "Are you going up to New York?"

Lawson replied, "Yes, in about two hours. I've been in touch with the State Police and the FBI. We're going in by helicopter."

"I'd like to go," Jim said.

Lawson replied, "No way! You're staying here!"

"Did you think about why they ran?" Jim asked.

"Just nervous, I guess; too close. I think they wanted more space."

"I think they knew the e-mail would be traced," Jim replied. "They must have planned to move as soon as they sent the message."

Lawson replied, "That makes sense. They don't know about Miss Cramwell's phone, and they ran right after sending the e-mail." After a brief silence he continued, "We've done some checking on the two tenants your daughter rented to, Al Bartles and Tim Downs. They're from New York City and they've lived in your daughter's apartment building for just about two months. And they moved out in a hurry."

Jane spoke up, "Ellen told me about them. I didn't like her description, but she needed tenants. The apartments were vacant for several months."

Lawson responded, "Do you know much about them?"

Dave replied, "I haven't meddled in Ellen's business dealings. She handles all of the business issues dealing with rental, taxes, permits, and maintenance. She's always had two or three tenants, and she didn't talk to me about the current ones at all."

Jane responded, "She wanted desperately to show you she could manage the business. I should have told you, but she asked me to say nothing about her problems."

A grimace covered Dave's face. "This is one time when I wish I had pried into things more. She..."

124

Lawson's voice interrupted, "There's a good chance those two are involved, and that they're with her now. If Dulles is right, they may not want to send any more e-mail messages; but you'll hear from them. They'll react to your response some way, maybe by mail or from a payphone. Leave your computer on and keep checking it regularly. And we have an advantage that they don't know about. Stay by the phone in case your daughter calls again or for calls forwarded from your office. I'm going up to work on locating her. I'll call when I have something."

"Thanks, Mr. Lawson. Bring our girl back, please." Jane spoke with tears rolling down her cheeks.

Jane picked up the phone after one ring. "Hello. Yes. Oh, yes. Hello, Dorothy." She whispered to Dave, "It's your secretary."

"What kind of a package? Express, you say? Would you, please? Thank you, Dorothy. No, no news since yesterday...thanks for your concern."

Jane hung up and spoke to Dave. "There's an express mail package for you. Dorothy will have a courier bring it over."

The doorbell rang half an hour later. Dave entered the room while opening the large envelope. He removed a single sheet of paper and read the message aloud.

"Mr. Cramwell:
WE KNOW YOU LOCATED THE HOUSE AND TRIED TO SURPRISE US. THAT WAS A MISTAKE. IF YOU ARE CONCERNED FOR YOUR DAUGHTER, DO AS WE ASKED. YOU WILL GET NO MORE COMPUTER-MESSAGES. YOU HAVE TODAY TO GET THE MONEY AND TOMORROW TO DELIVER IT ELECTRONICALLY. WE WILL MONITOR THE ACCOUNT. WHEN THE MONEY IS RECEIVED YOU WILL GET A MESSAGE TELLING WHERE TO FIND YOUR DAUGHTER. IF YOU DO AS WE SAY, SHE WILL NOT BE

HARMED. OTHERWISE, YOU WILL REGRET YOUR DECISION."

Dave stared at the unsigned paper trying to extract more meaning from the words. He looked at his wife. "I have to get the money now and send it."

"Before you do, call Detective Lawson," Jane's voice had the sound of a plea.

Jim chimed in, "The envelope and paper are important. Be careful with them, you may destroy fingerprints or other evidence. You may want to make a copy of the letter."

"You're right, Dulles."

Dave removed two tissues from a dispenser and picked up the message and envelope. "I'm going to copy this. Get Lawson on the speakerphone."

Jim keyed in the numbers. After two rings the voice answered, "This is Lawson."

"It's Jim Dulles. The Cramwells received an express message."

"What does it say?"

"Just a second, Mr. Cramwell is making a copy in his library office. He'll read it to you."

Jim waved at Dave finishing the copy. "I've got him, Mr. Cramwell."

Dave handed Jim a large envelope and signaled to put the evidence inside, took the phone and spoke, "Hi. Let me read the message."

When he finished, Lawson asked, "What have you done about the money?"

"I called Walt Baran, my banker, last night at his home. Walt and I are good friends. He said we could get the five million by noon today."

Lawson answered in a firm voice. "We need time to track them down."

"But they may harm Ellen if they find you're still looking for them!"

"What they do is out of your control. They may harm her even if you send the money. You can't trust these people."

"We want our daughter back! It's our money!" Jane's raised voice contrasted her usual, quiet manner.

"I can't stop you from sending the money, but a federal crime has been committed, and we're obligated to pursue the criminals."

Jim spoke, "Are you in touch with the Banque Suisse? Do they have any obligations concerning the account?"

"They have been contacted. Once the money is received they'll inform us."

Jim replied, "Yes, and it's likely that it will be disbursed electronically to one or more other locations immediately. If the money is sent, you may not get it back."

"But we'll have our daughter," Jane said.

"If, they release your daughter," Lawson's voice sounded emphatic, and he emphasized the, if.

Jim said, "Ellen says she doesn't know who they are or what they look like. They want to keep it that way. As long as the Cramwell's comply with them do you think they'll harm her? Maybe they just want the money."

Lawson raised his emphasis another notch. "Stick to your computers, Dulles! And keep your opinions to yourself!"

Dave made the decision. "I'm getting the money."

Jim had a thought, "Mr. Cramwell, we may be able to send the money without sending it."

"What do you mean?"

"With the cooperation of the Banque Suisse, we might be able to make the transactions appear to be real, but not actually occur."

"What do you mean?" Lawson said.

"Is the FBI there with you?" Jim asked.

"Yes."

"Talk to them. I'll call someone in the Financial Industries Group at my company and see what can be done."

Dave reacted, "And if they find out, the risk to Ellen increases. I'm getting the money. We'll deal with the transaction later. If I want it to be real, it will be real."

Lawson's voice interrupted, "Okay, calm down. You go ahead, but keep me informed of any action you take. I'll send someone to pick up the message. Give him the envelope, too. You made a copy, didn't you?"

"Yes," Dave said.

Lawson's voice barked out more commands. "Dulles, find out what you can about this electronic transfer idea. I'll get the FBI involved. It's about 10:30 now. I don't know if we'll find where they're holding Miss Cramwell this evening or tomorrow. I'll call back around 2 o'clock or sooner if we need to talk to any of you. Mr. Cramwell, call me if you get any more messages or calls from your daughter. Remember, they said you have until tomorrow to send the money. Don't take any actions unless I know about them. So long for now."

Ellen completed another routine of exercise and a run on her imaginary track. This, along with the privacy of a meager bathroom, even with its ice cold water, improved her outlook. She ate everything they provided, and for warmth pressed against large tepid radiators or paced the room wrapped in the blanket. Her only contact with her captors occurred when they passed food through a small opening at the bottom of the door.

The chain jangled as Ellen walked to the window. With her cheek against the icy glass she peered at a view that she might enjoy under other circumstances, a cloudy afternoon, snowcapped evergreens, and a few falling flakes. She dialed 911, sent the call, and waited. After a minute without response she cleared the number and tried again. A disturbing red glow appeared next to the word, Battery. *Now it's up to them.*

She walked to the bed and sat, wrapped in the blanket. She leaned back against the rusted metal rods, hid the phone and tucked her knees to her chin. *Maybe it's up to me.* Placing her hands on the metal ring around her ankle she felt the chain. Then she removed her sneaker and sock and tried to slide the ring over her foot, but without success. After a few tugs at the strong chain she turned to the head of the bed, to the chain, wrapped around the tubular metal frame and secured by a laminated metal lock. She leaned back again. It looked futile.

At Mayfair, Ellen learned the academic basics of educating young children as well as the special teaching methods for which the school was known. Willing to experiment, she brought the sophistication of new art forms to her young students in first, second, and third grades. She arranged trips for them to the Philadelphia Art Museum and Academy of Art, to Chadd's Ford, where the Wyeth's art legacy resided, and to the Barnes Foundation. Classroom parents volunteered to assist her with these trips, and when she ended each year with a highlight trip for the older children to the New York Metropolitan Museum of Art, the parents clamored to be part of it. She charged forward, consumed by her love of art and for children, blossoming under the Mayfair flag, impressing Dr. Suskind with her creative ideas, and emerging as a solid elementary school teacher.

As the years at Mayfair passed Ellen further explored her own art. Peggy Charles, the teacher who helped her with her Mayfair interview, became a close friend. She and Peggy sailed the Chesapeake during the summer and visited Ellen's parents in Connecticut during the holidays and for a few weeks each summer. A few other acquaintances resulted through Annie's theater group. She accepted a number of introductions by Mayfair teachers to brothers, cousins and friends, but none of these bore the fruit of a significant relationship.

Ellen explored Philadelphia and became familiar with the city and its surroundings. She observed the progress in Annie's career, which included several lead parts in Arbor Theater productions, and a number of TV commercials. Ellen also traveled with her to New York with Annie on a number of occasions. Annie landed a role in an afternoon Soap Opera taped in New York, and located a small apartment there to share with actor friends. Ellen programmed her VCR to tape Annie's premiere Soap Opera appearance, then took a personal day from school and took a train to New York to watch the taping. She presented a beaming Annie with a bouquet of roses afterwards. Back in Philadelphia, Ellen taped the full series of Annie's appearances.

When the premier episode ran, Ellen and Annie sat on a sofa eating popcorn as it started. Ellen spoke, "This show's gonna be swell!" a line from an old Mickey Rooney and Judy Garland movie.

Annie giggled the tune "There's no business like show business!" as the videotape started.

A sequence of beautiful people wandered into and out of scenes during which at least seven convoluted plots evolved. Ellen and Annie dipped into the popcorn making comments as the story unfolded.

Annie: "This one's a real floozy."

Ellen: "Really, or just in the story?"

Annie: "Both."

Ellen: "Where do you find guys who look like that?"

Annie: "On soap operas."

Ellen: "Isn't this where you, or should I say, Tiffany, comes in?"

Annie: "After the commercial."

Ellen: "Aren't there any normal people?"

Annie: "No; we're all beautiful. Oh, oh. Here it is; my entrance!"

Annie (Tiffany) wearing fashion designed clothes facing someone named Brent wearing a tuxedo. He tries to convince her that infidelity is the way to go.

Annie: "You rat! But you're so tempting!"

Ellen: "Does he have a brother?"

They continued in this manner through the hour, and for several evenings to follow as the plots evolved until Annie's role diminished and she disappeared from the story.

On the last day of school before the Christmas break at Mayfair, Ellen stood at bulletin board removing the holiday art from the walls of her classroom and packing it away for next year. After five years she accumulated a colorful portfolio of artwork and associated memories. Ellen's haul of gifts, another of the standard benefits of the holiday season, sat on her desk. Teachers scurried in the halls with excitement of the season, peeked into her classroom, and stopped at her desk to wish her a Merry Christmas and a great vacation.

Two hours later, with her car filled with unopened school gifts and other Christmas purchases, Ellen headed north on Interstate 95 to spend the holidays in Connecticut. A fall of several inches of snow in the Northeast heightened her anticipation of a White Christmas.

That evening, the Cramwell family dinner started the traditions of the holiday season. As the family sat among festive surroundings in the dining room, Ellen began to unwind from the hectic pace of the school's holiday activities and the excitement of the children. From across the table, Dave asked, "Any new developments at Mayfair?"

"Not really. It's a comfortable place, like college; Dr. Suskind recruits a new round of young, straight A graduates every year who are her new freshmen."

"What does that make you, a senior?"

"I guess it would put me in graduate school."

"Has it been that long?"

Ellen spoke in a cautious tone, "Yes it has...I might be looking for another position, Dad."

Jane, perked up at this announcement and chimed in, "Now, Ellen, don't make any quick moves. Mayfair seems like such a nice place."

131

Ellen turned to her mother, "It's nice, but I'm hitting my limit there. I've learned a lot about teaching art and I can handle a classroom, but I can get a better salary in public school systems in the Philadelphia suburbs. I had dinner with one of the teachers who left last year. I was amazed at her salary and at the benefits. I'm not getting any retirement accrual. She suggested I start looking around."

Dave asked, "Would you consider looking around here?"

Recognizing her father's attempt to seize an opportunity Ellen replied, "I like the East Coast; sure, why not?"

"I think I can help you out. I have some contacts with the school board."

Ellen knew he would not waste time.

Dave called Ellen a few weeks after the Christmas holidays. "I've got an interview set up for you."

"Really? Where? When?"

"Down near Saybrook; it's close to our summer house. You can arrange it at your convenience, anytime before April. That's when they start to hold open interviews."

Ellen felt discomfort. "You mean I'm getting special treatment?"

"It's like a special sale, before they open it to the public. You won't be the only one they're talking with in advance; then they post the position openly if it hasn't been filled."

"What's the job?"

"You can call and find out about it for yourself first, then schedule the interview if you're still interested."

"Sounds fair enough. I'll do it. Thanks, Dad."

She made the call and scheduled a trip to Connecticut at the end of February.

Ellen arrived the day before and spent the night with her parents. She woke early, had breakfast with Jane, then left for her interview at Ethan Allen Elementary School, called Ethan A or Allen. The interview differed in many ways from her session at Mayfair, but much the same, Ellen found herself with an offer when it ended. She accepted on the spot.

Ellen opened the door to find Jane in the sunroom, reading the *Hartford Courant*. Jane looked up. Ellen sat next to her with head down, while Jane leaned forward, as if looking for a clue. Ellen turned slowly toward her mother, maintaining a grim demeanor, staring into Jane's apprehensive eyes. Then she burst out "I got it!"

Jane replied, "You! Devil!" and drew her daughter into her arms.

That evening the Cramwells ordered Chinese food, one of the traditional Friday night choices. After a buffet style dinner, Ellen sat in the living room with Dave and Jane while Maria served coffee.

Dave opened this discussion with another surprise. "Now that you have a job here, you'll need someplace to live."

Caught off guard, Ellen stopped at mid sip and returned her cup to the table. She didn't reply. *Here it comes, an offer to live at the summerhouse.*

Dave continued, "I have a deal for you, Ellen."

Ellen began preparing her defense, but his follow through surprised her again. "There's an old house for sale on Sunrise Lane near the summer house; do you remember where that is?"

"Sure. I remember."

"My bid was just accepted and I'll be closing on the house in about four weeks; it needs a lot of work, but it would be perfect for you. You can live there, and there's still enough space to create three other apartments that could produce income. I'll put down ten per cent and give you the place. You make the mortgage payments, run the rental business, and take the income. If you get two renters the mortgage and expenses will be covered, and if you get three you'll make money, or you can pre-pay the mortgage with the profits.

Taken back by his offer she said, "Dad, would you do that?"

"Why not? Think of it as an early inheritance; and, you'll be running a business."

"You're a devious one," she said with a smile. "But I'd like to take a look at it first. Okay?"

"Okay!"

Jane watched the exchange with a smile. "You'll love it, Ellen! It's the old Bradford House; remember?"

"Sure; large, white with green trim, two or is it three floors? A great old house."

Jane took the lead in moving this deal to closure. "It's spacious and old New England. Let's go take a look!"

They drove from Hartford to the Connecticut shore along Long Island Sound in an hour. Then Ellen spent two hours exploring the historic building, climbing stairs, looking out windows, opening closets, and experiencing the thrill of discovery amid the wonders of an old, vacant mansion. Then she went outside and walked around the property, three acres of woods with a lawn area. Ellen spotted an old outhouse that sat behind the mansion amidst a flower garden. Rather large, about ten feet square, its architecture matched the house, clapboard walls and gingerbread trim around the roof.

Ellen pointed at building and walked toward it along a loose stone path. "Can we look inside?"

"Why not?" Dave replied.

While Dave removed the padlock and swung open an old, wooden door, Jane stood at a distance along the path, seeming to dread what would appear. Ellen peeked into the dark building, then stepped inside. It had been converted into a work shed, resting on a concrete slab floor. A few rusted tools lay on a bench and some dusty work clothes hung on wall hooks; a bicycle with a flat tire stood in a corner next to a small utility cart. Ellen walked to the square window and peered out through yellowed, lace curtains. She scanned the walls and said, "I'll have to figure out what to do with this."

"Does that mean you're in?" Dave asked.

"I'm in the Cramwell business, I guess, one way or another."

A beaming smile crossed Dave's face. When Ellen came out, Jane moved closer to peer into the building. Jane laughed, "I hope it wasn't the outhouse that sealed the deal!"

In Dr. Suskind's office two weeks later, Ellen faced her first resignation, ever. With heart pounding, she tried to picture the reaction to her announcement. They sat in the comfortable area of the office Denise used for conversing.

Ellen's mentor started, "Good morning, Ellen!"

"Good morning."

"What can I do for you?"

With throat, dry from the tension, Ellen struggled for the words. Then she said, "Dr. Suskind, I have appreciated the opportunity to work for you and with your staff. I've learned so much, and I find this hard to do, but I've decided to accept a teaching position in Connecticut."

Without hesitation, Denise smiled and replied, "Ellen, you've done well here. I understand, and I expected that some day you'd make this decision. I'll bet your parents are pleased. How far away will you be?"

"About an hour's drive."

"That's just about right, don't you think?" she replied, through an understanding smile.

Ellen caught the meaning. "Yes, I think you're right."

"Tell me about the new job."

Ellen had seen Denise Suskind in action; she knew how to suppress her reaction to a surprise. Ellen admired her way of looking ahead through adversity, without demonstrating disappointment. Now, her immediate questions, friendly and with sincere interest, turned an unpleasant experience into a comfortable chat.

Ellen gave an overview of a position at Ethan Allen Elementary School. She would lead the special adaptive art program for grades one through four, with an opportunity to move into a regular classroom as a second grade teacher within two years. She finished her description with, "It was a great offer."

"It sounds wonderful. We'll have to find someone else, of course, and we'd like you to be a part of that. I have a few candidates in mind I'd like you to meet." As expected, Denise took the hit and shrugged it off, almost as if she anticipated Ellen's decision.

"Thank you, Dr. Suskind; I like idea of having a role in helping you select a replacement."

Denise smiled. "Ellen, replacement is the wrong word; you do that with a tire. Teachers are individuals, too, like their students. You can't be replaced, but we can fill the position with a successor, one who will have to impart her individuality on the position, just as you have."

She had now transformed Ellen's dread into exhilaration. With a feeling of absolute relief, Ellen replied, "Dr. Suskind, I appreciate that," "When will you be moving?"

"At the end of June when my lease is up; my Dad will be coming down to help me move."

With a smile covering Denise's lips and a twinkle in her eye, she said, "Make sure he stops by to see me."

Ellen smiled and nodded, request, "I will." *I wonder what that's about.*

Ellen's Mayfair friends gave several goodbye parties during the last two weeks of June. Annie, not one to miss a party, came to two of them. As the last of these wound down Peggy raised her wineglass to signal the others. "Here's to Ellen: a teacher, an artist, a friend..." after a short pause, with a wink at Ellen she said, "a heck of a sailor and a lady!"

A chorus followed, "To Ellen!"

With glassy eyes, Ellen said, "Peggy, my Mom and Dad would appreciate that ending. Thanks."

As the day of her departure neared, Ellen began packing for the move. Annie helped Ellen fill numerous boxes and bags with the accumulated objects of five years at Mayfair. Standing amid this chaos Ellen spoke, "You know, this is a lot of work! I have lots of stuff! Like George Carlin says, I'm moving to a bigger place where I can take all my stuff, and have room for more stuff!"

Annie giggled, "Yeah! It's all about stuff!"

Ellen sat down amid her, stuff, and replied while laughing, "I am tired! No cooking tonight; how about pizza?"

"Depends; what kind of stuff are we putting on it?"

"The usual stuff!" They doubled up with laughter.

After a short time Ellen spoke, "Annie, I'll miss you. We've had so much fun!"

"Yes, we really have."

Ellen looked at her friend through moist eyes. "I'm going to cry."

"You do and I'll go into my, *Hard Knock Life*, routine again."

"No, not that!"

"And so will I miss you; we have to be thankful for the time we had, more than eight years now; but we'll see each other. Don't worry!"

The doorbell interrupted their reminiscing. "It's my Dad." Ellen pressed the buzzer to open the door.

The familiar voice sounded from the small speaker, "Hi, I'm here!"

"Hi, Dad! Come on up!"

After coffee and a discussion on the day's plan, they packed Ellen's belongings onto a rental truck and drove to Mayfair. The sun peeked through a white puffy cloud as Ellen drove into the parking lot, followed by Dave at the wheel of the truck. When Ellen stopped and opened the door, she spotted Denise Suskind crossing the parking lot with her long, determined, strides.

"Bit of a comedown from the Jaguar, Dave," she said, pointing to the old truck.

"Business is tough," Dave responded.

Denise replied with a smile, "That's not what I read in the *Wall Street Journal!*"

He laughed and returned a grin as he lifted an orange dolly from the back of the truck.

Annie started on the path to the building. "Come on Ellen, let's do it!"

Dave pulled down the truck cargo gate and locked it, then started pushing the dolly to follow; he stopped when Denise touched his arm. In a soft voice she said, "Dave, let's take a walk. The girls can handle the packing."

Ellen looked first at Denise, then at Dave, who seemed surprised by the request. Ellen shrugged, took the dolly from her father, and rolled it away, following Annie along the path.

"Ellen!" her father called. "Here!" She turned and caught the keys he tossed. "We'll take a walk. Let me know if you need help."

It took only half an hour for Ellen and Annie to fill the space reserved for Ellen's school things at the rear of the truck. After Annie slammed and latched the truck gate, Ellen snapped the lock into position and looked off into the distance; she spotted them strolling along a tree-lined walkway, a scene, somewhat disturbing.

Annie echoed Ellen's thought. "I wonder what that's all about."

Ellen concealed her feeling, "Oh, they knew each other in college; probably a trip down memory lane."

Ellen began waving at the strolling pair, pretending not to notice Annie roll her eyes. After catching their attention, Ellen watched Dave and Denise start across the lawn toward the truck. When they arrived, Ellen announced, "Well, we're finished."

"Time to go, Denise," Dave said. "It was nice talking to you." Dave and Denise exchanged a friendly embrace and then Dave climbed into the truck. Annie scampered into Ellen's car.

Ellen walked over to Dr. Suskind and shook hands, and then finished off with a hug. "Do well," Denise said.

Ellen replied, "Thanks for everything. It was a great experience. I'll never forget you, and the opportunity to work here." Then she finished with a comment about the young teacher who would replace her. "I think Sarah will be a great addition to your staff."

"I'm glad you feel that way, Ellen. It's nice that you agree with our choice."

Nostalgia seized Ellen at her departure from this friendly place, one that helped her grow and mature. She recalled that day when her car first turned into the Mayfair driveway. *What happened to the time? I'll miss this place.*

She followed the truck down the drive, and into her new life, with Annie, at her side Annie engaging in small talk. They stayed away from the obvious subject. *Maybe it was more than just one kiss. Or maybe he had more of a role in my getting that job than I realize.*

Jane picked up the ringing phone. "Hello. Yes, Mr. Lawson, any news. Oh, I'll put the speaker on so we can all hear. Mr. Dulles," she paused, "Jim, he wants to talk with you." She pressed the speaker button.

Dulles leaned toward the phone, to Lawson's voice. "Dulles, I want to arrange a discussion with you and the FBI about this money transfer thing."

Jim replied, "I've spoken to one of our financial types, and I think he should be involved.

"Okay, can you have them available, say four o'clock? We have a specialist from the FBI, but they're in favor of having some outside opinions on this."

"I'll call him again. He's doing some homework for me; I have the CEO of ECD aware of what's happening, so we should be able to get all the help we need. And a good friend of mine, Aaron Moskowitz, specializes in financial transactions over wide area network communications. I think his opinion would be useful."

"If you think so, fine."

"How do you want to make the call?"

"Take this down." Lawson provided a phone number and password for a teleconference.

"Okay we'll call in at four o'clock." Jim cradled the receiver.

Ellen dozed, waking to the sound of footsteps outside the door. Through bleary eyes, she stared at the small portal, about a foot square, like a dog exit, sliding open at the bottom of the door. A small bag passed through the opening and the door closed. Dragging the chain, she shuffled to the door and reached down to open the bag. *Coke and a Big Mac; gourmet dining.*

After finishing her meal she tossed the paper and cup into a wastebasket. Then she extended the length of the chain from the bed frame to the window, and back again to the bed, where it ended at her ankle, so that its full length lay on the floor. Starting at her ankle she examined the first link, then the second; continuing in this manner with each one, she kept a mental note of the count. On her journey to the final link, numbered 253, she made a special note of those numbered 14, 83 and 127, the candidates for her plan.

Ellen sat on the bed, placed her hand on the head frame, and began tugging at the first thin metal bar and then the second. After trying them all she selected the fifth bar, which seemed to move a little more than the others. Placing her feet against the head frame she grasped the bar and tugged at it. After five minutes of pulling at the bar and wiggling it from side to side, she measured progress as minimal. She stopped her efforts, exhausted.

Ellen rested for a short time and then resumed the work and rest cycles several times. Finally, as the bar loosened she whispered an excited "Yes!" With mounting enthusiasm, she kicked at the bar and it flexed. When she kicked again her foot slid off and struck the wall behind the bed with a loud thud. *Damn!* She sat waiting for a sound from below. When it came, she jumped from the bed she started to run in place. Rapid footsteps pounded on the stairs and the door swung open. A hooded figure appeared, ominous, standing in the doorway. Ellen continued to run in place for a few steps, conscious of her observer. Then she stopped and began to jump, pounding her foot on the floor with enthusiasm. The hooded figure watched for a few seconds and shook his head, turned, and closed the door. After several minutes she slowed down the strenuous activity and began pacing the room. Then she sat on the bed and exhaled a long sigh. *Too close!*

Jim keyed in the conference code number. A voice message requested the call code. He entered it and two beeps from the speakerphone signaled connection to the call. He nodded to Jane and Dave and said, "We're in."

"Anybody there?" he asked.

"This is Agent Matt Bremmer. We also have Larry Walczak of FBI Information Technology and Detective Lawson on the line."

Two more beeps sounded over the speaker. "Who just joined?" Bremmer asked.

"This is Ray Pierson from ECD, and I have Tom Jenkins and Gina Palazzo with me."

Another pair of beeps and another voice, familiar to Jim, sounded in, "Aaron Moskowitz here."

"This is Bremmer. I'd like to set an agenda. We'll start with introductions and then a briefing of the situation by Detective Lawson. After that we'll have Larry give us his view of things. Then we'd like comments and maybe ideas from the rest of the folks. Lawson, you're up."

Detective Lawson provided background on the situation and then on the status of the search. "We've covered about forty percent of the cell area; we expect to be finished by Tuesday afternoon. We can't do very much at night without arousing a lot of suspicion if we happen to get near the location where they're holding Miss Cramwell. We may be lucky and find the house in the next two hours, before it gets too dark, or we may still be looking at noon tomorrow. We'll call the Cramwell's as soon as we've found it."

Jane spoke, "What will you do then?"

Agent Bremmer responded, "Mrs. Cramwell? We'd like to discuss that a little later. We want to focus on the electronic transfer alternatives here. Could you bear with us for a while?"

"Yes, but Ellen's safety is the most important thing."

"We all agree with that Mrs. Cramwell. Please let us continue. We need to use our time in the best way."

Shaking his head at Jane, Dave mouthed, "Not now."

Jane said, "Okay, go ahead."

Bremmer continued, "Larry, you're next."

"We've been in touch with Banque Suisse Federated through Interpol. Since a felony is in progress they have certain liberties with their accounts. They can monitor the transactions and advise us when it has been received from the Cramwell's bank. They can monitor withdrawals, and identify where and when they were made. It's likely that the withdrawals will also be electronic, and could be triggered almost immediately to several other banks. Since we don't know which banks, we can't deal with the deposits from that end. We could stop withdrawals, but that would tip our hand. It's not likely that they'll release Miss Cramwell until they have the money in hand."

"Anything more?" Bremmer asked.

"No, that's about it."

"Who's the spokesman, or spokesperson for ECD?"

"That would be Tom Jenkins," Jim said. "Tom?"

"Thanks, Jim. I'm from Electronic Business and Gina is from Financial Industries. We have different perspectives but agree, in general, with what we've heard. Gina?"

Gina spoke, "Hi. I've got a couple of thoughts on this. First, are we still in touch with the captors by e-mail?"

"This is Dave Cramwell. No, they've stopped sending."

"Have you stopped sending?"

"We sent the one message back, acknowledging Ellen's e-mail. They haven't answered it by e-mail, but they have sent a message by FedEx, a warning to comply with their demands."

"Do we know how they would verify the deposit?"

Jim spoke, "Not directly, but they might be able to access their statement and obtain the balance through the Internet."

"But we don't know for sure?" Gina asked.

"Anybody?" Jim asked.

Lawson replied, "I guess they could always phone Banque Suisse."

Gina continued, "How about this? We could send a message with each withdrawal by electronic transfer, advising the receiving bank that the funds are part of a felonious extortion, and to notify Banque Suisse when they have been received. We'd need to talk with the technical people at Banque Suisse about it, but it would be a simple program."

Aaron identified a potential flaw. "If there are only a few of them, it wouldn't be too bad, but suppose they send the money to thirty or forty different banks? Also, the secondary banks may receive requests themselves; kind of a cascade."

Gina had an answer. "It wouldn't make the messaging process any more difficult, only the manual follow up. If they use fifty banks and there are only a few people involved in the kidnapping, it will take them time to round up all the cash, and I assume that the time would be useful to the FBI. The take for each of them has to be large enough to make this added complexity worthwhile. My guess is that there are a few of them and they will use only a few secondary banks for deposit. They want to have cash in hand as quickly as possible and head their separate ways."

Bremmer reacted, "That's not a bad assumption, Ms. Palazzo."

Aaron chimed in, "Gina. Just to clarify, if we knew the kidnappers were checking the balances through the Internet we could give them access to a fictitious balance statement at the Banque Suisse. We could do that, too, in principle, with all the secondary banks, but we might not have enough time to alert them and install the software; they're not likely to have the same in-house software so we'd have to deal with them individually."

"You're right, Aaron."

Lawson spoke, "Could we wait until we find out how many secondary banks there are before we act?"

Gina again, "Yes, and there's one more thing. We have overnight to deal with the secondary banks. The deposit will be made by close of business on Tuesday, which is about 10 or 11 PM in Switzerland. The transaction won't be credited until Wednesday, and it won't appear on the statement until Thursday morning. I'm not sure the kidnappers thought all of that through. They may just have someone try to withdraw the money directly from the Banque Suisse."

"Sounds to me like we've covered a lot of contingencies here," Bremmer said. "Why don't you technical folks continue to talk about this and then give us a briefing on what you recommend. How about two hours from now?"

A round of, Okays followed.

Bremmer closed the discussion, "We'll reconvene, same number and code, at 6:30 Eastern. Thanks, everyone."

After Dave disconnected Jane shook her head and said, "What does all that mean, Jim?"

Jim answered, "It's not going to be easy. If we knew they would only check the balance at Banque Suisse from Ellen's computer, we could lead them to believe there was a transaction when there wasn't one. If we knew the names of the secondary banks, we could probably do the same with them. There are too many unknowns right now. Maybe they'll think of something better over the next few hours."

Dave said, "I spoke with Walt Baran after lunch. There will be five million dollars in our account this afternoon, and it can be withdrawn tomorrow either as cash or electronically. Unless I get a warm feeling that the computer people know what they're doing, I'm going to follow the instructions and turn over the money."

Ellen's dinner consisted of a cheese sandwich, potato chips, and a bottle of sweet orange soda. Afterward she walked to the bed, raised the head frame and pushed the bed from the wall in small increments, taking precautions to minimize the sound. Satisfied with the separation she lay down on the bed and continued her negotiations with the head frame. After an hour of short kicks at the bar, followed by periods of waiting to listen for reaction downstairs, the thin bar loosened enough for the next step. She got off the bed and sat with her back against the wall behind the head frame. She placed her feet on the frame and then drew her knees to her chin for a final attempt. With a quiet grunt both feet struck the weakened bar at the same time driving it out of the frame. It fell with a soft plop, onto the bed.

Ellen sighed, "Finally!"

She sat for a few seconds, listening for sounds. Hearing none she rose from the floor and reached for the dislodged bar. She lay down on the bed, perspiring from her efforts. *Never thought of this as a way to get a good workout.* Raising the bar above her head, she examined the tool, smiling. She closed her eyes.

Ellen sat up, startled. *How long has it been?* Her shirt gave the answer. She shuddered from its dampness. *Don't blow it now!* Moonlight streamed through the window creating shadows. Voices, faint, came from downstairs. Nothing seemed unusual.

Ellen sat up and placed one end of the bar into the opening at the bottom of the frame, and then wedged the other end along the top of the frame until it clinked into place. When she tried to remove the bar again, it came out with ease. She repeated the process a few times, now confident she could access the tool with ease.

She rose from the bed and walked to the bathroom with her chain jangling on the floor like the *Ghost of Christmas Past*, bringing a slight smile to her lips. Without electricity moonlight would have to suffice. She stripped off her sweat-laden shirt and sports bra and the left leg of her skin-tight running pants. She pulled down the right leg of her pants and slid it down through the anklet shackle and over her foot. Then she pulled it back up and out through the shackle, freeing the left leg of the pants. Next, she used this same little trick to remove her panties.

Ellen reached into the shower, turned the hot water handle, and placed her hand in the icy stream, allowing the water to run. After a few minutes she tested it again, feeling a slight temperatures increase, Then she took a deep breath, closed her eyes and stepped into the dark, freezing chamber. With clenched teeth, she pressed her hands to the tile walls, suppressing an instinct to scream. The water ran down her back and legs to the cold floor. She stood for a few seconds until, accustomed to the chilly water, she slid her hand along the wall beneath the showerhead until her fingers felt the small bar of soap.

After washing, she wrapped herself in the damp towel, refreshed and tingling from the experience. Then she picked up her clothes and placed them on the radiator, and spreading her arms, she hugged the lukewarm mass of metal to draw its meager warmth into her body. A while later she tiptoed to the window and looked out at the moonlit night. *That's good.* Then, she looked downward at a light, fresh layer of snow. *This could be a problem.*

Returning to the bed, she dragged the mattress to the floor, then into the bathroom, until it touched the radiator. She removed the towel and wrapped the blanket around her trembling body. Then she squeezed herself into a fetal position and squirmed to create friction. Soon the shivering subsided. She needed sleep for tomorrow, a big day.

Bremmer convened the second teleconference. "Well, here we are again. Hi, everyone. Lawson, why don't your describe the situation."

"We've covered about sixty per cent of the cell; no luck yet. We've stopped for the night, but we're planning our activities for tomorrow morning. We have about ten hours of daylight to work with."

"Larry, what's the electronic situation."

"We have two recommendations. We've contacted Banque Suisse Federated and we have Mr. Jacques Heilmann joining our call."

With a German accent Heilmann spoke, "Hello. I vill help in any vay I can."

Larry continued, "Banque Suisse will alert us that the transaction has occurred. It will not be recorded until the next business day; that's normal protocol, so it shouldn't raise suspicion. Attempts made all day Wednesday to transfer will receive a standard message indicating the deposit has been received and that transfers from the account can be made on Thursday."

"What about withdrawals?" Jim asked.

"Attempts to withdraw in person will meet with the same rules. Agents will be stationed at Banque Suisse to follow anyone who makes such an attempt. It's not likely they'll try a withdrawal in this way. We'll prepare a message to follow all electronic transfers from the numbered account to other bank accounts. Banque Suisse will have five phones standing by to respond to inquiries at the phone number provided in the message. The FBI and Interpol will be available at Banque

Suisse to speak with callers from the secondary banks to verify the criminal nature of the transactions."

Aaron asked, "What if they try third level transactions, from the secondary banks other banks?"

"Those will be held for another day, giving us the weekend, but once the time has elapsed, we're back to the same situation. A transaction could be delayed or stopped, but the kidnappers would get suspicious."

Dave spoke up, his voice emphatic. "You mean that even if I send the money, I can't control what happens once it gets to Banque Suisse? If I send it, I want it paid and we want our daughter back. I don't want the FBI or anyone else to hold up the delivery and jeopardize my daughter!"

Bremmer replied, "Once you've sent the money to Banque Suisse, it's out of your control. We have to do what makes sense after that."

"What makes sense to you may not to me. If I don't have control, I shouldn't send the money. Maybe I can exchange it directly in a bag or something. I don't like the odds. It's like throwing it up in the air and hoping the wind will blow in the right direction."

"Not quite as bad as that," Bremmer said.

"Would any of you send the money if you were in my position?"

A long pause followed. Nobody spoke.

Aaron broke the silence. "It sounds like you have some things to set up. The question is who makes the decision? Do the Cramwells control the flow of money or do the banks? What leverage do they have to ensure that the money will flow and that it will go where they intend to send it?"

Bremmer replied, "I'm afraid the answer is, none. Once they make the first transfer it's in the hands of the FBI and the banks."

Ellen's blinked her eyes in the darkness. She stretched beneath the wool blanket, feeling its scratchy surface on her bare skin. Coming out of a deep sleep, the excitement of the plan filled her with pleasant anticipation. Wrapped in the blanket, she pressed against the radiator. She reached up and ran her fingers across her clothes; she felt a trace of warm dampness.

Dropping the blanket to the floor, she sat next to the radiator to absorb its meager warmth while reversing the puzzle of dressing. The running outfit, although light in weight, provided comforting warmth. Now dressed, she tied her shoes, rose, and dragged the mattress back to the bed. Then she removed the tool to start the next phase of her plan.

At the window, she reached down and counted links, each little more than one inch long, until she found the fourteenth. She lifted the chain to the moonlight and found the flaw, the reason for its selection. She inserted the bar into the link and tried to pry it apart, like using a crowbar, but found difficulty in obtaining leverage. After several attempts without a sign of progress she stopped. *That would have been too easy*. The next link on her list, 83, would give her a longer and heavier burden to carry. She found the same difficulties; the chain was too strong. On the third link, exerting maximum effort, the bar slipped away and clanged against the radiator, piercing the silence of the building.

"Oh, no!" she whispered to herself. She sat for a few seconds and heard stirring from below. *Damn!*

Ellen lifted the bar and length of chain and tiptoed to the bed. She replaced it in the head frame and threw the blanket on the bed as footsteps pounded on the stairs. Again on her toes she carried her metal tether into the bathroom. Just as she lay down on the floor next to the radiator, the door opened and she heard someone entering the bedroom. They footsteps stopped, and then continued.

A circle of light appeared on the bathroom threshold. She traced the beam back to a shadowy presence. Ellen lay on the floor, moaning, and held her knee in her hand. The chain lay

149

against the radiator. Ellen looked up at the hooded figure. "I tripped on the way to the bathroom," she said.

The figure reached down and shined the light on her ankle, then tested the chain connection. He lifted the chain and passed it through his hands, tracing it back to the bed frame. Ellen crawled a few feet and peeked around the doorway at the figure. He yanked at the chain and the bed jumped. Ellen closed her eyes. He yanked once more, but the chain remained secure. Returning to the bathroom he shined the light on Ellen; she moaned softly, squeezing and rubbing her knee. The figure moved the beam onto the shower, toilet, and basin. After shaking his head, he grunted, and turned away toward the door. Then he stopped and walked back toward Ellen, and extended his hand. Ellen froze, not knowing what to expect. He motioned again and then reached down, took her by the shoulders, and raised her from the floor. She continued to nurse her knee. He pointed toward the bed and reached to lift her.

She shook her head and pulled away. "I haven't gone to the bathroom yet," she said.

The figure shrugged, turned, and left the room. The door lock clicked.

Ellen stopped her ad lib knee massage and took a few deep breaths. *Have to be more careful.* Then she smiled. *Acting!*

Jim woke with a start. How long had the music been playing? He rolled over and looked at the clock. *I should have been there already!*

After a shave and a quick shower he dressed. As he closed the door he heard a ring. He re-entered the room and picked up the phone.

"Jim Dulles," he said.

"This is Dave Cramwell. Are you coming over?"

"Sorry, I was just leaving. I'll be there in a few minutes."

"We're going to transfer the money today. I want to talk to you before we do."

"I should have been there. I know. Give me a few minutes."

When he arrived at the Cramwell residence two cars stood in the drive. Maria opened the door as Jim approached the entrance.

"Good morning, Mr. Dulles."

"Good morning, Maria."

"Would you like something to eat?"

"You read my mind. All I've had is coffee. Some toast, or a roll would be fine."

"How about some scrambled eggs?"

"That would be better."

Maria nodded and led him to the office where Dave and Jane sat with two other men. The accumulated strain of six days had taken its toll. Dress and grooming couldn't overcome the worrying and lack of sleep. He said, "Sorry, I got up a little later than I should have."

Dave stood and introduced the two men: Fred Gantler, from his bank, and the other, Allan Borski from the FBI.

Borski looked at Jim and spoke. "Mr. Cramwell wants to send the electronic cash transfer this afternoon. We understand you were involved in planning how we deal with the transfer. Mr. Cramwell would like to have you around in case there are any changes or developments. If we locate the house today there will be a need for some quick decisions."

Jim spoke to Dave and at Jane with concern. "I'll do what I can."

After Ellen finished her sandwich, she placed the dish near the door. She sat on the bed and thought about her failed effort. *Almost caught.* There was a better way. She removed the loose bar from the head frame and sat on the floor, between the bed and the wall. After placing the bar beside her on the floor she gripped the chain to keep it from jangling and kicked at another of the bars. She waited for a few seconds, then repeated the process several times until she felt the bar loosening. With both legs on the bar and her back to the wall she applied maximum pressure until a second bar came loose and fell onto the bed.

Ellen sat in silence, overcome by a feeling of exhilaration over her accomplishment. After a while, she rose from the floor and sat on the bed, holding one bar in each hand. Too exhausted from the exertion to continue with her plan, she inserted the bars back into the head frame.

At the Cramwell residence awaiting developments, Jim stepped outside to break the monotony. His breath condensed in the crisp, clear air as he walked along the paths, through the gardens behind the house. Even on a dreary February afternoon the property had character. He looked to the west at the sun giving off an orange glow between the clouds, low and approaching the horizon. Darkness would soon arrive.

He became aware of someone approaching. When he turned, Maria, called out, "Mr. Dulles!".

"What's happening?" Jim asked.

"The place has been located; the one where they're holding Ellen! Come inside!"

Following Maria's quick steps, Jim returned to the house. He approached Jane and reached for her hand. "Good news?" he asked.

She smiled and raised hers to his comforting squeeze. "Yes." He sensed her feeling of hope.

Dave and Borski sat next to the phone. Borski spoke, "So you're going in to get her tonight."

Bremmer's voice replied, "Yes, but it will take a few hours before we're ready to move in. We're stationed almost a half mile away, out of sight."

"Where are they?" Dave asked.

"A small cabin west of Lake George."

"Are you sure you have it right?" Dave continued.

"About 99%; but there's not much activity and we want to be sure, to get as much information as possible before storming the place. We need another hour of direct surveillance to be sure, and then we have to get a team in there without making too much commotion. We don't want them to run. They've done that once already, and it won't take much to get them nervous."

"Then we have to send the money," Dave said, looking at Jim.

Jim offered his opinion, "I think it's the right thing to do. It looks like the FBI has found the right place. They'll probably be in there before the cash is transferred out of Banque Suisse."

Bremmer responded, "We don't have them yet; and it might not be the right place."

Jim replied, "You must be close even if it's not the right place. I thought you said 99% and you were almost finished combing the whole cell. You don't want them to get nervous. If they check and the transfer has been made, they'll think that everything is moving according to plan, and take steps to get the cash. I assume that's what you want."

"Okay, you seem to have the right idea," Bremmer said. "Mr. Cramwell, it's about as late as you can wait to do this. Mr. Gantler, can you see to it that the transfer takes place?"

Gantler spoke, "I'll call our office right now. They're standing by after working hours tonight. It'll take five or ten minutes."

Ellen lay on the bed planning her next steps. She stiffened to the sounds on the stairs, then watched as a hand reached through the opening in the door. The remains of her evening meal disappeared. After a few minutes she rose again and removed the two loose bars. Then she threw the blanket over her shoulder, and with one bar in each hand, she walked to the window in short, quiet steps. She folded the blanket into a thick pad and counted down to the fourteenth link. She placed one of the bars through the link and wedged the bar along the floor, under the radiator and on top of the blanket. She passed the second bar through the link, creating an angle between the bar and the floor. Placing her foot on the extended bar she pressed down and felt the link's resistance. The bar wedged under the radiator and the second bar created a pair of levers, acting in opposite directions on the link, like opening scissors. She put more pressure on the link for several seconds, then stopped. Removing the bars, she held the link to the window. *Nothing. Well, let's try the next one.*

Ellen repeated the process again on link 83, this time firmly securing the first bar before starting with the second. After several attempts, she raised her foot, intending to apply her full weight standing on the bar. She hesitated. *No, too dangerous!* Instead, she sat on the bar and supported her weight by placing both hands on the floor. Reducing the pressure on her hands, her buttocks settled against the bar, causing a sudden movement downward ending in a quiet thud on the blanket. She waited, then slid her hand down the bar until she touched the link. Raising it to the moonlight, she saw the small gap in the link. A start; she wanted to scream with joy.

She reset the two levers again into the weakened link. This time, the experience of her first attempt made process easier. With less effort and without a sound, she spread the link further. After the fourth attempt, when the gap was large enough, she removed the link. With satisfaction at her accomplishment, she stood and gathered the severed section of chain in her hands and walked around the room in newfound freedom. After a few minutes, she replaced the bars in the headboard and reconnected the segments of chain with the broken link. She lay down on the bed to rest, covered the broken link with the blanket, and waited.

Ellen heard a noise from below, a series of shouts and loud laughter, the first she had heard since the start of her captivity.

Something's up! Some kind of news! What if they decide to move me again?

—8—

Although the house had a long history, to Ellen it signified a new life. Dave had enlisted the services of a few Cramwell Industries workers to help unload the moving truck in exchange for case of beer and pizza.

When they had finished unpacking, Annie visited with Jane Cramwell, whom she hadn't seen for some time, while Ellen went out on the porch to sit with Dave. They sat on the steps, side by side, gazing out onto the spacious property on a warm summer day. After a short time, Ellen decided to ask him, "Dad, what was that with Dr. Suskind?"

"I wondered when you would ask," he said. "What did you think it was?"

Embarrassed at her thoughts, Ellen stared out across the lawn, avoiding eye contact. "I don't know. Something between you two?"

"Yes, Ellen."

She froze, looking over her shoulder.

He continued. "She wants Cramwell Industries to help finance a part of her new science wing."

After a huge sigh she said, "Dad, you should write a suspense novel! Why all the secrecy?"

"Dr. Suskind," he was being formal, "is looking for ten companies to put up $500,000 each. She plans to make a big announcement in the fall and didn't want anyone to hear it but me. She claims to have five already, but they may not all be firm. I might be the first with real money."

"Did you agree?"

"I'll take it into consideration. She'll send some information describing the budget and purpose and if it makes sense to me, I'll put it before the board."

"She didn't say anything about this before, did she?"

"No, this was the first time I knew about it."

"It was nice of her to wait until I was no longer an employee."

"Denise Suskind knows how to keep things proper, but she's not afraid of being aggressive."

"I watched her during the five years at Mayfair. She has a sense of timing."

After a short pause in their conversation, Ellen asked, "Did you talk about anything else? You two looked pretty friendly out there."

"Yes, we did. We talked about you, and recalled old times, long ago."

"She's actually a very nice person. What did she say about me?"

"That she expected you to impress her, and that she wasn't disappointed."

"What about the old times."

He turned to Ellen, smiling, "An Englishman..."

Ellen laughed. "I guess you're entitled to your secrets. Maybe someday you'll tell me about it.

"Maybe. Someday."

Over the following weeks Ellen said nothing about her new information to Annie. Ellen struggled to keep the secret through the summer. Two days before the public announcement appeared in the newspapers, she called Annie with the news.

"Wow, $500,000! The Arbor Theater could use that kind of money!" exclaimed Annie. Then, with an impish smile she continued, "I thought maybe they were fooling around."

"Annie, life is just one big soap opera to you!" Ellen replied, but she said nothing about that part of the talk with her father.

Throughout the summer, Ellen spent her days with the contractors as they converted the Bradford House into a four-apartment complex. She exerted her influence on the design for the renovation, spending many evenings reviewing ideas and changes that occurred as the workers uncovered the mysteries of the old structure. Disliking the cold feeling of walkups and high-rises with long dark corridors, where people entered and exited but never knew each other, she wanted her renters to feel good about living in her building. The Bradford House would be different. The design called for one apartment on the ground floor, along with a small office. It included a community sitting room off the ground floor that any of the guests could use, with a large-screen television, a small refrigerator, card tables, soft chairs, and a bookshelf. Ellen's apartment and two others were fashioned out of the second floor, including storage space on the third floor for each of the apartments.

The building stood in a residential community near a middle school. She planned to convert the large outhouse, now work shed, into a coffee and ice cream stand. It would be a stopping place for students after school. The architect flinched at her thought, then pointed out the need to face zoning issues. She ignored his challenges until after a while, working together, they developed an attractive design for the small building and presented it at the next town meeting. The Outback Coffeehouse caused quite a buzz. She stated her intent to maintain the Victorian style, and to add a landscaped pathway to the tree-lined street. The design had a charming appeal. She pointed to the absence of any other such gathering place for students, and that it would also be a convenience for commuters from the nearby train station. The motion passed. The following morning Ellen's phone began to ring as kids from the high school began applying for jobs. She had no difficulty in hiring a both students and retirees to work at the Outback.

Ellen lived in the Cramwell's summerhouse until she moved into her new apartment at Bradford House in mid-October. The remaining apartments on the second floor were ready for occupancy in November, and the one on the ground floor was completed by the end of the year.

Ellen advertised Bradford House in local newspapers, at school, and at Cramwell Industries. A teacher from Ethan and her husband rented one of the apartments; an industrial product salesman learned of the apartment through Cramwell Industries and rented another. By the end of the year the combined income from rent and the Outback were enough to cover Ellen's expenses and mortgage payments. The third rental, to a young newlywed couple, made Ellen's business very profitable. When Ellen announced, with pride, her cash flow position, her father smiled with approval at her use of this financial term. Dave didn't pry into Ellen's business activities, leaving her to make all the decisions.

After three years the salesman departed and a year later, so did the young couple. Ellen filled their vacancies without difficulty, and felt fortunate to have upstanding replacements. After the fifth year, Ellen's luck changed. The local business climate experienced a downturn and the teacher friend from Ethan retired and moved away. For several months, mortgage payments for Ellen's vacant building began depleting prior profits, but she kept her plight from her father.

One evening in January, Ellen sat reading in front of the fireplace when the doorbell rang. When she opened the door, two men, one tall and thin, the other shorter and heavier stood in the doorway. "Are you here about the apartments?" It was as much a hope as a question.

"Yeah; can we take a look?" the thinner man said.

Ellen examined the pair with some uneasiness, but after an awkward silence she said, "Follow me." She showed them the ground floor apartment and the community room and then took them up the stairs. "Look around. They're very nice. Are you looking for one or two apartments."

"Two," the thinner man said. "Yeah. We'll go upstairs and look around."

She wondered about these two, different from her past renters, but visions of an improved financial picture overcame her concerns. She led them upstairs, opened the door to each apartment, and then stood in the hall as the two men walked from the first apartment to the second, exchanging quiet comments. After a short while they emerged from the second apartment.

The thin man spoke, "We'll take the two upstairs."

Ellen took a deep, silent breath. "When do you want to move in?" she asked.

The thin man announced, "Next week."

"That'll be fine," she said, trying not to demonstrate the joy of an improving financial picture.

In the first-floor office Ellen opened a file cabinet and removed two lease agreements, handing one of them to each man. "Look these over and let me know when you're ready to sign," she said.

"We'll be back tomorrow," said the thin man. They left.

Al Bartles, the spokesman and Tim Downs, returned the following evening to sign the agreements and paid the escrow and first month's rent. Ellen used the Cramwell Industries financial organization to run credit checks and found nothing unusual. They moved in one day while Ellen was at school.

One evening a few months later, Ellen stepped from the shower and wrapped herself in a towel. Taking a casual glimpse out the window into the twilight she noticed a small red dot. Leaning closer, she recognized the glow of a burning cigarette and a puff of smoke rising above the face of a man standing in the shadows of a tree. *Is someone looking up at the window?* Ellen twisted the plastic rod to close the blinds. She turned out the light and moved one of the slats, enough to see outside. He was gone.

One afternoon short time later Ellen arrived home after a day of teaching and opened the front door of Bradford house to find her renters in the community room. Several beer cans sat on the table and the television set blared. Through the smoke, the screen presented four hulks bouncing around a ring while the referee struggled to control the chaos.

"Please clean up when you're finished," she said. "And please smoke outside."

They grunted in response.

The next morning Ellen descended the stairs for her morning run she confronted the stale smell of beer and cigarettes, and a mess of cans, cigarette butts, ashes, and crumpled bags, from consumed pretzels and potato chips. Cleaning the mess forced her to shorten her run that morning. Ellen arrived few minutes late for school that day, cursing these inconsiderate slobs, and remembering her misgivings about them on the day they arrived.

Loud music and other noises from their apartments, beer cans and cigarette butts on the driveway all served to increase Ellen's anxiety about her new tenants. She thought about talking to her father about the problem, but decided against it. She'd take care of it herself. When her parents came to visit she'd spend hours cleaning up and often placed messages in the mailboxes of her troublesome tenants to advise them of her visitors. This seemed to work, and they curtailed their behavior on those days. And Ellen's improved financial situation was enough to keep her from making more of the situation.

The night watch at the Cramwell's included Dave, Jane, Jim, Maria, Jane's sister, Sandra, and the FBI agent, Borski. Dave reached for the ringing phone and switched on the speaker.

"Hello."

Bremmer's familiar voice sounded through the room. "There has been an inquiry to Banque Suisse about the funds transfer."

"What information did they request?' Jim asked.

"There was an electronic inquiry into the status of the numbered account at around 7:30. The call came from an airport pay phone in New York. It was a query on the account transactions. Here's the reply to the query."

As the audience huddled around the phone Bremmer read in a slow, clear voice:

"EFT DEPOSIT NOTIFICIATION FOR ACCOUNT, and then the account number

A DEPOSIT ON 02/23/99 FOR $5,000,000.00 HAS
BEEN RECEIVED TO YOUR ACCOUNT.
ALTHOUGH RELEASED BY HARTFORD FIRST
BANK THE FUNDS MAY NOT BE POSTED UNTIL
THE NEXT DAY. THE FUNDS WILL NOT BE
AVAILABLE FOR WITHDRAWAL UNTIL
OPENING OF BUSINESS ON 02/25/99. YOU CAN
IDENTIFY THE TRANSACTION AS 910420572.

That's it."

Dave replied, "That means we have until Wednesday night before the money could be sent by EFT to other banks."

"That's right."

"Maybe we should wait until we've heard from them before you send your men in. They may free Ellen now that the money has been sent."

"I wouldn't count on it, but it would be better if she wasn't under their control when we take them."

"Can't we at least wait? If you have them under surveillance they can't go anywhere."

"We'll make our decision around midnight. It's taking a little longer than we expected to get everyone in position for the assault."

"What's the weather like up there."

"There's a fair amount of snow on the ground."

"I guess we'll just wait to hear from you."

The conversation ended.

Ellen strained to understand the words of the muffled voices. There was something up. They sounded excited. When would they go to sleep?

She removed the phone and dialed 911. A ring and then a crackling sound broke up the response into incoherent segments.

She spoke in soft tones. "This is Ellen Cramwell. I'm going to break out tonight," Crackling, but no reply.

"Did you hear me?" again in a whisper.

The red light cast a glow in the room, Battery low. She heard more static noise sounds but incomprehensible voice sounds.

"Guess not," she said in a whisper. Ellen replaced the phone and then stretched out full on the bed. She created a mental schedule of the next steps of her plan, listened for sounds, and tried quell her anxiety. After almost half an hour of silence she decided to make her move.

Ellen coiled the segment of chain still attached to the bed in a circle near the headboard, covering it with the pillow. She lifted two legs of the bed and placed them on the blanket, then lifted the other two legs and slid the bed in short segments until she headboard stood alongside the window. She grasped the segment of chain attached to her ankle, ran it along her leg, and then wrapped it into a band around her waist several times. Then she crammed the loose end into the chain band and took a few soft steps around the room, stopping at the window. *I'll be carrying almost ten pounds of excess weight.*

Then, she removed the loosened bars from the headboard and carried them to the door. Kneeling, she rested the end of one bar on the floor and placed the other end at an angle against the door. She pressed her foot on the bar until one end made a notch in the floor and the other dug into the door, then repeated the process with the second bar. She tried to wiggle the struts. Satisfied with the structure, she stood and returned to the window. *Maybe it'll give me half a minute.*

She returned to the window and removed the blanked from under the legs of the bed, and placed it on the bed. She unwound the chain and also placed it next to the blanket. Then she took the pillow and held it against the glass pane and began striking the pillow with the heel of her gloved hand in short strokes, first light taps and then with increasing intensity, near the edge of the window. After several tries she heard the clink and felt cold air pour through a small triangular hole. Success!

With gloved right hand, she gripped the broken pane, thumb inside and fingers outside. She closed her eyes, broke off another piece, and placed it on the floor. Continuing for almost half an hour she removed enough glass to create a jagged hole, the full width of the window. Then she removed glass from the lower edge until only a few short pieces remained, too short to grasp, leaving a rough, sharp surface. She placed her head and shoulders through the opening and looked up at the moonlit sky, then down at the dark windowpane below. A few small pieces of broken glass lay in the snow, next to the building. As her heartbeat quickened she struggled to control the anxiety that drove her to move faster. *Stay with the plan.*

Ellen pulled her shoulders back in from the opening, folded the blanket several times, and then lined the bottom and sides of the hole with the blanket's thickness. She lifted the coiled chain segment attached to the bed and placed it on the cushioning blanket. *Ready!* She began lowering the chain down the side of the cabin, one link at a time. The chain began swinging in a slow pendulum motion and made a soft clink against the window below. She stopped, allowing the motion to dissipate, then continued until the chain, still attached to the headboard, hung free. When she heard a sound from downstairs she decided make caution a second priority. *Time to go!*

Ellen placed one leg through the window and straddled the opening, perched on the blanket and grasping the chain. As she lowered her head and moved it through the opening she felt a sting on her forehead "Damn it!" she cursed in a whisper. Looking back at the jagged glass she blinked as wetness blurred her eye. "Too fast!" Then she heard more noises on the stairs.

With her head out in the cold air, she removed one hand from the chain and pulled at the blanket, caught in the ragged edge of broken windowpane. Freeing the blanket, she rolled it under her arm and slid her second leg out the window, and with the aid of the chain she repelled down the wall. She heard more noises and the clicking of the bedroom door lock, then the sound of anxious voices. As her head pressed against the dark window of the first floor, she wiggled her feet searching for the ground. The window before her filled with light and a face peered out through the glass. Ellen gaped, into the eyes of Kevin Reardon! Confusion raised thoughts about times past. She gathered her wits. *Not now, time to get out of here!* She released the chain; the gawking face rose as she dropped the final five feet. She struck the ground and rolled over on her side in a pile, with the blanket and chain; her face sunk into the soft powdery snow. She raised her head, staring down at the red stain. Rising to her knees she touched her forehead, a reflex. She lowered her stained glove from the source of the blood.

The Cramwells prepared for an all night session, anticipating their daughter's planned rescue at 2 AM. Jane lay on the sofa with eyes closed while Sandra sat nearby. Jim paced the hall peeking into Dave's office from time to time. Dave and Borski were out on the porch to getting some air. The clock showed 12:18. The phone rang as Maria entered with a fresh pot of coffee. Jim picked up. "Just a minute," he said, turning toward Dave and Borski as they entered the room. Jane sat up, exchanging glances with Sandra.

"Something happened. It's too early," Jim said. He pressed the speaker button.

"This is Detective Lawson. I have some news. There's some kind of commotion at the cabin. Lights went on, shouting, men running outside. We're not sure what happened. We're moving in closer to find out before taking action."

"Did anyone see Ellen?" Jane asked.

"No. We had to stay out of sight. They come and go through the front door. Our position is several hundred yards away, facing a corner at the rear of the cabin; whatever happened was on the other side and at the front."

"What do you think it could be?" Dave asked.

"The assault team has moved closer to investigate. It could be some sort of conflict between the captors. Now that they know about the transfer of funds, maybe they're arguing about the money; or it could be a fire, or anything. But that's only speculation."

"Should we stay on the line?"

"No. We'll be in touch as soon as we know more. But we wanted you to know about this because it'll probably affect our plans for 2 o'clock. We'll call again when we have something definite."

"Thanks Mr. Lawson." Dave broke the connection.

Ellen's mind raced as she rose, wiping her bloodstained glove against the front of her windbreaker. *Kevin Reardon! How could he?* She hadn't thought about him for years. He had his faults, but a kidnapper? *Can't think about this now!* She threw the blanket over her shoulder. From her observations through the bedroom window she deduced that the road from the cabin headed north. She raced across the snow, along side the house, past the porch and out onto the road. About a hundred yards away from the cabin she glanced over her shoulder; a door opened onto the porch, which was illuminated by light.

Running in the open air gave her confidence. The moon provided enough visibility to deal with the unfamiliar road. She picked up the pace, sensing her advantage. *They won't catch me, even with this added weight.* Shouts and screams broadcast the confusion of her captors. Now, about two hundred yards away, Ellen looked over her shoulder again, at a beam of car headlights reflecting from the snow. An engine cranked.

On the road she'd lose her edge. Black silhouettes of trees loomed on both sides, contrasting the snow. *Which way?* The terrain and trees indicated mountains, possibly the Berkshires of Massachusetts. *East.* Turning right she left the road and sunk into the deep, fluffy snow. After breaking through a few pine branches the darkness of the quiet forest made her stop. She remembered an uncle proclaiming the advantages of a snowfall during hunting season. Looking down she realized why.

After only a few minutes, Dave answered the expected call. Lawson spoke, "It looks like Ellen has escaped. We don't know how, but after the cabin lit up a car drove off. Then it stopped a short distance away from the cabin and the driver and another guy went off into the woods. One of the agents heard someone shout, 'find her!' That's when they moved in on the cabin and captured one of them. We're not sure how many more were in there."

Jane reacted, "Oh, God! What will happen now?"

"Where are you?" Jim asked.

"Do you have a road map of New York State?" Lawson asked.

With a questioning look, Jim leaned toward Dave.

"Just a minute," Dave said. He rose and crossed the room to a file cabinet and opened a drawer. "I'm glad I save these when I travel."

"He's looking," Jim said.

Dave returned to the desk and spread out the map. Lawson described the location. "It's west of Lake George, near Thurman. It's barely a dot on the map of New York."

"Got it," Dave said.

Lawson continued, "Good. The state police are here; they have detailed maps of the local area. We'll find her."

Ellen scanned dark patches of sky that appeared through the trees, searching the sky for the moon and stars. She wanted to continue east, in a straight line, away from the road. A trail of telltale footprints revealed her path. *This won't do.* She continued forward in the deep snow.

Shouts from the road and a slamming car door penetrated the quiet. "Here's where she went in! We need a flashlight! I'll go back and get one!" An engine revved and the car drove away. Now, separated by only a few hundred feet, she expected the distance could close.

Ellen trudged through the snow dodging bushes, low handing limbs and the snow-laden pine tree branches. She had to keep moving, but she also had to find a way to hide her trail. She passed beneath the branch of a large tree that looked like a maple standing against a number of large pines. After about a hundred feet she stopped when she heard the rushing sound of a running stream. A short distance ahead, the trees disappeared into a black abyss of darkness below and starlit sky above. She stooped near the edge of a gorge, listening to the sound below, louder than the faint sounds of her pursuers. *I have some time.* Crawling and holding onto the trees lining the gorge, she dented the snow with her feet and arms and slid down its slope. Then she grasped a small bush, stopped her slide, and climbed back to the top. She rose with care and placed her feet back into her prints, walking backward toward the maple tree.

The thick limb loomed over her head, about eight feet off the ground. She unwound the coil of chain from her waist, then draped the blanket over both shoulders and tucked the loose ends under her armpits. She looked upward at the limb. Swinging the chain in a circular arc, she allowed it to gain momentum and then released it upward and over the limb. She covered her head as the chain dropped down on the other side of the branch; its free end stopped a few feet from the ground. Ellen grasped both ends of the hanging chain and pulled herself up. She threw her blanket over the branch and sat down, feet dangling. She gathered the chain into folds and over her shoulder. Looking up she found the moon and the North Star. She touched her head, wincing at the feel of a rough crust. *What next? Too low; have to keep going.*

Ellen moved along the branch toward the trunk of the tree, then climbed around the trunk and up to another branch on the other side, extending toward more pines and away from her tracks. When the branch began to sag, she stopped. *Far enough!* Unwinding the chain from her waist she wrapped it over another limb, higher. She moved further out on the sagging branch while tugging the chain above to support her weight, reducing the load on the limb below. She stared at branches of nearby pine tree, covered with snow, as she moved forward.

When Ellen felt she had gone far enough she pulled down on the free end of the chain until the other end began to pull at her ankle. She clenched the loose end, allowing it to hang below her hand. With both hands she grasped both chain segments until they held all of her weight, unloading the limb below. Hanging from the higher branch, her arms strained as she allowed the links of the chain to slide over the branch above. In a slow, controlled ascent, like an elevator, the free end of the chain moved downward while she and the end attached to her ankle moved upward.

When Ellen neared the higher branch above, she clasped her hands around it and climbed up to a sitting position on the branch. Then she coiled the chain, stood, and began to move outward again, while grasping another of the tree's branches. She continued her movement, away from the trunk, until she could almost touch one of the adjacent pine trees. Standing on the thick maple branch, she heard the faint sounds of voices growing louder. *Close enough.*

Now, well onto the far side of the maple tree, she reversed the process, using the chain in the same manner to descend from the high limb. When the last links of the loose end reached her left hand on the downward path, her knee touched the branch of one of the pine trees. *Here goes!* She released the chain and began to fall. With closed eyes and spreading out like a skydiver she crashed into the branches of the pine tree. As the branches slapped at her face and chest, resisting her fall, she grasped at them until she could hold on, stopping the descent.

Ellen opened her eyes and looked back up at the limb above. After regaining her bearing she looked down where the chain hung from her ankle to the snow on the forest floor below. Ellen shinnied around to the opposite side of the pine, further away from the maple tree. Satisfied with her position, she released her grip on the snowy pine branches and slid through and over them, downward, striking the ground with knees bent, and for the second time, tumbling to rest in a snowy heap.

Ellen sat for a few seconds moving her arms and legs, searching for unusual pains. *Still in one piece.* The tree-scaling episode had deposited her behind a row of pine trees more than thirty feet from where she had first climbed the maple tree. In the dark, she hoped it would be far enough. As she planned her next move, the distant sounds of thrashing, shouting and cursing penetrated the quiet forest.

Bremmer called again confirming Ellen's escape. "When the FBI and State Police advanced on the cabin they found the room where they held her. There was a piece of chain connected to a bed and a broken window. She must have climbed down. They're holding one of the captors, Tim Downs."

Jane exclaimed, "He rented one of her apartments!"

"That's right!" Bremmer said.

"Where is Ellen?" she asked.

"We haven't found her yet. At least two of the kidnappers chased her into the forest. We're following them, but it's heavily wooded and dark. We've asked for helicopter support."

"We're coming up there!" Dave's voice raised to a level that surprised Jim.

"I wouldn't advise that," Bremmer replied.

"We're coming! My car has a cell phone, and it's about a six-hour drive. We'll stay in touch from the road." Dave wasn't asking.

"Okay, if you insist. I think you'll be able to find an inn near Lake George. When you do, after you check in, call me." Bremmer recited his cell phone number.

Ellen sat beneath the pine tree testing her muscles and rubbing her arms for warmth. She stood and uncoiled the chain from her waist, then draping the blanket around her shoulders she wrapped the chain around it as a belt for her makeshift cape. After a short time she rose and looked up at the sky. To the east, the ravine presented a barrier to escape and west would take her back to the road, and possibly into her pursuers. After encountering the ravine, they would head north or south. Heading south could lead her directly into them, and across her own path of entry into the woods. Her only choice, north, the direction in which she had started, would preserve any separation distance she had gained.

Darkness and the merciless cold now presented another challenge. The snowbound woods seemed endless as she climbed over stumps, branches, and drifts. Although she maintained strength and tone in her muscles, they began to feel the effects of her irregular movements. Aching, she longed for an opportunity to break out of the woods and run. *If I could find a road maybe a car might pass by, or it might lead to a house.*

She no longer heard the sounds of pursuit, but a different, faint noise broke the silence. She stopped to listen. It grew louder, like the thumping of an engine or an airplane, no, a helicopter! She imagined the dread of recapture. *They're coming after me in a helicopter!*

Taking cover under a large bush she began to scan the forest canopy, but the aircraft remained out of view. After a while the thumping stopped, returning the wintry forest to its earlier serenity.

As Ellen continued her journey, the blackness turned to gray as the thick woods before revealed an opening. She moved forward, approaching the edge of a clearing. A barbwire fence stood between her and an expanse of snow. On one knee, she crouched near a large evergreen. She placed her hand on a fence post and scanned the open area ahead. Less than a quarter mile away sat a house.

In her elation Ellen climbed between the fence wires and out of the forest cover. In knee-deep snow, she started to run toward the house. After only a few paces she stopped. The thumping sound returned and began growing louder. Then, realizing the mistake, she retraced her steps back to the fence. A light from above illuminated the glade. She climbed over the fence and scampered back into the forest. Squatting under a large pine, she peered through the branches at a circle of light darting in random movements across the snow. The helicopter hovered over the opening, then began moving closer to the house.

Ellen broke a branch from the tree. On hands and knees, she crawled out into her fresh tracks in the open snow. Then moving the branch in arcs over the snow surface, like an eraser, she smoothed the snow while retreating into the woods. The beam of light, swinging from the house and along the fence line, approached her position. Back in her hiding place Ellen watched the moving light trace the perimeter of the forest opening. The aircraft hovered again for a short period and then thumped away.

Ellen sat for several minutes, listening. When the quiet had returned, she rose and began to move toward the house. This time she worked her way around opening, on the forest side of the fence, until she approached the rear of the dark, silent building. A small garage stood between Ellen and the house. A snow-covered driveway and path to the porch lay before her. Dead tired, she welcomed the thought of shelter.

The moon had dropped below the tree line. She stepped into the shadow of the house and into an eerie darkness. Nearing the back of the building she crept forward with arms outreached, her eyes focused on the window ahead. She raised her arms, reached forward, and leaned her face toward the window. One more step met with emptiness as the ground disappeared. She and felt the sensation of falling, then a sharp pain in her head, and blackness.

Jim sat next to Dave, who gripped the wheel as his white Jaguar as it raced north along Interstate 91 toward Springfield. Jane rested with her head on a pillow in the back seat.

Examining the map, Jim said, "We should be there around noon."

"That's about right," replied Dave. "We've spent time in the Adirondacks, but not recently. Lake George is about five hours in good weather."

"Roads look clear. I think I heard Bremmer or Lawson say they had some snow."

"Maybe we'll find some in New York. Why don't you get some sleep? I'm turning the driving over to you in a couple of hours."

"Sounds good. We've all been up a long time. Just let me know when you've had enough." Jim leaned the seat back and closed his eyes.

Dave's voice rang out, "Okay, your turn." The car door slammed.

Jim woke with a start at the sounds. He raised his head to observe Dave negotiating the octane selection. The smell of coffee completed his transition to confused awareness. He muttered, "I just put my head down. What time is it? Where are we?"

Jane answered, "About twenty to nine. You've been out for over two hours. We're just south of Albany on the New York Thruway."

Jim blinked and turned to the back seat, toward the aroma.

"Here, this should wake you." Jane offered a steaming cup.

"Where did that come from?"

"Maria packed a basket of sandwiches and two thermoses of coffee. We didn't want to stop and waste time."

Jim accepted the cup. The warmness felt good in his hand. He took a sip. "Wow, that's strong coffee," he said.

"Maria is from Colombia. She knows how coffee should taste."

An icy gust of air rushed into the car. Standing by the opened door Dave leaned down to look into Jim's eyes, "You're on."

Ellen peered through a long tunnel surrounded by whiteness. She raised one foot, feeling the resistance of oppressive weight and restraint to her step. Befuddled by the difficulty of the simple task and by the unfamiliar surroundings, tears streamed from her eyes. Jane and Dave appeared in the distance, but oblivious to her presence. She called out but her voice made no sound. She heard a crackling noise and then the words "Where are you calling from? Can you please speak up?" She screamed in frustration.

Ellen woke shivering. *What happened?* Her head throbbed and her toes ached with numbing pain. Cuddled up in a ball with hands tucked in her pockets, she opened her eyes. To her left, a thick wire screen spaced in one-inch squares covered a large window. Her back pressed against a curving brick wall laced with vines in a semicircular pit surrounding the window. She glanced upward at another window above, the same size, the one she remembered approaching, and then to a gray sky. Her eyes blinked at invading snowflakes.

Ellen tried to stand but her body felt like concrete. She struggled to wiggle her fingers, to unclench fists, frozen closed. With painful effort she forced them open. Huddled in the icy pit, she strained to recall the sequence of events: running, a helicopter, walking toward the house, her last memory. Then it fell into place, a basement window surrounded by a window well, hidden by the snow and the dark.

Her head pounded, and she had newfound pain in her right wrist. *I must have bounced off that screen.* She reached up to a sore cheek. *And scraped my face.* She heard no sounds of life, only the howling of a cold winter wind.

The thick gage screen, designed for security, blocked the direct route. Mustering all of her strength, Ellen rose to her knees. The movement caused a massive throb in her skull. She discovered new aches in her ribs and in her back. After a pause she raised her hands and gripped a vine, pulled herself to a standing position, and leaned forward. Her chin rested on the top of the curved, brick window well. Under normal circumstances, climbing out would be easy; now the wall seemed insurmountable. *How do I get into the house? I have to climb out of this pit or freeze.*

With Jim at the wheel the white sedan sped north. The car phone speaker emitted a chirp. Dave pressed the send button. "Hello."

A voice responded from the speaker, "Bremmer."

"This is Dave Cramwell. Any news?"

"We caught another one of them. Claims his name is Frank Meade, heavy set and dark hair, about five-nine. Does he sound familiar?"

Jane leaned forward from the back seat and replied, "No; he's not one of the Ellen's tenants. I don't think we know him. Any news about Ellen?"

"We've found her footprints in the snow about twenty minutes ago. We've tracked her to a ravine and it looks like she may have fallen down in the dark. We've started searching."

"Oh, no!" Jane reacted, reaching over the seat and grasping Dave's hand. "She could be hurt! Or..." Jane's words trailed off.

"Now let's not assume anything," Bremmer said. We haven't been looking for very long. She may be with the one we haven't caught yet. We know there's at least one more loose somewhere in the woods near the cabin."

"That could be Bartles," Jane said "the other tenant."

"Where are you?" Bremmer asked.

"We've just gotten off Interstate 87. We're about 20 minutes from the Mohawk Inn," replied Dave. "That's where we'll stay."

"Call me when you get there. That's all we have for now. Our operation is set up about an hour from Lake George. You'd best get some sleep. I'll call you there when we have something to report."

"Okay. We'll call you after we've checked in," Dave said.

"Have you gotten anything from the one you caught?" Jim asked.

"He's in custody and they're questioning him and Downs."

"Any idea who is the mastermind behind this?"

"Probably Bartles, the one we haven't caught yet."

Standing in the small, brick-lined pit, Ellen flexed her shoulders and raised her knees. As feeling returned to her numb body, pain gripped her icy hands and feet. On tiptoes, she stretched her arms over the edge of the brick wall. She searched for something to grasp, to pull herself up over the well and out of this new prison, but without success. Weakened by exposure and with the added weight, she knew that a direct route wouldn't work.

Ellen unwound the chain from her waist and tossed the blanket and the loose end of the chain over the wall. The immediate weight reduction gave her hope. *I wish it were always that easy.* She pressed her back against the wire, window screen and her right foot against the curved wall. Grasping the screen with her fingers, she lifted her back up along the screen, then raised her left foot and pressed it against the wall, spanning the gap between the window and the wall. Then she moved feet and hands in sequence, rising upward a few inches each time. She smiled. *Spiderwoman*. After a few cycles she stopped to rest, then continued until her toes reached the top of the wall and her shoulders neared the top of the window screen. With body horizontal, suspended more than four feet above the floor, Ellen stopped again. *If I place my feet over the edge, I'll fall. How do I complete this silly plan?*

After a few seconds she lifted her chained right leg over the left leg and started to rotate her body, until she faced downward, hands grasping the screen and feet pressed against the arc of the wall. A few gnarled vines in the wall gave her feet added leverage. Next she raised one foot over the edge of the wall, and then the other. She pressed her hands against the screen, extended her arms, and pushed so that her legs, just below the knee, rested on the edge of the wall. Grasping the screen, she began moving sideways, to her right. The gap narrowed on its circular path to the window allowing her knees, thighs, and then her hips over the top of the brick wall. Then she released her grip on the screen and rolled her exhausted body to rest. Warmed by the exertion, she lay in the soft powdery snow, satisfied by her accomplishment, catching snowflakes on her tongue.

Jim entered the small room and dropped his shoulder bag on the floor. After three steps he collapsed on the bed. He started to doze but forced himself to stand and walk to the basin. He washed his face with cold water. The phone rang.

He listened to Dave's instruction, "Jim, I've called Bremmer. We're going to stay here for a while."

"I think that makes sense, at least until we've heard something."

"Jane and I are going to try to rest. Get something to eat and maybe some sleep. Just stay in your room; we'll call when we hear anything."

"Okay. I'll do that."

"Jim?"

"Yes."

"And thanks for being here."

The trace of a smile formed on Jim's lips. A few seconds ticked by as he searched for a response. "I'm glad to help," he said. I know how you and Jane must feel."

"We'll be in touch." The phone clicked.

Jim dialed "7".

After a few rings, a voice said, "Room Service."

"I'd like a pot of coffee and a sandwich. Turkey on rye, lettuce, mayonnaise."

"It'll be about fifteen minutes."

"Keep knocking if I don't answer."

Half an hour later Jim had finished his sandwich and sipped a cup of coffee. He felt the stubble on his face, stood and walked to the mirror. "Pretty grim," he said to himself.

He stripped and climbed into the shower, the universal refresher. Afterward, with a towel around his waist, he shaved and greeted his image with, "Better."

When he finished, he walked to the bed and pulled back the bedspread, revealing crisp white sheets. He sat on the bed and then slid under the covers. It felt like he had climbed into heaven. *What was it like right now for Ellen? She must be miserable.* His comfort began to feel uncomfortable. *She could be freezing.* Soon, sleep overtook his guilt.

Ellen climbed the stairs to the elevated porch. A white cottage with red shutters, it looked like a typical vacation house, occupied through the warmer months and vacated during winter.

It would be cold, but better than the outside. She couldn't face the thought of trying to walk farther. If there were houses nearby she'd look later; now, she needed rest and warmth.

Knowing what to expect, she approached the solid, red door and tried the knob. Then she took a few steps and pressed her nose to the glass of the large picture window. The furnishings seemed modern and comfortable. *I've already done breaking and exit. Here goes, my first attempt at breaking and entry.*

She unwound the chain and doubled over a segment three feet long and allowed it to dangle from her hand. Swinging the chain in a circle, she increased the rotation speed and then eased toward the window. Then she covered her face, closed her eyes, and slammed the chain into the glass. The window shattered and streaks spread outward from the gaping hole in the glass pane.

Ellen dropped the chain and began picking shards from around the hole to clear a segment along the bottom of the window frame. When she completed the job she gathered the chain into several loops, picked up her blanket, and crawled through the large opening into a dark room. As she stepped on the glass fragments she drew the blanket around her shoulders. It felt colder inside.

Ellen stood in a living room furnished in a casual, contemporary style. A few pictures hung on the walls, but shadows made their content unclear. She walked through to a small dining room to an oval table surrounded by six chairs, all dark wood. Next, she came to the kitchen. She lifted the receiver of a black wall phone, listened to silence, and replaced it. White cabinets hung on two walls, beneath one a sink, the other, a counter. Ellen approached the electric stove on the third wall and turned a switch; nothing happened. She returned it to the off position. She walked to the sink and turned the faucet handle; nothing again. *I wonder if anything works.*

She opened a white drawer filled with kitchen utensils and gadgets, another contained knives, forks, and spoons. A third finally produced something useful. Ellen struck a match and lit a candle. She removed a glove and placed her hand near the flame. After a few seconds, she warmed the other hand.

Ellen noticed a room behind the hanging kitchen cabinet. She bent down and looked through the opening. She walked around the cabinet and into a den. *A fireplace!* A stack of firewood sat in a brass log carrier next to a pile of newspaper. She knelt, leaned in and peered at a black ring at the top of the fireplace opening. She yanked the ring, felt the cold air, and looked upward at dim light.

She twisted a few pieces of paper and lit them. After a few minutes, flames wrapped around the kindling and it began to burn. Ellen placed one of the logs onto the grate. In a short time, she sat before a blazing fire, one that would make her father proud.

Ellen ventured up a flight of stairs to a hallway where she found a bathroom and three bedrooms. A variety of sheets, pillows, and blankets sat in a bedroom closet. Gathering the bedding materials in her arms she, she returned to the living room and dropped them onto the sofa. She covered her shattered entryway with her old blanket and moved the remaining bedding into the den, next to a fire, now at full strength. Upstairs, she explored the remaining rooms, and located some towels.

Next to the kitchen she found a pantry containing a few cans, half a box of cereal, and a box of crackers. She searched through the drawers to locate a warming pan, spoon, and a can opener. She opened a can of vegetable soup, poured it into a pan and placed it on the fire. She remembered camping when girls would turn up their noses at a similar meal. Today, the hot soup and some crackers, next to the crackling fire, would be a feast.

After finishing the soup she threw another log into the flames, wrapped herself in the bedding, and lay down her head on a pillow, next to the fire. Her eyes closed. *A little nap and I'll be ready to go looking for someone. The worst is over.*

Jim fumbled to find the ringing phone. After a few seconds he located the receiver and placed it on the pillow next to his head. Half-awake and in a raspy voice, he said "Hello."

"Jim, this is Dave. I just spoke with Bremmer."

Jim paused to process the message. Was it Dave or Bremmer?

"Jim?" The voice asked.

He connected. "Yes. Sorry, I was really out. Yes, Dave. I'm just re-joining the world. What's up?"

"We slept pretty well, too. Bremmer called and they're still looking for Ellen. They sent a team down the ravine and didn't find anything. They're still searching. It looks like she fell over the edge but climbed back up the hill. The snow is fresh but they can't find tracks leading away from that spot. They just seem to end right there. Doesn't make sense, but at least she's not down in the ravine. They know that, for sure."

"What about the other guy? Any luck with him?"

"They've found another set of tracks, different and separate from Ellen's. They're concentrating on Ellen right now. The going is slow; it's a thick forest according to Bremmer. But it'll be getting dark again soon, and we have another decision to make. Could we see you? We need to talk, and then call Bremmer back."

"Give me ten minutes, I just need to get dressed."

"See you around 3:45; in the coffee shop. We want to get out of the room for a while."

"3:45; okay."

Ellen tucked the blanket to her chin, the start of a slow awakening to the burnt carbon aroma of a spent fire. She opened her eyes and stared at the dark at the gray ashes and charred wood. A few embers displayed their dying red glow. She stretched her aching muscles. *How long have I slept?*

She reached for a log and placed it on the gray ashes, along with a few pieces of kindling, waiting for signs of re-ignition. A flicker and then a small flame brought a smile to her lips. When she rose and raised her arms to stretch and bent to touch her toes the ever-present chain jingled. She reheated the remaining soup and ate it with a few more crackers. Then, after a short warm up exercise she wound the chain around her waist and started for the front door. She clicked the dead bolt and stepped out on the porch into a wintry wind; the sun hung in a cloudy sky, its position said mid afternoon. *Can't go too far.* Down the stairs she crossed the snow toward the road stretching into the thick woods. She stopped, then extended her arm to measure the elevation of the sun. *When it's halfway to the horizon I'll turn back.*

When Ellen estimated she had gone a little more than a mile, the road ended at a tee she turned right, placing the sun and the wind at her back. In fresh snow, almost knee-deep, she trudged forward, glancing from time to time into the forest silence. Her only companion led the way, a familiar gray presence matching her movement across the white surface, growing longer as the sun dropped from the sky. Today's expedition, fruitless, had started too late. She decided to turn back.

When the house came into view, she anticipated a return to the warmth of another fire, something to eat, and a good night's sleep. With an early start in the morning, she'd make a serious effort to find a way home. Nearing the house she looked upward at the darkening sky, scratched by the trails of a jet airplane, almost invisible as it chased the sun, and the only sighting of her journey. *If there were only a way to contact them!* She looked back down, startled at the sight of footprints, merging with hers, and leading toward the house.

She crouched low in the snow. *Who?* Scanning the quiet landscape she saw something, a dark blot in the snow on the porch stairs, someone sitting, or lying down. She stared at the motionless figure for a few seconds, then rose and started an indirect approach toward the side of the house, watching for movement on the stairs. Her cautious approach brought her to the side of the house, and a porch railing, about twenty feet from the stairs. Prepared to turn and run, she called out, "Who's there?"

The shape stirred and a head raised from the stair. As it made a slow turn in her direction, she recognized the face. Prepared to turn and run, she stood and watched lips moving but without sound. An arm raised, beckoning her.

Ellen opened her windbreaker, grasped the chain and allowed a segment to hang loose from her hand. She took two steps in the direction of the figure; she heard a whisper, "Ellen?"

"Kevin?"

His reply, an almost inaudible, "Help me!"

She thought of the irony, rescuing another man in distress. She walked to the bottom of the stairs, watching with care, ready to react to Kevin as he lay on the stairs. He extended his arm in her direction. A frost-covered beard and mournful eyes signaled his frozen helplessness. He wore ice-crusted sneakers, a thin windbreaker, and a pair of dark slacks. He had no cap, and his hair was matted with snow. She draped the chain over her shoulder and approached.

When she knelt next to him, a dam of emotion burst as she screamed, "Help you? Help you! You bastard! You lousy piece of humanity! You and your pals grabbed me off the street and scared the hell out of me! You covered my eyes and tied me up; took me God knows where!" She beat the heels of her fists against his shoulders and back.

After a few gasping breaths, she continued, "You let me piss myself and gave me junk to eat! You chained me up like a damned criminal in a freezing room with cold water baths! I froze! I almost died out here last night! And you want my father to pay you five million dollars for this treatment! Help you! I should let you freeze out here!" She shook him by the shoulders. "You're pathetic!" Consumed by an emotional turbulence, she stood over him with tears in her eyes. "Damn you! What did I see in you? I gave myself to you! How could you...do this?"

He shook his head and replied, "I'm freezing!" Then he tucked his knees to his chin, a defeated hulk.

Ellen sighed, knowing what she had to do. A night in the cold had sapped his strength. She reached down and extended her hand. "Come on, get up." She helped him to his feet, "Go on, up the stairs." She pushed as he lifted one foot up to the first step, teetering for an instant, and then the other up to the next step. He seemed overcome by exhaustion, and no longer a threat. When he reached the porch she moved around in front of him, opened the door, and led him into the dark room. She placed an arm under his and helped him into the den. He stopped, squeezed one hand with the other, and rubbed his feet on the floor.

Pointing to the bedding on the floor she said, "Wrap yourself in this. I'll make a fire."

Jim sat across the table from Dave and Jane, a cup of coffee in his hand. While they exchanged a few words Jim puzzled over Dave's statement, "We want to talk with you". He waited for the explanation.

Dave started, "Jane and I have been wondering about your participation in all of this. You hardly know Ellen. It just seems strange."

Jim thought for a few seconds. A week ago he didn't know them or their daughter, and now he had been involved for six days helping them deal with these bizarre circumstances. *This is strange*. Then he began his explanation. "I know that you and Jane are close. I can tell you that Ellen and I hit it off." He nodded at Jane and continued. "I don't know how long it took for you to know you were meant for each other; and I'm not saying that's how it is with Ellen and me; but I think there's a chance that it could be. Her last words when I left, I can still hear her saying them, were, 'call if you ever get back here'. I remember the look in her eyes when she said them, and how they made me feel. I called her from home the next day. I didn't need any other reason for coming back here except to see her. I might even have come this weekend. I wanted to get to know her better. Now I'm here under circumstances that are more than strange. It's so frustrating...and what's happened to her? I..." His voice trailed off. He shook his head and ended his statement. "I guess that's it."

Jane's eyes fixed on Jim through his monologue. When he finished, she waited a few seconds and then said, "Ellen hasn't had many men in her life, at least not serious relationships. Oh, she dates, but hasn't found anyone yet that fits her...expectations. She came close to marriage once, but we're glad she didn't go through with it. That young man, what was his name...Kevin?"

"Reardon," Dave said.

"Yes, Kevin Reardon. They broke up, I guess it was more than ten years ago. She hasn't really been involved with anyone since then."

Jim replied, "I didn't know. We went out just that one time, and we didn't talk about personal things, mostly about likes and dislikes, jobs, and college; and running, that's how we met." Jim went on to describe the morning in the fog, his fall, and how he stayed an extra day just to have dinner with her. Jim felt good to see Jane smile when he described his actions on Yellow Day.

After listening to Jim's story, Dave looked directly into Jim's eyes, "You know, when you first called we were very suspicious. You were a voice on the phone, a matter of hours after her disappearance. The police suspected you and we thought you might be involved. I really didn't want you around here." He paused and continued. "Now we're both glad you came."

Then Jane spoke, "How about you, Jim. You must have had some involvement with women; and I would say you're older than Ellen."

Jim smiled at a mother's intuition, then recalled his reaction to Ellen, about the eighteen children. "Yes. Married, three children," he answered. They both stiffened his reply, and then

185

as he continued, "my wife died seven years ago, cancer," they sat back.

With a consoling look Jane said, "We're sorry to hear that. It must have been hard on the children."

"Yes, it was. Gail had a daughter before we were married. Long story, but the five of us were very happy, a wonderful family situation. After her death we struggled, but then we realized she'd want us to go on with our lives."

Jim opened his wallet and placed a set of photographs on the table. Jane smiled and nodded as her eyes moved from picture to picture. "What a lovely family," she said, glancing at Dave, who leaned over her shoulder to look at the pictures.

Dave said in a low voice, "We wanted Ellen to have brothers and sisters, but it never worked out."

Jane elaborated, "What he means is that after Ellen, I couldn't have more children."

"I'm sorry," Jim said.

With far away looks in their eyes, Dave and Jane seemed to retreat into their own thoughts. A silence followed while Jim sat, thinking. *The randomness of life has thrown us together to share a time of crisis. These are nice people. They don't deserve this. But you don't always get what you deserve. You have to deal with what you get.*

A waitress appeared next to the table, "More coffee?"

They each woke from their reveries and refused the offer.

"Let's call Bremmer," Dave said.

A few minutes later they sat in the Cramwell's room. Dave and Jane huddled at one extension and Jim held the other. Bremmer spoke, "Darkness is going to make things difficult, but we can't stop. Another night out in this cold would be hard to survive. I have to be realistic, Mr. and Mrs. Cramwell, if she hasn't found shelter by now her chances aren't good."

Jane responded, "Can't you do anything more?"

"We're doing all we can, Mrs. Cramwell. We found them and then they ran. We didn't expect that. If only she had stayed in the house."

"You can't blame her for what she did," Jim said. "She didn't know you were nearby, and you have to admire her escape. You said she broke a chain?"

"That's what it looks like," Bremmer replied.

Jane's face contorted with her response. "Can you imagine being chained? Like an animal? Anyone would want to get away from that."

"Well, I guess you're right. We were so close when she bolted. It was just a bad break."

Dave spoke, "What's your best guess as to what's happening?"

"She's either out there alone or she's been recaptured and..." his voice trailed off.

"And what?"

"Depends. They'd be upset with her for trying to escape. Now they're on the run and may not get the money. It's an unstable situation. They could act from anger and emotion." After a brief silence Bremmer continued, "Or, they could come to their senses and check on the money. From their inquiry, they have learned that the money has been transferred. They could release her. But I'd guess they wouldn't do that until they have the cash in hand. We aren't in control; that's what I mean by unstable."

Dave said, "So Ellen could be out there freezing alone or, or back in their captivity, or worse."

Bremmer didn't respond.

Dave continued, "Well, I think we understand the situation. Call us if there's anything more."

A candle rested on the fireplace mantel held upright in a small glass. The flickering of a comfortable fire bathed the room in warm, yellow glow. Ellen rationed logs to provide heat through the night. She wanted to be ready for a long walk tomorrow. She found more bedding to share with Kevin, and cooked two cans of soup and a can of peas. Kevin slept. She knew he needed that more than food.

Ellen finished a portion of the food and then placed the leftovers next to the warming fire. As she stepped back from the fireplace she tripped over the chain. She reached for her shackled ankle. *I have to find a way to take this thing off!*

Holding the candle at arm's length, Ellen walked to a door in the kitchen and turned the knob, exposing a set of stairs leading downward to blackness. The candle cast a flickering light on the narrow stairway. After a few steps down, the dark cellar evoked an aura of mystery; in a scary movie, this is when she closed her eyes. She stopped, torn between continuing and turning back. When her sight adjusted to the limited light, at the bottom of the stairway she saw a dark, gray floor, and continued down the stairs into a low basement.

She saw a few boxes and some chairs stacked in a corner, a water heater and stove. On the floor in one corner a small stack of firewood sat next to a large table. Above the table, hanging from the wall, a pegboard displayed screwdrivers, a hammer, wrenches, pliers, and other tools. She screamed with joy, "Just what I need!"

Among the tools Ellen found a chisel, and a vise attached to the table. She put the candle on the floor, raised her leg, and placed her heel on the table next to the vise, with knee bent. The third link gave her the right leverage, so she placed it on the vise and set the chisel. After a few bangs with the hammer a small notch formed in the link. She continued her efforts, examining progress between intervals of hammering, until the chisel drove through the chain. Then she clamped the severed link into the vise and hammered until the opening spread. When the excess chain rattled to the floor she smiled with satisfaction. The shackle and two links remained, dangling like an ankle bracelet.

She coiled the chain and threw it over her shoulder; then she picked up the candle. She started for the stairs but decided to explore the basement further. A window in the center of one wall turned out to be the trap, where she had spent the previous night. Next to the window she spotted a cabinet; when she opened the door the corked tops of five wine bottles pointed at her. She smiled again. *What a break!*

After examining the selection, she chose a California Merlot from the rack. She closed the cabinet and tucked the bottle under her arm, and headed back up the stairs. At the gadget drawer she rummaged around for a corkscrew, and also a small knife. She removed the cork and found two wineglasses, then poured one glass and took a small sip. *Not bad.* With her new find, Ellen entered the den. *Oh, for some cheese to go with those crackers!*

In silence, Dave and Jane picked at their meals, and Jim pushed his food around the plate. Dave broke the silence, "Let's call Bremmer again."

A few minutes later they assumed positions at phones in the Cramwell's room. Dave asked, "Any news?"

Bremmer's voice carried an unusual excitement. "We have something! We've found another set of tracks, easier to follow. They're not your daughter's."

"How can you know that?" Dave asked.

"They're large prints; a man's. And, luckily, the searchers haven't trampled them. They ended at a road by a set of tire tracks. We think he may have gotten away in the car."

Jane said, "Maybe Ellen is with him in the car. At least she'd be out of the cold."

"That's not likely, her prints weren't around, unless he picked her up further down the road. But then she'd still be captive and subject to his or to their whims. Considering how cold it is out there, you're right; it might be a better alternative to being lost in the woods. Exposure for this period of time is serious. Realistically, another night out there will be very hard on her."

Jane shook her head, burying her face in Dave's chest. He held her in his arms. "We'll find her," he said.

Jim replied, "So, what are you going to do now?"

"We're continuing to search. If we find new tracks we'll let you know. We're also flying the area with a helicopter. It's not much good in the forest, but along the roads we may locate her or find houses where she could have gone. Someone could have taken her in, but there are few houses in this area, and only a few inhabited during the winter."

"If someone did, wouldn't they have called the police by now?"

"Probably; but it could happen at any time," Bremmer said. "We have to consider every possibility."

Jim said, "What about the electronic funds transfer? The last guy, the one with the car; couldn't he get the money tomorrow?"

"That's right."

"Are you doing anything about that? He's the only one who might know something about Ellen. He might even be with her."

"We have an idea what the car looks like, but from the way it was parked we couldn't get a look at the license plate. Also, we have the cooperation of Banque Suisse, and the authorities associated with each of the secondary banks are ready to apprehend anyone who tries to withdraw the money."

"What will you do tomorrow, when you have some daylight?"

"We have dogs scheduled to arrive here later tonight, and they'll start from the cabin with Ellen's scent, about two or three in the morning."

"Aren't they supposed to be pretty good at finding people?" Jane asked.

"They're very good. We called them in late this morning. They weren't of any use until now. We'll give them the scent at the cabin and see where they take us."

"At least it's something," Dave said.

"Yes, something," Jane commented.

"Call us at any time at the inn if you hear anything," Dave said.

"Will do," Bremmer replied.

After they disconnected Dave spoke to Jim in a voice that sounded tired, "We may as well call it a night. I'll phone you if we hear anything."

"Okay; you both should try to get some sleep," Jim replied.

"I doubt if we'll sleep," he said.

"Yes, I know," Jim replied.

They exchanged goodnights, and Jim left.

—9—

The level on the Merlot bottle showed through the glass at the midpoint of the label. Ellen sat in the warmth of the den, sipping her wine, feeling a rosy glow. The sleeping figure in front of her stirred. She watched as his eyes opened and met hers.

"What time is it?" Kevin asked.

"My guess is, maybe ten."

"What's that smell? It smells good."

"Chicken soup; want some?"

"Yeah, I haven't eaten in a day."

"Poor baby!" She knew he caught her sarcasm. She pointed to the pot sitting near the fire. "There it is."

He rolled over and reached for the pot of soup with his right hand, keeping his left tucked in a pocket. Using the spoon in the pot he gulped the warm nourishment. Ellen dropped crackers wrapped in wax paper into his lap. After a minute he slowed down and said, "What's that you're drinking?"

"A nice Merlot. Goes well with canned chicken soup and crackers." She saw his pleading look. "Okay, here," she handing him a glass. Then as she poured, she said, "You don't deserve this."

He finished the soup and they sat in silence.

Ellen decided to confront him. "Okay, Reardon, what's your story? How did all this happen?" She noticed his surprised look.

Kevin took a sip of the wine, then he said, "Here's my story."

"It better be good," she replied. She leaned back against the sofa and closed her eyes.

Kevin began with the night she left, starting with his anger when she walked out the door. "I was surprised by your strength. You never behaved like that before. You were always submissive; tried to please; easy to control; no strong opinions. "Suddenly, you were different. I didn't like it. It was unsettling."

"You lost control over me on that day, and I grew up. But what you've done during the past two weeks has been repulsive, Kevin. What brought you to that?"

"I tried to call you a few times, but you didn't answer."

"No, I didn't. It was over. I couldn't invest anymore of myself in a hollow relationship."

"Well, after that I started drinking."

"Started? You were an experienced boozer all along. Don't try to hang that on me."

A sheepish look covered his face.

Ellen continued her scolding, "And look at you. You were a good-looking guy, and a pretty decent physical specimen. Now you've got a potbelly and a double chin."

"Okay, okay! Just stick to the rotten personality. Stay away from the physical stuff."

"Alright, go ahead. Who were those other characters? Your Klansmen in the hoods?"

"Al Bartles was the guy behind it. Tim Downs is an actor."

She leaned back and breath whistled through her lips. Then she said, "I knew those guys were no good! How did you get involved with them?"

"Let me tell it my way. I'm going to jail for this, at least let me tell you why."

She nodded, beckoning with her left hand to continue.

"Okay, so I ratcheted up my drinking, and even tried some drugs."

"God, Kevin! You really went to pot!"

They laughed at the double meaning, then he said, "Yeah, well; so I continued with the acting, and I didn't do very well; a few beer commercials; one for a Health Plan. I did some Summer Stock in New Hampshire and Vermont. Then I decided to try California."

"When was that?"

"Let's see; '91; no '92."

"I was in Philadelphia then. Living with Annie."

"Annie! I forgot about her. How's she doing?"

"Not bad; some Soaps; a few small parts in the movies. She's a regular with Tommy Conlan's Arbor Theater in Philadelphia."

"Conlan! He screwed me!"

"You screwed yourself, Kevin. Conlan was just better than you." Ellen felt good to speak her mind. When she and Kevin were an item she kept her feelings to herself, always found a way to be soft on him.

Kevin looked toward the crackling fire and said, "Well, let's not argue about it. I'm supposed to be telling my story here."

He was on, acting a role. He wanted to be the star, here in these bizarre circumstances. She shook her head and closed her eyes. "Go on. It's your line."

Kevin drained his glass and held it out to her. She refilled it.

"Okay, so I'm in California, it's the '90s. I have a shot at a big role in a Schwarzenegger movie.

"I'll be back," she mimicked. Then she stood. To his questioning look she said, "Really, I'll be back; I'm going downstairs for some firewood."

She returned in a few minutes with three logs under each arm. After placing one of them on the grate and the others in the brass holder, she said, "Okay, continue; the Schwarzenegger movie."

"Well, not a big role but a start. I was supposed to get the final word on a Friday, but I didn't hear anything. My agent called me on Monday and said it fell through. After that things got worse. I waited tables, parked cars, worked as a lifeguard, and scrambled from day to day. After a year I really got into drinking. I gained weight and started looking pretty shaggy. I had forty-five bucks in my pocket and decided to come back to the East Coast. Hitchhiked across the country sleeping in trucks, at rest stops and anywhere I could. It took me three weeks.

Then I hung around Boston for a while and that's where I met Tim Downs, an actor. Believe it or not, he was worse off than I was. We got some parts around New England, nothing big. We'd sit around at night drinking beer, envisioning the big break. After a few months Downs introduced me to Bartles, a guy that he knew in high school. Bartles was always doing some sort of deal. I never knew what he did, but he always had more than a few bucks in his pocket. We started trading memories one day and I told them about you. Bartles perked up when I mentioned your family money."

Ellen sat back, listening with her eyes closed. Although the wine had made her mellow, at this point in his narrative her senses awakened. "What did you say about it?"

"I described the first time I saw your house, and Cramwell Industries; and that we were close to getting married. He asked me, what happened." Kevin stopped and looked into the fire.

"And? What did you tell him?"

After a short pause he said, "I told him I dumped you."

"Figures," Ellen said. "You had to be in control. Macho image and all that."

"Anyhow, he calls me a jerk for passing up an easy mark. Then he comes up with the scheme."

"And you go for it, just like that?"

"Not exactly. I was shocked at first, and then when he started talking about five million dollars..."

"He set the number?"

"Yeah, and the money was on the way when you broke out."

Ellen opened her eyes, staring at Kevin. "My dad paid it?" *He paid the five million dollars! My dad paid five million dollars!* Ellen's eyes began to glaze.

Kevin replied, "Yeah. Bartles checked and the transfer was made. We were pretty excited."

She recalled the sounds downstairs, before she broke out. Then she said, "Okay, okay. So then what?"

"Bartles promised that you wouldn't get hurt, that I wouldn't be identified, and that it was just a money thing; your father could afford it. He designed a scheme to keep you from seeing anyone so that we could drop you off someplace when it was over. We'd be on our way before it all got sorted out."

Ellen sat up and glared at Kevin. "Just a money thing? My father could afford it? You idiot! You've committed a felony! And how could you be sure something wouldn't go wrong, and that I wouldn't find out who you were? I did, by the way! Do you know how stupid this was? But that was your style. Contacts and quick hits; that's Kevin Reardon. I can't believe I thought I loved you! God, was I stupid!" She sat back again and to regain her composure. "So, what was your take?" she asked.

"A million," Kevin said.

"Everyone got a million?"

"No, there were only four of us. Bartles got two and a half and Downs and Meade were in for three-quarters of a million each. Bartles figured out the split. He did all of the planning, set up the bank transfer, and arranged for the houses where we kept you. He was the brains."

"And you found the mark so you got a million."

"That's about it. Downs and Mead did the muscle work.

"They're the hooded guys?"

"Yeah; except once. I came up when you hurt your knee."

Ellen suppressed a smile and shook her head. She didn't have the heart to tell him. "How did you decide on where and how to capture me?"

Kevin thought for a second and replied, "That plan changed more than once. Bartles wanted to establish a normal residence in your apartments and then sneak you out of house at night. Meade and I would hold you while he and Downs continued to live in their apartments as the investigation went on. He figured that by carrying on, as usual, he and Downs would escape suspicion.

"So, why didn't he do it that way?"

After a while Bartles started to play devil's advocate with his own plan, and a few things made him change his mind. First, he was worried about being spotted leaving your house. And he was afraid of a struggle and maybe you'd run. You impressed him...as an athlete. That created too much uncertainty. Then, he expected that he and Downs would be questioned, so he started to coach Downs in how to handle himself. Downs started acting funny, asking stupid questions, and sounding like he'd panic during the questioning. Bartles figured that Downs would crack, so he decided on grabbing you in an, out of the way, place; after that, he and Downs would scram."

When Kevin paused, Ellen asked, "And how did you decide on my morning jog?"

"After deciding to change the plan, Bartles started looking at your daily routine. You jog almost every day, so we started to watch. Your schedule is very predictable, and we timed it to the minute. After a couple of weeks he even had statistics. Bartles said this would be a strict timetable operation. We decided on the wooded area because it was the most desolate. Downs said we should just jump out of the car and take you at gunpoint, but Bartles rejected that. Again, too much uncertainty. You run, someone shoots...Bartles didn't want you injured, or worse. Then we worked on the details."

"What details?"

"First we picked a spot, at the midpoint. Then we rehearsed the thing at least five times?"

"Rehearsed?"

"Yeah, that was my idea, just like the theater. Bartles really liked it."

Ellen shook her head, thinking back to that first rehearsal, where she met Kevin.

Kevin continued, "Bartles ran from the entry point to the mid point of the stretch; Meade drove and Downs worked the stopwatch. Meade followed Bartles, caught up to him, and stopped the car right where I was waiting, along side the road."

"So you grabbed me!"

"I didn't want you to get hurt, so I volunteered to do it."

Embellishing the words with sarcasm, Ellen said, "Very considerate of you, Kevin."

"Anyhow, we did that a dozen times until Meade could stop the car at just the right place."

Ellen interjected, "On his mark; for Kevin's entrance."

"I guess you could put it that way."

She replied, "Sounds like you were getting ready for Broadway, Kevin. You chose a wonderful way to put your theater training to use. If only you had put that kind of energy into your career." *I wonder if he'll ever get it.*

Kevin reacted to her comment with an intense gaze. After a while he continued, "So we had the plan down, and something else happened. You didn't show up."

Ellen sat back and asked, "What do you mean?"

"Bartles wanted to do it on a Monday, so that the bank could deliver the money by the end of the week. We were all set and then you didn't show. All of our timing and scheduling went out the window."

Ellen smiled. *I was having coffee with Jim!* "Whose car was that outside my house that morning? It wasn't the same one you put me in when you grabbed me."

"No, that was mine; Meade was driving it. We agreed that if anything went wrong with the timing, Meade was to pick me up and we were to call Bartles. When you didn't show up I called him from the car, and he said you weren't back yet. He instructed Meade to make one pass along your course and see if you were out there, but to stay out of sight. We couldn't figure out where you were.

"We took a slow drive all the way back to your house. We parked down the street, across the intersection, and called Bartles to report we couldn't find you. He said to leave; that's when I saw you in the rearview mirror, coming over the hill. Meade wanted to hightail it out of there, but I thought that would be a bad Idea. We scooted down in the seat and hoped you wouldn't see us. After about ten minutes I took a look, and called Bartles again. He said you were in your apartment, and that you couldn't see our car from there. That's when we drove away."

Ellen felt a chill, thinking about the incident. *So they <u>were</u> in the car. I remember, too far to get a good look from my office window. And Bartles was watching for me and heard me go into my apartment. I had no idea all this was going on!* She returned her thoughts to the present. "So then what?" she asked.

"We were ready again the next day, but Bartles called when you didn't leave to run and we had to wait one more day."

"Yellow Day."

"What?"

"That was Yellow Day. Never mind; it's a school celebration, and I had to be in early, so I didn't run."

"Oh. Well, by then, Downs was climbing the walls. Bad omens, he'd say; too many things going wrong! Downs was the weak link. But Bartles said, tomorrow is a go."

"I feel like a cancelled space shuttle launch."

"Kind of like that. Well, that night we were all nervous. What else would happen? The morning finally came and we went ahead with it. But it messed up the timing on the bank transfer. Bartles knew he'd have to wait into the following week to get the money."

Ellen asked, "Why the electronic transfer?"

"Bartles talked us through the alternatives. The rest of us wanted a direct exchange of cash, but he said it would be too easy to trace, and it would place us in jeopardy of being nabbed. That would create a link back to all of us. We suggested having the money delivered by car to a pay phone, where follow-up instructions would lead to another pay phone, and another, until one of us would take the money."

Ellen interjected, "I think you saw that one in the movies."

"Maybe. But Bartles said with a GPS, a global positioning system, and a cell phone a car would be too easy to track. He said that sending it through an overnight courier company or mail would identify an address, and wouldn't work either. So, he settled on an electronic delivery, and a cascading scheme where it would be spread out to other banks. He said, this way, we'd be able to pick up the money in smaller pieces before it could be traced."

"Clever idea. How would the money be picked up?"

"That part he didn't tell us. He just said that he knew some people who would do it for a piece. I think that's where he spent some of his cut."

"What about the hoods? Whose Idea was that?"

"Bartles again. You knew three of us, him, Downs and me. He didn't want you to recognize us, so he devised the scheme of silence and the hoods. Remember, in the original plan, he and Downs would stay in their apartments and act normal, for a few days. After we got the money we'd drop you far someplace far away so we could head in our own directions. After the plan changed Bartles and Downs would be prime suspects, so it really didn't matter if you saw them. But they were still afraid of linking themselves to me, so we kept them, anyhow. He thought they were kind of scary, too, and would intimidate you."

"They were scary, when I saw them that first time, when I sat at my computer."

"Yeah, I know. When we first got the hoods, Downs sneaked in wearing one and scared the hell out of me." Kevin managed a weak laugh.

"God! You guys really were a bunch of clowns!" Ellen shook her head at Kevin's comic description, then asked, "Why did you move me? Why didn't you just stay where you were?"

"First, Bartles came up with the idea of an e-mail ransom message because it was slower to trace than the phone. He figured the police would be expecting a phone call, but if he used your computer to make the call, we wouldn't be traced immediately. The call would be first be traced through your service, then to the house. So he ordered the phone in an anonymous name, and planned to move you as soon as the message was sent, before they could trace the call location. He spent a lot of time thinking things out."

Ellen asked, "Did my Dad reply right away?"

Kevin thought for a second and then proceeded. "Meade and I drove you up here. Bartles and Downs waited for the return message and then left. But Bartles was surprised at how fast the house was located. When we left, we passed some police cars in the neighborhood and called Bartles. He saw them, too, less than an hour later. I think Bartles was shocked; he couldn't figure that one out, but he said we wouldn't have to worry once we got to the cabin, they'd never find us there. After that, he sent a warning message by overnight mail telling your Dad he knew they located the house, and to just follow instructions and not try that again."

Ellen thought about revealing her secret. *He's a felon, and I'm not safe yet; better not.* She replied, "So what happened when I broke out? I heard lots of shouting and a car. Later I heard a helicopter. What was that all about?"

"Well, first, seeing you through the window almost blew me away. Then, when I found out the cops were there...when you ran off, I thought I'd have a heart attack."

"What?"

"I think they must have been ready to move on the house and you surprised them. We wouldn't be sitting here if you hadn't run."

"You saw them?"

"Yeah; I was in the car with Bartles. He dropped me off and I started in to the woods after you, then he drove back to get a flashlight. A while after that I heard strange voices and saw some guys in uniform and others in plain clothes. There must have been about ten of them. I figured out it was the police. I waited for a while until I was sure they wouldn't see me; then I gave up chasing you and started to run. I never saw Bartles after that. Either he saw them and ran, or else they picked him up. I don't know."

"So the helicopter, that was the police."

"Yeah."

"I hid when I heard it, thinking it was your crowd."

Kevin shrugged. "What will you do now?" he asked.

201

"I'm leaving tomorrow morning to find somebody. Where are we, anyhow?"

"New York State, near Lake George."

Ellen nodded. "Now it's a federal crime. The FBI is probably involved. Reardon, you're career will be doing Christmas shows in some federal prison."

"Jeez! FBI!" he said.

Ellen coughed through the tightness in her chest. Then she said, "Look, I'm tired. If you don't do anything else stupid you might get a break." He posed no real threat, but the chain was a precaution. She knelt next to him and said, "This is so you stay put," then she reached for one of his sneakers.

He rolled over, and with a surprised look said, "What's this?" As she continued he moaned in response and grimaced, "No! The other one, please!"

"What's the matter?"

"Too much pain, please."

She removed the sneaker from the other foot, unlaced it, and then cut the lace into two pieces with the kitchen knife. Then she wrapped one end of the chain around his leg and wove a piece of the shoelace through the links to fasten the chain securely to his ankle. "Just keeping you honest, Kevin. I don't think you're in any shape to walk out of here."

He nodded with closed eyes and a look of pain.

Ellen placed two more logs on the fire from the dwindling supply. Then she tied the other end of the long tether to her wrist with the remaining piece of shoelace and said, "This is to be sure you don't try." *It's not perfect but, if he tries to move I'll know about it.*

Kevin rolled over and turned his back to her, facing the fireplace.

She wrapped herself in blankets, watching him, and said, "Get some sleep. I'm going to look for help tomorrow; it looks like you need it more than I do."

He replied with a whimpering, "Okay."

"See you in the morning." She closed her eyes.

202

Jim stretched in the warmth of the bed after a restless sleep, thinking of Ellen, out in the cold. Could she survive another winter night? After two days in the woods, there'd be pain, frostbite, or worse. He felt helpless. *What else can I do?*

He wandered down to the coffee shop and decided on a bowl of hot cereal. After his first spoonful the Cramwell's arrived. They spotted his wave and crossed the room to his table.

"Hi, Jim. How long have you been here?" Dave asked.

"Just a few minutes. Any news?"

"We had a call at six o'clock. They started out with the dogs this morning from the cabin where Ellen escaped. They tracked her to the ravine, and then after a few minutes they lost the scent. It was as if she disappeared into thin air. The dogs are running around in circles. Bremmer will call back if they pick it up again."

Ellen woke with a cough and pressed both hands to her chest. Her lungs felt raw. The pain of a sore throat made her swallow and provoked another cough. She sat up and gazed at the few remaining embers. Kevin faced the fireplace; his quiet moans indicated discomfort or pain. The tether connecting them remained in tact.

She untied both ends of the chain and shuffled to the kitchen. The dwindling food supply included three cans of soup, one container of crackers, and the untouched, half box of cereal. She chose a can marked, wild rice, and opened it, then returned to the den and poured the contents into the cooking pan. Six logs remained; she placed two of them on the grate and stirred the embers and watch while the wood began to smoke. In a short time flames licked at the logs.

After finishing breakfast Ellen walked over and nudged Kevin with her foot. "Okay, Rip van Winkle, it's time to wake up." When he rolled over and looked up at her. With ashy, pale complexion, bloodshot eyes, and shaggy, red stubble covering his chin, he looked awful.

"Morning already?" he said in a raspy voice. He reached down to rub his foot.

"Yes. The sun is up; I think it's mid morning. I want to get going."

"Are you leaving?" Kevin exclaimed.

"No, not yet." She put on her gloves and cap. "I'm going out for a minute."

She went into the kitchen, found two cooking pans and a funnel, and went out the front door. She walked to a snowdrift and filled the pans with snow. She returned and placed them near the fire. After a while, she poured a few drops of the water into the empty wine bottle and rinsed it out, then filled the bottle with water. She replaced the cork, went back outside, and returned with two more snow-filled pans. She set them next to Kevin and said, "Drink some of this from time to time; and you may want to munch on the cereal." She handed him the box.

She brought the last two cans of soup and the remaining crackers from the kitchen and placed the scant supply of food on the hearth, next to him. "I'll open the cans and leave them here, too." Then she said, "I brought the last few logs up from the basement. Use them sparingly; that's all there is. I'll send help as soon as I can." She paused, then said, "I don't suppose you have any idea which direction would be best."

"No," he said in almost a whisper. Bartles did the driving. I have no idea where we've wandered to, or where the cabin is from here."

She filled her windbreaker pockets with crackers and wrapped the blanket around the bottle. She compressed a blanket into a tight roll and then tied it with Kevin's shoelace and tossed it over her shoulder. "Well, I'll just have to fake it," she said, turning to walk away. She looked at him and said, "So long." She started for the door.

"Ellen?"

She stopped and turned toward him.

He continued, "Take care of yourself. Don't get lost; and come back if you can't find someone."

She nodded and started to leave.

"Ellen!" he called out again.

Now what does he want? She looked back again at his defeated, tired face. Their eyes met for a few seconds. When Kevin's raspy voice managed the words, "I'm sorry," she thought back to their time together, and realized they were words she never before heard him say. Then Ellen turned and walked away.

Dave spoke with animation while Jim listened on the extension. "You've picked up Ellen's trail! That's great!" Jane stood at Dave's side with her ear next to the phone.

Bremmer responded in an even voice, "Took a while but they found a new set of tracks somehow disconnected from the others. It's as if she flew to another spot and started out again. She can't be too far away, unless she's with the guy in the car; but that's not likely."

"When did you find her new tracks?"

"Just a few minutes ago. I've got to run now."

"We'll wait for more news. Call us with...anything." Dave hung up the phone.

Jim spoke, trying to be optimistic. "It shouldn't be much longer now. It's daylight and she can't be more than a few miles away. Let's pray she's handling the cold."

At the word, pray, Jane's eyes met Jim's.

"Ellen's a survivor," Dave said. "She escaped from them. I'm sure it was a complete surprise. The cold is her greatest enemy now. She could use nourishment, but she hasn't been without food for that long. It's the cold. It can wear down your body, and your spirit."

Jim detected the forced optimism as Dave continued, "Ellen would know to keep moving unless she found shelter somewhere. She's in good shape. If she can stay dry and keep moving she'll come out of the woods sooner or later, or the dogs will find her."

Jane finished off the discussion. "I like your idea of praying, Jim." She sat and closed her eyes.

Ellen started out on her journey by retracing the path she had taken the day before. She had one last pack of crackers in her pocket. The blanket roll rested on her shoulder, held in place by her right hand. Warm and dry with cap pulled down to her eyes, her sneakers dented the powdery snow at a brisk walking pace. She controlled an inclination to break out in a run, knowing that long-term stamina would be the key to survival. Intending a full day's effort, she would turn back only if nothing hopeful occurred by mid afternoon.

After a while, clouds began to shield the sun. Then a few snowflakes began to appear. She stopped to look at the darkening sky and guessed that it was about noon, another five hours before darkness and falling temperature would present another problem. Then the wintry wind pierced her thin clothing, so she stopped to unroll the blanket, remove the cork from the bottle, and take a small sip of the water. Reaching into her pocket, she pulled out a cracker and placed in her mouth. Another cracker and sip of water ended the meager lunch. She wrapped the blanket around her shoulders, like a poncho, and tied it to her waist with the shoelaces. She tucked the water bottle under her arm and resumed her trek.

As the afternoon wore on Ellen's coughing became more persistent, and soon it was accompanied by a pounding headache. When she placed her glove to her forehead, it encountered a sore scab. The physical discomfort raised competing thoughts. *Maybe I should sit down and rest. No! I have to keep moving and stay warm; there has to be someone out here! And I have to conserve energy.* She continued, but reduced her pace to a slow, methodical trudge.

They gathered again for more news. Jane looked at Dave with anticipation as Bremmer delivered his message. "They tracked your daughter to a house in the woods!"

Dave replied with excitement, "Is she safe?"

"She wasn't there, but someone else was inside, man, semi-conscious, with a fever. It appears he may have frostbite, too."

"Did they talk to him? Any information?"

"No, he was barely coherent. An ambulance took him to a nearby hospital. They'll try to get some information after they've taken care of his pain. It looks like he was one of the kidnappers."

"What's happening now?"

"The tracking team is sure that Ellen was in the house, and that she left this morning. Her footprints were on the steps; snow has started to cover her tracks leading from the house. The dogs have her scent and the team has started out after her, along the road."

"How about the weather?"

"Getting worse. The snow has increased. There's a real storm is brewing."

Jane grasped the phone and pulled it to her lips, "How much more does she have to go through? Can't you do anything else?"

"The forest is very thick and the roads are narrow. With this snow we can't see much from the air. The search team followed tracks through the woods and came upon the house. Now that she's on the road we're trying to get a few vehicles in there. For the time being we have to stay on foot and rely on the dogs."

"Why do you think she left the house?"

"The firewood was exhausted. I guess she didn't want to just sit around and wait. She probably wanted to take advantage of daylight."

"That sounds like Ellen," Dave said.

"There were a few opened cans of soup, and some cereal, but they were almost out of food. It looks like the guy we found was in bad shape and needed medical help."

"When did you find this place?"

"About 2:30."

"When do you think she left?"

"Can't tell for sure; probably mid morning, several hours earlier; maybe four or five."

"So she could have been ten miles away by then."

"That's right. Maybe more."

"Can you do anything else?"

"Well, we think don't think the guy in the house, the third kidnapper, had the car. Now it seems there may be a fourth, who escaped in the car. We can make a public announcement on radio and television, but he may still be out there, and he might hear or see a broadcast. But it's not likely that he's with your daughter."

"Then there seems to be little risk in getting the announcement to the news. Do it! It might save her life!"

"Okay; turn on your TV, it won't take long."

Dave clicked the remote control and the screen flickered to life. He found the local station showing Oprah in the middle of a book review. They watched for almost ten minutes until bulletin notice appeared on the screen. A woman sat behind a desk. "We have a developing story. Ellen Cramwell, daughter of industrialist David Cramwell of Connecticut, is lost in the area west of Lake George. It is reported that she is on foot in a snowstorm. The location, near the village of Athol, is sparsely populated. She was last known to be heading north on Harley Road, and could be on any of the roads in that area. Police are tracking her and ask residents living nearby to keep an eye out and to call 911 with any information. She'll be seeking shelter and may possibly have been overcome by cold. Further reports will follow as the Police release information. We return you to the program in progress." The screen flickered and Oprah reappeared.

Dave turned the sound to mute. "Let's hope someone sees her. In a few more hours it gets dark."

"It's better to make this public," Jim said. "At least there's a chance someone will spot her. It's hard to believe she could be out there on the road for hours and not come across anyone."

Dave replied. "Off the main roads it's pretty desolate. After November, only a few true residents remain. Some come back for a few days of hunting and for some skiing; but the homes are far apart and most are empty this time of year."

Jane looked out the window. "I need some air," she said.

"Good idea," Jim said.

Jim and Jane walked out on the porch along the front of the inn. They looked out at the snowstorm, gaining intensity. Several inches on fresh slow covered the cars in the parking lot. Jane looked up at the sky at the worsening weather and shook her head. Jim thought of himself in this situation, one of his children at the mercy of a snowstorm. He empathized with a parent's concern. A few minutes later the door closed behind her and Jim stood alone on the porch. Flakes landed on his eyelashes and in his hair as he gazed into the falling snow. He thought about Ellen's courage and all that she had faced since he last saw her. He had withheld his true feelings, trying to maintain a positive attitude with the Cramwells about Ellen's chances. He struggled with himself to maintain that attitude.

Ellen wanted to delay the decision, just a little longer. Her shadow grew longer as she approached another road, intersecting her path. She stopped at the crossroad and looked left, then right through the falling snow, for a signal to help her decide; keep going, or return to the house to the vision of a warm fireplace.

The last few logs were probably gone by now, and the soup, as well. She wondered about Kevin, in bad shape and with a severe chill. *Could he even keep the fire going?*

There were no vehicle tracks to provide a clue. Returning to a cold house didn't seem like an option. *Tomorrow, I'd just have to come back here.* She had three left, keep going or turn? Which way? From the sun, she knew the road ahead headed north, and it looked like more of the same. The crossroad sloped downward from left to right. She decided to turn east, and downhill. *The main roads are in the valleys.* Now, there would be no turning back.

After a short time the road flattened, then resumed its gentle downward slope. The snowflakes fell faster and the buildup of powder crunched beneath her feet. *A car or a house, anything would look so good right now!* The raw feeling in her chest ached with each cough. If she stopped, it would be a difficult night. The blanket roll wouldn't provide much shelter. As tears began welling up she suppressed a moment of weakness. *Don't lose it, Ellen.*

Another mile or so, and now she struggled through a raging snowstorm. Staying on the road became a major effort. The cold, dry snow, almost to her knees, exerted an icy grip on each step. Without warning, she felt her left sneaker loosen. She knelt in the snow and removed her gloves. Her fingers stung when she cracked the icy coating from the lace, frozen rigid. She tightened and tied the lace, then switched positions and did the same with the other sneaker. When she finished, she cupped her hands and exhaled into the small hole formed by her thumb.

She rose after the brief stop and plodded forward. Between coughing spasms, puffs of breath streamed from her mouth like the exhaust from a steam engine. Then, a movement in the distance brought her to a halt. Squinting through the swirling snow, she raised her gloved hand to fashion a visor. The picture came into focus; a magnificent stag stood along side the road, full-grown. She had never seen a deer with such large antlers in the wild. Awestruck by the appearance of the creature, she continued her motionless stare until an involuntary cough broke the silence. The deer turned, and with tail high, bounded off through a white curtain of trees.

Amid trembling spasms, she cursed the enemy, relentless cold. But movement was her ally. She resumed the arduous journey and began to think about the worst case. *What if I find nothing before darkness?* Huskies survived by burrowing into the snow, even in the bitter Arctic cold. The snow produced an insulating effect. But they also had thick fur; with thin blanket, and a low body temperature, it might be too late for that option. *Be thankful it's not raining.*

Ellen stopped again for a brief rest. The light gray sky dissolved to dark; she stood at the fringe of night. *Should I try to build a shelter before it got dark? No, not yet. Another half-hour, I have to keep going.* She tightened the blanket around her shoulders, trying to shut out the howling wind, and summoned a burst of energy to pick up the pace. After a while the exertion wore her down; she slowed again. Then another coughing spasm forced her to stop. She removed the cork from the bottle and drained the last drops of water. She placed the bottle upright in the snow, in the middle of the road, then pointed the neck in the direction of her course, and started off once more.

Ellen's teeth began to chatter. Darkness surrounded her when she noticed a faint glint through the falling snowflakes. *Please, let it be someone!* Her heartbeat increased as she focused on the blurry light. As she neared it, the glow of a window illuminated the fallen snow below.

"Thank God!" she rasped.

She plodded forward, stopping in the road in front of a large, stone house. The light of a lamp shined through lace curtains behind the panels of a large bay window, like a scene from a Dickens novel. Tire tracks swung in a graceful arc from the road into a driveway, ending at the rear wheels of a utility vehicle parked next to the house. Ellen stepped into the tracks and followed them down the drive, then into a set of footprints leading to a door at the side of the house. She approached a large, white, six-panel door. Above the door the enticing glow of light shined through a set of small, square windows. She raised her arms, took a deep breath, and pounded at the door with her fists. Shivering and coughing in the bitter cold, he stepped back from the door, awaiting a response.

After a clicking sound, the door opened a crack. Ellen held a fist to her mouth to suppress a barking cough and peered through the narrow space. First, a face surrounded by gray hair appeared and then the door opened, revealing the figure of a woman; she wore an apron. Gazing into the woman's kind eyes, Ellen pleaded, "Help me!"

The woman turned her head and called over her shoulder, "Earl!" Then she reached and grasped Ellen's arm, "Come in, please."

Ellen took two steps and stumbled into the vestibule. She gazed into a mirror, stupefied by the image: purple lips, raw, red cheeks, white eyebrows, a white-crusted cap, and clutching a blanket, thick with snow. She sprawled on the floor and her entire body began to shake. She heard footsteps in the hall and a man's voice, "What's this?"

The woman spoke, "It must be the girl they talked about on the news."

"Clara, I think you're right! Let's get her into the living room by the fire."

The man knelt next to Ellen and helped her sit up; then he placed his arm under hers and raised to a standing position. Ellen placed an arm over his shoulders, then she staggered down a narrow hallway, supported by the stranger, into a large room where a fire blazed.

"Sit down, child," said the woman, steering Ellen into a rocking chair. Let's warm you up."

Ellen nodded, "That sounds wonderful." A captive and then a fugitive, living in constant uncertainty, she had guarded each action, suspected danger at every turn. Then, she battled with the raging winter storm, controlled her fear, and struggled not to give up. Now, as she relaxed, the safety of her surroundings unlocked the emotions she had suppressed for more than a week. Unguarded tears flowed down her cheeks, and she began to sob and cough without control.

Dave, Jane and Jim sat in one of the few occupied tables in the quiet dining room, picking at their food; thoughts were not shared. From time to time they glanced out at the howling storm, under normal circumstances a beautiful work of nature, but tonight a vicious threat to Ellen. The windblown, near-horizontal motion of the snowflakes glided across the darkness outside the large window, reflecting the light from the cozy lamp that sat on the table. Jim searched for a comforting comment, but decided against it. *They wouldn't want to talk right now.*

The waitress approached the table and Dave reached for his wallet. "Mr. Cramwell?" she said.

"Yes, here you are," Dave said, handing her a credit card.

No, not that; there's a message for you at the desk," she replied.

Dave glanced at Jane and rose to his feet. "I'll be right back," he said. "You two stay here." He rose and followed the waitress across the floor.

When Dave rounded the corner to the lobby, Jim turned to Jane; with eyes closed and head down, she gripped the edge of the table. *Think of something to say!* There was no clever way to deal with this. He reached across the table and placed his hand on hers; his voice seemed hollow. "Let's hope for the best."

She raised her head and stared into his eyes. "Thanks. I'm praying for that."

After a few seconds Jim looked away. As they sat, waiting, hands touching, Dave reappeared and approached the table. "They've found her!" he exclaimed with a broad smile.

Jane moved her right hand to cover Jim's; then she gave a loud sigh and sat back. She seemed to be waiting for the next sentence.

Dave continued, "She must have walked more than fifteen miles! When she found an occupied house the owners realized who she was, from the television bulletin. They said she has a very bad cough and seems weak, but otherwise, okay."

"Thank God! Can we go to her?" Jane asked.

"The FBI has called in an ambulance. They're taking her to Adirondack Hospital, about twenty miles from here. After all the exposure to the cold, she'll need some time to recover. Let's finish up here and get ready to go. I have the directions."

—10—

Ellen's awoke amid clean white sheets of a warm hospital bed. A transparent fluid wound its way from a plastic bottle to her left arm; a bandage covered the right side of her forehead. A woman wearing a white coat stood at her bedside. The woman spoke. "Ellen, good morning; nice to have you with us." The name, Dr. Connie Ashton, appeared in script above the breast pocket on her coat.

Ellen stretched her aching body and replied, "Hi. Where am I?"

"You're in the hospital. You've had a rough time."

"Tell me about it," Ellen replied. "What day and time is it?"

"Thursday evening; almost nine thirty."

"It's been a long day. The last thing I remember is stumbling into that house."

"I'd like to hear your story, but when you're a little stronger. You have pneumonia and you're suffering from exposure. In two or three days you should be feeling better. And I want a plastic surgeon to take a look at that scar on your forehead."

"That all sounds good to me," replied Ellen through a weak smile.

"From what I've heard, you've been through a lot. You must be a survivor."

"I never realized some of things I knew until the past few days," Ellen replied through a series of coughs. As she drew her knees into a bent position a realization struck her. "What happened to my...anklet; the lock?"

"Oh, someone from maintenance came over and removed the lock, with a pair of metal cutters. Your ankle was a little raw, and we've bandaged it."

"Feels good to be rid of it. I hope they tossed it out."

"No; actually, the police have it, for evidence."

"Oh, I guess they would want it. The rest of it, the chain; I left that in the house."

"The police, or I should say FBI, need a few minutes with you." The doctor looked over her shoulder, "Mr. Bremmer, you may come in now. Not too long, she needs rest."

A tall man with blond hair entered the room followed by another, shorter man. The tall man spoke. "Miss Cramwell, I'm Agent Bremmer of the FBI." He flipped open a leather folder revealing an identification card. "This is Detective Lawson of the Connecticut State Police." The second man waved a badge and a wallet at her and nodded.

Bremmer continued, "We know you're tired but we'd like to get a few facts right away."

Ellen nodded, "Sure. What do you want to know?"

"Can you tell us how you were kidnapped?"

Ellen provided a two-minute wrap-up of the events along the Shore Road, how they blindfolded and transported her, and her experiences when they held her in Connecticut.

"Did you see any of them? Can you describe them?"

"They wore hoods and chained me to the bed. They were very careful about that. But during my escape, I saw one of them."

"Who was that?"

Ellen hesitated, and then said, "Kevin Reardon. I knew him in college; graduate school at Yale."

"When did you see him?"

"Twice. First, when I was escaping I saw him through the window; and later, when I broke into the house where I stayed for two nights. He showed up on the second day; seems he was running from you while I was running from them. He seemed to be in bad shape."

"Weren't you afraid of him?"

"He looked horrible. He could barely walk and in obvious pain. I helped him get through the night and left for help the following morning."

"You say you helped him. Even after all you had been through? Weren't you worried about him?"

"I was cautious, at first. But then I saw that he was exhausted; he didn't seem to be much of a threat."

Bremmer glanced at Lawson. "Kevin Reardon; so that's who he is. We tried fingerprints but he has no record of being printed."

"Is he okay?" Ellen said, sitting up.

"Yes. We tracked you to the cabin and found him there, barely conscious. He's here, in the hospital, now." Bremmer continued, "Do you know how many of them there were?"

"I talked with Kevin last night," she said, sitting back in her pillow. "He told me there were three others. Two of them rented my apartments, Al Bartles and Tim Downs. Downs was an actor friend of Reardon's, and the third, Frank Meade, was a friend of Bartles. Have you caught them all?"

"Meade and Downs are in jail and Reardon is under custody here. We don't have Bartles yet."

"Bartles is the brains behind this deal," she said.

"How do you know that?"

"Reardon told me. I guess it makes sense that he's the only one on the loose. They started after me in a car when I broke out; Reardon confirmed that Bartles was driving. He went back to get a flashlight, but Reardon never saw him after that. Reardon wasn't sure whether you caught him, or he got away. I guess I know the answer, now." Then she said, "There were some others, too, helping with the transfer of money. Kevin called it cascading; but he didn't know who they were. He said Bartles took care of that."

"Yes, we figured he had some other accomplices." Bremmer changed his tone, "Miss Cramwell?"

"Yes."

"Did they harm you?"

"Not in the way you mean. They scared me, but they weren't rough...or anything."

217

Bremmer nodded. "Good. You've got a lot of spunk, getting away like that. How did you do it?" The two lawmen nodded at her description. Bremmer commented, "It's an impressive story. Where did you learn all that?"

"My Dad, mostly. I guess I made some of it up as I went along, like *Indiana Jones*." She grinned at her impromptu analogy.

Bremmer reacted with a smile of his own. "You sure had us fooled. And the dogs, too."

"That wasn't the idea. When Kevin told me the police were in the area, looking for me, I couldn't believe it. And I hid from your helicopter."

"We were that close?"

"Yes. And Kevin said Bartles was shocked that you found the first house so fast. Thank God for that phone."

"Did you tell him about it?"

"No. I didn't think that was such a good idea."

Bremmer nodded, "Good." After a short pause, he said, "We'll be going now, but we'll need you to identify the three of them soon. Your doctors want us to leave now. Get some rest."

"Thanks," replied Ellen.

As Bremmer and Lawson left, Doctor Ashton returned and stood next to Ellen's bed. "You have more visitors," she said, motioning toward the door with a nod and a glance.

Jane and Dave's smiling faces appeared over the doctor's shoulder. They approached Ellen's bedside and leaned over in a prolonged embrace. Jane's smile turned to tears, and the trio enjoyed a silent moment, a shared happiness that could not be improved upon by words. After a while, Ellen spoke first, "Mom, I want you to know that through it all, I was a lady."

Jane replied with a playful jab at Ellen's cheek. "Of course! You're my daughter!"

Then Ellen turned to Dave and said, "And Dad, without your survival skills I don't think I could have gotten through it."

"I'm proud of you, Ellen," Dave replied. "I'm sure it must have been very tough. You can tell us about it later. It must be quite a story."

"I just told the police that one of them was Kevin Reardon."

"Reardon! I can't believe it!" Dave said.

"Reardon?" Jane shook her head.

Ellen described her own shock at Kevin's involvement. After about ten minutes Dr. Ashton entered again. "This is a happy occasion, I know, but she really needs to rest. Pneumonia is nothing to take lightly."

"Just one more thing," Ellen said. "Dad, did you find out who lived there? Whose house did I break into?"

"Not yet."

"I smashed the window and used their wood, and food, and a bottle of wine. It saved my life."

"I know. We'll take care of it, Ellen. Don't worry."

"Dad, did you hear anything from Ethan A? What do they know about this whole thing?"

"The police met with Mrs. Stuart, you Principal and filled her in, but only after she agreed to maintain the information in confidence. They made up a cover story that you were taken ill and we were caring for you. We got a few calls, and kept up the appearance. The police didn't want any information to get out that might jeopardize you."

"Have the Ethan A staff learned the true story yet?"

"Yes. After it was announced on radio and TV, the police said I could tell her the truth. I called Mrs. Stuart and explained."

"What was the reaction?"

"Shock, of course. Lots of questions and concerns. She planned to advise the staff the next morning. I called her again in the evening, when they brought you here to the hospital."

"I'm glad they know. I wouldn't want them to worry."

"I'm sure you'll be the center of attention when you return."

"For sure!"

After giving Ellen one last hug, Dave and Jane prepared to leave. As they started toward the door, Ellen saw Jane whisper to the doctor, who nodded and raised her hand and spread five fingers.

As her parents exited, Ellen lay back on the pillow, ready for her first good night of sleep in more than a week. She began to doze off, but opened her eyes at the sound of a gentle knock. She looked toward the door, at a man wearing a yellow sweater, smiling at her.

She seemed thinner than he remembered, but understandable after what she had been through. That enchanting look on her face; how could she ever suspect that he'd be here? With open mouth Ellen shook her head in disbelief. He crossed the room, taking slow steps, searching for the right words. At her bedside he still didn't have them. Then he leaned forward and watched her eyes close, accepting his soft kiss. "We have to stop meeting like this," he whispered.

She seemed overcome by the situation and replied, "But how? Why?"

"It's a long story, but it started when the police picked me up, and I've gotten to know your parents."

"Police! Why? You know my parents?"

"Your doctor won't give me the time, now. Tomorrow; get some rest."

"But now I don't want to rest!"

"You don't know how glad I am to hear that. But rest is really what you need. I'll come back tomorrow morning."

"How did you meet Mom and Dad? I can't believe this!"

Jim replied, "We're practically old friends by now." He spotted Dr. Ashton at the door, motioning to wrap it up. I'll tell you about it tomorrow." He brushed the knuckles of his hand against her cheek; Ellen smiled and leaned her head, pinning his hand between her face and shoulder.

"Good night, Ellen. I mean that, do have a good one. You deserve it."

"Thanks. You, too."

Jim walked to the door and waved. He had only enjoyed her company for a few hours, but now he felt like an old friend. He turned for one more look, at her closing eyes, and at the smile on her face.

Jane sat at Ellen's bedside, chatting about the events of the past two weeks. "He just wanted to come here and help," Jane said.

"And how long has he been here?" Ellen asked.

"Let's see. He arrived on Saturday; almost a week."

"And he's been with you since then?"

"Yes; every day. He even helped the FBI with the money transfer to and from the Swiss Bank."

"He did?"

"But mostly he was considerate and understanding in helping us deal with all of this; our concerns for your safety."

Ellen shook her head. "We went out just that once. I thought I might never see him again."

"But you wanted him to call again."

Ellen nodded. "Yes, I did."

"Well. You got your wish."

"I don't know much about him."

"He didn't tell you about his wife?"

Ellen's mouth opened as she gawked at her mother.

"A very sad story. She died about seven or eight years ago. He has three children."

"He never said anything! We never got into a serious discussion about families. He wasn't wearing a ring. How did he tell you?" She shook her head at these new discoveries about Jim.

"It was right after he arrived. He was very forthright about it. He guessed we weren't too happy about his presence, at first. He told us about your Yellow Day."

Ellen smiled. "Yes, that was nice."

"Ellen, I don't know where this is going, but he seems like a fine person. I can tell you're upset, and maybe I shouldn't have said anything. Talk to him. I like him, and you know I'm pretty fussy."

"No, Mother, not you!" They both laughed then Ellen continued, "Three children! How old are they?"

"I think I've burst enough of the bubble. You talk to him about it."

"I will." Ellen nodded. "I will."

When Jim arrived in the hospital lobby he spotted Jane reading the *New York Times*. "Hello Mrs. Cramwell; anything interesting?"

"Jane." She rose to shake his hand. "There's a nice story about Ellen," she said with a smile. "But they've suppressed a lot of the information."

"I'd like to read it. How's she doing...Jane?"

"She seems to be progressing well. I was with her a short while ago. The doctors are doing another examination."

"Any idea when she'll be out?"

"Not yet."

"Is it all right if I go up?"

"Of course. Just talk to the nurse at the desk." After a pause she said, "Jim, I'm glad I caught you before you went up. You should know I told Ellen about your family. I didn't realize you hadn't talked to her about it. She was quite surprised."

"I'll bet. Thanks for the warning."

"Don't think of it as a warning. Just friendly advice; I guess you'd call it a, heads up." She smiled.

Jim smiled at her choice of words. Like Ellen, easy to talk to and genuine in her conversation, Jane was a person of quality; he liked the thought of their friendship.

"Go on up. I'll wait here," Jane said.

He nodded and started for the elevator.

Ellen smiled when Jim entered and crossed the room. She wondered how he would approach the situation.

Jim pulled a chair to the side of the bed. "Hi. How's it going?" he asked.

"Okay. Lots of probing and measuring; they seem satisfied with my progress."

"You look better today; rested, I'd say."

"Thanks. I slept like a hibernating bear."

"More like Goldilocks in the right bed."

Ellen laughed. "Actually, I felt like Goldilocks when I was prowling around in that house I broke into."

"I want to hear about that, soon."

She paused, thinking about Jim's family. She wanted to be stern with him, but couldn't bring herself to take that tack. She started to ask a straightforward question. "Jim?"

Before she could complete it he interjected, "I have something to tell you."

Relieved that she didn't complete the thought, she asked, "What is it?" She knew what to expect; but it would be interesting to hear how he would proceed.

"I have a story, about a wife and children to tell you about. This seems like the right time. Maybe I should have done it sooner."

Ellen paused before answering, "Go ahead, Jim. I'm listening."

He started from the day he met Gail, on the beach, his reaction to her child, their life together, and then her illness. Then he told her about his trip to Hawaii, his new job, and went on right to the present. It took almost half an hour. Ellen nodded and asked few questions, accepting the story in Jim's words.

He concluded with, "And then I was on the ground and heard a dog barking, and there you were."

When Jim stopped she saw that he wanted her reaction.

"That's quite a story," she said.

"I thought it was a little much for our Yellow Day. I hope you don't mind my keeping it from you. I didn't want to scare you away."

She wanted to say something about his choice of words, but before she could respond he said, "I was almost scared away from Gail, when I found out about Tracey. I was a kid, and the thought of an instant family was overpowering. I hadn't lived yet."

"You found something wonderful with her, Jim. I know it was horrible, but the real tragedy would have been if you hadn't made a life with her."

He sat for a few seconds, and then he said, "Nobody ever put it that way before. We were all too close to her to be that objective. But we're all better for the time she was with us; and the kids wouldn't have existed without her."

"They might have had another mother."

"No, they wouldn't have existed. Different persons would exist. I've thought about that a lot. We are all conceived at a point in time and space that is unique. Even a heartbeat sooner or later is a different conception, creating a different person. It's actually eerie to think how accidental or statistically improbable our individual existences are." He stopped and paused, "I'm getting too deep here."

She eyed him with a quizzical look. "Jim Dulles, there's a lot to you. I want us to spend some time exploring that thought further."

"You're on. I've never discussed it with anyone before; just mulled it over in my mind."

"It's ironic, Ellen. Now I'm the one with a ready-made family."

"That you are; and I'm the one who should be scared."

"Are you?"

"Yes, I am. When I told the teachers about you they used the words, fast track. We've spent what, four hours together? Five?"

"Four hours and thirty...eight, no nine minutes," he said, looking at his watch.

She grinned at him "You're like my Dad, always thinking in numbers."

"That's another story. We'll have to set some time aside to discuss that, too."

"I'll have to create a schedule to deal with all of these new subjects."

"I can't think of a better way to spend some time." After a pause, he continued, "Well, maybe I can."

Ellen felt herself blush, "You're terrible!"

He looked into her eyes and shrugged, tilting his head, with a silly grin on his face.

A voice sounded from the doorway, "Okay you two, visiting time is over!" Dr. Ashton, five feet two, walked over and turned her face upward to meet Jim's eyes. She spoke with intensity, "She's doing great and we don't want to slow the progress. She needs some rest now."

"Okay. I'll be going," Jim said. "When do you think Ellen will be ready to go home?"

"Day after tomorrow, if you give her some rest."

"And if not?" Ellen said.

Dr. Ashton shook her head and returned a wry grin.

Jim waved at Ellen and walked toward the door. As he passed Dr. Ashton he said, "I'll be good." Then, to Ellen, "See you tonight for a while. Day after tomorrow you're going home." He made his exit.

Ellen sat back, sinking into the pillow, looking forward to the many long conversations that she hoped they would have.

225

The dying wind lifted swirls of snow across the icy walk as Jim walked down the hospital steps. Having Ellen safe changed things. Now the FBI could deal with finding Bartles, the last conspirator, and on recovering the money. Jim approached this afternoon's appointment with eagerness, pleased by Dave Cramwell's invitation.

He drove the Cramwell's sedan along roads covered by snow, drifting in the wind, and arrived at the inn an hour later. When Jim opened the door, a gust of cold air followed him into the lobby, where Dave Cramwell, Bremmer and Lawson sat in a lounge area. Dave extended his arm in a wave from across the room. They exchanged greetings and then Dave led the group down a hallway to a small room. They sat at a conference table while a waitress poured coffee.

Agent Bremmer took charge. "Here's the status of the funds that Mr. Cramwell sent by electronic transfer. The Banque Suisse acknowledged receipt of five million-dollars through electronic transfer and a message from the Cramwell's bank account. Using Ms. Palazzo's suggestion, and with the cooperation of Banque Suisse, the account was flagged, so that requests for withdrawals were intercepted. An attached message notified receiving banks that the funds were obtained through felonious extortion, and that a person's safety was in jeopardy if the funds were not transferred. The message asked the banks to cooperate in tracking subsequent transfers or withdrawals, and identified Jacques Heilmann as a contact at Banque Suisse to assist the banks in dealing with the situation."

When Bremmer paused in his narration, Jim asked, "How many outbound transfers left Banque Suisse?"

"A total of seventeen," replied Bremmer.

"That's quite a number, and almost $300,000 per bank! Harder to track and follow-up; Bartles knew what he was doing.

"Yes, he did; and it caused a problem keeping tabs on the money. Some of the secondary banks were slow in responding and cash was withdrawn before they connected with Banque Suisse. The transfers were in differing amounts. Some of the seventeen banks re-transferred to a third tier of banks in smaller amounts."

Jim spoke up, "What's the status of the funds now?"

"A total of $3,987,000 has been stopped and the rest has not yet been accounted for or withdrawn from the third tier banks."

"Over a million still out there!" Dave exclaimed.

"Yes, that's right."

Jim asked, "Any other information?"

"No, but there may have been other accomplices. We're still tracking all of the transactions. Bartles may have used a dozen or more people to help him take out all of that money in cash."

"Any news on Bartles?"

"Nothing at all. He disappeared. The car hasn't been seen and we haven't had any reports of anyone seeing him, either. Seems like he had a good plan for an escape route, and for dealing with glitches. He could be anywhere by now."

"He also knows that the funds have been intercepted. It's a good thing we have Ellen," Dave said. "Who knows how he would have reacted if she hadn't escaped."

Bremmer answered, "You can never tell; but considering all of the planning he did, I would say he'd be very displeased at losing four million dollars."

Jim thought of the choice of the word, displeased. A better description would be, really pissed. Jim didn't like the picture of Ellen in the hands of Bartles under those conditions. "Ellen was very brave to escape and take away his option," Jim said.

After a brief silence Bremmer said, "We'll follow-up, and the money that we recover will be returned to your bank account, Mr. Cramwell."

Dave nodded, and then Bremmer continued, "I'd like to thank you and ECD for your help, Mr. Dulles. We'll be sending a letter to you."

"This has been an experience I'll never forget," replied Jim. "I'll pass this information up the chain in ECD. I'm sure the top brass will be pleased to get the acknowledgment. I'd like you to write a letter to our CEO, if you could."

"Sure, just give me the address."

"I guess that's it, then," Dave said. "As soon as we can get Ellen out of the hospital we'll be heading back home."

"No reason to stay around here. We'll keep you posted if anything develops. Your daughter will be asked to testify when we get to court."

They stood and shook hands; then Bremmer and Lawson left the room.

"Thanks again for everything, Jim," Dave said.

"This is a story for the grandchildren," replied Jim. Then, realizing the faux pas, he blushed.

Dave maintained a straight face, "Yes, it is."

"And it looks like it may cost you a lot of money."

"Ellen is more important than the money."

"You never seemed to think twice about paying the price. It could have been the full five million."

Dave looked straight at Jim, and said, "Jim, how much would you have paid to get your wife back?"

The question hit Jim like a brick. He thought of all the good times, Gail's influence on the children, her sense of humor, and the vacuum caused by her departure from the family. After only a few seconds Dave's strong gaze began to focus on him. Then Jim said, "You're right; every penny I could get my hands on."

A trace of a smile crossed Dave's lips, followed by a nod.

A woman's voice urged, "Miss Cramwell? Miss Cramwell? Time to wake up." The gentle shaking motion stopped as Ellen opened her eyes from a peaceful slumber. As Ellen focused on the words, Hospital Volunteer, in white letters, on a young woman's blue working coat as the woman asked, "Lunch time; are you hungry?"

Ellen rubbed her eyes and answered, "Yes, I really am. What time is it?"

"Just noon."

"I guess I do need the rest. I was out. It felt great."

"Dr. Ashton said to wake you. You need food as well as rest."

Ellen sat up to a tray containing a small piece of chicken and mashed potatoes, a salad, roll and butter, a dish of chocolate ice cream, and coffee. "This looks great!" she exclaimed. The woman smiled when Ellen picked up a fork without hesitation. In a short time Ellen licked the last drops of chocolate from her spoon. *I must be getting better.* Then she reached for the coffee. A few minutes later she placed the empty cup on the tray, lay back on the pillow and closed her eyes.

When she woke the clock said 3:15. *God, I slept three more hours!* She lay in the bed for a while, working sore muscles and stretching, then pushed back the blanket. Across the room, a bright cluster of yellow roses sat on the dresser. After opening the small envelope she smiled and placed the card back. She turned to the movement at the doorway; a wheelchair rolled across the threshold; a policeman followed.

Kevin asked, "Had enough sleep? I've been here four times and you've always been sleeping." His right hand and his left foot were bandaged.

"Following doctor's orders," she said. "You look like you've had a rough time, Kevin."

"I'll be okay. How about you?"

"Pneumonia, but I'm getting better. What's with the bandages?"

"I'm short a piece of finger and two toes from frostbite."

"Oh, Kevin, I'm so sorry! You didn't seem to let on that it was that bad when I left!"

The policeman wrinkled his face at this exchange and stepped out of the room.

Kevin replied, "I had a lot of pain, but the wine and your company, that evening, made me forget it. It could have been a lot worse. Besides, you had enough problems."

"How will it affect you?"

"I'll be able to walk, and it's only the tip of one finger."

"When did they find you?"

"Late afternoon. About six or seven hours after you left. I used up all the wood, and made my mind up to start burning furniture; then I went into kind of a daze. I heard some dogs barking and then some voices; it was kind of confusing. I can't remember what happened or what I said." He paused, and then asked, "How did they find you?"

She described her experiences that day leading to the discovery of the occupied house. Then she asked Kevin, "What will happen to you?"

"Jail. But he lawyer said, because I'm a first offender and I've agreed to assist the FBI with their investigation, maybe it won't be too bad."

"Did they catch the rest of your gang?"

"Just Meade and Downs. Bartles is still out there somewhere. He had the car."

"Yes, I remember. Any idea where he went?"

"I've been helping the FBI, telling them the plan. They don't want me to talk about it. If they find Bartles it could be good for me, with the trial."

"What about the other two?"

"The FBI doesn't want me to talk to them at all. Who knows what they're saying; they just followed orders."

"Are you sure he'd have followed the plan? If the FBI hadn't showed up and I hadn't gotten away? He bailed out on you as soon as things got tight."

"You're right. I didn't think that far ahead. He knows his way around; he planned his own getaway and left us to look out for ourselves."

Ellen saw him as an overgrown child; looking for the easy way, no strategy to his life, just a series of tactics. "He's a criminal, Kevin! He was always thinking ahead. Do you really think each of you would have gotten your splits?"

His jaw dropped, and after a few seconds he changed the subject. "I'm glad you're okay. Who was that guy in here this morning?"

"A friend," she said. *More than that, I hope.*

"Just a friend?" He pointed to the roses.

"You wouldn't understand, Kevin."

"Well, maybe not." He seemed to search for the next words, "Take care of yourself, Ellen."

A beep sounded and the policeman removed a pager from his belt. Then he said to Kevin, "Time to go."

Kevin turned his chair and started to roll away. As he neared the doorway, Ellen spoke, "I'll be leaving in a day or so. I don't know why I'm saying this, but good luck."

He rotated the wheelchair to look at her. "I don't deserve it; but thanks, same to you. I realize, now, that I blew it, Ellen." Then he turned again, and propelled the wheelchair out the door.

A series of images formed in Ellen's mind, of Kevin receding into the distance. She recalled her excitement and anticipation when she watched him swagger down the street, the day she first saw him on the stairs, then her trepidation when he shuffled away after she ended the relationship. This time, as a criminal facing prison, his broken figure rolled away; she watched with sadness and pity. *He wandered back into my life once; I wonder if I'll see him again.*

Jim joined Jane and Dave their table and scanned the menu while a waitress poured coffee. After he placed the menu on the table, Jane looked at him and said, "We want to ask you something."

He sipped the coffee, then said "What is it?"

"We want Maria to bring some clothes for Ellen, and a few things for me. She'll come up this evening in my car."

Jim nodded, not quite understanding the need for his consent. Then she continued. "We were wondering if you'd mind driving one of the cars back."

He envisioned himself driving back with Ellen. "Of course," he replied with a smile.

Jim dropped his coat on one chair, then pulled another to her Ellen's bedside. When he sat down, she wanted to start right out, but he spoke first, "Had a great conversation with your mother last night. Oh, your dad was there, too."

Taken back by his comment, she replied, "You two are getting quite close, aren't you? When was that?"

"Last night, after dinner."

"And where did you dine?"

"A place called Capriccio's; great Veal Marsala!"

"Well; she must be getting serious."

"I guess so. I saw the check when your dad picked it up."

"Regular part of the family now, are you?"

"No, just old friends." They both laughed.

"Now I have something to tell you," she said.

Ellen sat back against the pillow, looking straight ahead. She searched for the right start, and then began with a flat matter of fact voice. "I wan to tell you about Kevin Reardon. He was one of the kidnappers. He and I were an item in graduate school. And when I saw him again for the first time in, maybe, fourteen or fifteen years just the other day, I was shocked."

"So you knew him, too."

"I saw his face through the window as I was escaping. I couldn't believe he was involved. Then he showed up the next day on the steps of the house, the one that I broke into. I was so mad at him I couldn't see straight. But he was freezing. I dragged him inside by the fire. We had a long talk. He described how this all happened."

Ellen reached for the glass of ice water at her side and took a sip through a bent straw. She set the glass back on the table and proceeded with her tale, the gang of four, and their botched operation. "Kevin was just a pawn. When I left him alone to seek help, he looked pitiful. He's here in the hospital. Yesterday he came by to visit and told me that he lost part of a finger and some toes." She shook her head, "To think that I considered marrying him".

After a pause Jim said, "How different was he then, fifteen years ago? What happened between you two?"

"He was handsome. Swept me off my feet. My first love. But after a little over a year, it went sour and I left him."

"Any regrets?"

"None," Ellen said without hesitation.

"How about him?"

"Yes, I think he has some regrets. You know, after all of this, I feel sorry for him. He was much worldlier than I was, then. I had a hard time breaking off our relationship, and had some uncertainty about it right afterward. But that only lasted a few days. My friend, Annie, saw to that."

"Annie?"

"Annie Nowik. She's an actress. I lived with her when I was going with Kevin."

"So, how did she fit into it?"

"Kevin's an actor. She introduced us."

"So she felt responsible."

"Yes, but she didn't push him and she didn't pull me away from him. She just did her Annie thing."

"Which is?"

"You'll have to meet her. We've been friends since high school. Annie is a free spirit. I learned a lot from her."

"I think she'd probably say the same about you."

Ellen didn't respond at first. She thought about his statement, and then gave a slight, almost imperceptive nod.

"So, we both have pasts," Jim said. "Ellen, I know this has been about the strangest two weeks I've ever spent, and that it doesn't begin to compare with yours. Maybe it's fate, or destiny, or luck, but it's one of those events that will shape the future. I want to know all there is to know about you, or at least try if you'll let me. But I don't want to go too fast, to make you uncomfortable."

"I feel the same way."

"Would you let me take you to Philadelphia to visit my family?"

Ellen thought about the question, searching ·for the right answer. After the short silence, Jim asked, "Too fast?"

"Maybe. Let me sleep on it. We'll talk tomorrow."

"The doctor said you'd be released then. I'll have to be getting home and back to my family and my work, soon."

"Oh, that's right. How have you been managing?"

"I'm used to this. I've been working out of my room at the inn. Everything is moving along. I've called home a few times but not always successful in finding anyone there. I've left some messages."

"And it's been costing you a lot of money to hang around here."

"You're worth it." He raised his hand to her face and then ran his knuckles from her lips to her ear, and then to her hair, as she leaned into the caress. "Like the Clairol commercial."

Ellen liked this little move of his, the same as yesterday. She reached for his hand and held it to her cheek, as he moved closer. "Just give me a little time, Jim. This seems too good. It's scary."

Jim nodded. "I forgot how good it could be."

After chatting for another hour Ellen's eyes closed and her responses deteriorated to nods and sighs. He waited for her to answer one of his questions. After a few seconds, Jim rose and backed away from her bedside. When she didn't react, he turned and walked out into the corridor.

He stood by the elevator, thinking about their conversation. He understood Ellen's caution; she had just experienced a physical and emotional upheaval, then hospitalization. Now, when she wants things to return to normal, he shocks her by his appearance and then informs her of his family. Maybe he was coming on too strong. But she was such a joy! It just felt right. *Here I go, again. Slow down, Jim!*

The doors opened and he stepped into the empty elevator; the numbers lit in decreasing sequence. On the ground floor he walked toward the sign, Information, on a desk in the lobby. Behind the desk, a woman in a gray dress read a paperback novel; she looked up as Jim approached.

"Can you tell me where Kevin Reardon's room is located?" he asked.

She turned to keyboard and tapped a few strokes, then looked up at him again and said, "That room is restricted. No visitors."

"Are you sure?" Jim asked. He leaned over the desk and nodded at the message; his eyes dwelled on the screen.

"Says so right there," she said, pointing to the computer.

"Thanks," he said.

Jim sat in the lobby for a short while reading an old issue of *Sports Illustrated*. An elderly man approached the receptionist and began to converse. Taking advantage of her distraction, Jim rose and returned to the elevator. He pressed the number, 3, and the doors closed. When he got out, a sign on the wall said 301-315; an arrow pointed left. As Jim turned down the corridor a policeman rose from his chair, eyeing Jim's approach.

"Hi, I'm looking for Kevin Reardon," Jim said.

"Sorry. No visitors," said the policeman.

Before Jim could respond, a wheelchair emerged from room 311. "What is it, officer?" asked the occupant.

"You're to have no visitors, Mr. Reardon," said the policeman.

"What do you want?" asked Reardon, staring at Jim.

"I'm a friend of Ellen's."

"I know. I saw you in her room yesterday."

The policeman, glaring at Jim, raised his voice, "You'll have to leave!"

Jim faced the policeman, "Officer, could you please call your superior, or the FBI, or whoever is in charge. I'd like to talk with Mr. Reardon."

The policeman looked at Kevin. "Reardon, get back in the room!" Then he turned to Jim. "You, what's your name?"

"Jim Dulles. I'm a friend of the Cramwell family."

Kevin swung his chair around and retreated to his room. Jim backed away as the officer steered him down the hallway.

"How did you find this room?" asked the policeman.

"I just took a chance that he was here when I saw you on that chair."

"Well, you're not going any farther. Stay here."

The policeman ushered Jim the short distance to a nurse's station and picked up a phone; he kept an eye on Jim while he made the call. The policeman spoke with nods and gestures. After a few minutes he hung up the phone.

"Let me see some identification," he said to Jim.

Jim opened his wallet and provided a driver's license and two credit cards.

"Okay, you have ten minutes in the room. The door stays open. I'll be standing right outside."

They walked back to Room 311 and Jim entered. The policeman took a position in the doorway.

Kevin sat in his wheelchair, watching Jim approach. "So, what is this all about?" Kevin asked.

Jim sat down in a chair next to Kevin. "I guess you heard, I'm Jim Dulles. Ellen told me about you. I just wanted to see who you were, that's all."

"What's it to you?"

"Look, We have a few minutes. You're not getting many visitors. I'll leave if you want, now that I've seen you." Jim started to rise from his chair.

"No. Stick around. When I saw you visiting Ellen, I wondered about you, too."

"Wondered what?"

"It looked pretty serious between you two, but she said you were a friend; that's all."

"You're right, we're friends."

"How long have you known Ellen?"

"I just met her, the day before...you and your buddies grabbed her."

"That's only a little over a week ago!" exclaimed Kevin, a look of disbelief on his face.

"That's right."

"So what brings you here, in the middle of all this, if you just met her?"

"You wouldn't understand."

"That's what Ellen said."

"She's right." After a short pause Jim spoke again, "How could you bring yourself to do that to her?"

"I needed money. Her father has plenty and I didn't think she'd get hurt or anything."

"She's in the hospital, and so are you. It could have been worse. You both could have died out there!"

"I know, but I didn't think...." Kevin's words trailed off.

"Damn it, Reardon, that's your problem! Not thinking! She didn't deserve what you did! It happened because you didn't think! And after all of this she feels sorry for you! Wake up! Think about that!"

Jim didn't know what to expect when he decided to meet Reardon. Now he saw a rather pathetic guy who didn't seem to care about his actions, and didn't have any idea how to gage their potential effects. Jim stood up. "I'm going now; just one more thing, though. I know you're cooperating with the FBI, but you'll do some time for this. Spend some it learning how to think while you're in there."

Jim rose and walked toward the police officer. Kevin called out, "Dulles!"

Jim turned and replied, "Yes."

Kevin spoke in a choking voice, and with damp eyes.

"You seem like a good guy. I really am sorry about what happened. I know you may not believe this, but yesterday, maybe for the first time, I realized what I could have had. Take care of her. I wish I did, when I had the chance."

Jim nodded; then he walked past the police officer into the corridor.

Ellen emerged from the small, private bathroom. Jane sat in a small chair, next to Ellen's bed and Dave stood by his wife's side.

"I feel good to be wearing my own clothes," Ellen said. "It was nice of Maria to bring them up here."

Jane replied, "She really didn't seem to mind. She couldn't wait to see you."

"We had a nice chat last night. I told her the whole story."

Dave said, "You must have the story down pretty well by now."

Ellen laughed, "I keep making it better."

Dave replied, "I'll bet." Then he said, "Well, are we ready?"

Just then, Dr. Ashton walked into the room. She said hello to the Cramwells and smiled. Then she started a sermon on dos and don'ts for Ellen during the next week. "She still needs rest, and keep the visitors down to a small mob. And be in bed by 9:30 at night. Keep that up until for a few days and you'll be ready for a little exercise. Walking and some stretching. But don't start running for another week, and only if you're really up to it. Don't push yourself. You may think you feel good, but your body has been through a serious stress. If you don't take care of yourself you'll be back in bed just like that. I think they have hospitals in Hartford, don't they?"

Ellen laughed and she sat down in the wheelchair that a nurse rolled over to her. "I think we have one, or is it two?" Ellen replied.

After saying their good-byes to Dr. Ashton, the small caravan started its exit. Inside the elevator Jane said "We'll meet Jim in the parking lot and he'll follow in his car to Hartford."

"Alone?" Ellen asked.

"No, I'm riding with Jim," Jane said. "You'll be with your father and Maria."

"You two are getting quite chummy," Ellen said with a smile.

"We have to be polite, Ellen. Besides, we have a lot to talk about."

"Oh you do! Mind telling me what?"

"Things mothers want to know."

"Which would be?"

"Things they don't tell their daughters," replied Jane, as the elevator doors opened.

Ellen reacted with a grin, then looked up to see Jim, as they stepped into the corridor. "Hi," he said. "How are you doing?"

"Can't wait to get home," replied Ellen. "I understand you're having company on the drive back."

"We have a lot to talk about."

Ellen smiled at this rapport between Jim and her mother. They were playing along with each other, teasing her. She found this new situation curious, but also pleasing. No one she dated had ever gotten close to her parents. She pictured Jane and Jim during the long drive home. *I'd love to hear that conversation.*

The Cramwell's Jaguar rolled down the interstate ramp. Ellen sat next to her father and Maria sat in the back seat. Ellen turned her head toward Maria and asked, "Everything okay back there?"

"I'm fine. I'll just enjoy the scenery and maybe doze a little. I'm still a little tired from the drive up here. I'm not used to doing that."

Ellen replied, "Fine. Let us know if you want to stop."

Thinking back on the events of the past week, with her father at her side, Ellen savored the comfort and security of the car. For a while she just kept her eyes closed, silent, remembering times past in other cars with her mother and father, skiing vacations, the mountains in the summer, sailing, travel overseas, and college visits. Dave recalled a few of their special incidents that they alone shared, and which Ellen treasured. From time to time she leaned forward and stared out at the rearview mirror to catch a glimpse; they followed, a short distance behind. Each time one of them seemed to be in animated conversation, smiling at each other, or laughing.

"They've really hit it off, haven't they," she said.

Dave glanced in the mirror, "Yes, they have. He has a nice way of relating to her. I like him, too."

"I thought so. He seems so at ease with her, with both of you. I can't believe he's spent a week up here with you."

"I think you know him better than you realize. You just haven't had much time together."

Ellen sat back to think about her father, always the cautious one, so different from her mother. She had never spoken to him about the men she dated. But his comments gave her an opening. "Dad, what do you think? About Jim and me?"

The odometer rolled off a few tenths before he answered. "You know I take my time about these things, and a father feels nobody is good enough for his daughter. But at least this guy is worth any time you invest in finding out who he is."

Wow! That was a lot for Dad to say! She replied, "What about the family thing? How do I deal with that?"

He took a few seconds to answer. Then he said, "Head on. You meet them and they meet you, and you like each other or you don't." Ellen absorbed the thought and he continued, "You've got tough competition. They lost a mother and you can't replace her. You bring wonderful qualities to the table, but it may not work out, who knows?"

"You make it sound so logical, Dad."

"Well, it's an adventure; you can choose to take the ride or to watch. And you may find some things that frighten you if you ride. But I think you'll ride, and it will work itself out."

"Remember that old amusement park, when I rode the carousel and tried for the brass ring? Where was that?"

"Somewhere in New Jersey. I remember the time you had collected about five of the steel ones, but never got the brass. You were so excited. When the ride was ending you came around and tried to toss them in the bag, and missed. Rings were flying everywhere and the attendant had to pick them all up. You were so embarrassed."

"You remember that? It's one of my regular nightmares of embarrassment. Maybe I'll get the brass one this time."

Dave grinned, "Could be; or maybe just a handful of steel ones."

"Dad!"

Jim expected an interesting, if not memorable drive. Jane had engineered the seating arrangements, so he decided to play defense and let her have the ball. She started with small talk, comments about the snow and the beauty of the Adirondacks, then switched to her relief at having Ellen back, and going home. Jim listened and nodded, made a few relevant observations, and maintained a safe following distance behind Dave's car.

For a while the conversation paused; they sat for a few minutes while the miles slipped by. Jim did the driving, but Jane took the time to shift gears. "Having three children must keep you busy, Jim. We had our hands full with one."

Here we go! Jim followed her down the expected path. "It's interesting and demanding, especially now that they're older. People at work talk about their problems with toddlers and kids in elementary school. I always tell them that it doesn't get easier. Parenting never stops. Witness how you've spent the last week."

241

"You're right, Jim, an astute observation."

"Sometimes I think back to the days when they were infants. Piece of cake, by comparison. The problems always seem to get tougher."

Jane nodded. "Tell me about them, your children."

Jim thought about her request; then he decided to start from the top. "Tracey's the oldest. She lives in Philadelphia and works for a financial investment firm."

"How old?"

"She's twenty-five, almost twenty-six."

"Married?"

"No, but very eligible. Nothing serious, at the moment; lots of interested guys."

After a silence Jane asked, "And who's next?"

"Elise; she's eighteen and a freshman at Princeton."

"That's not far from Philadelphia. You must like that."

"I do; it's only an hour drive." He paused, and then continued with the family basics, "And the third is Michael, sixteen."

"Is he home alone?"

"Most of the time my trips are only one or two nights; I have a neighbor look in on him, or he spends some nights with friends when I'm away. Because of all the uncertainty this week, I've asked Tracey to stay with him. This has been a, longer than normal, departure for me. I've been checking in by phone at night to keep in touch, but I haven't had much luck in talking with him, or with any of them. I've left one or two messages for each of them."

"Do you see much of Tracey?"

"Quite a bit. She's a good kid. Worries about me like a mother; comes over on weekends and makes breakfast."

"It must have been hard for her; your wife's death."

"Yes, she and Gail were very close. Tracey had a hard time, but she was the first to bounce back. She gets her strength from Gail."

"And what does she get from you?"

242

Jim thought for a second, then said, "No quick answer to that one. Maybe my sense of humor, and an analytical way of looking at things. She's very good in math."

"A good skill for a financial analyst. And what about Elise, what is she taking at Princeton?"

"She's keeping her options open, but we may have a lawyer brewing there."

"Has she said anything?"

"Just a few casual comments; she has always been interested in politics. But she still has time to decide."

After a short silence Jane asked, "How do you think they'll react to Ellen?"

Jim realized she'd find a way to move into this zone. Now they were there. He took a deep, silent breath. *Don't try to finesse her.* "Good question," he said. He bought some time by checking the rearview mirrors, then continued, "I'm not sure. You think you know them, but they can surprise you. My guess is they'll have mixed feelings. On one hand, resisting change and on the other, wanting what's good for me. I think it will be harder for Ellen, three of them and only one of her. But she is very likeable, and I think they are, too."

"You know, Jim, being our only child, we've sheltered Ellen a lot; and, in your words, parenting never stops. I guess we can't stop worrying about her now."

"You're making me think forward to a time when Tracey or Elise brings someone home with serious intentions." The words were out before he could retrieve them.

He wasn't surprised when she picked up on them with the jugular question, "Then your intentions are serious?"

"You know, Jane, this is really interesting. I haven't even talked to Ellen about this; but here I am, I'm telling her mother that they are."

She turned to him. "Jim, that doesn't surprise me. But we should change the subject. This is an area for you and Ellen to discuss. I'm sorry."

"Don't be, Jane. It's just parenting."

Jane laughed. "Yes, I guess it is."

Ellen dozed after lunch; she woke just as they started down the driveway.

"Up time!" Dave said.

She rubbed her eyes and asked "Home?" Then she looked over he shoulder at Maria, who also appeared to be waking. Jane's car followed into the drive. *Have they been talking all this time?*

"Yes, here we are," Dave said, as they rolled to a stop.

While Jim and Dave unpacked the cars Ellen took a seat on the sofa near the fire. After a while Jim sat down beside her and Maria rolled in a teacart.

Ellen turned to Jim and asked," When will you be heading back to Philadelphia?"

"I'd like to stay around here for a few days, if you don't mind."

"I'd love it, but how's work? Aren't you behind?"

"Not too bad. I've been keeping up with things. Using all the gadgets."

"I'm glad. This has really been a disruption for both of us. I have a hard time believing all this happened. Two weeks ago we didn't know each other; and now...."

He completed the sentence, "we're involved."

She took a few seconds to ask, "Are we?"

"I care about you, Ellen," he reached for her hand.

She felt his warm squeeze and returned it. "I like hearing that." She leaned forward and took a sip of tea. "Jim, you asked me something yesterday; about meeting your family."

"I shouldn't have pressed on that. Maybe you're not ready."

"At the time I thought maybe I wasn't, but now I think I am. She sipped her tea and then continued. "When you walked away that first day, I wondered if I'd ever see you again. And what has happened since then, well, it's like a dream. I shudder to think of what the outcome could have been. I think when I'm a little stronger, I'll come down by train."

"Ellen, I have something to tell you."

"You've changed your mind."

"No, not at all, I think it's a great idea, the train, whenever you're ready. But you're right, you need some time to recover. Weekend after next?"

"Maybe too soon; how about the one after that?

"Okay, it's a date." He smiled.

After a short silence, she asked, "Then what is it?"

"I met Kevin Reardon yesterday."

Her jaw dropped. "You did? How? Why?"

"On the spur of the moment, after I left your room. I located his room, but a policeman was sitting in the corridor; he didn't want to let me in. But I asked him to make a call and check me out; he did, and then gave me ten minutes. I probably spent less than that."

She stared at him, shaking her head, "Why did you want to see him?"

"After your description, I just wanted to meet him once, the guy who could have changed my future."

"What do you mean?"

"If you and he had stayed together, your week of torture wouldn't have occurred. I wouldn't be sitting here. You wouldn't be coming down to visit next week."

"This sounds like we're moving into one of those deep topics again."

"You're right."

"So, what did you think?"

"Strange guy; he got into the deal without ever thinking about what could have happened, where it might have gone. He seems to think about one minute out front"

"If that. What else?"

"I wanted to be mad at him, but I felt more like a counselor. I yelled a little, but once I got my anger out, I left. I kind of felt bad for him."

"He has a way of doing that, evoking pity. That's it?"

"Well, not quite. As I was leaving, he called to me and said he was sorry. Then he asked me to take care of you, and wished that he had."

Ellen's heart jumped. Kevin; he could be shallow, devious, mean-tempered, inconsiderate, and thoughtless. But what might have happened if, so long ago, he had shown just a little of what he did yesterday? She felt herself going down one of Jim's hypothetical paths.

They established a schedule over the next few days. Jim woke early and worked in the morning. Dave made his home office available to Jim, where he had computer access to his network of contacts as well as a phone and a fax machine. Ellen slept late and joined Jim for lunch. Then Jim returned for another two hours of work while Ellen did a few exercises and read. After that Jim and Ellen took a walk around the neighborhood.

On Thursday, during lunch, Ellen made a surprise request. "Jim, would you like to take a ride?"

"Are you up to it?"

"You'll drive, and it'll be relaxing. I know it sounds strange, but I want to show you where my adventure started; the place where they grabbed me."

"Are you sure? That may be a little stressful."

"No, I want to do it. It's a beautiful place, but they've spoiled it for me with the memory of what happened. I want you to see it, and then put that memory behind me."

Jane expressed her concerns, but Ellen overcame her protests, and by 1:30 Jim and Ellen started the short drive to the Connecticut coast. Jim made a few phone calls on the way while Ellen took a short nap.

At 2:30 Jim nudged her, "Ellen, we're almost there. Where do I go from here?"

She opened her eyes, looked up at the highway sign, and said, "Keep going; one more exit. A short time later she said, "Okay, turn here; this is the road." Jim swung around a corner onto a tree-lined road. "Slow down." Ellen leaned forward, pointing to the left side of the road. "Okay, stop; this is it."

Jim pulled to the edge of the road and moved the shift lever to Park; the car sat, idling. "Let's get out," she said.

Jim stood in the road watching Ellen pace the left-hand edge. Then she exclaimed, "Right here! I remember the tree. And the car was about where your car is, a few feet further down the road and more toward the middle."

Jim walked to her side, "Are you sure you're okay?"

"With you here, I am. I didn't want to come alone. That would have been too much."

"I see what you mean by quiet place," he said. "And on an early, foggy morning, it must have been spooky."

"I never thought of it that way before. And I don't know if I ever will again, but I'm glad I came." She extended her gloved hand to him.

He took it in his and drew her into his arms. "I like your quiet place," he whispered.

Her chin pressed into his shoulder and she replied, "Thanks Jim, for helping me with this."

He turned his face toward hers and smiled at her. He leaned toward her as she raised her chin. Her eyes closed. Sensing her soft lips on his, he suppressed a laugh.

"What is it?" Ellen asked.

"Your lips are soft, but your nose is cold."

She giggled, "And my heart is warm."

Jim's Saab crossed the Tappan Zee Bridge in a steady flow of westbound traffic, while crawling vehicles heading east toward New York City queued for tollbooths. He liked crossing the Hudson River. His thoughts returned to grade school days, reading tales of Washington Irving like *Rip van Winkle* and *Sleepy Hollow*, and family trips to the Roosevelt mansion at Hyde Park and to West Point, further north. He scanned the wide expanse of river, often filled with sailboats, but not today, on a cold morning in March.

Passing through New Jersey, Jim reflected on the events of the past two weeks and on plans for the weeks ahead. Ellen would be coming down in two weeks. He wondered how his family would react to her arrival. *Time to find out.* He pressed the speed dial number and his access codes, and then listened for the ringing on the speaker.

A female voice answered, "Hello."

"Tracey?" he replied.

"Dad! Where are you?"

He raised his face to the speaker mounted above the rearview mirror and spoke in a loud voice. "On my way home; just crossed the Tappan Zee Bridge. I've called a few times; I finally got through to you."

"I only got the one message."

"I hung up the other times, when I heard the click to the machine."

"How is everything going? I've been staying with Michael but it seems that every time you call I'm out. He told me about your being involved in something,...a kidnapping."

"He got that part right. The Radnor Police came over one morning; they thought I had something to do with it. They brought me in for questioning."

"That's what Michael said. Who was kidnapped? He couldn't remember the name."

"A friend, Ellen Cramwell. I met her in Connecticut."

"So why did the police think you were involved?"

"They found my fingerprints in her house and witnesses saw us together the night before."

"Dad, you never told us about her."

"I just met her on a Monday....And she was kidnapped on the following Wednesday morning. I told Michael about it before I left to come up here."

"Yes, but he didn't remember the details. Why did you go back up there?"

Jim hesitated for a few seconds. "I wanted to clear it up; that I wasn't involved."

Tracey responded after a pause, "Is that all?"

"Well, not quite. It's a long story."

"I'll bet. Did you clear it up? Did they find her?"

"Yes and yes."

"Okay, now the long story."

Jim delivered a narrative of the adventure that had consumed him for eleven days, while Tracey interjected comments at points in the monologue. He downplayed his feelings for Ellen and maintained a neutral voice as he spoke.

When he had finished, Tracey said, "She sounds like quite a person."

"She is."

"So that's it, you're coming home now?"

"Not quite."

"Aha! I knew it!"

"Knew what?"

"Come on, Dad. You didn't go up there just to clear your name."

"You're good, Tracey. More like your mother every day."

"Okay, so what's the story."

"Well, Ellen is coming down to Philadelphia in two weeks. I want you all to meet her."

"Kind of like meeting the parents?"

When he said, "Tracey! I don't get no respect!" he unconsciously put his finger in his collar, his Dangerfield move. They both laughed. He continued. "Yes, Tracey, like meeting the parents. Can you come over on Saturday morning, when Ellen visits?"

"Do you think you could keep me away?"

249

"Could you call Elise for me; tell her I'll talk to her when I get home?"

"Sure."

"I'll be picking Ellen up at 30th Street Station around nine o'clock Friday night. I'd like Friday evening to be quiet; maybe you can come over for breakfast on Saturday. And you can ask Elise if she can make it then."

"Does she know about this?"

"She knows a little about what's happened. I'm sure she's talked to Michael and I've left her a few messages, too. I just don't want her to overreact."

After a few seconds of silence Tracey replied, "Dad, you haven't done this before. This is different."

"I know. It's hard to explain. I'll try do that when we have some time together." *You'll like her.* He stopped from saying it.

"So she's a teacher, huh?"

"Yes, she is."

"So what's on the docket, as you would say, for Saturday and Sunday? When is she leaving?"

"I thought we'd have breakfast together and maybe a nice dinner on Saturday. Sunday I'll take her back to the train station around 2 o'clock. She has to get back to teaching the following Monday."

"What are you planning for dinner?"

"Duling-Kurtz out in Exton. I think she'd like that."

"Who wouldn't?"

"Look, I'm almost in Pennsylvania; we've been talking for almost a hundred miles. Don't forget to call Elise."

"Okay, Dad. See you Saturday."

"Maybe we'll talk before then."

"Okay. Bye."

"Bye." He pressed the red END button, CLEAR, and then started another call. Time to get back to business.

Later, at home, Jim sat at his computer terminal reading and deleting e-mail messages. A door slammed with a loud thud. A voice sounded, "Dad? Dad?"

Jim replied, "I'm downstairs." He looked up at the sight and sound of sneaker-clad Michael running down the stairs.

"Hey!" Michael said.

"Hi!" Jim replied. He rose and hugged his son. "How have you been?"

"Fine. Tracey and I had a few games of chess and scrabble, rented some videos, went out for pizza. It was fun. So, what's the deal with you?"

"Sorry I didn't talk to you more often, but I've never had a couple of weeks like this."

"I figured that out. You're usually pretty regular with the calls. How did everything go? Did they find her? Did her father pay the bucks?"

"Yes, it had a happy ending, except she got pneumonia, and he did pay the bucks. But she escaped and they got most of the money back."

"She escaped? How?"

"All right, sit down. I wish I had taped this when I told Tracey."

"Tracey knows?"

"I called her from the car a few hours ago."

"You did? Well, fill me in. There was a small article in the paper here, but it didn't say much. Boy, the guys at school will love this! Dad involved in a big time kidnapping operation!"

Jim shook his head. He rewound the mental tape and started the story from the beginning. When he finished Michael let out the teenage vocabulary staple, "Awesome!"

"There's more."

"There is?"

"Ellen will be coming down for a visit in two weeks, on Friday night."

"Oh. Well, I'll be at a basketball game and I'm spending the night at Bob's house."

"Tracey will be coming over Saturday morning. I'd like you home then."

"We'll be sleeping in."

"I'd like you to meet her. You'll have plenty of time to spend with Bob."

"Okay." Michael turned and left the room.

Jim continued cleaning up e-mail when the phone rang.

"ECD, Jim Dulles", he said.

Jim smiled at hearing her voice, "Dad? It's Elise."

"Hi, good to hear from you."

"I just spoke with Tracey." She said nothing else, leaving an uncomfortable pause.

Jim replied, "Did she give you the story?"

"Yes, most of it."

"Anything more you want to know?"

"Do I have to come home on that Friday?"

Jim sensed a tone of resistance in her question. "No, but I'd like you to. Is it a problem?"

"We have a game."

"How about Saturday?"

"A group of us are going up to New York."

"What's the occasion?"

"There's an off Broadway show we want to see. A friend of a friend has the lead role."

"I'd like you to meet Ellen."

More silence. "Do I have to?"

"No, you don't have to do anything, but I'd like you to."

"Can I call you back?"

"Sure, but try to do it by next Wednesday."

"What's the deal with you and her?"

"No deal. She's a friend. I've known her for a few weeks and she's been through a lot. She'd like to meet you."

"That's all? Do you like her?"

"Yes, she's a nice person." He smiled to himself. *You'll like her.*

"You've never done this before, Dad." She sounded like Tracey's echo.

"I know. So this is a first. I've never..." he stopped at mid-sentence.

The line was quiet and then she said, "Do you love her?"

Jim's closed his eyes and took a deep breath, "Heavy question, but I've only known her a short while."

"But you're bringing her home."

"She's not like some prize I'm bringing home. You've brought friends home and so has Tracey. Michael will, too, when he goes to college. She's a friend I want you to meet." *I don't think she's buying it.*

"I'll call you, Dad. Gotta run. Bye."

He heard the click before saying, "Bye."

After a week of pampering, Ellen began feeling like herself again. She did floor exercises several times a day but made sure to be in bed whenever Jane showed up. The small scar on her forehead served a reminder, but the plastic surgeon said it would fade in time; for now, she could covered it with a little makeup. Her strength began to return; she looked forward to running again, and to being back in her class at school.

Ellen faced her visit to Philadelphia with some doubts. What were his children like? How would they react to her? How would she respond? She hadn't yet said anything to Jane or Dave about it. Time enough for that, once they saw her looking healthier.

Ellen picked up the phone and pressed, one, and then ten more digits. After a few rings she heard the familiar, "Hello."

"Annie?"

"Ellen! I called last week and left three messages. Then I called your Mom and Maria answered. She told me an unbelievable story about you."

"Unbelievable, that's good description."

"I read a newspaper report, but it didn't say much of anything."

"The investigation is still underway, and the FBI doesn't want to say too much."

"Tell me about it."

"How much time do you have?"

"All that you need."

Ellen went on to describe her two weeks while Annie punctuated her story with exclamations; "No way! Amazing! FBI! A chain? Kevin Reardon? Five million dollars! What a story!"

When Ellen finished Annie asked, "So, what happens next? Back to work?"

"I'm going back on Monday." She decided to drop the other shoe, "Then in two weeks I'm going down to Philadelphia to visit Jim and his family."

"You are? His family? Is this serious?" Then Annie asked, "Can we get together when you're here?"

"I'll find a way to spend some time with you. I'm coming down by train on Friday and returning Sunday afternoon. I'll know more about how serious it is by Sunday. He has three children. I 'm not sure what to expect, and a little afraid of how it might go."

"Three children! When you said, family, I thought you were talking about meeting his parents."

"That would be easy."

"How old?"

"Teenagers to mid twenties."

Ellen sensed the pause, and then Annie said, "Maybe we could meet on Saturday afternoon for a while."

"I wanted to go out and visit Mayfair School; maybe we could have coffee afterwards. How's that?"

"Sounds good. I have a matinee at two o'clock and should be finished before five. How about the White Dog Café?"

"We'll see you there at five thirty. I'll call if the plans change."

"No changes. I'm meeting this, Jim, of yours next Saturday. Got it?"

"Got it." *There's no resisting Annie!*

"Ellen. It's good to talk with you again."

"You have no idea, Annie."

They exchanged good-byes and hung up.

—11—

Ellen spent most of the following week with her parents; on Thursday they drove her back to Bradford House. After the police assured her not to worry about destroying evidence she entered the two apartments vacated by Bartles and Downs. She found that they had removed all of their personal items; only a few pieces of skimpy furniture and some kitchen utensils remained. She called her cleaning agency to clean the apartments and placed an, apartment for rent, ad in the newspaper. She relaxed for the rest of the weekend.

On Sunday evening she began to think about her first day back at Ethan A. It had the makings of chaos. Everyone would want to hear the story. *Maybe I should just schedule a lecture in front of the whole school with Q&A afterwards; or videotape it.* She smiled at the thought.

The next morning Ellen eased her car over the speed bumps on the winding drive into the Ethan A parking lot. The dashboard clock showed 7:33, earlier than her usual arrival time; she would get into her classroom without fanfare. Only one other car sat in the lot, Jack's; an appropriately named Jack of all trades, he kept Ethan A going, always there when you needed him.

Ellen inserted her magnetic card into the slot and removed it when the green light blinked. The comfortable corridor led to her room; she smiled at the familiar sign, *Miss Cramwell, Second Grade*. She swung open the door and switched on the light, illuminating the room. When she stepped inside, instead of the usual artwork, a massive sign circled the walls in letters that looked three feet tall. Her face filled with a grin; she stopped and shook her head at the sign, WELCOME BACK MISS CRAMWELL! WE MISSED YOU!

"We did." A voice came from the open door. She turned to see him smiling at her.

"Jack! Hi! Nice to see you."

"Hi. You had a real time of it."

"Yes, I did. It feels good to be back." She pointed to the sign, "Quite a welcome!"

He nodded, waved and left; just like Jack, no questions.

Nothing but questions filled the rest of an all day party, and the kids would only accept one story to at story time. She smiled to herself as the children listened intently, with eyes tracking her while she paced the floor relating her adventure. They cowered at the mystery of her circumstances and broke the silence with cheers at her escape. *I am making it better, every time.*

The lunch crowd got into the real details. Overlapping comments and questions barraged Ellen from all sides, interrupting her narration. "Hoods; tied up! How did you feel?"... "Can you explain again how you broke that chain?"... "The scar doesn't look too bad. It'll go away.".... "You never told us about Kevin Reardon!".... "I'm getting a cell phone!"... "And Jim just drove up to help out; I want to meet this guy!"... "That must have been awful, I hate the cold!"...

Ellen glossed over a few parts. She didn't disclose the five million dollars, just leaving it at a lot of money, most of it recovered. Her announcement of the upcoming trip to Philadelphia unlocked a whole new set of friendly kidding. After a while she adjourned the session; they dispersed to resume classes, leaving many unanswered questions.

The afternoon included a visit from the Principal. During the course of the day, each of Ethan Allen's teachers made a point of stopping by to wish Ellen well, and to learn, first hand, about her saga. After three days Ellen's luncheon group began conversing about other topics, but her celebrity at the school continued through the remainder of the week.

Each day, after school, Ellen took short walks in the neighborhood around Bradford House. At midweek, pleased with her progress, she included a few, she interjected a few short trot segments within the walks. Ellen felt good to be getting back into shape, but not yet ready for her usual morning run.

She also knew Bartles was still out there. The thought made her uneasy.

While cleaning her desk on Thursday evening Ellen noticed a movement, someone standing in her doorway. Looking up from her desk, Ellen raised her arm and made the familiar, come on in, motion to Karen. Since Ellen had returned to school, she had not found a minute to spend alone with Karen.

Karen neared the desk and said, "Big week."

"Yes it has been. I'm still not caught up with everything. That'll take another week, at least."

"Getting ready for your trip?"

"That's why I'm here. I'd like to enjoy the weekend, knowing that next week's lessons are planned ahead. I don't want to feel guilty."

"When are you leaving?"

"Right after school, tomorrow."

"Need a ride to the train station?"

Ellen sat back at the offer. She planned to drive and park at the station. Having a driver would reduce the departure pressure. She replied, "That would be nice, Karen, but I'll be getting home on Sunday and I'll need my car."

"I'll pick you up."

"I don't want to trouble you."

"Not trouble. Besides, I'll be getting first hand news. You know me; I have to know everything."

"You said it, not me. I should have realized you had a motive. Sure, thanks; I appreciate your offer." They laughed.

"Ellen, we've known each other since you started here. What is it, six years?"

"That's about right."

"I can't remember your being involved with anyone in all that time, at least not anything serious."

"You're right. Not since I've been here."

"So, to me this looks serious."

"Could be. We seem to have clicked, but it's been such a short time. I don't want to go too fast."

"Anything you'd like to talk about? Say no, and I won't be offended."

Ellen paused. Except a few brief sessions with her parents, she hadn't talked to anyone about Jim. She liked Karen; a talk might do her some good. "How about a coffee after I straighten up and finish writing out my plans for Monday morning; fifteen minutes."

"You're on."

They sat in a pair of soft chairs at a local coffee shop, taking their first sips; hot coffee on a cold winter evening, just the right setting for a talk between friends. Karen asked a few light questions about the travel arrangements. After a while, Ellen started. "I'm scared about tomorrow."

"Scared? Why?"

"Jim Dulles entered my life less than a month ago. I could never have imagined it...frightening, exciting, exhilarating, like a roller coaster. Through it all Jim showed how different he is from anyone else I've known. He took time from his work for a week, helping me, although I didn't realize it at the time. He became a friend to my parents before I got to know him, and spent more time with them than with me. Our time together has been wonderful, and..." Ellen paused and looked out the window at the falling flakes of snow.

Karen said nothing, and then Ellen continued, "He has a family." In her description of Jim and her planned trip, Ellen omitted this important detail.

Karen eyebrows raised. "A family?"

"Yes, three children. That's the scary part. She died about seven or eight years ago."

"Ellen, if he was still married, that would be scary."

"Karen, a family! I'd be getting involved with an established family. I always imagined creating a family, not being assumed into one. How will they react to me? They had a mother. I'll be a threat to them." Ellen stopped, waiting for a response.

259

Ellen looked for a reaction; Karen sipped her coffee. She seemed to be gathering her thoughts. She put her cup down and looked at Ellen. "I can see why you're scared. It's hard enough dealing with a man, let alone his children."

"I want to go down there, but I feel as though I have to impress them. With Jim and me, there's been no pressure. It's hard to explain; we've been so comfortable together. You know how it is; you're usually putting up a front with a new guy and he's doing the same with you, acting; both afraid to say the wrong thing or do the wrong thing, unable relax."

"I've been there a few times. More than a few."

With Jim I <u>have</u> relaxed, and now I'll have to be on guard, and start acting."

"Why? Why can't you be yourself? You like kids."

"I love my second graders. I'd know how to deal with small children, in elementary school. We're talking about teenagers and young adults. I was supposed to go through a learning process before I had to deal with teenagers. I can't bring a few teddy bears, books, and a video game to break the ice."

"My guess is that Jim has broken the ice by now. How old are they?"

"Tracey, his wife's daughter before Jim married, is 25; Elise is a freshman in college, probably eighteen or nineteen, and Michael is about sixteen or so."

"So Jim adopted Tracey?"

"Yes."

"And he faced, in some way, the same situation as you are. He'll understand."

"Tracey was a small child. That was a little different; easier."

"Ask Jim how easy it was."

Ellen sat back to digest Karen's comment. Jim's situation with Tracey seemed easier because of her own comfort in dealing with young children. For Jim it would have been just the opposite. In his early twenties, what did he know about children? He would have been scared to death. Then Ellen replied, "You're right, it must have been scary for him."

"So talk to him about it."

"I should."

"And be yourself; no acting. I know it's easy for me to say, but if they're anything like Jim, you'll all get through it. And don't expect instant adulation, like you extract from those second graders who all love you."

"Oh, come on, Karen!"

"If you could hear the real story around Ethan A, it's that all the kids and parents love Miss Cramwell."

Ellen felt herself blushing at her colleague's observation; she shrugged and said nothing.

Karen continued, "Plan your interactions with them, but not too carefully. You want to be prepared but spontaneous. That's when you're at your best. Too much preparation and it'll come off as phony, like acting. None at all and you'll always be reacting. That could disarm you and make you nervous."

"I don't want to threaten them."

"They'll be threatened. You can't stop that. They've had Jim to themselves for a long time; they'll be possessive. And they want what's best for him. You can't replace what they've lost, and they'll want you to know that. I don't know what kind of kids they are, but they may test you."

Ellen looked down at her cup. "Sounds like I've got some preparation to do." Then she asked, "I wonder what she was like?"

"Has Jim talked about her?"

"Not much, but I think he wants to."

"Do you know, anything?"

"Not really. They met in college, when Tracey was four. She died after a long illness, cancer. Her name was Gail."

"Ellen, your adventure is just starting. You're going to have some fun, some excitement, surely some uncertainty, and probably some anguish. Expect that. I know you can deal with it."

Ellen hadn't talked to Karen like this before. She now saw Karen as sincere and helpful, more than just a colleague. Outside the classroom and away from professional duties, she found a caring person, a true friend. Pleased by this opportunity to grow closer to Karen, Ellen would think more about her advice.

That evening, after dinner, Ellen removed a pair of traveling bags from her closet and set them on her bed. She planned for a relaxed weekend, maybe go running with Jim. She included her running clothes among mostly casual things, and one, dress up, outfit. She finished packing and set the larger bag by the desk in the common area of Bradford House. Then she read for a while and fell asleep, thinking about the upcoming weekend. What would it bring?

The excitement of travel often kept her awake. She wandered in and out of sleep until the merciful buzzing sound of her alarm clock ended her attempt at sleep. She climbed out of bed, somewhat groggy. One of her school standards, slacks and a sweater, lay spread out on a soft chair. *I'm glad I picked this last night.* It would also be a comfortable travel outfit. After breakfast she finished packing the smaller cosmetic bag. A short time later, she checked the night-lights and the door-locks.

Ellen stood on the porch next to her luggage, ready to face the big day. She walked to the railing at the end of the porch and looked onto the empty street, staring at the spot where the mysterious auto sat on the morning of Yellow Day. *What if I had called the police?* She raced through a mental scenario in which the kidnapping didn't occur. *Would I be heading to Philadelphia today? Ellen, you're starting to think like Jim!* She cleared her head, looked at her watch, and walked back toward the stairs.

A few minutes later, headlights appeared at a distance. The car came to a stop at the curb. Karen's face appeared above the descending window and she called out, "Ready to go?" The trunk unlatched and raised a few inches.

"Sure am!" Ellen placed her bags in the trunk and climbed into the car. "I really appreciate this, Karen."

"No problem. You have enough things to think about."

The school day dragged until, at 3 o'clock, she ushered her students into the adjacent classroom. Leaving fifteen minutes early required placing her students in responsible care; Judy had accepted the chore.

Ellen led the group of eighteen anxious, giggling second graders down the hall, and peeked into Judy's classroom. "Here they are!" she said, smiling at Judy.

Judy replied, "Going somewhere?"

"Judy!"

"Oh, I forgot." Ellen could tell that Judy was into it now. She watched in wonder as Judy raised her arm to focus the students' attention. When she brought it down the complete assembly of tiny voices resounded with, "Have a nice trip to Philadelphia, Miss Cramwell!"

Ellen nodded at the group and then whispered, "Judy, you devil! Where do you find time for this stuff?"

"We try to do our best."

"When I get back you can tell me how you got my kids into that act."

Judy winked at Ellen's students and said, "We have a secret."

"Well, I'm out of here!" Ellen turned with a wave and hurried off.

A few minutes later Karen's car exited the Ethan A parking lot into a chilly, gray evening. Light traffic, an hour before the evening rush, made it a pleasant drive to the station. Snowflakes fell on the windshield and flickered through the headlight beams. They chatted about the arrangements for pickup on Sunday night and then about the upcoming weekend. As they neared the New Haven, Ellen recalled memories of her two years at Yale, and shared college experiences with Karen.

After a break in the conversation, Karen said, "Well, soon you'll be on your way. How long is the trip?"

"About five hours. I should be in Philadelphia around nine o'clock. I splurged on first class seats."

"Well, that should be nice."

"I want to relax, have a nice meal, and be ready for, as you call it, the adventure."

Minutes later they exited I95 and arrived at the train station. Ellen opened her door and Karen jumped out of the car and lifted the bags from the trunk. She placed them on the curb and put her arms around Ellen. "Knock 'em dead," she whispered.

Ellen returned the friendly squeeze. "Karen, thanks; for everything."

"Be yourself; no acting. I'll see you Sunday, around 7:30. Have fun!"

Ellen smiled and nodded. She picked up her suitcase and the smaller bag and started toward the station door amid the commotion of Friday evening travelers. She glanced over her shoulder; Karen's smiled face and gave a final wave. As Ellen continued toward the station, she raised her left arm, the one holding the small bag, up above her head, in a thank you farewell to her friend.

Ellen wove her way to the gate, recalling Jim's advice to take the train. On a snowy Friday night, the airport would be hectic; flight delays could easily be one or two hours, and possibly more. She didn't need uncertainty to add to her stress, and first class on the train cost less than an airplane coach fare.

As the attendant placed her bags on the overhead rack Ellen settled into the single, soft seat on the left-hand side of the aisle. She wanted to be alone, to think, and to use the time preparing for her important weekend encounters. Lying back on the seat she felt the push forward of the train's acceleration. White flakes raced across the window and the glowing buildings of New Haven faded away, soon replaced by the occasional lights of the countryside. The attendant asked for her choice, and then placed a small glass of white wine on the tray before her, next to small ramekin of warm nuts. After a few sips she took a deep breath. *The trip is now on. Forget school; it'll still be there on Monday. Time to get ready for what's ahead.*

She closed her eyes between sips and recalled Karen's coaching session about preparation, the key to success in any endeavor. It reminded her of her father. When she reached to take another sip she discovered a full wineglass. She leaned out over the aisle and caught the eye of the attendant, smiled, and raised the glass in a salute. With a broad smile on his face, he nodded back.

Ellen traveled only on occasion during the school year. Looking out the window at the falling snow, she applauded her choice, the alternative to a cramped center-seat on an airplane runway waiting for clearance to take off, or perhaps a cancelled flight. She would enjoy the train ride. *This first class travel isn't too hard to take.*

After half an hour she picked up the menu placed on her tray by the attendant. She reviewed the choices and selected a vegetable lasagna and salad, topped off by a chocolate chip cookie. She sat with eyes closed, opening them only to sip her wine until the meal arrived. When it did, she sat up and looked with pleasure at her choice, eyeing the chocolate chip cookie. When she finished, the attendant took her tray and raised the bottle of wine before her with a questioning look. She thought for a second, then shook her head. *They're small ones, but two is enough.* She glanced at her watch, almost seven o'clock.

Ellen closed her eyes, holding the stem of the glass as the train's gentle rocking complemented the glow of the wine and induced a feeling of contentment.

Ellen glanced up to the sail filling with wind as the boat skipped over the blue waves on a starboard tack. Across the water, a man at the tiller of another boat, like hers, tugged on the line that trimmed his sail. Behind by three or four lengths and exhilarated at the speed of pursuit, she planned to overtake him in a series of three or four more tacks. Pulling hard at the tiller her boat swung behind his into clear air; his boat covered her tack, maintaining its position. She countered again but the quick, experienced responses preserved his lead.

As Ellen planned her next maneuver, another boat crossed her bow and swung into a position ahead, between her boat and the one she trailed. A woman, somehow familiar, manned the tiller of the interloping boat. Frustrated by this new threat, Ellen struggled to determine the right response. All three boats maintained parallel tracks and consistent spacing as they approached a marker. A group of observers stood on a pier. Some watched through binoculars while others just cheered the maneuvering boats.

Ellen pushed the tiller and slid behind the two boats, ducking as the boom swung across. The woman did the same, responding to Ellen's challenge, then she turned and smiled at Ellen. Narrowing her eyes in the bright sunlight to make out the woman's features, Ellen recognized the face of Denise Suskind. With athletic, tanned arms, wearing a white cap and sunglasses, and with look of confident pleasure, Denise seemed to be in charge. Startled by the surprising sight, Ellen raised her hand to wave. Then Denise's face became unfamiliar, that of a stranger. The tiller slid from Ellen's hand and her sail aligned with the wind. Ellen's boat stalled. Helpless, looking toward the pier, Ellen's father shook his head as his eyes locked onto hers. A group of teenagers standing on the pier laughed as boats slid by Ellen, leaving her alone, out of the race.

"Miss? Miss, it's your stop!"

Through sleepy eyes Ellen asked the attendant, "Where?"

"Philadelphia, five more minutes. There'll be an announcement in about two minutes."

"What time is it?" She looked at her watch.

"Eight fifty," said the attendant.

"Thanks...for waking me up."

266

"We wouldn't let you miss your stop," he said. He reached up to the overhead rack for Ellen's bags and carried them to the front of the car.

Ellen rose and moved forward along the aisle toward the small rest room at the front of the train. She closed the heavy door, into stainless steel surroundings, and looked at the face in the mirror. *This is awful!* She recalled her first day of captivity, the scene in another bathroom as she raced to clean up. *That was worse!* She pressed the small water taps and splashed her face with hot, then cold water. She heard the sound of a click followed by the message, "Philadelphia, three minutes! Philadelphia Thirtieth Street Station, three minutes!" Opening her purse, she did the powder and lipstick, ran a comb through her hair, and turned her head from side to side to admire her work. *Not bad!*

The train slowed to a crawl while Ellen worked her way against the line of departing passengers, prepared for a quick exit. The station platform raced past the windows and the train ground to a halt to the sound of squealing brakes and the smell of metal on metal. She put on her coat, slid the purse strap over her shoulder, and stood ready to depart. As she exited the car, the attendant smiled. She returned his smile and said, "Thanks, nice trip," while handing him two folded dollar bills.

He lifted the suitcases and handed them to Ellen. "Thank you."

Ellen merged into the line of passengers, heading for the exit. Then, as she stood on the rising escalator, Ellen thought again about Karen's coaching.

Jim eased his car into the parking slot beneath the station and glanced at the digital dashboard clock, 8:45; he had a few minutes. He climbed the stairs and entered the spacious hall of Philadelphia's 30th Street Station, a historic relic of the golden age of rail. Renovation had produced a marked change from the seventies and eighties, when it had deteriorated to a sorry state. The restrooms had become an embarrassment and the place had few redeeming qualities. Now, dramatic change included a bright and clean appearance. The beautiful cavernous ceiling showed off refinished squares of gold and maroon that, along with the long, vertical chandeliers, created an impressive setting for travelers. Jim appreciated the vertical space, and variety of eating-places and shops added to the traveling experience.

Jim spotted the large clock at 8:52 and then the Status Board, showing, WASHINGTON METROLINER, ON TIME, 8:58, TRACK 4. Making his way around the line of passengers, he took a position near the top of the escalator and glanced at the clock again: 8:53. He thought about Ellen, and wondered if the events of the past few weeks created an unreal situation. *How will we react to each other? I wonder if we'll be as comfortable with each other under normal circumstances? And the kids, what will happen there?* Elise had called on Wednesday, as planned, but with little enthusiasm. Michael displayed only negative signs all week about Ellen's visit, and Tracey, a little more upbeat, but maybe just due to curiosity.

As Jim continued watching the clock, his heart took an extra beat when the status column of Ellen's train changed to the word, ARRIVED. A short time later he scanned the complement of passengers rising on the escalator and spotted her familiar face ascending toward him. She smiled and waved. Jim pressed his way through the mass of people like himself, crowding in, eager to greet their weary travelers. Ellen stepped from the escalator, jostled by the continuous flow of passengers through the limited space. Jim took the bag from her hand, drawing her into a clumsy hug. "It's great to see you!" he said.

"Me too; I mean it's good to see you, Jim."

"Right on time. How was the trip?"

"Wonderful. I rode first class."

"Oh, that's nice. I've done it a few times to Providence and Boston.

"Very relaxing; I'd do it again."

"There's something about a train."

"I found that out."

"Well let's go." He guided Ellen toward the parking garage entrance.

Ellen looked up at the ceiling. "The station used to be a mess. It looks amazing."

"It really does. Maybe on the way back we can take a little time to look around."

A short time later Ellen sat at Jim's side as he maneuvered through the garage, up the ramp, and out into the falling snow. After a few turns he merged into the traffic on the Schuylkill Expressway, a Dutch word pronounced, school kill, skookil, or skewkle, depending on the particular Philadelphian doing the pronouncing.

"I always liked that sight," Ellen said, pointing at the lights of Boathouse Row coming into view, a series of buildings along the east bank of the river owned by rowing clubs. Strings of white lights framed each, like Christmas decorations, providing a distinct Philadelphia landmark. Ellen smiled, remembering the sight from her Mayfair years. She turned her head to take in the view, looking back over her shoulder until it faded away.

"It is nice, especially in the dark with the snow falling," replied Jim.

"So, how long of a drive is it?"

"Fifteen, maybe twenty minutes. Traffic is light; you arrived at a good time. Are you hungry? We can stop."

"No thanks. I had a full meal...and then some."

After a few minutes Jim broke the silence. "Would you like to hear what we have on the docket?"

"Sure; and I have a few things to add." She glanced at Jim for a reaction, but he just nodded, and his eyes didn't leave the road.

He replied, "Okay, I'll give you my list if you give me yours."

"You first."

"Well, tonight we'll go home and just relax. I'm not sure when Michael will be there. Elise may arrive tonight or she may come in the morning. Tracey will be over to make breakfast tomorrow. We have a free afternoon and I'm taking you to a nice dinner tomorrow night. Sunday is open. You may want to take a ride or something. How does that fit?"

"I have three items. I've started running again, and I'd like to do that first thing tomorrow. Are you up to it?"

He nodded, "Yes."

"Then, in the afternoon I'd like to drive out to take a look at Mayfair School, where I taught. And I promised Annie we'd get together for coffee at five thirty. I'd like you to meet her."

"Looks like a good fit. What time do you want to run?"

"Around seven."

"Have you ever run at Valley Forge?"

"No, I've been there, but not to run; could we?"

"It's less than two miles away. We can get there, run, and be back in an hour."

"Sounds like fun. I remember some hills."

"It's a nice jog. You'll lose me without trying. I usually run near the house, but you'll like the park better. Now, what about Mayfair?"

"I'd just like to walk around and see how it changed; maybe look in the windows. I'll tell you about the time I spent there. Someone may be around, but I haven't contacted the school about coming over. If it had been a weekday, I would have."

"We can go after lunch."

"What time is dinner?"

"Eight o'clock." .

"We could go into Philadelphia and meet Annie after Mayfair for coffee at the White Dog Café."

"If we're back by seven, we'll be fine."

"It's a full schedule. I think Sunday should be a relax day."

"How about a late breakfast and read the paper."

"Perfect."

"What time is your return train?"

"Two thirty; I wanted to get home at a reasonable hour. Monday morning it's back to school."

Ellen saw the green sign with the words, Conshohocken, 2 Miles. "Must be getting close," she said.

"We're almost there," Jim replied. After exiting the expressway he wound through a number of quiet, wooded, and hilly roads. When he pulled into a driveway, Jim said, "9:25; we made great time."

Ellen swung the car door open and stepped out into the crisp air. A pair of lights next to the front door illuminated the drive and lawn revealing an inch of new fallen snow. Jim climbed a few brick stairs and dropped her suitcases in front of the entrance. He turned the key, and bumped the door open with his hip. He stepped inside and flicked on a light. "Come on in."

After she stepped through the door, to the right, the entrance hall opened to a large room that caught her attention. Jim took her coat and guided her to a sofa into the living room lit with a few soft lights. Before she could react he struck a long match and placed the flame into a stack of wood, lighting it in several places. When flames began to char the wood, Jim stood up "Would you like anything to drink?"

"Decaf coffee, if you have it."

"Make yourself comfortable," he said, "I'll be back in a minute."

Large impressionist paintings hung at each end of the room, and another over the fireplace. She sat in the farther of the two small sofas, at right angles to the fireplace, separated by a coffee table. A few soft chairs filled the corners of the room. Ellen's gaze locked on a shelf of photographs. She looked to be Ellen's age, perhaps a little younger, with thin features and a beautiful oval face framed by long, dark hair. She wore a black sweater with a single strand of pearls, and stared back with a faint smile, like the *Mona Lisa. What a beautiful woman!* Ellen shook her head. *And what a tragedy; I wonder what she was like?*

Ellen walked closer to the shelf and turned her attention to several other photographs of Jim, his wife, and the three children. The oldest, a girl, the image of her mother, while the younger daughter resembled Jim. The youngest, a boy, had facial features that blended the looks of both parents. In another picture, Jim and the three children leaned against a log with an orange sunset in the background. Ellen's eyes returned to the woman. She thought of Karen's words, be yourself. After two minutes in her house, this beautiful and haunting ghost, whose smile seemed to signify a dare, confronted Ellen with an intimidating presence.

Jim rounded the corner carrying a tray and placed it on the table. "Sit down and enjoy the fire." Ellen returned to her seat and Jim sat across from her, in the other sofa.

The flickering flames and dim lights created a cozy atmosphere and the aroma of burning wood added to the setting. "What a lovely room, Jim! I love fireplaces."

"So do I. I noticed you were looking at the photos."

"Yes. You have a good-looking family. "She paused and then continued, "That picture is striking. She was beautiful, Jim."

Jim looked at the gallery of photos and nodded. "That, she was."

They sipped coffee and chatted. Jim described his work and family and Ellen recalled her days living in the Philadelphia area. During a quiet lapse, the sound of an opening door interrupted the silence, followed by the call of a male voice, "I'm home!"

"It's Michael," Jim said.

A female voice added, "Me, too!"

Jim turned to Ellen and said, "and Elise". Then he looked back over his shoulder and called, "Come on in!"

Ellen watched over Jim's shoulder, while the sounds of footsteps and the closing of closet doors completed the announcement of their arrival. *Here goes!*

Elise entered first glanced at Ellen, for just a second, then said "Hi, Daddy!" A few quick steps and she hugged her father.

Michael turned the corner. "Hey!"

Jim released his daughter and held her by one hand, waving Michael toward him, "Elise, Michael, I'd like you to meet Ellen Cramwell."

Ellen rose and extended her hand and said "hello," first to Elise and then to Michael. The teenagers each shook her hand and replied with a nod and hi.

"So how did you two get together?" Jim asked.

Elise replied, "When I called Michael about coming home he said he'd be at Bob's; so I picked him up."

"When did you leave Princeton?" Jim asked.

"I caught a train about five. Tammy picked me up; we hung out for a while, and then had something to eat. You weren't here when I came home to get my car."

"Tammy and Elise were inseparable in high school," Jim said, turning to Ellen. "How is Tammy?" he asked Elise.

"Same as usual; another boyfriend, four point oh grades, starting on the volley ball team."

"Where does Tammy go to school?" Ellen asked.

"Penn," replied Elise. Then she said, "I'm tired, Dad. Do you mind if I go up?"

Ellen watched Jim's reaction, "No, go ahead," he said.

"I think I'll go up, too," Michael said.

Ellen thought of the phrase, they had broken the ice. Now she felt the coolness on the other side. *I wish they were second graders.*

After Elise and Michael left, Ellen sensed Jim's discomfort with their rapid departure. She yawned to give her own signal. "Jim, it's been a long day. It must be after eleven o'clock. I could use some sleep. Don't forget, seven tomorrow we'll be running."

"You're right. Let me show you your room, and then I'll come down and lock up."

After taking out a nightgown from her suitcase Ellen noticed several photographs on the shelves of a hutch, all pictures of Tracey. In the first she sat on horseback, facing the camera with confidence; the second with another girl, dressed in 1920s costumes, a picture that would have been taken at an amusement park. In the third she held a diploma and wore a college graduation gown and beamed with a broad smile. In the last picture she stood against a railing with her mother. Tracey seemed to be about thirteen or fourteen, and a small note said, Vacation '87. *I was just starting at Mayfair.* She'd have to face Tracey tomorrow.

Ellen took the clock from the nightstand and set the alarm for 6:30. She changed into her nightgown, picked up her cosmetic case and opened the door. In the dim hallway, a small night-light glowed near the floor and a sliver of light escaped under the door at the far end of the hall; she heard voices. She found the bathroom door on her left and turned on the light. Afterward she opened the door, peeked out, and started back toward her room. On her left, as she crossed the stairway opening, she saw Jim rising up the stairs, halfway to the top. Startled, her eyes met his. She stood still, watching as he rose toward her.

Jim took Ellen's hand and he led her into her room. He swung the door in a slow, quiet arc while holding the brass handle down. After the door closed he allowed the·handle to rise in a soft, click. Ellen placed her cosmetic bag on the bed and stood with arms at her sides, facing Jim. He walked to her and placed his hands on her shoulders, then slid them down and under her arms, and eased her into his. The gentle scent of her hair and then of her perfume, and the feel of her soft cotton nightgown, like magnets, almost intoxicating. It had been a long time.

Ellen spoke first, drawing a sharp breath, "Jim, this is dangerous. We shouldn't do this. What if they come out into the hall?"

He brushed her cheek with his, and brought her lips to hers, one soft kiss; he could taste the mint on her lips. She didn't resist. He wanted to continue, but knew she was right. He whispered. "I didn't plan this. I just found it hard not to seize the opportunity."

As Jim's hands pressed against her back. Between deep breaths, Ellen said in a soft voice, "Let's not threaten them any more than they already are. You don't know how much I don't want to stop, but not now."

He slid his hand down the curve of her back to her hips, along the softness of her body. "You're right," he replied, opening his arms and releasing her. "But I want you to know, this is a struggle for me." He stepped back and turned out the light. Then he opened the door a crack, peeked out, and looked at her over his shoulder; he closed the door and stepped into the hallway. After a few soft paces on the carpet runner he turned and waved. Ellen returned the wave and touched the index finger of her right hand to her lips, then disappeared behind the closing door.

In the dark room, Ellen's deep, quick breathing gave way to a calmness and feeling of mild ecstasy. A dim light shined through the mullions of a colonial style window. Imagining where it might have gone, she listened for signs of activity. Hearing none, and still excited by the brief encounter, she walked to the window and raised it few inches. She knelt and inhaled the cool air that rushed in through the opening.

After a while she climbed into the bed and pulled up the comforter to her chin. Her feelings hadn't diminished nor had his. And his restraint pleased her. Or did it? She remembered her feeling the instant after he had turned out the light and before he opened the door. *I thought he was...*

She closed her eyes, reviewing her day's activities: Karen's counseling, the train trip, the station, and the cool reception from Jim's kids. Her thoughts lingered on the pleasure of the past few minutes. It had been a long day.

His questions about how they would react to each other were answered. Jim stopped at the door to Elise's room. He couldn't hear their specific words, but guessed the subject. Raising his hand he started to knock, but halfway through the motion he stopped, dropped his hand, turned and placed it on the door handle to his room, and closed the door behind him.

Encountering Ellen in the hall and whisking her into the bedroom made him feel like a kid, hiding from his parents; it aroused a sense of excitement he had not felt in this house for many years. He wanted her, but Ellen was right. She wanted them to accept her. An embarrassing situation could have occurred, stressing out everyone. He admired Ellen's words of concern, the threat to Elise and Michael. She had the presence and the sense to disengage. *What would I have done if she hadn't?* Now he needed to find a way to dissolve the tension in the household and let them see Ellen as he did; but he knew it wouldn't be easy. And he had to, go slow.

Jim climbed into bed with thoughts racing through his head. He stretched his leg and back muscles and took deep breaths to clear his mind. The image of running with Ellen in the morning emerged. In a few minutes he fell asleep.

—12—

Ellen reached for the glowing dial, where the morning greeting said 6:30. She tapped the top of the clock. The buzzing stopped and she lay back on the pillow with eyes closed. *Five more minutes.* It seemed like a minute and the sound returned. She rolled over and pressed the alarm switch, then climbed out of bed. A gray morning peeked into the room from around the window shades. Ellen raised a shade and looked out at new, thin layer of fresh snow hanging on trees and covering the yard. *This should be fun.*

In a few minutes, dressed in her running clothes, Ellen started down the stairs. The aroma of coffee greeted her as she reached the first floor. When she walked into the kitchen, Jim sipped from one mug; another mug, empty, sat on the counter near the coffeepot.

"Good morning," he said. "Sleep well?"

"Yes I did. How are you? Do you always get up this early?"

"Only for special visitors. Actually, I'd be up by seven-thirty or eight on a typical weekend."

She filled the mug and took a sip. "Umm! This is good! Ready to go?"

"Take it with you," Jim said, starting toward the door.

Sipping coffee while Jim drove, Ellen spoke little along the way. Snow muffled the road sounds of the car as it wound through a number of turns on a traffic-free road. A flock of Canadian Geese passed overhead in a lazy V, honking their mutual encouragement. After short time the car crossed a bridge and entered the park.

Ellen gazed out onto the patches of wooded areas amid a great expanse of open, hilly grassland and remarked, "Here already? What a beautiful morning!"

"I thought you'd like this," Jim replied.

He parked the car on a hill near the Memorial Arch, smaller replica of the Arc de Triomphe in Paris, and a monument to the encampment at Valley Forge. Ellen and Jim started their warm-up schemes, stretching and loosening muscles. After a few minutes Ellen asked, "Which way?"

"Follow me." Jim started down the hill at a slow trot. "And feel free to leave me behind whenever you'd like."

Nodding she moved to his side. Their shoes beat in concert on the fluffy snow as they trotted down a gradual, tree-lined slope. They passed a few of the historic markers that identified officers and their brigades, participants in the historic winter encampment called the crucible of the revolution, a test of the fledgling nation's will. They approached a series of small log cabins alongside the road, fortifications and cannons on the other side. Condensed breaths spilled from Ellen's lips as she remarked, "I can't believe the park is so empty. I haven't seen anyone."

"It'll pick up a little later," Jim replied between short puffs.

Ellen glanced at her watch at intervals and noticed Jim doing the same. When they turned a gradual bend in the sloping road, a sight appeared that caused them both to stop. A doe and three small fawns stood just a short distance off the road. In a classic pose, the animals turned their gazes toward the runners. "They're beautiful!" Ellen said, in a low voice.

"Lots of them around here," he whispered back. They slowed to a walk, watching the deer. "There's a movement to hunt them, there are so many."

"No!" exclaimed Ellen. "The poor animals!"

"All of the building around here is consuming open space. Ten years ago you never saw them during the day, and only on occasion, at night. Now, it's common to see them at any time."

The deer started to move, first at a slow pace and then faster. Jim and Ellen resumed their run as the deer continued, parallel to the road; then the deer made a sharp turn across the path, in front of Jim and Ellen to the other side of the road.

"Their speed is amazing," she said. "And they're so graceful. Look at those little ones." When she glanced over at Jim and noticed the smile on his face she said, "This must be old hat to you."

"No; I always like to see the deer; but it's more fun with you, to see your reaction, too."

The deer raced across the field toward a wooded area, almost out of sight. Ellen picked up her pace. Jim kept up, but after a while he looked at his watch once more and slowed down, "You go ahead, this is where I turn back."

"Okay. I need another five or ten minutes."

"Be careful!" he called. "The hills might be slippery!"

Ellen smiled. She liked his concern; he sounded like a parent. With a wave, she ran off; Jim turned and started back up the hill.

Jim stopped to observe Ellen glide away. His heartbeat, already strained by the run, increased at the sight of her slim hips, and her dark hair, bouncing with each graceful stride. He liked the excitement she added to his life, and recalled their chance confrontation the previous night. When she disappeared over a hill, he resumed his trudge, upward toward the arch. *What will breakfast be like? Not as bad as last night, I hope.* Ellen's acceptance by Elise and Michael needed work, and he wondered about Tracey's attitude toward Ellen, still unclear.

After ten minutes Jim puffed to a stop back at the Memorial Arch. He looked back down the path, straining for a sight of Ellen on her return. He walked under the arch and then once around at a slow pace to cool down. Then he began to pace in nervous steps, looking out toward where he expected her to appear. Ellen had been abducted while running and Bartles was still out there. *How could I have left her alone? What if he was tracking her? He had done it before.*

Jim started back down the hill again along the path of their run; his pace increased to a trot and then to running speed. He hit an icy patch, slipped, and tried to regain his balance; reeling like a slapstick comic he stopped short of falling and stopped. His pulse pounded as he tried to gather his composure from the near fall. Then a bouncing head appeared over the hill. After a sigh of relief he took several deep breaths and started back up the hill.

He stood at the top of the hill, watching Ellen's approaching image grow. He nodded in admiration as she closed her run with a last surge, an athletic sprint of expended energy; and then, at his side gasping for breath, she bent over with hands on her knees. Jim asked, "How was it?"

"Terrific! I'm getting back in shape." Ellen raised to a standing position and took a few steps.

"You looked great to me."

"A challenge, especially the uphill part. I saw a fox! It was lovely, bouncing through the snow. I stood and watched for a while."

"You don't see too many of them," Jim said.

"This has been a real communion with nature. I'm glad we came here, Jim."

"We'll do it again." Then, starting toward the car Jim asked, "Hungry?"

"Yes; I guess I am. But can we take a look around at the arch?"

"Sure."

They walked around the monument, while Ellen read the inscriptions. When she finished and walked toward him, he extended his arm and they locked gloved hands. "This has been fun," she said.

"Glad you liked it. I thought you would." He removed his key ring from his pocket and pressed the black button on the remote lock control. A soft beep and two blinks of the car lights signaled, doors unlocked.

When they reached the car, she turned to him. Before he could react she kissed him quickly on the lips, then pulled back and reached for the car door, a broad smile on her face. "I'm starved," she said.

He saw her gesture, a pleasant surprise, as another signal of the comfort in their relationship. Overcoming his first reaction, to reach out and take her in his arms, Jim smiled and squeezed her hand as she climbed into the front seat.

After a shower, refreshed, Ellen reached the bottom of the stairs with hair in a ponytail, wearing just a little lipstick. Her usual Saturday outfit, designed for comfort, consisted of blue jeans, a white turtleneck, a dark blue sweater, and loafers. At the end of the hall she found the kitchen. White walls, flowered tiles, beige natural cabinets, and modern appliances extended an invitation to enter. Large windows on three sides allowed in natural light and looked out on the snowfall, adding to the appeal of the room. A woman with her back to Ellen and wearing black slacks and a green sweatshirt worked at a counter. The woman raised her head and turned at the sound of Ellen's footstep to say "Hi."

The face, with the same quizzical smile, stopped Ellen in her tracks; her jaw dropped and her tongue floundered for a response. After a noticeable delay she responded, "Hi; I'm Ellen."

The woman extended her hand and said, "Tracey."

Ellen found herself staring at Tracey as she grasped Tracey's hand. She had lost her mother but had captured her looks, the dark hair and bright eyes, and that beautiful smile. Ellen blurted out, "You look just like your mother; the picture!" Then Ellen regained her composure, and realizes she still held Tracey's hand. She released it with embarrassment.

Tracey replied with a smile, "That's a compliment, you know."

Ellen paused, thinking for the right words, then replied, "I'm sure it is."

Tracey turned back to her work and said over her shoulder, "Want to help?"

"Have to earn my keep," Ellen replied. "What do you need? And what's for breakfast?"

"Pancakes." While she continued her preparations, Tracey pointed to the cabinets and drawers and enlisted Ellen in setting the table and pouring the juice.

Ellen felt good to be busy. *That wasn't so bad.*

While Ellen completed her chores Tracey asked, "Where were you this morning?"

"Running at Valley Forge Park. It was wonderful!"

"Dad usually runs around the neighborhood. I'm always after him to go to the park."

Ellen set five glasses on the counter and reached for the container of orange juice. She began to reply to Tracey's comment when Jim entered. "What are you ladies up to?" he asked.

"Pancakes; and Canadian bacon from Farmers' Market."

"I didn't know we were having health food," he replied.

Ellen laughed at the comment and Jim continued, "I'll get the paper." After a few quick steps the door closed behind him.

"He's in good spirits," Tracey said, then, "I wonder why?" with that smile again.

Self-conscious over her blushing, Ellen didn't look up but continued pouring the juice. *She sure has her father's impish sense of humor.*

After he came in, Jim asked, "Are we ready?"

Tracey replied, "Just about. You can call them."

Jim walked to the stairs and called out, "Elise! Michael! Breakfast!"

After a short wait, Michael replied, "I'm coming, I'm coming!"

Then Elise, "I'll be right down!"

After several minutes Ellen heard their footsteps on the stairs. "Good morning Michael, Elise," she said. Michael replied with a "hey" and Elise with a "hi."

Ellen sat across from Tracey and next to Jim, who sat at the head of the table. Michael took a seat next to Tracey, on one side of the table and Elise accepted the remaining place next to Ellen. Eyes turned to Jim, who seemed prepared to say something. With his hands on his lap he started, "Thanks for our family, a lovely morning, a great breakfast, and new friendships."

Tracey smiled and nodded at Ellen, who replied in a soft voice, "Amen."

Michael had three pancakes on his plate before anyone could move; Jim shook his head and shrugged, smiling at Ellen.

Pancakes were an uncommon item in Ellen's diet. A taste of Pecans made these different, and she remarked "These are good, Tracey. Great idea!"

"Hang around here long enough and you'll find all kinds of things in your pancakes," Tracey replied. "I mean good things." Then she asked, "So, what are you and Dad doing today?"

Ellen recited the agenda, noticing that Michael and Elise seemed to take an interest in the schedule.

"You'll be busy," Tracey said.

Tracey's attitude surprised Ellen. She didn't know why, but she had expected her to be the hardest; not true, so far. But the other two were like clams; Ellen had to figure out how to open them.

During breakfast, Ellen's questions directed at Michael and at Elise met with short responses. They seemed unwilling to extend themselves. After a while Ellen felt her efforts becoming forced. She decided her skills at communicating with teenagers were just as much of a problem. Soon, knives and forks rested on syrup stained dishes.

Tracey announced, "I know Dad wants to read the paper," and then nodded to Ellen, "and the kitchen crew is going for a walk." She finished with, "You two can clean up."

As Michael and Elise groaned in response, Tracey stood and said, "Come on Ellen, I'll show you the neighborhood."

Ellen glanced at Jim's open mouth, evidence of his astonishment. An encouraged Ellen, answered "Let me put on my boots, and I'm ready to go." She rose and headed for the stairs.

Jim's surprise turned to relief. He whispered to his daughter, "Nice idea, Tracey."

Then Tracey turned from Michael to Elise, and whispered, "Hey guys, let's lighten up. You're scaring her."

Before Tracey's comment, Jim planned to say something. He started to offer his view, but then stopped. *Tracey's doing fine. No piling on!*

Ellen tugged on her boots, pleased by the breakthrough, at least on one front. Her kitchen time started the process moving. Now she would have an opportunity for a private conversation with Tracey, someone she could deal with, given half a chance. Ellen pulled on her blue stocking cap and zipped her windbreaker and then started down the stairs with a bouncing step. She stopped on the fourth step, for some unknown reason recalling her mother's lesson and constant reprimand, 'Walk, Ellen; don't bounce.' She continued at a, ladylike, pace toward Tracey, who stood at the front door, again with her mother's smile, looking up at Ellen.

They walked up the drive and then began a slow uphill climb along the quiet street, making fresh tracks along the edge of the road in the fresh, powdery snow. The neighborhood had a beautiful, wooded setting. Ellen asked, "How long have you, or your family been here?"

"About eighteen years. We moved here right after Elise was born."

"It's so peaceful."

"Yes. It was fun growing up here. Lots of neighborhood kids. It was like a big compound. I live about half an hour away; I come over a lot to visit with Dad."

The conversation moved from Tracey talking about growing up in the neighborhood to Ellen's description of her ordeal in the Adirondacks. Then to Tracey's job as a financial analyst. When they reached the bottom of a steep hill Tracey advised, "This is the halfway point; now it's uphill for a couple of streets."

Halfway to the first intersection Tracey asked, "Dad said you're a teacher; which grade?"

"Second."

"Must be fun."

"Yes, it is. I really like the kids at that age."

Before Ellen could continue Tracey asked, "Any children of you own?"

"No, not yet."

"Have you been married?" asked Tracey.

The two bold questions surprised Ellen. "No, I haven't." Now, the pleasant walk and Tracey's efforts gave Ellen the impetus to share her concerns. "I'm having trouble connecting with Michael and Elise. Teenagers are not my strength," she said.

They continued up the hill in silence, approaching the crest of the hill. Then Tracey answered, "Michael and Elise, had a hard time dealing with Mom's death."

"You must have, too."

"Yes, but I was older. It was hard, though; she was a special person. Has Dad talked to you about her?"

"Not really; no details, just a few essentials."

"They wanted to have more children, but she had problems. It must have been early stages of her illness." After a short pause, Tracey continued, "She was only 33 when it was diagnosed."

"Tell me about her, please."

"Dad fell in love with her before he knew about me. I was four when they met. He had a hard time dealing with it. I remember Mom said, at first he couldn't handle the immediate family."

"So, what happened?"

"He came to the house, to Mom's party when she graduated from college. That's when I first saw him. Afterwards I told her I wanted him to be my Daddy, but Mom said he was just a friend." Tracey paused and they continued along for a few minutes, nothing said.

"So, what happened?"

Tracey laughed. "You're persistent. Mom said he fell in love with me, too. They got married the next summer. I was a little bridesmaid, five years old."

Ellen replied, "What a lovely story!"

"It is, isn't it? It was wonderful; I had a father. He adopted me a year later and Elise was born two years after that, then Michael two years later. It was great having a brother and sister."

A silence followed as they climbed another hill. Tracey seemed to be searching for words, and Ellen decided to let her proceed at her own rate. Tracey's age was deceiving. Under different circumstances, she could have been a teaching colleague, or perhaps a good friend. And her maturity, it must have been strengthened by the two tragedies of her life. *What an admirable girl!*

After they reached the top and started down a long winding hill, Tracey picked up the conversation again. "It was wonderful after that. We went so many places and were always doing things together. Mom was the planner, always wanting to do family things. Dad figured out how to get there. Then Mom got sick. We denied it at first. I couldn't get used to the idea that she'd never get well. Dad prepared us, as well as he could, for the inevitable. It was still hard to believe when it finally happened. She was so young."

"Tracey, I'm so sorry. You must have been very close to her."

"Each of us was, in our own way; but I think I had a special link. We were alone, together. You know what I mean? Until Dad came along."

"I know. There's a special bond when you share a hardship."

Tracey stopped and turned to Ellen, "You know, Dad has never brought a woman into the house before. That's what's unique, here. He wouldn't invite you for a weekend if you were just any, I guess the word is, Jane."

"Be careful, that's my mother's name," responded Ellen, grinning.

Elise smiled. "Sorry. You get the picture. The fact that you're here means something; at least to him."

This put the situation in perspective. She replied, "And to me, Tracey he's not just any, Joe. They both chuckled at the analogy.

"I'm pretty fussy," continued Ellen. Then after a few seconds she added, "I'd think women would be all over him."

"Not as many as you think. Having three children has been a deterrent. Look at my Dad, he was almost scared away by me. You should be terrified; there are three of us for you to deal with."

"Tracey, I've thought about myself as a threat to each of you and to all of you, as a family."

"It's the fear of the unknown, I guess," replied Tracey. "We've grown comfortable having Dad to ourselves, and now it could be changing. And it might seem that, somehow, Mom is being forgotten."

Ellen thought for a few seconds and then said, "I can't compete with her, Tracey. That's a contest nobody can win. She occupies a part of you that no one can touch."

They walked along, saying no more as they approached the Dulles' house. Ellen spoke again, "Thanks, Tracey. I enjoyed our talk, and getting to know you. Maybe we can do it again sometime."

When they turned at the top of the driveway Tracey stopped and extended her hand. Ellen took the cue, accepted Tracey's grasp and turned to her as Tracey said, "Ellen; there's one more thing." Ellen waited for the next words, and then Tracey finished her thought. "You're only about ten years older than I am. I always wanted a big sister. If some day you and Dad get together, I'd like to think of you that way."

What a powerful statement! It made Ellen tingle. She had come further in just a short time than she ever could have expected or hoped for with Tracey. Truly, this beautiful young woman would be more like a sister than she would a daughter. Tracey had turned the age situation around, showing Ellen that she wanted to reach out, to end the threat. With a lump in her throat Ellen said, "Tracey, I was an only child. You don't know how nice it is of you to say that." Their eyes met, Tracey took a step toward her. Then, at the top of the driveway, standing in the cold winter morning air, they each extend their arms and came together in a warm embrace.

Jim looked up from his newspaper at the sight of Tracey and Ellen turning from the road into the driveway. He rose and started toward the door, watching through the window as they started down the shallow hill. His curiosity aroused by Tracey's initiative and Ellen's willing reaction, Jim wanted to greet them and to hear about their talk. When he saw them turn toward each other and embrace, he hesitated. *Not a time to disturb them.* He returned to his chair, buried his face in the newspaper and waited for the door to open.

He heard their voices and then the jiggling of a key. When the door opened, Jim looked up, "How was the walk?" He almost said, the talk.

"Great!" Ellen replied with a smile on pink cheeks.

"Nice day; refreshing," commented Tracey. Then she said, "Dad, I hope you don't mind, but I have to leave in a little while."

"No, I understand. I'm glad you could make it for breakfast, and got to meet Ellen."

"We had a nice talk," Tracey said, glancing at Ellen.

While removing her windbreaker, Ellen replied, "Yes, we did." Then, she smiled at Jim along with an, almost, imperceptible nod.

"Good," Jim replied. He waited for elaboration, but neither Tracey nor Ellen offered any. He decided not to probe. As Ellen started up the stairs he asked, "So, are you ready for a drive over to Mayfair?"

"Sure give me a few minutes."

Jim followed Ellen up the stairs. When she turned left at the top, he turned right. He stopped at Elise's door and knocked.

The door opened. "Hi, Dad," Elise said.

"Where's Michael?"

"He's at Bob's."

"What are you planning today?"

"Tammy is home for the weekend, so we're getting together."

"Will we see you this evening? You can bring her over."

"No, I don't think so. We're going to a movie, and it'll be late."

"Well, Ellen and I will be out for the afternoon, and then for dinner tonight. But let's make sure we get together tomorrow, before Ellen leaves."

Elise's replied with a passive, "Sure."

A short time later, after Tracey drove off, Jim and Ellen left for Mayfair. Along the way, Jim listened to Ellen relate her experiences at Mayfair as a new teacher. He looked for an opportunity to switch to the subject of Ellen's walk with Tracey; but none arose, so he stayed with Ellen's line of thought.

"Sounds like you enjoyed those years," Jim said.

"Yes, I became an adult; on my own, free, learning the business. And there's no better place than Mayfair to do that."

"Tell me about Dr. Suskind."

"She was a whirlwind, and a terror, but not in an intimidating way; no ranting and raving, and she never belittled or criticized her staff openly. She just had the highest goals and wouldn't accept less. And somehow, her charges elevated their standards to her level. She'd raise money that nobody thought she could, and get, I guess you'd call them, big hitters to donate and become associated with her school. She always challenged the staff, and she invited speakers and educators who were out on the leading edge of their professions to give talks and seminars. She had a powerful influence on my formative years. It was exciting, and it made me believe all schools were like that."

"But you found otherwise."

"Well, yes. Talking to teachers from other schools and districts I was appalled by some of their stories. I had to suppress my own experiences and just listen. I would have embarrassed them if I told them about Mayfair. It made me feel lucky to be there." Ellen paused.

"But?"

"No, not really any buts. It was my first job; I couldn't have done better. And the money wasn't important to me; I appreciated the freedom to explore and learn. I guess it may have been different if it was a breadwinner job. The pay was adequate, and most of the young teachers, like me, treated it as a boot camp. Some older ones worked part time and used it as a gateway back into the workforce. She had a few full-time staff, associates who helped start Mayfair and they probably did better from a financial standpoint. But most of her older teachers were from two income families and could get by."

"So, what prompted you to leave?"

"After five years I learned a lot, and the changes each year were becoming incremental. I started to prepare myself for a move. One day I mentioned it to my parents and my Dad swung into action; hence, Ethan A."

"Nice story. You know, at Mayfair you were only a few miles away from where we live."

"I've thought about that."

So had Jim. After a short silence, he replied, "I wonder if we were ever closer than that?"

"What do you mean?" Ellen looked at him with a puzzled stare.

He continued his thought, "In the same place at the same time; at the same event, movie, or shopping center; or at the same intersection."

"Jim, you certainly have an imagination! That's another interesting thought. We could have met then, when you..."

He picked up, "were married and had a family."

"Yes. I wonder how that would have felt."

"Now you're getting it. Let's put that on the conversation list." Jim spotted the Mayfair sign and guided the car into the drive.

Ellen began to formulate possible instances where she might have met Jim. *I wonder if...*but the driveway onto the campus brought her back to thoughts of Mayfair, to that first trip up this same drive on a beautiful spring day. Her thoughts accelerated through the five years, then to Ethan A, the encounter with Jim, and to the present. She ended her reverie when the car stopped.

They took a short walk around the campus, romping in the snow like children.

"Remember the term, good packing?" Jim said.

"Yes."

When Jim reached down she anticipated his move. She dodged the snowball, retaliating with one of her own and then ran away from his next. Standing at a distance, she watched while he made a third snowball; but this time he dropped on the ground and began to roll it in the snow. Ellen picked up the hint and started one of her own. After a short while they had the makings of a snowman, and stood back to admire their creation.

"I haven't done that in a while," Ellen said.

"Either have I; used to build them all the time when the kids were small."

Then Ellen started to take careful steps in the unspoiled snow behind the snowman as Jim watched. When she finished, the message said, ELLEN CRAMWELL WAS HERE!

"Maybe Dr. Suskind will see this on Monday," Ellen said. She stepped again through the letters from the exclamation point to the first E, taking care not to destroy the message. Then, after a small jump away from her sign, to preserve identity of the E, she walked around to the snowman. Looking back to admire her sign Ellen said, "She may be upset that I didn't call her about coming. Maybe I should erase it."

"No! Give her a call on Monday and explain. Once she hears your story, I'm sure she'll forgive you."

"She probably read about it already. But you're right, I should call her."

On the way back to Jim's car he reached for her gloved hand, and she tucked it inside his. "This was fun," she said.

Inside the car they shared a soft kiss, and Jim asked, "How about something hot to drink?"

"You read my mind."

At a small restaurant near the school, Ellen ordered hot chocolate and Jim had coffee; they shared a club sandwich. They drove to Philadelphia, took a short walk on the Parkway, and spent a few hours at the Art Museum. Afterward, they headed for to West Philadelphia to meet Annie, as planned.

Annie, wearing a black turtleneck sweater and jeans, sat at a small table near a back window. With an animated movement of an actress, she rose to greet Ellen. Her light hair and bright eyes caught Jim's attention; he had pictured her differently.

"So you're Jim!" Annie said.

"So you're Annie!" Jim replied.

"So I'm Ellen!" They all laughed.

Jim and Annie clicked instantly. Annie seemed a perfect best friend for Ellen; he could see how she and Ellen fit together so well. The conversation started with the excitement of Ellen's past month, her health, back to school, and then to the weekend with Jim. Annie got a few barbs into Reardon along the way. It switched to Annie's acting career, which seemed to be on the rise, a lead in an Arbor production and a small Broadway role later in the spring. The time passed quickly; laughs seemed to be the order of the day.

After a while, Ellen looked at her watch. "Time to go, Annie; but first I have to visit the powder room."

Anticipating the usual, me too, from Ellen, Jim expected them to leave together to compare notes. But when Ellen rose from her chair, Annie didn't respond to the implied invitation. Jim sensed Ellen's hesitation; Annie said nothing and didn't move. Then, with a questioning look, Ellen walked away.

After Ellen turned the corner Annie looked straight at Jim and said, with stage presence, "So you're Jim!"

He laughed again. "This feels like a rehearsal," he said. Then, "Line!"

She smiled and said, "Jim, you're okay."

He responded with, "I'll bet you say that to all the guys."

"Not all of Ellen's guys."

"Oh? Just some of them?"

"None. I've never talked to any of them like this."

"You seemed pretty tough on Reardon; and you knew him before Ellen did. You must have talked to him about her."

Annie seemed to consider Jim's remark, then said, "Ellen asked about Kevin and I arranged for her to meet him. I didn't know him very well then. We were in a few classes together; he had a reputation as good time guy. After a while, as their relationship evolved, it became clear that Ellen was in over her head. It found it hard to keep my mouth shut, but she needed to make her own decision. Too many of them had been made for her. I was glad when she broke it off. I think she's more careful now, more particular. She's a wonderful person, Jim; take care of her."

Annie's candor disarmed Jim; after a few seconds he replied, "I'd like to do just that. But she does seem so cautious."

Annie nodded. "It's your family, Jim. This is hard for her. She had hopes for a fairy tale marriage, and bringing up her own children. You have three already. It's a little overwhelming."

"She can still have children," he said.

"But she can't ignore yours, and Ellen could never be comfortable if they resented her. She tells me that, your wife...Gail, must have been wonderful."

Jim digested Annie's comments. He could relate to Ellen's fears. He remembered his own feeling of panic when he first learned about Tracey. But Tracey was one little girl, and he had time to get to know her during her formative years, when she needed a father. Ellen faced a different situation, three grown children with memories of a wonderful mother, and the challenge of building relationships with them.

He picked up on Annie's comment. "She really was." Then he said, "I think Ellen made some progress with my oldest daughter, Tracey today."

"How's that?"

"They went for a walk. I think they got along well."

"How old is Tracey?"

"She's almost twenty-six."

Annie reacted as if it were a cue. "She could be Ellen's sister!" Then, she wrinkled her face and said, "Oops! Sorry."

Annie's red face turned downward at the table. "So, you're Annie!" he said.

Annie looked up. "Line!" she said.

Ellen left the table expecting to have a powder room chat with Annie. It would be the only opportunity to talk alone with her friend, but she chose not to take the hint. Now returning, she spotted them laughing, and engaged in conversation.

"What have you two been up to?" Ellen asked.

Jim stood and said, "We've been solving the problems of mankind."

"In five minutes?" Ellen replied.

Annie chimed in "We only solved half of them."

Then Jim, "We're saving the other half for next time."

They roared at the ad-lib humor while Ellen watched. She didn't have to wonder about Annie's opinion of Jim. "Who writes this stuff for you two?" she said.

Jim and Annie looked at each other and simultaneously said, "Line!" followed by more laughs.

Ellen found the friendly interaction between Annie and Jim both amusing and puzzling. Although Annie had introduced Ellen to Kevin, she had never shared a friendship with him. With Jim, she seemed to have established one already. Her best friend liked this guy, a nice feeling.

Ellen agreed to call Annie when she returned to Connecticut, and to bring Jim to see Annie at the Arbor Theater in a production called, *Give Me a Break!* The title fit her well.

In the street, Annie and Jim shared a short hug, and then Annie and Ellen, a long one. After good-byes, when Jim turned onto the expressway, Ellen turned to him and said, "Annie was blushing when I came back. She never blushes. You two must have gotten into some interesting topics."

"Yes, we did," he replied. Silence.

Ellen noticed the teasing smile. She decided not to ask, but to play his game, and just looked ahead at the weaving cars leaving Philadelphia.

After a few minutes Jim started to feel self-conscious. How could he tell her? It might threaten her more. The silence grew thicker. He started to squirm and then the pressure of his thought won out, and he released it. "We were talking about Tracey; when I told her Tracey's age, Annie said Tracey could be your sister."

"She said that? No wonder she turned red!"

"Then she apologized and we started laughing. That's when you came back."

"Jim," she said, "Annie's right. Tracey and I talked about the same thing."

"You did?"

"Yes, we had a nice talk. She's quite a girl,...young woman."

"You talked about your ages?"

"No, but Tracey came to the same realization that Annie did, but without the blushing. Tracey said, if you and I got together, she'd like to think of me as a big sister."

"I knew you two had a nice conversation, but it was deeper than I thought. How did you react?" He glanced back and forth from the windshield to her eyes, waiting for her response.

Ellen placed her hand on his arm. He removed his left hand from the wheel, reached across, and covered hers. Then Ellen replied, "I said, I always wanted a sister."

Jim gazed ahead. What could he say? Nothing; he caressed her hand and then gave a gentle squeeze.

That evening Jim made an effort to recapture their Yellow Day experience with a quiet dinner at a country inn. Ellen remarked at the similarities. Jim ordered an expensive red wine, took a sip and nodded to the waiter, a young waitress wearing black slacks, a white shirt, black bow tie, and a dark green apron. "Very nice," he said. The girl poured a glass for Ellen and then filled Jim's. He raised his glass, and Ellen followed his lead to a gentle clink. "To us," he said.

Ellen nodded and they each took a sip. He looked into her eyes and asked, "Are you sure?"

Ellen placed the glass on the table and stared down into the deep red liquid. "I was going to ask you the same thing."

"Ellen, I don't want to waste time. I've faced a major life tragedy, but I've also been fortunate. I know what love is, and I thought I could never find it again." He paused. "Now I have." He waited and then said, "You haven't answered my question."

With eyes still downcast she replied, "I only have one concern. I'd like them...your children, to be comfortable with me; with us."

"That would be nice, but I'm willing to let that happen later, if necessary. We'll give them some time. Don't expect to get it all done in this one weekend. But at some point, we'll have to do what we want."

Ellen nodded. "I know, but I want it to be perfect, Jim."

"Perfection is a high goal."

"One worth striving for; and I've waited a long time for this opportunity to strive."

"Me, too. I had it once, and..."

She reached across the table and placed her hand on his. Their eyes met. "I can't replace her, Jim."

"Yes, I know." He decided to tell her, "But she told me about you."

With a puzzled look, Ellen asked, "What does that mean?"

"At the end we talked. Gail wanted me to find you. But she said, not too soon."

Ellen's eyes glazed. "She really was special."

The waitress returned to discuss menus, and they ordered. The conversation moved to the future and making a life together. They agreed to give his children time to get used to the idea. Ellen would stay in Connecticut until the right time, and then Jim would talk to them about their decision, to make a life, living together, after they were married.

They shared a dessert, a hot fudge sundae on a warm brownie, and had coffee. Jim looked into Ellen's eyes and said, "A great evening, Ellen."

"Yes, it was. This is a lovely inn, and the food was scrumptious!"

"One thing we have around here is a number of good restaurants. In time, we'll explore lots of them."

"And talk philosophy," she replied.

The following morning Ellen rose at 7:35, dressed, and packed for her return trip. She ran a brush through her hair, thinking about yesterday's welcome surprise, an enjoyable walk with Tracey. She looked at the reflection in the mirror. *Today I'd like to connect with Elise. Even a few words would be nice.*

Anticipating a fresh cup of coffee, Ellen reached the bottom of the stairs. She entered the kitchen with a cheerful, "Good morning! You guys sure do a good job with coffee!" Michael looked up at her from the table, elbows resting on a newspaper, without response. Sensing his embarrassment and feeling her own, she recovered with, "Oh, I'm sorry, I thought your father was down here."

Michael replied, "No, he's at church," turning his head back down to the newspaper.

Church! Jim never said anything about that. Her parents, Catholic and Episcopalian had not pressed her to go to church. On occasion she would go with one of them, and always at Christmas and Easter. *Jim went to church on Sunday! He was an old-fashioned guy.* She reprimanded herself for the thought.

After recovering from Michael's revelation, Ellen poured a cup of coffee, then asked, "Michael, would you like a refill?"

He looked into his cup, then at her, and nodded.

She filled his cup, wondering about her next move. Then she asked, "Does your father plan on a big breakfast today?"

"No, but he'll probably bring home some bagels."

"When do you expect him?"

"He went to seven o'clock mass. He should be home a little after eight. Elise and I went at five o'clock last night."

They went to church, too? She controlled her surprise at this unsolicited revelation. "Elise still sleeping?" she asked.

"She didn't get in 'til 1:30 this morning."

"Hungry?" she asked.

"I can wait for the bagels."

"Mind if I cook something?"

"Go ahead."

Ellen scoured the refrigerator and a short time later an appetizing aroma filled the room. Out of the corner of her eye she noticed Michael glancing at her. "Sure you don't want some?" she said.

"What is it?" he replied.

"Omelet."

"We usually just have scrambled eggs."

"Last chance!"

"Okay, I'm in."

Ellen made a tactical decision; Michael would be her next target. Remembering the adage about the shortest way being through the stomach, she would take special care to make this a masterpiece. She removed the mushrooms and ham from the skillet; then, before starting to pour the eggs, she stopped. "Mushrooms, cheese, tomatoes, and ham," she said. "Take your pick."

"Hold the tomatoes," he said.

"Okay. Two minutes."

She poured the eggs and added Michael's selections. In a short time, she flipped the omelet to completion. When she placed the plate before Michael, the perfect yellow fold surrounded by two slices of raisin toast brought a smile to his face.

"Where's yours?" he asked.

"Coming up. You start."

When she sat down to join him, he started the second slice of toast; a small piece of omelet sat on the plate. "Well?" she asked. "How was it?"

"Awesome!" Michael said, with a smile.

Progress! "How about another?"

"Yeah, but I'll wait for Dad. Maybe he'll want one, too. You finish yours first."

"Okay." She took her first bite.

"So, Michael, what's today's news?"

"I'm reading the sports page; Flyers lost."

Ellen was not into hockey. She thought about her reply and then asked, "What's your sport, Michael?" A gamble; maybe he just watched but didn't play.

"I mess around with the guys playing basketball and a little hockey, but I'm on the cross country and track teams at school." he answered. "How about you? Dad said you're a runner."

She suppressed her elation. "Yes, I did a little bit of running in high school and college."

They discussed Ellen's running experiences. Michael asked lots of questions and she gave the answers. "Olympic tryouts! Wow!" Michael exclaimed.

When the engine stopped Jim lifted his warm package and climbed out of the car. The descending garage door made its unique sound as he opened the family room door. Ellen and Michael sat the breakfast table, taking him by surprise. "Bagels!" he called, waving the bag. "What are you guys having?"

"Omelets, Dad," Michael said. "Want one? I'm having seconds."

Ellen looked up from her plate with a mouthful, a shrug, and a smile. A few minutes later Jim and Michael began spreading cream cheese on their bagels while Ellen delivered a fresh round of omelets. Michael devoured the second with the same gusto as the first.

"I didn't know you liked omelets, Michael," Jim said.

"A nice change from pancakes and scrambled eggs," replied Michael, rising from the table.

As Michael rinsed the plate in to the sink, Jim leaned over and whispered, "You're good, Cramwell; very good."

Ellen grinned, jabbing a clenched fist at an invisible target.

Jim made another fire and spent the morning with Ellen reading the *Philadelphia Inquirer*, drinking coffee, and munching on the bagels. Elise came down at 10:30, waved, and returned with a cup of coffee. "Hungry?" Jim asked.

"Bagels will be fine," she replied. She brought one back and took a spot with a section of the newspaper.

After a short while, Jim asked Elise, "How was your evening?"

Another short response came from behind the newspaper, "Fine."

The trio sat in silence, reading, and after a while Jim asked, "Ellen, what time is your train?"

"2:10," she replied.

"It's about 11:30 now. If you'd like to spend a little time at 30th Street Station, why don't we leave around 12:30?"

"Okay, I'll go up soon and get my things ready."

Jim nodded and returned to the *Inquirer*.

A short time later Ellen returned and resumed her reading. She looked up from the magazine section when Jim stood and said, "I'm going to talk with Michael." After a while she heard Jim and Michael discussing the state high school basketball tournament. Jim's high school team, a perennial powerhouse, was making a run at the state title again.

Ellen's eyes turned to Elise, face buried in the newspaper. *What's the signal? She could have left, but she's still sitting* there. *Does she want to talk? How do I start?* Ellen turned her eyes back to the newspaper but not at the words. Her mind raced for an opening. Each time she thought of a question or comment, second thoughts led her to remain silent. Her anxiety increased as the seconds passed. The ticking of a small clock on the mantel seemed to be getting louder. She cleared her mind and tried to concentrate on the situation.

I wonder if she's really reading, or waiting for me to say something. For heaven's sake, Ellen, she's half your age! Her father's girlfriend is sitting across from her, and she's probably petrified. But she's not leaving. Damn! This teenage stuff is hard!

Ellen raised her head from behind the newspaper, and glanced at Elise, hidden behind the Entertainment section. "When do you go back, Elise?"

"This evening," Elise replied without looking up.

"Driving or train?"

"Train."

"Oh, what time?"

"Around seven."

Ellen's questions continued for a few minutes, but met with one and two word responses; but like sparks on wet straw, a fire never started. The stilted conversation stalled; Elise seemed reluctant to share thoughts or demonstrate enthusiasm. Ellen began to feel self-conscious. *I'm trying too hard. Maybe she just wants to read.* Ellen stopped turned back to the newspaper. An uncomfortable silence followed.

Ellen sighed with relief when Jim returned a short time later. When he sat down Ellen said, "Think I'll pack." When Ellen rose and started out of the room, she noticed Elise's face rising over the top edge of her newspaper. *What was that? Anger? Fear? Was it resentment?* But looked more like a plea.

Ellen came back a few minutes later with bags in tow and placed them by the front door. "Ready when you are," she said to Jim, returning to her seat.

"I'll load them now and we can leave in a little while," Jim said. As he stood to leave, Elise dropped her paper on the coffee table and rose to her feet, following Jim and leaving Ellen in the middle of her "Okay" and alone with the newspaper.

A short time later Ellen stood by the door, ready to depart for Philadelphia. Jim called out, "Michael! Elise! We're leaving!" After waiting for a response, he called out again. Ellen heard doors open and close, and Michael and Elise appeared and came down the stairs.

Ellen extended her hand and said, "Nice meeting you, Elise, Michael."

Michael shook her hand and responded, "Thanks for the omelet."

"Glad you liked it," Michael replied.

Elise gave a quick handshake and brief nod.

Jim and Ellen spent almost an hour touring the bookstore and shops at 30th Street Station, finishing with coffee for Jim and tea for Ellen. At 1:45 they sat side by side, on one of the wide, curved-back wooden bench seats common to old railroad stations. They leaned against each other and began the small talk, watching the clock move. Jim had that feeling of melancholy, on the edge of an imminent departure. "The time went too fast," he said.

"It always does when you're having fun. I enjoyed the weekend, Jim," Ellen said. When she pushed a little closer to him he returned the pressure.

"I'm glad; and you were able to spend some time with Annie, too."

"You two didn't seem to have any trouble getting to know each other."

"I don't think I've ever met anyone as outgoing. I felt as though I had known her for a long time. You have a nice friend, there."

"And, she lives here, so you can see her perform and get to know her better."

He nodded, thought for a few seconds, then decided to ask, "What did you think of the kids?"

Ellen took a second, then answered, "For a first trip, I think I made some progress with Tracey."

"Your cooking didn't hurt you with Michael, either."

"Yes, that was fun. He seemed to enjoy it, and we did chat a little. But, I couldn't get Elise to talk at all. I made a stab at it, but she seemed reluctant to engage. I only got a few words at a time. Of the two, I thought Michael would be the hard one."

"She's going through first semester shock, and now she meets with another surprise. It's tough on her."

"I wonder how she and Michael really felt."

"I think Michael is fine. Two out of three; not bad," Jim said, raising his eyes to the board showing arrival and departures. He found the words, BOSTON METROLINER-2:10-ON TIME. The clock said, 1:51.

As they sat, surrounded by the movement of winter clad travelers hurrying across the spacious floor, the announcer's voice a message, difficult to interpret in the spacious, echoing station.

"You'll have to come up to Connecticut for a weekend," Ellen said. Let's schedule something in a few weeks. Do you think your children would want to come?"

"I'll talk to them about it, maybe..." Jim's reply came to an abrupt end. He noticed a distinct, directed motion, a clear bright signal within the random scurrying. It moved toward Jim and Ellen, something familiar about it. He leaned forward to focus on the disturbance. Then, smiling, he nudged Ellen and nodded in the direction from which it came.

Ellen looked first at Jim, then turned to the clue of his nod. Her mouth opened at the sight. Tracey led the pack with rapid steps in their direction, wearing a yellow windbreaker along side, Michael in a matching sweatshirt and Elise, complementing her siblings in Jim's Yellow Day sweater.

Elise spoke first, "I hope you don't mind, Dad," pointing at his sweater.

Ellen sat back shaking her head; grasping Jim's hand, she rose to greet the arriving trio, and her eyes welled with tears. The Sunshine Gang stopped, and stood before Jim and Ellen, grinning. Then Elise took a step forward toward Ellen.

As Ellen accepted her embrace, Elise whispered, "It was nice to meet you. I'm sorry, but..."

Ellen whispered, "I know." She closed her eyes with pleasure at the increasing strength of Elise's squeeze.

When Elise stepped back, Ellen perceived the embarrassment of young girl, in a situation for which there could be no preparation, struggling for the right words. Before Ellen could convey her empathy, they spilled from Elise's tongue, "I know you're leaving, but the Dulles family welcomes you!"

Ellen replied with a simple, "Thanks!" Then she leaned toward Jim and whispered, "Three for three."

Jim folded Ellen and Elise into a package in his arms and returned a whisper, "Four for four." Then he winked at Tracey, always the ringleader, and said, "Nice job, Tracey."

Soon all five formed a huddle hug, a message of love amidst the haphazard movement of travelers hustling across the open expanse of floor; many of them slowed their pace to watch, while others stopped and smiled.

—EPILOGUE—

On a crisp October afternoon, with rich sounds of a classical organ reverberating through the spacious church, Jim stood beside Michael and Aaron in traditional morning dress. The music stopped; after a pause, the familiar march melody began. The audience, family and friends, teachers and second graders, rose and turned toward the aisle. Jim's eyes transfixed on his approaching bride.

Dave, eyes moist, raised the lace veil and kissed his daughter. He squeezed her hand and then placed it in Jim's. Ellen kissed her father's cheek and turned, radiant in white, to a position at Jim's side. Jane smiled at the scene, dabbed her eyes, and grasped her husband's hand as he stepped into the first pew. Annie, Tracey, and Elise, maids in soft yellow, glowed with joy as shining beacons of Ellen's Yellow Day.

ABOUT THE AUTHOR

As a Penn State professor, systems engineer, and now a consultant in the computer industry, Bill Douglas has produced numerous publications relating to his work, including journal articles and a book. Consumed by the challenge of writing fiction that elicits both smiles and tears, has created *Yellow Day*, his first novel. Bill enjoys reading mysteries, jogging, playing golf, traveling, and watching college football. His wife, Joan, a teacher and avid reader, collaborates in his writing. They live in Strafford, PA, a suburb of Philadelphia, and have three grown children.

Printed in the United States
1991